THIS NEVER HAPPENED

○●○

THIS NEVER HAPPENED

a novel

by

R. Tim Morris

EMPIRE STAMP

Empire Stamp trade paperback edition: April 2019
ISBN 978-1-7750598-1-3 [eBook]
ISBN 978-1-9990728-1-0 [Paperback]
ISBN 978-1-7750598-0-6 [Hardcover]

For my boys.
May you always find your place in this world.

"It's not me but the world that's deranged."
—Haruki Murakami, *1Q84*

●

TEN THOUSAND YEARS LATER

"I shouldn't be here."

This is what you tell yourself upon waking, as the white light of unconsciousness begins its slow fade out. The light dissipates, and you find yourself missing it already.

Your face burns, blood pools in the pockets of your mouth, and your jawbone clicks unfavorably. You unpeel yourself from the curbside, momentarily piecing back together your reason for being here in the first place. The neon sign crackling above you reads *The Starfish Room*; its cartoony sea star flickers, trying to decide whether it wants to shine purple or blue.

Out here on the worst street in Brighton Beach sits this most unpleasant bar. Its origins are murky, but somewhere along the way the Starfish Room went from being a seedy watering hole for Russian alcoholic perverts to a stopover for their Manhattan-bound, club-hopping sons, daughters, and grandchildren. Although the establishment's generous selection of imported vodka is well-known into the farthest reaches of Brooklyn, its seamy nature has always been enough to keep the majority of finer connoisseurs away. It's also notorious for never checking ID's, so it continues to find popularity with the underage crowd. Right now, you're wishing they had checked yours.

You journeyed to the Starfish Room tonight to try something new. When one is lost and confused and likely in desperate need of a change, sometimes the best thing to do is stretch one's boundaries. Quite often though, that very same decision can be the very worst move to make. Case in point: your blood dripping on the sidewalk. But there was something about the evening's misty, hot summer rain that made it easier for you to stretch yourself beyond familiar comfort zones. There was a certain feeling in the air; like having a fresh opportunity; a second chance; or being born again.

Tonight's brilliant rebirth found you kissing a girl you'd only met some ten minutes beforehand. She didn't ask you what your name was, but to be fair you didn't think to ask her either. You didn't even find her all that attractive when you first noticed her inside, slumped disinterestedly in a dark corner — what with the too-skinny face, her lazy eye, and the way she spat a little when she spoke to you — and she was even less appealing outside. Make no mistake though: some girls will come into your life and you'll know instantly they've come for a reason. Undoubtedly, this girl will not fall into that category. She was only ever at the Starfish Room to be forgotten by you. But you kissed her anyway. The aftertaste of strong vodka on her tongue repulsed you immediately. Her skin felt rough; scratchy in your hands. And then something hard stapled you violently in the neck, then your face, and you hit the ground like fresh dough on a granite countertop.

And now, as you shake the last of the light from the back of your eyes, you realize the gruff man who hit you is still here.

The muscled, young, bear of a man snarls at you in his broken English. He asks, "You got something dumb?" The boyfriend, you presume. You'd spotted him sucking on the girl's neck earlier, but when he soon vanished altogether you must have mistaken his momentary disappearance for something more permanent.

"I'm sorry," you say for lack of anything more original. "I think this was a mistake."

He proceeds to kick you firmly in the ribs. He spits on you before blurting something unknown in Russian and then he disappears again, this time with an arm wrapped around his ambivalent companion to somewhere unseen.

Consider this. When your relationships with girls — as few and far between as they've become — started to feel increasingly more distant and awkward, you deliberated upon the idea that perhaps you'd been going about it all wrong. *"Maybe try worrying less about making mistakes, and just let the mistakes happen,"* is what Dr. Griffin had suggested last week during your session. *"You might soon find those mistakes avoiding you, rather than the other way around."* So, bring on the mistakes. Your therapist's expert advice is what brought you here tonight. It's what led to your blood on the crumbling sidewalk. Maybe a cracked rib or two as a parting gift. You even had the night off, and this is what you chose to do with it. Right now, the puddle from the evening rain feels good on your burning skin, so you remain on the cracked sidewalk, its surface still warm from the long day's heat.

You work for a laundry and linen supply company; Brooklyn Whites, it's called. Sounds like a racist sports team but it's really not. You pick up and deliver tablecloths and napkins and uniforms and floor mats from restaurants all over the city. It's dull, but you don't ask for much more. And you just about took that extra shift tonight too. Much better to be cleaning up your face instead of dirty tablecloths, right? A lot of bad decisions can be made over a ten-thousand-year span.

For the first time in months, you think of your mother.

Some mothers tell their sons they will be someone special someday. Some tell their sons they are the smartest in their class. The most handsome, maybe. Your mother only told you that you were born ten thousand years too late. She would say it with a crooked smirk on her face, sometimes after a little joke you never understood. Always when your father wasn't home. *"Oh, you wouldn't get it,"* she'd say. *"You were born ten thousand years too late to understand."*

You always wondered if there was some great event that occurred ten thousand years ago; something worth your mother's blasé indifference and flippant explanations, but you have no idea what that might have been. Where might you have fit amongst those Neolithic people of 8000 BC? Who can say? You do know for certain you've never once felt as though you belonged where you actually were. But perhaps you're no different than most young men.

Ten thousand years ago, people were building their world's first cities. You imagine the number of mistakes they might have made along the way which probably went unnoticed. Nothing like today, where everyone's watching and waiting for you to screw it all up. But way back then, Earth's citizens had begun living in mud-brick domiciles. They were just starting to learn how to deal with noisy neighbors and domestic disputes.

You live in Coney Island, a subway ride away from Manhattan. You share a crusty two-bedroom apartment on Mermaid Avenue with your father. It very likely has the approximate dimensions and appeal as those original mud homes. You have neighbors on either side of you, above and below, and you know them as well as most anyone can really know their neighbors. The woman who lives on the top floor of the building runs a tai chi studio in her living room and she claims the amount of psychic energy her students generate is enough to calm all the world's aching souls. You never once imagined that could possibly be true since the world has as many problems as it does.

You sit up on the sidewalk now, convincing yourself that your head must actually hurt a lot more than it does. You barely feel it due to the handful of Sinequan you swallowed earlier. You keep the 100-count bottle of 25mg doxepin capsules next to the water glass on your bedside table so you remember to take four of them every night. Usually before you sleep, but in tonight's case it was before you made the decision to head out on this poorly-planned pursuit. In some state of pathetic yearning. Emotional delusion. You took the drugs in addition to the 10mg Vivactil tablet and the 20mg of OxyContin.

There's an echo of a woman's voice from somewhere around you. "Are you okay?" she asks from what almost feels like high above. But you know instantly this is not some higher power. No angel would be coming for you tonight, that much is clear. It's just the ringing in your ears that makes her seem so far away. You hadn't even heard her footsteps approaching, and you usually notice things like that. She crouches beside you and places a hand on your own, the one clinging to the still-fresh pain in your ribs.

You don't have the energy to even turn to her. "I've seen worse," you say.

"Me too," she replies with some aloofness. "Working in a place like this, I feel like I see something worse every night." You can smell the smoke from her cigarette before she holds it out, offering you a puff.

"No, thank you. That stuff will kill you."

"Oh yes," she says. "And you're doing so much better without it." Without asking, she sits down beside you and crosses her legs in some odd yoga fashion, not caring at all she's wearing such a short skirt. Her spiky hair is dyed seafoam green, but her faerie-like face belies any punk rock vibe she gives off. Craning her neck in the direction your assailant ran, she asks, "So what was that guy's problem, anyway? Why did he attack you like that?"

"I think I kissed his girlfriend." You try rubbing the crick out of your neck from where the man's meaty fist landed. "Though I guess she could have maybe been his sister? I have no idea."

She straightens her legs out defensively now, like you're some sexual miscreant. "Sounds to me like you should be a little more certain about these kinds of things next time."

"Tell me about it."

"So, what's your story then?"

"My therapist told me I should try new things. You know, experiment."

Again, she holds her cigarette out in an attempt to sympathize, but still you refuse. "You sure he meant for you to put the moves on chicks like that in dive bars like this?"

"He wasn't all that specific in his suggestions." You wipe some more blood from the corner of your mouth with the sleeve of your hoodie.

Dr. Griffin has also recommended writing down your dreams as personal therapy. Daydreams too. You daydream when you're working. When you're not working, you like to lie on your bed and dream. In your dreams, you're not cleaning up the messes others have left behind. In your dreams, you knew what to do after high school. Decisions were easier for you to make. In your dreams, you don't live on Mermaid Avenue; you live in the country. Not like the Hamptons, but maybe someplace like Bowling Green or Elizabethtown. In your dreams, everything is perfect. You're just as you want to be. You're everything you missed along the way to where you are now. It's only when you wake up that you seem to experience the backwards reality of it all. In your dreams, your mother didn't leave both your father and you.

"You're pretty young to be needing a therapist though, yeah?" this girl asks. You don't imagine she could be much older than you, but you've never been all that adept at guessing ages.

Still, you can't seem to find it within you to answer her.

She takes a deep breath in and stares up into space. Her focus is intense, like she's trying to remember the lyrics from some song not listened to for half a lifetime. "Mmmmmm," she hums pleasantly to herself.

Your eyes find their way to her legs. She has a tattoo on her calf written in a scribbly font which appears to spell *REMEMBER*. There's a long white scar just below her kneecap. She scratches mechanically at the other knee with her free hand; not so much like it is an actual, legitimate itch, but more like an unconscious tic. You want to keep going, to look farther up her leg, to her thighs and higher, but you know it's only because you're so alone tonight and you always seem to regret decisions like that coupled with feelings like these.

You ask, "Did you say you work here?"

"I did," she replies, still looking off somewhere far away. "I do." Slowly, she raises an arm above her head and holds her hand open as though ready to pick an apple from a tree. Her eyes follow something in the air for a moment longer before snatching it in her fist. She squeezes her closed hand a little tighter, then opens it up for a look. Some sort of insect, you think it's a mosquito, falls to the sidewalk, as lifeless as you're feeling right now. "There's so many of these fucking things in the summer," she complains. "It's the heat." She stamps what's left of the already dead thing with her foot.

Same as the one you'd just kissed, this girl has not entered your life for any reason but to be soon forgotten. And yet, through it all, there remains a pleasant feeling of safety with her. You know for certain you've never met her before now, but it's not because you can't place her face. It's unfamiliar, sure, but not really a surprise for you. You're used to unfamiliar. It's the more intricate filigree of detail you always look for when meeting someone unrecognizable: the angle at which her shoulders rest; the one front tooth which is a little too long; the smell of her chosen brand of cigarette; the slight scratchiness in her voice, playing like an old record player; the tattoo and the scar. These are the things you would have remembered if you'd met this girl before tonight. They are the details you'll remember should the two of you ever cross paths again. The details you'll look for when you surely won't be able to place her face in the future, like anyone else could very easily do.

Your condition is called prosopagnosia — those who prefer to not get tongue-tied might also call it face blindness — a cognitive disorder which makes it nearly impossible for you to recognize and remember faces. Of course, yours is a fairly mild form, in that, other than forgetting people you've met before, you can still function on a day-to-day basis. In some cases, a person suffering from a more debilitating form of prosopagnosia will not recognize their *own* face in a mirror, and they might even forget details such as places, events, and inanimate objects. Some might say you're lucky, but you still have to take mental notes when you're with people — like the

slight way their head might lean or how fast and frequent their eyes blink —
to act as memory triggers.

"So, what's your name anyway?" she asks.

Your name is Cepik Small. *Seh*-Pick, it's pronounced. You often tell people it's like septic without the T. The name is Polish, though you have no idea which of your ancestors was the last to actually set foot in Poland. It's doubtful you could even point to it on a map. Friends call you Epic for short even if it's the exact same number of syllables. But you don't feel like you have so many friends anymore.

"It's Epic," you mumble.

Turning to you now, her expression is something as scattered as the fading stars above. "Right," is all she responds with, like you're really trying to get at something else.

It's all part of the same story though: some forgotten friends; a stupid name; a crummy apartment; an uninspired career; a broken heart. Some might assume you're alone, and it's true. But you're not really lonely. At least not all of the time.

There was a girl you used to know. It was three years ago. You were seventeen. Her name was Reya and the situation you met her in was much like this one. Reya had just been mugged exiting a subway station in Manhattan. You can't recall which station, only that it was somewhere in Midtown. You saw her on the sidewalk, wiping blood from an open wound on her shin. She was missing a shoe and her stockings were torn. There were specific things about her you immediately picked up on, things you found yourself gravitating toward. Like the curl of her fingertips and the way she squinted, but only a single eye like she had a constant, pounding headache.

The first time you heard her voice it was familiar, wasn't it? The two of you talked for a while and when you finally worked up the courage to ask her if there was anything more you could do, she said you could go get her something to help ease the pain. She pointed to the Duane Reade directly across the street from where you sat. You wasted no time in agreeing to help her any way you could because Reya was genuinely nice to you, especially considering how she was attacked by strangers only minutes before you happened to come along.

Strange, but there was no traffic that night, not even a taxi, and you crossed the street without having to dodge a single car. Once inside the pharmacy, you found the appropriate aisle, but were quickly overwhelmed by the selection of over-the-counter medications:

Lidocaine.

Non-steroidal anti-inflammatories.

Topical treatments for psoriasis and eczema.

Anti-fungal creams.

Sunscreen.

All the little rectangular packages looked exactly the same with their colorful boxes and stupid names in bold, white font. You had no idea there could be so much choice, so many decisions to make, for something as mundane as this. Now, of course, you're doped up on so many meds and psychopharmaceuticals it's hard to recall a time when you were so *un*familiar.

After a moment of deliberation, you selected a bottle of children's fever relief and a one-page pamphlet of aspirin dosage recommendations. When you returned with your chosen product, Reya looked you up and down with those green eyes of hers; a kind of disseminated expression on her face, obviously wondering what could have possessed someone to make such a curious selection. But you know it was in that moment where she decided you were just weird enough to take a chance on.

And it's the exact same look the girl from the Starfish Room is giving you now on this Brighton Beach sidewalk. It's a look you log away as another memory trigger for the barmaid, should you cross paths again someday.

You and Reya had something great. She even told you she loved you, didn't she? You made enough of a connection on that first night, that it hurts so much more when you think about it now. In your dreams, you and Reya never made it to the part that hurt, did you? Somewhere, someway, things took a different turn.

And now this girl, the one with the distracting legs, comforts you and your own wounds. She has the perfect eyebrows of a SoHo mannequin and the pouty lips of a photoshopped cosmetics ad. Her lipstick, eyeliner, and fingernails are all black; dark enough for you to realize you'd be better off if you just got out of there. One stupid mistake is enough for tonight. You make a note to talk to your therapist about this tomorrow. Dr. Griffin will be happy to know you tried stepping outside your comfort zones, but he will also be proud of you for stopping before things got any worse.

Your body is sore, but you manage to peel yourself off the sidewalk in spite of the pain. An extra OxyContin or two tonight won't hurt, right? Routinely, you take two 10mg oxycodone hydrochloride tablets every morning when you wake up, usually with a few more throughout the day. No big deal.

"Where are you headed?" she asks, though you're not sure if she really, truly cares.

"Maybe tonight is not the night for meeting someone new," you say to her as you walk away, supporting yourself upon the brick storefronts for a couple more blocks.

You're not sure what it was you were meant for, but you know it's not what you've been given. Your father told you he wished you might have everything you ever wanted in life, yet his own life has always seemed so barren and meaningless. The two of you barely have enough money to get by. You've always felt as though you were a spectator in life, rather than a participant. You've felt this way in everything you've done and everywhere you've been. In your dreams, you are definitely a participant. In your dreams, you weren't an outcast in high school; you were just normal enough to go unnoticed. In your dreams, you fell in love, didn't you? In your dreams, you are everything your father really wanted you to be. Everywhere you were meant to be.

ooo

When you get back home, the apartment door seems to creak louder than usual. You pull the chain above your head, turning on the only light in the room: a bare 60-watt bulb smack-dab in the middle of the ceiling. There's no light switch on the wall, just this long, dangling chain which sometimes hits you in the face when you move around in the dark. The light is yellowed, like an old newspaper left in the sun. You feel only slightly more relevant.

A sweaty haze from the Coney Island heat fills the room. The hot smell of briny sea water and half-dead fish. The only walls within the ping pong table-sized apartment are for the small bathroom and the second bedroom

— your father's tiny room — and you can walk from the front door to the window in seven modest steps. You have the bare bones of a kitchen in one corner, complete with a child-size refrigerator, and a Murphy bed, which is, more often than not, pulled down leaving a void in the wall and making it feel like there's another room to be had. Aside from a coat rack, a dresser, and a desk and chair, you don't have much else to call your own. *"Imagine no possessions,"* John Lennon would have said, but even if *he* decided to pop by for a visit, you're certain he would have been tempted to add one of those long, hollow rain sticks or a decorative egg timer at the very least. As shitty as this apartment is, you continue to remind yourself it isn't as bad as the last one. It's progress.

You turn on the aging computer before taking a cold shower and when you're out of the bathroom, the computer continues to grind away. Still, it helps drown out the shouting voices from the all-night fried chicken dive on the street corner below. Searching the refrigerator for some hidden treasure you might have forgotten, you find a bottle of grapefruit juice you squeezed fresh three days ago. The pulp has sunk to the bottom like flakes in a forgotten snow globe. You pour some into a cracked plastic blue cup — it makes everything you drink look like some strange sort of space juice — and then sit down at the desk, your computer having almost finished deciding whether it wants to continue living or not.

Like a lot of things, your computer puzzles you. If asked to explain how the device works, even the very basics of it all, you wouldn't know where to start. If you opened it up, you'd be incapable of identifying a single piece inside. In your dreams, simple things don't confuse you. The computer conundrum helps to alleviate the biting memory of everything that transpired tonight. Why did you make the decisions you made? What came over you? Whenever you're faced with something like this, with exasperating thoughts that don't make any sense, you always try to think of everything else in the world you'll never know. The secrets of your computer, for example. You consider the number of things in your apartment alone which defy logic: the lock inside the door, the mechanics of the light above you, even the plumbing. And then of course there's a billion more in the world outside, things that exist only to exist:

Smartphones. Inner tubes. Prisms. Laminating machines. Shower curtains with maps of the world on them.

Thinking about it all helps you focus as the computer finishes powering up. In your inbox, there's the confirmation message to meet with Dr. Griffin tomorrow morning, as well as the usual variety of penis enlargement offers and another spam email inviting you to sign up for some new Massive Multiplayer Online Gaming experience. An MMORPG, they're calling it. All they're waiting for is your credit card information. There's an unread email from your father which has been sitting there collecting digital dust for nearly two weeks. He hasn't been in this apartment for more than a month now.

You keep an ongoing journal in a notepad application saved onto the desktop. You click it open and try to piece together the events from this evening, like the conversation with the girl outside the Starfish Room and, most importantly, the memory of Reya. Your entry from this morning is a smattering of scattered dreams from the night before:

In my dreams, I'm reaching for a jar. I knock it over and it hits the floor but doesn't break.

In my dreams, I'm riding the bus.

In my dreams, I'm staring up into a tree. It's tall, maybe a poplar? Beyond its browning leaves and twisting branches there's nothing but bright, blue sky.

In my dreams, I smell a summer storm inching closer. The pond frogs and katydids chirp madly with anticipation.

The mundane nature of your dreams does not elude you, yet there remains something exciting about them you can't explain. Your jaw pulsates with pain; that guy who clobbered you has likely already forgotten about what happened tonight but you keep feeling the reminders.

You recall the white light of unconsciousness that permeated your vision. And you remember it in other ways too. It's peculiar, but that light reminded you of being born. People say it's impossible for babies to remember the moment of their birth, but you remember the light that day. It wasn't a brilliant, bursting flash, a soft luminous luster, or anything else that might come to mind when one thinks of light, but you know that's what it was. You remember it easily because it has haunted your dreams countless times since. Over and over. And when you're not dreaming, you're sometimes still reminded of that wonderfully frightening flash when the F-Train bursts out over 4th Place. Or when the sun is caught within the steel web of the iconic Parachute Jump at Luna Park. You can't help from remembering.

But people will still tell you they don't remember the day they were born. They can't comprehend what it must have been like to see that light — the light that bathes them all in their most vulnerable of moments — for the first time. You don't have the heart to tell them you remember every horrible second of it. And what's worse, you know for sure it's also the very same light they tell you to walk toward when you're dying.

Although the water from the bathroom tap refuses to get cold, it still feels good to splash your face in the sink. The mirror laughs at you: its crack winding through the center splits your face in half. There does seem to be two sides to you sometimes, doesn't there? But you can't put your finger on it. You never have been able to. Looking deeper into the broken glass, you attempt to pull out an answer but there's nothing forthcoming. Soon, you lose it entirely. You stare long enough into your own reflection and your recognition of yourself will inevitably slip away. It's the same for everyone. They are all strangers to themselves eventually, no wonder it's nearly impossible for others to figure you out. Of course, it's all so much more difficult when living with prosopagnosia.

You've asked your landlord a few times to have this mirror replaced, but you and your father don't seem to sit too high upon Stanley's list of priorities.

The bed springs creak when you sink into them, the bare mattress releasing a dusty wheeze. Letting go of itself a tiny bit more. Your sheets are still in a laundry bag on the floor, as you'd washed them at work the night before. The ceiling seems to be vibrating, as if to the beat of some sinister music. You don't hear any music though, sinister, angry, or otherwise. Mistakes you've made flash through your mind once again, the same as every night. Why did you venture out to Brighton Beach tonight on such an irrational quest? You should have known nothing good could possibly come out of it. You've been searching for happiness, for some kind of relief from this debilitating malaise for so long now, but you don't know if it will ever come.

Tomorrow, though, is another day. Maybe tomorrow.

In your dreams, happiness comes every moment of every day.

You look around for the four missing 25mg Sinequan doxepin capsules beside your bed and curse to yourself when you remember you'd already taken them earlier, before having your lights punched out.

LOVEHUNTER

Your father never had much in the way of advice or words of wisdom to share, but one of the things he always liked to remind you of was this: *"It's not officially summer in Coney Island until the start of the Mermaid Parade."* This is when people will finally begin to unwind and enjoy the sun. Today is so muggy and sticky and sweaty, you feel as though you're sucking air in through the exhaust pipe of a car that just ran the Daytona 500. The haze conjures up something like one of those cartoon mirages. Deserts and palm trees with big coconuts. Stuff like that. Your rubber shoe soles want to fuse with the sidewalk and asphalt. It's too hot to simply lie in your apartment hoping for a short, cruel gust of sea breeze; you need to stay moving just to keep the sweat coming.

The costumed crowds are holding Surf Avenue hostage and you have to elbow them out of your way to get through. It's a maddening assortment of mer-creatures (both *maids* and *men*) and various representatives of undersea royalty which number into the thousands. Topless women painted in blue. Dogs wearing clam shells. And then there's all the kids running around like they own the place.

When you were a boy, you reveled in the annual festivities much like anyone else, mostly by making mischief with friends of yours: Barton and Reilly. These were the kind of friends everyone had in middle school, the ones who always got you into trouble but you kept calling them your friends because it's not like you had any other options. You don't remember all that much about them now except for random details; like when he was younger, Barton had always wanted to be a concert pianist, up until his music teacher told him his fingers were too short. So, arbitrarily, he became an avid reader of Hitler's Mein Kampf instead. He enjoyed eating licorice babies, but mostly for their racial connotations. As for Reilly, all you can really recall was that he had an incredible collection of plastic dinosaurs. It's funny, the things you choose to remember about people.

During the annual Mermaid Parade, the three of you would sneak your way onto parade floats only to surprise the crowds by tossing eggs at them. Cartons of eggs were simple enough to stow away in your school bag and you could usually count on throwing half a dozen before being spotted by anyone with any sort of authority to direct you elsewhere. The hope was that you might even get lucky with the opportunity to hit someone you knew; someone you'd waited the entire school year to nail with a surprise egg in the face. Reilly's family owned a bakery, so the three of you had a nearly-unlimited supply.

But their wrong-side-of-the-track antics unavoidably escalated in levels of cruelty: from throwing eggs to flooding the school bathrooms and breaking car windows. To stealing wallets and torturing the neighborhood dogs. The last summer you spent together, you told Barton and Reilly you'd had enough. You wouldn't be taking part in any of it anymore. It was time to grow up. It was time for all of you to grow up, you said. As it happened, the two of them ran up Fifteenth Street, right to your father's shoe store and burned the place down. How's that for growing up then? You didn't speak to Barton or Reilly again until high school. The Smalls went bankrupt shortly after the loss of the family business, and things have only been spiraling downhill since then.

The latest example being this morning: you showed up for your regular Saturday appointment with Dr. Griffin. The receptionist was new (you didn't recognize her, at least) and when you gave her your name she simply stared blankly like she didn't believe you. But maybe it was just the purple bruising taking up one-quarter of your face that had thrown her off. You took that punch two nights ago and the colorful side effects are really starting to set in.

"I'm sorry, Mr. Small, but Dr. Griffin will not be able to see you today."

"*He can't see me*? But I have an appointment."

"Did I not call you this morning?" She looked over some scribbled paperwork in front of her, more mumbling to herself than talking to you directly. "I'm sure I had you on my list here—"

"I wouldn't be standing here if you had called me."

"I'm sorry," she said again, as though saying it a second time would mean something more to you.

Throwing your arms up into the air, you entwined your fingers together atop your head; your sweaty palms lazily tried to crush your cranium. And you wondered what it was you should do next.

The receptionist (you finally noticed her name plate read "Kerrigan") shifted her dark eyes back and forth quickly. She lowered her voice to a hush and said, "I probably shouldn't be telling you this—" She took another peek behind her, "—but Dr. Griffin is *dead*."

Your arms deflated back down to your sides, and you hurt your boney wrists when they slapped the rivets on your jean shorts. "*Dead*?" you asked, flabbergasted.

"Shhhhh!" Kerrigan clicked her pen quickly a few times and wrote something on an unseen notepad. The darting, shifty eyes and the vigorous pen-clicking might prove to be future memory triggers, so you made sure to log them away.

"When did he die?" you asked, lowering your voice just enough.

"This morning." With her pen, Kerrigan pointed over her shoulder. "They told me it was a suicide." She said they like there was some secret society plotting against her on the other side of the wall. "Though I think it was his wife. Maybe his brother? His brother always seemed a bit suspicious to me. I'm thinking poison. Or like an overdose of prescription drugs, you know?"

"You've certainly come up with a load of theories considering he only died this morning."

"I have a lot of time on my hands. Plus, I just saw 'Murder on the Orient Express' last night. So, you know."

You smiled a little, but only in the hopes that the conversation would be over sooner. "Should you really be telling me all of this, Kerrigan?"

"Yeah, probably not."

You considered what the chances might have been that Dr. Griffin perhaps took his own life because he could no longer handle the problems of his anxiety-laden, manic depressive clients. And what might the probability have been that Dr. Griffin killed himself specifically because of your *own* problems? Like he had to do it this morning before *you* showed up.

"The fact remains," Kerrigan continued, "you will no longer be able to see Dr. Griffin. I can make an appointment for you to see someone new if you'd like?"

Of course, who's to say he was even responsible for it? It could have been an accident for all you know. "But Dr. Griffin is the only therapist I've ever seen. He knows *everything* about me."

"I'm sorry," she said one more time. She took a look over some sort of document in front of her. If this was actually pertaining to you, whether it was anything relevant at all, or if it was completely unrelated to your presence there, you had no idea. Maybe it was the instruction manual for that desktop fan of hers which was obviously not working; blowing its air at the wall, trying to oscillate but stuck in that *click-click-click* position. "I know there's a guy in your neighborhood who's eager for new patients. He'd be a great match for you. I've got your file right here. I'll send it to him."

As it happened, he *was* eager; eager enough that he'd see you the exact same day. Almost immediately, in fact. So, Kerrigan transferred your personal information from the office of the late Dr. Griffin to the office of the unknown Dr. Gideon and you made your way there.

Now you're right in the middle of the Mermaid Parade. The office is above a furniture store, beneath the subway tracks, and across from the Luna Park entrance. The amusement park gate's giant blue and red pinwheels and crescent moons are unlit during the day and only help with the feelings of abandonment and neglect that go hand in hand with this part of town.

You have to push a guy in a giant sea star costume aside to get to the front door. There's a buzzer, but it's missing the metal plate around it which likely held the building's list of tenant names. There's no identification on it whatsoever, as though the place were vacant. It feels more like an incomplete movie set; maybe the buzzer plate is still somewhere inside a poorly-labeled box in the back of one of the prop trucks. Nevertheless, you try the handle and the door swings right open. You slip into the building quickly, separating yourself from the insanity outside.

The office upstairs is empty. There's a reception desk, but no one here. Everything in the room feels new yet there's a sense of someone having been through here recently, like an IKEA showroom. The wallpaper appears longer than the height of the wall; it's peeling up over the ceiling and you wonder if there was always too much paper or if the walls have been slowly shrinking. A framed campaign poster of Ronald Reagan seems both topically and chronologically misleading, as do the stack of kitchen decor and boating magazines from the 1990's. At least the temperature is welcoming; if the crowds outside knew that standing in this office felt like being on an arctic ice flow, the Mermaid Parade wouldn't be nearly as popular this year.

You rap a fist upon the reception desk and hear a wet cough from behind the door, as though you've just woken this someone from a nap. After some rustling of papers, a man emerges from the next room. A lanky but slight frame with a bit of a beer belly, he's wearing flip flops, shorts, and a t-shirt which says "Surf Tofino" with a picture of a camper van and a surfboard on it. His hair is short and wavy, dirty blonde with graying temples. And a long, pointy nose almost seems lengthy enough that he might touch it with the tip of his tongue should he lick his lips too vigorously.

"I'll be right with you, Mr. Small," he says, identifying you as though it would be impossible for anyone else to have walked in right now. You thank him and he disappears behind the door again, leaving you behind to wait in one spot until called upon. You take another look at the poster. "People First," it reads. It's obvious now it's a picture of Clinton, and not Reagan like you first thought. You don't know how you could have made a mistake like that.

He calls for you to enter the office and you walk in guardedly. The serenity of the front reception is immediately lost upon entering Dr. Gideon's office. The open window facing Surf Avenue allows for every sort of festive cacophony to invade what should be a peaceful setting. The heat has returned also, seemingly tenfold, prompting your questioning of why the therapist's office could not be in the front reception — and vice versa — at least just for today.

"I like it in here," the man who led you in responds with before offering a seat on the sofa. He seats himself at the desk, puts his feet up, and places his hands behind his head in victorious fashion, as if just winning a thousand bucks at the horse track.

"I'm sorry," you apologize. "I didn't realize you were Dr. Gideon. I thought you were maybe the receptionist."

"I don't have a receptionist, so I can understand your confusion. But please, it's just Gideon."

"Oh. Okay."

"I mean, I'm not actually a doctor."

"You're not? But the sign in the hall says Doctor."

"You know what? I told the guy not to put Doctor on it. Ah, but you know how it goes. Nobody ever listens, right?" He kicks his hairy legs off the desk like he's all done with the idle chit chat and is ready to get down to business. His desktop is clean aside from a pen, a lilac-colored journal, a manila folder, and an empty, stained coffee cup. Gideon (you wonder, *Was this a first name or a last name?*) opens the folder and flips through some different-colored papers. "Lexapro. Sinequan. Pristiq. Vivactil. Boy, they've got you on a lot of shit, don't they?"

"Well, Dr. Griffin prescribed all of those to me himself. He knows me better than anyone."

"Better than you know yourself, is that how it goes?"

"Yeah. I suppose so."

"And this thing: your proso...prosopang...pangno—"

"Prosopagnosia," you say. It took you a while to learn the stupid word too, didn't it? "It means I don't remember faces."

"Do you remember *me*?"

You stop. "Have we met before?"

"I don't think so." With his little finger Gideon digs around inside his nose, not caring that you're sitting directly across him, or even that the two of you are in the middle of a serious conversation. You always thought picking noses in public was a faux pas, but you could be mistaken. He looks at the tip of his finger before wiping whatever treasure he found onto his shorts. "I heard this Griffin killed himself. Is that right?"

"That's what his receptionist said. Though she had some other theories too."

"Yeah. She told me. Confidentiality seems to go out the window with that one, doesn't it?" Comically, he makes a clueless sort of face and swishes a hand past the top of his head. "Well, you don't have to worry about that with me. There're some things I like to keep from even myself." He winks, though you have no idea what he means by that. "I should tell you, however, that some of my patients have described my therapeutic methods as being very unorthodox."

"Unorthodox?"

"Yes."

"Can you give me an example?"

"Not really. I'll just throw some shit at you and see what sticks." You're starting to wonder why Gideon was the first therapist Dr. Griffin's receptionist suggested to you. Did she have any *other* names on that list? "So, where do you want to start?" he asks.

"Where?"

"I have the list of psychopharmaceuticals you're taking, Cepik, but I know virtually nothing else about you. Where does your depression stem from? Childhood? High school? David Lynch films? *Lost Highway*, did you ever see *that* one? Boy, that's a mindfuck, right there. What other issues are we looking at here? And where the heck did that nasty bruise of yours come from?"

You rub your jaw, embarrassed. His barrage of questions hits you unexpectedly, not unlike the sucker punch you took two nights ago outside the Starfish Room.

"A mistake, no doubt?"

"I kissed a girl in Brighton Beach the other night. Her boyfriend was none too pleased about the whole thing."

Gideon takes a quick look over some of your paperwork, scratching at his scalp with the pen. "Not a very bright move. Why the hell would you do *that*?"

"Aren't you supposed to help me figure that out? Isn't that what you're here for?" His movement is almost imperceptible, but you sense shrugged shoulders, as though he's not really sure himself. Slumping back into the sofa even farther, you release a heavy sigh and bury your face into your sweaty palms. "God. It feels like such a waste."

"What's a waste?" he asks, pen at the ready.

"I mean, I already went through all of this with Dr. Griffin. I've been seeing him once a week for the last *two years*. And now I have to start from scratch again? I don't know if I can do it."

"Well, Griffin certainly didn't do you any favors by offing himself this morning, that's for sure. But I'll get you back to where you were, maybe even further. I promise you. Who knows, we might even consolidate your medication too." Gideon scribbles some notes into the lilac journal, taking his time. From outside, you hear bottles breaking and people yelling at one another. But even though the open window unapologetically allows for the invasion of the parade's racket, it still feels like this room is in some sort of extended silence. Like it's waiting for something about to happen. You feel uncomfortable. This searing heat and the pain in your jaw are making it worse, too.

As he continues to write, Gideon asks, "You know a griffin is a mythological creature, don't you?"

"I guess so. Why?"

For whatever reason, he picks his nose again; this time with a different finger. Maybe he knows about your memory triggers and is trying to throw you off by switching the details? "That means it doesn't actually exist."

"I know what mythological means," you say.

Without any further comment, Gideon jots something more down in the journal. Nervously, you take a look around the office, the details of which feel pretty typical with the standard bookshelves, area rug, and a potted fern. But there is one item on the wall behind you that sticks out. It's an album cover, an original dust jacket framed under glass. It's the cover for Whitesnake's *Lovehunter*, obvious only because the band name and title are clearly written across the top. You certainly would not have known otherwise. The wacked-out cover art is of a naked woman straddling a monstrous snake between her legs, and it goes far past the point of sexual innuendo. A very strange thing to have on the wall. You think, *Aren't therapists' offices supposed to be free of distractions like this?* Dr. Griffin's office was all eggshell and earth tones. Forgettable couch upholstery. Nothing this jarring in the least.

Nothing at all.

Finally, he finishes writing. He catches you staring at the album cover, but doesn't comment. Instead he says, "I've got a question for you, Cepik."

"I'm sorry, but can you call me Epic? Everybody calls me Epic. Not Cepik."

"Who's everybody?"

You recoil a little with the cognizance of how few people *Everybody* actually is. And you ask instead: "What was the question?"

"I was going to ask if you would rate yourself for me."

"What do you mean *rate myself*? Is there a specific category?"

"There is no category. Just rate yourself. Please give me a number between one and ten, excluding seven."

"Why not seven?"

"That doesn't matter."

"Um, ah—I guess a six."

"Six? Very interesting." Gideon's voice trails off as he writes some more down.

"Is that bad?"

"No, no. This is a good start."

What the point of this exercise is you have no idea, but it kind of feels like you're with some fifth-grade girls and they're deciding who you're going to marry based on the number that comes up on their origami finger puzzle thingy. He's right. This is very unorthodox. The naked woman on the large snake behind you is certainly not helping matters.

He says, "I find that given the opportunity, the majority of my patients will pick seven in their P-R-E: their *Personal Rating Evaluation.* If I eliminate the seven it forces them to choose between the two closest options: six or eight. They either have to knock themselves down a notch or bump themselves up. That says a lot about their personal reflection."

"But what if I intended to pick six anyway?"

"That's not my point."

This might be a bad sign, but you've already hit a complete and total state of confusion. To relieve your befuddlement, you do your best to think of something else you could never understand:

Curling irons. Garage doors. Hypodermic tubing. Van de Graaff generators.

Anything at all:

Coconut water. Staple removers. Two-way mirrors. Streaming music. Baby headbands.

That's better, isn't it?

"Epic? EPIC?"

But then it's back to reality. "I'm sorry, what?"

"I was asking about your mother and your eyes just kind of rolled back into your head."

"What about my mother?"

"I like to get the whole mother thing out of the way early since that's where most of my patients' problems will stem from."

"My mother left us. But that was years ago. I was only five."

"See? *This* is exactly what I was talking about." He points at you with his finger, jabbing excitedly. "That's it right there: the mommy issues!"

You recoil slightly into the sofa. Truthfully, you don't really think about your mother much anymore. Other than maybe a passing *What if?* fantasy once every year or so.

There was a man who came by your apartment all the time. You'd see him there on weekends or days you weren't in school. Never when your father was home. You weren't suspicious about this man as a child, but when your mother finally did disappear altogether one day and your father sat you down to explain that it was doubtful she'd ever come home, you began to put the pieces together. You were angry, but still not old enough to be *justifiably* angry, which is much worse. Basically, you grew up with your dad. That was family. Mom wasn't in the equation, so you didn't dwell on the fact that she hadn't had enough love for either of you to make her stay.

So, when you tell Gideon your mother left, you just say it without any coaxing. Some people have mothers, some don't. This is just the truth of it all. Why is he being so accusatory? Why is he treating this as some giant breakthrough? And worse, only mere minutes into your first session.

"There's really not much I can tell you about my mother," you say to him bluntly. "She's not a factor anymore."

You're not sure if he believes you or not. Gideon just scribbles some more in the notebook. "Well, this is why I like to get the mother thing out of the way early," he reiterates, though you can't tell if this is the end of it or not. All you know is you'd rather just move along. Gideon stops writing for a moment to draw a heavy line across the page. He adds another stroke or two for emphasis. Is he crossing out something irrelevant or underlining something important? His tongue juts out of his mouth as if he's concentrating exceptionally hard on scraping this line into the paper.

For whatever reason, you tell him, "My mother always told me I was born ten thousand years too late."

His pen slips from his hand, rolling off the desktop and onto the floor. "What did she mean by *that*?"

"I don't really know. But I remember she said it to me a bunch of times."

Gideon stands up slowly. He shuffles around to the other side of the desk to retrieve his writing utensil. "Well, I wouldn't put too much stock into that. Sounds like crazy talk to me, Cepik."

"Epic."

"That's what I said." As he sits back down Gideon rubs his temple like he bonked his head on the desk reaching down for his pen. "Tell me, have you ever had made-up arguments in your head? Where you get angry at strangers for no obvious reason?"

"I don't think so."

He holds one of the colored papers up, a ways away from his face as though his vision is failing him. "These drugs you're on? Pristiq. Lexapro. Vivactil. Why was Griffin prescribing all these? A lot of them are basically for the same thing, just tailored toward the needs and preferences of different patients."

"I don't know. It's just what he gave me."

Every morning you take one 10mg Lexapro escitalopram oxalate tablet, one 100mg Pristiq desvenlafaxine tablet and two 10mg OxyContin oxycodone hydrochloride tablets. You take one 10mg Vivactil protriptyline hydrochloride tablet during meals, at breakfast, lunch and dinner. Also, with your dinner you have two more 10mg OxyContin tablets. Before bed, you toss back four 25mg Sinequan doxepin capsules. And throughout the day, depending on a variety of factors (among them, headaches and boredom), you might also have some aspirin and Tylenol here and there. Maybe some indigestion relief, too. You've got a prescription for some cannabinoids as well, but you've never used them; they go directly from your hand into the pocket of Armand Bester, a co-worker of yours.

"Why not list your symptoms for me? Everything you told Dr. Griffin."

"Ah, I don't know." You've never been very good at talking about yourself. Or more specifically, your faults, weaknesses, and deficiencies. Gideon puckers his lips as though wanting to say something he shouldn't. You don't give him the chance. "Depression, mostly. I guess insomnia. Chronic pain. Headaches. Feelings of not belonging. A lack of focus, maybe."

"Paranoia?"

"I wouldn't say so."

"Have you ever had thoughts of suicide?"

You lean back a little, hands on your arms like a gentle hug. You're unsure of how best to answer but manage to sputter, "Hasn't everyone?"

"It's a serious question, Epic," says the man picking his nose and wearing the wrinkled *Surf Tofino* t-shirt.

"I *was* being serious. I just mean, it's probably a fairly common thought.

That's all. I would think it's highly improbable these days that you could find somebody who *hasn't* considered killing themselves."

"I haven't," he says to you, almost boasting. "Not once."

"I'm sorry, but I don't believe you."

"Do you find that strange?"

"Of course I do! With all the crap being shit upon us daily I find it impossible. Actually, it's inconceivable to me."

"How far did you get?" he asks, and jots a few more lines down in the book. Before you have an answer for him, Gideon rearranges his question: "How close did you come?"

The heat is intensifying. It's unstoppable. Outside, you hear some vehement banging of metal on metal, like somebody hitting a mailbox with a lead pipe. Car horns sound more like cries for help. You imagine the airplane droning in the far distance is actually nose-diving straight toward the earth. Maybe heading directly for you. Even the couch cushions feel more intimidating now, though you can't seem to stop yourself from sinking ever farther into their plushy hold like there's a weight tied to your foot and you're in the middle of the Atlantic. You try to collect your thoughts. There's something concrete in there somewhere but it eludes you. You're having a hard time placing it. Your mouth is so dry.

How close did you come? "Not very." You rub your throat and ask, "Could I please get a glass of cold water?"

"In a minute," he says, scribbling madly in the journal. Still writing and without looking up, Gideon asks, "Have you ever contemplated alternative methods of suicide? For example, jumping in front of the subway? Hanging yourself? A bullet or crossbow bolt to the head?"

A crossbow bolt? That is grim. You try to put yourself into the shoes of any such alternative suicides, but all your brain can come up with is: Anatomical Models. All-weather tires. Car mufflers. Pasteurized honey.

"Epic?"

You open your eyes and see there's now a glass of water on the table beside you, a bulbous pool already formed beneath it due to the humidity. "Oh. Sorry."

"You know, pills are probably the *worst* way to go. If you're just hoping for the easiest way out of this, that is. You could be suffering for hours. Days, even. Or worse, you could wind up in the intensive care unit on suicide watch with nothing to do with your time but think about how horribly you failed. And now you're even *more* screwed. That is not what I would call the easy route."

You stare at him, wondering how he could be so rude and so honest at the same time.

"Well, it's true. Go on, tell me it's not."

You guzzle all of the water in the glass at once and wipe your mouth with the long sleeve of your hoodie. "I suppose I haven't really thought about it that much."

"You should. If you're making a commitment like suicide, something that's going to affect so many people down the line, you need to put as much thought into it as you can."

A *suicidal commitment*? That sounds funny, you think. More humorous than *alternative suicide*, even. There's already some form of commitment though, isn't there? Isn't everyone resolved to the fact that death is irresistibly unavoidable? You'll be dead and Gideon will be dead and Reya will be dead, so what does it matter, really? Everything dies eventually. But there's something tantalizing about possibly being in control of it. Setting your own deadline.

"Have you ever looked forward to something so much that you wished you wouldn't have to wait any longer? Like a movie or a dinner date with an awesome girl."

"Of course."

"That's kind of what the thought of death is like for me. But the trouble is, I'm not suicidal. It's not in my programming. It doesn't seem like an easy thing to do, even though doing it would mean not having to wait any longer."

"That's an interesting perspective. But why is it you say you *look forward* to death? I mean, there's no indication things would be any better. In fact, all signs seem to point toward things being much worse. You know, with the fires of Hell and all that."

"I'm not sure."

"Perhaps there's more; the possibility of something in your life holding you back. Your mother, maybe?"

"I already told you. My mother is not a factor any more. She barely ever crosses my mind."

"Your father then?"

Right now, your father is lying on a bed in a cancer ward. Brain cancer, they told you, without saying much else. You wouldn't say the two of you have had a close relationship, but you certainly don't hate him. Maybe though it's because you haven't wanted to exit this world before him? Like it would be selfish of you? Maybe once he's gone it will be easier?

Still, you want to remind Gideon there are plenty of examples of pills being an effective method. When it works, it works, right? But you don't wish to dwell on this. It's not like you think about suicide every day. Why can't he just move on? Why is it so fucking hot in here? You hold out the wet glass in your hand. "Could I please have some more water?"

"Let's move on," he says. Oh, thank god. "You mentioned earlier about a sense of not belonging? How would you describe that?"

Not belonging. Now this, this you feel every day. "It's not so much a social thing, more like a feeling that where I am is not where I'm meant to be. In a geographical sense." You feel it every minute of every day.

"Where would you *rather* be?" he asks.

In your dreams, you live in the country. You hear horses in the distance. You smell corn fields on the breeze. You see an old wooden fence, longer than the eye can see; the kind of fence that's just a few tree branches held together with rusted wire and nails and looks like it's been stretched across the land for two hundred years.

But you don't share your dreams. Where would you rather be? Maybe it's not so much a *where*, as it is a *what*. Maybe you should have been *something* else. Like an octopus or a sea sponge that just sits there on the ocean floor. To be able to sit with nothing to do and nothing to worry about, to not even be aware that the concept of relationships or the very act of worrying about them existed in the first place would be so relaxing. Sometimes you think admitting yourself into a mental institution would be the way to go. You could just sit around all day, maybe read that stack of old science fiction that's been piling up. Maybe read some of them more than once. But that part of your brain you hate the most tells you that would be the easy way out. It would be the way to go if you wanted to avoid life rather than live it. So instead you find yourself getting punched outside a dive bar in Brighton Beach, right?

Gideon gets up from his seat and you realize you still haven't answered his question. Seems like he's not too worried about it though. He goes to the open window and slides it closed, quickly muffling the ruckus from the street. Is he trying to set a better ambiance? Your thoughts have been a bit scattered. Maybe you'll be able to think more clearly now.

You notice the journal he's been writing in now lays closed upon his desktop. Its lilac hue is a very distinct color and there's some sort of imagery on the cover you can't make out from this angle. A beaver, perhaps? Some Medieval spiked maces?

You look back up. He's staring at you now, his back to the outside world, bum resting upon the windowsill. The way he studies you with his eyes makes you feel as though he'd planted the notebook purposefully and he's just waiting to see what you might do with the opportunity. But that can't be it. You can tell he's really just waiting for another answer to another question you've missed. Whatever it might have been.

"I don't know," is what you leave for him to disseminate.

"You don't know? It's a very straightforward question."

"Maybe you could ask me again?"

Gideon returns to his desk and reels the journal back in toward him protectively. *My precious*, you think. Pulling open one of the desk drawers, he slowly slides the journal, the folder and the pen away, like he's all done taking notes and whatever the question was he had asked was for no greater reason than to wrap things up with you. He makes sure to lock the drawer with a key you hadn't noticed before now, attached to a rubber band around his left wrist. How did you not notice that? Gideon crosses his arms, places his elbows on the desk and says, "I asked you if all of this is about a girl."

You don't wish to dwell on it longer than you need to, but you also did not foresee yourself answering so quickly. "Isn't it always?"

He unfolds his arms and steeples his long fingers together. Still without any indication that he's planning on writing any of this new information down, Gideon says, "So tell me about her then."

How do you just tell him about Reya? Where would you start? Her eyes were a wonderful electric green, like Kermit the Frog or the freshest pesto. Her wispy hair was always getting stuck in the corner of her mouth, wasn't it? You used to brush it away for her before you realized she didn't mind the loose strands. And actually, they were only helping to make Reya seem more like she was meant to be. Should you tell him about that wonderful gap between her front teeth? Or her laugh? Her laugh scared you, didn't it? The way she cackled maniacally but usually only when she heard the lamest of jokes. When something was really, truly funny though, she'd simply smile a gap-toothed smile and say, "*That was really funny.*" It's the way she appeared across a crowded room, especially in those moments when she didn't know anyone was watching her. There's a face people have when their guard is down and they're not paying attention; their muscles relax and they look sad or angry or simply approachable. Reya didn't have that face, did she? Hers was even more beautiful when she *wasn't* paying attention. She was always holding her elbows in her palms, like there was nowhere better for her hands to be.

But what if you told Gideon that Reya was the girl you felt you were always waiting for? Do you tell Gideon that she told you the same thing?

That you were meant to find her that night, after she was mugged outside the subway? Do you tell him how you miss her terribly?

You miss her, you know you do, but it also feels a lot like a *longing*. Like the hardest part is still to come. Kind of like there's still more missing to be had.

But then again, maybe you could just say what he wants to hear? Maybe you'll lie and tell him it was all very simple: you were in a shitty relationship that you knew would be shitty right from the start. Maybe she said her phone was acting stupid and she'd call you back later but then she never did. And then it was over. Just like that. Why not tell him that? Seems like it would be a much easier problem for the man to fix. That is what he wants from you, isn't it? He doesn't really want to put a lot of work into this; staying awake all night worrying about those unbearable, messed-up patients of his. Wouldn't a therapist honestly prefer the easy route? Someone who can be fixed with a single visit? *Here, take two of these! Great, thanks Doc. I'm all better now! Yay!* And you don't really want to be here with him either, do you? You'd rather Dr. Griffin hadn't killed himself so selfishly.

"She's gone," you say instead of everything else you're thinking. What you don't say is that except for the giant cavity in your heart she used to fill, it's like she was never really here.

"And so that is simply that?"

"What more could there be?" you ask him bluntly. "And what about everybody else? Isn't everyone left behind by someone else eventually?"

"Perhaps so." Gideon slumps a little farther into his chair, possibly trying to link your comments together with events in his own life. "Let me ask you this: do you ever find yourself jumping into things a little too quickly?"

"I'm not sure. I don't think I've ever thought of myself as being so impulsive or overly reactive."

"I'd think again. Consider the drugs you're on. Did you question Griffin's prescriptions at all or did you just run to the pharmacist and load up? How about that bruise on your face? Typically, one does not get punched in the mouth at a bar due to meticulously planned and well-thought-out actions. Your mother left you and it doesn't seem to have ever bothered you. I mean, I'd be contemplating that shit for a long time. Blaming myself. Most anyone would, don't you think?"

"I'm sorry. I don't really know what's normal for most people."

"You talked about suicide like it was nothing more than zipping up your coat on a cold day."

"Only because you asked me about it."

"Nevertheless. It seems as though your thoughts of suicide creep up on you pretty fast. Like it's no big deal."

"Well it's not like I've ever seen it through."

"Obviously. Still, I find it of particular concern."

You can't tell if what he's saying is just more psychobabble — leaning a bit heavier on the babble-end of things — or if it's all starting to make sense and you simply don't want to accept it. Either way, your thoughts default to something, to anything else:

Sports trophies. Combat Knives. Elliptical machines. Pink Lego. Sticky notes. Multi-colored sticky notes. Fun-shaped sticky notes.

It doesn't feel like you're out as long as usual since Gideon is still staring at you, in the exact same position he was before your eyes rolled back into your head.

Then he says, "Maybe all this zoning out you've been doing is what leads to the overwhelming feelings you have. Maybe you need to slow things down a bit. Try some pleasure delaying. I think maybe you're simply too quick to slip back into your comfort zones, whatever they may be. I'd suggest taking some time before making that decision. Let the potential repercussions of it all sink in a little first."

The last time you saw him, Dr. Griffin had suggested that perhaps you should be taking more risks, which is why you're sitting here now with this bruise on your face. He gave you a lot of suggestions for finding happiness, but this was the last one he offered before he killed himself. You don't tell Gideon that.

"Pleasure delaying," you say. "I'll consider that."

"Then I'd say we made some progress here," he proclaims, patting himself on the back. "Not bad for a Day One."

Progress. Oh, yes. Leaps and bounds. You can barely begin to imagine just how much your life is about to change.

Gideon unlocks his desk drawer and removes the journal, flipping it open to the page he had previously made notes on. "Now, how about I write up a prescription for a couple of new things?"

"You're giving me *more* drugs?"

"*Different* drugs. You won't be taking any more of that crap Griffin was giving you."

"Isn't that dangerous? To just stop the meds my body is used to?"

"If your body was used to the drugs, the drugs would be working, wouldn't they?" He takes a look over your sheet and considers the list of medications you're already on. "Here," he concedes. "I'll keep up your prescription for the Vivactil and the cannabinoids, but the rest have got to go. Let me just write these up for you at the front desk." Gideon takes the journal with him as he makes for the door. "This won't take long, Epic. Please, just stay seated here for a few minutes."

A gust of cool air from the front office gushes in as soon as Gideon opens the door. He slams it shut behind him; the *Lovehunter* album rattles against the wall and the naked woman on the cover has to straddle that snake a little tighter just to hold on. You only have seconds to enjoy what's left of the breeze before it's gone, consumed entirely by the humidity. Outside, the screaming from the wild parade intensifies. You don't know if Gideon had *literally* meant for you to remain where you were when he instructed you to stay seated, but you get up and move to the window anyway.

From the top of a giant purple octopus float, a half-dozen men are firing into the crowd with oversized water guns. There are hoses from the back of each cannon connected to a gigantic tub of ice water that sloshes about as the float slowly navigates over potholes. You feel like a kid again at the window, hoping they might take aim upon you. You'd certainly open this window if they did. Luna Park ripples in the background, the heat and dry air making it appear to be dancing along with the party on Surf Avenue. Heavy beats from dissonant music shake the building; the window pane vibrates a little with every reverberation.

And then you spot her.

No, it's not Reya. Not even close. Her short hair is bleached white, almost the color of apple meat, and a dark pink stripe is painted above her left ear. She wears big sunglasses. You see the tiniest glints of a pierced eyebrow, a nose stud, and a lip ring, all lined up along her left side too, making her face appear jarringly unsymmetrical. Despite the heat, she wears a green army jacket and, for good measure, a flannel shirt is tied around her waist. Like she thought it was 1994 and she was heading out to a Pearl Jam concert.

What catches your attention instantly however, is seeing her stand amidst the crowd. You can't tell if it's her presence or lack thereof. Even the water spraying madly from the float seems to be avoiding her, like she has an invisible force field surrounding her or she exists in a different plane of reality. She sticks out because she isn't watching the parade with the same kind of general interest and enthusiasm as everyone else. It's almost as though she's trying to figure out what the point of it all is. She's not dancing on the spot or eating candy floss or wearing some garish costume; this girl remains within her own, quiet pocket universe.

Just as you're about to turn away, she looks up. Even from behind the sunglasses she wears, you can tell where her focus is set. She looks to the window where you're so blatantly spying. You almost jump back out of sight but you don't move an inch. You stand your ground. There's a slightly crooked smile on her face. The only thing you're hearing right now is the near-silent buzzing of some bug in this office.

And she very cautiously raises her right arm, opens her fingers as slowly as a flower blooming, and waves at you. It's obvious she's not even sure why exactly. You can see the confusion on her face. People are constantly saying things like, *"I can read her like an open book,"* which you always thought was stupid and made no sense at all. But now you get it.

Ten thousand years too late maybe, but now you finally get it.

ooo

You dash out to the front desk where you quickly take your new prescription from Gideon. He seems oblivious to the fact he'd asked you to remain in his office, and prattles on about something or other for a moment longer before the two of you eventually agree to meet again in a week. He'll send an email, he says, placing the cool palm of one hand into yours and the other upon your shoulder. You're not really locking any of it in; you shake his hand, stuff the prescription into your pocket and bound down the flight of stairs which takes you back out onto Surf Avenue.

The parade is practically over by the time you're outside. The floats are all out of sight and the crowd is already thinning out, most everyone heading into the park. You try to find the spot where the girl with the white hair was standing, but it wouldn't matter if you were exactly where her awkward feet were planted. She is most definitely gone.

This is the part where you begin to question everything. What are the chances she wasn't really looking at you? Perhaps the timid smile and wave were meant for someone else. Was she even here at all? Is the heat making you delirious? It's entirely possible that your prosopagnosia has you fooled, and you're looking for someone you're falsely recollecting. Maybe you've completely forgotten her already and compensating with some made-up details?

You pick up a large, plastic trident from the sidewalk, discarded by who knows what kind of fantasy sea creature. The police crews and piles of garbage along the parade route are very nearly the only signs left of the festivities that blew through here just minutes ago. The memories you're hoping to find are perhaps only less real than the mermen and mermaids who presumably once-presided over Surf Avenue.

THE THIRD

There's a delicate electricity in the air tonight, a feeling like if one were to tread ever so far from where they were meant to be, sinister events might unfold. The clear summer twilight seems to hide dark clouds beneath it, rather than the other way around. Yet the same rancid, musky odor of Coney Island Station greets you as it always does, smacking all of your senses at once. Sure, it's still comforting in a way, but you feel like you need to put yourself outside of your comfort zone (as the late Dr. Griffin suggested) so you find a seat directly across from another passenger — in fact the only other person in view — rather than a shady spot in the back corner of the last train. The old man ignores you, he of the two-piece checkered suit and ascot, looking like Al Pacino from *The Godfather*. On his feet, he showcases a pair of worn bowling shoes, one noticeably larger than the other. His left arm rests upon a massive, black garbage bag, its contents unknown but enigmatic. The deviant smile on his face captures you for a moment; why is he smiling so? You want to keep staring, but you know you'd be utterly defenseless should he make any sudden eye contact. Thankfully, your hand glides against a newspaper on the seat beside you, which is enough to turn your attention elsewhere.

Every time you ride the F-Train you feel lucky. There's a fairly high chance that good luck has never directly befallen anyone who rode the F, but inevitably you will catch yourself thinking, *"This is the day something special will happen.*" Because of this, you don't take the F-Train very often; in fact, you avoid it as much as possible. Because too much good luck, too much eager anticipation for something unknown cannot be healthy. And how likely is it that good luck could be such a constant anyway? That goes against the very idea of luck. Maybe it's something akin to this pleasure delaying, as Gideon suggested yesterday? Still, based on the alarming fashion in which this train shook upon leaving the station there was no reason to believe good luck was on its way.

Certainly not in your direction at least.

Tonight, you're riding the F-Train to Roosevelt Island. You're meeting Armand Bester, a co-worker of yours, at The Salt Mine, a trendy new restaurant on Roosevelt's Main Street. The small island, slivered between Manhattan and Queens, has a dark and dirty history of penitentiaries, lunatic asylums, and holding pens for victims of Smallpox. But today, Roosevelt Island is slowly transforming itself into the latest of New York City's gentrified neighborhoods offering luxury condos for a young, affluent demographic. You were supposed to pick up the company van from Bester at the warehouse in Gowanus, but he called asking you to meet him on Roosevelt Island instead.

His message: "There's something wrong with the van."

You don't know the first thing about the inner workings of your single-slice toaster, but Bester apparently thinks you're the company's expert on vehicle repair. Your guess is he once again did a little off-roading through Queensbridge Park beforehand and simply requires an alibi before filling out the night's routine paperwork. But you also figure as long as he's spotting your subway fare it's all fine by you. Plus, you can deliver the medicinal marijuana, the stuff which is prescribed to you which you only get for him. The perks of having a messed-up friend with mental issues, right?

The copy of the Daily News beside you appears to have gone untouched, as if the Sunday edition had been delivered directly to this seat. You catch the words "Coney Island" right on the front page in big, bold, serifed letters. There's rarely ever front-page news about Coney Island, and if there is, it's only because of a tragedy. You take the newspaper for a closer look. Sure enough, there was a homicide yesterday; it happened during the Mermaid Parade, just a block away from Gideon's office. You try to recall if you heard sirens or screaming but it's almost like you weren't even there yesterday. Like Gideon had you under hypnosis or something. There are no names or much in the way of description; sensationalistic journalism at its best. A man in his late twenties or early thirties was strangled with his own shirt. He was discovered in an alley by a homeless man who had probably wondered at first who had taken over his turf.

And then you don't know why, but you suddenly think again about how long it's been since you've spoken with your father.

The next few pages are of no real consequence. You glance over them as the train stops at Avenue U Station. A penguin at the Central Park Zoo that was believed to have died yesterday was now miraculously alive again. Some gibberish about a coma-like condition called cerebral hypoxia. They also refer to it as hypoxic hypoxia. Simply glancing over the article doesn't give you any glaring insight, nor do you really find it interesting enough to read deeper. The rest is so mundane it feels the same reports have been printed over and over again. Effortless stories for the simple sake of daily dissemination: a sewage pipe burst in the Upper West Side; a new dog park opened in the Village; Hampton green tomatoes may reduce cervical cancer.

By the time the train reaches Avenue N Station, you've already tossed the paper aside, without bothering to fold it back neatly into its once-pristine condition. On the seat, there's a book which you hadn't spotted when you first took the newspaper. It is a novel, softcover and dog-eared in its condition. You almost wonder if somebody left it beside you as they passed by, but you're certain no one other than the grinning gentleman across from you has been in this car.

You pick the book up, and it feels only slightly heavier than you imagined it might. Just enough to seem significant.

The novel is entitled *The Third*. The cover is a painting of two identical left forearms with their wrists facing out. Someone has defaced the cover with a bright green marker, having drawn juvenile slits along the wrists with blood streaming out. Like they are bleeding guacamole or possibly belong to some sort of space creature who has assumed the form of a man. Checking the front matter, you discover this is an English translation of a French novel by the author Jean Trepanier, first published in the 1970's. This translation was some twenty years after that. The back cover offers no synopsis, no indication of what the reader might be in for. You've been meaning to read a new book since burning through that inane space opera trilogy, so without any consideration you simply open up the novel to Chapter One and start reading as the F-Train disembarks from Avenue N.

The writing is by no means extraordinary, but it may be due in part to the translation or maybe this Jean Trepanier was simply a bad writer. Or possibly both. Right from the start, the novel does not seem so out of the ordinary. It's about a young man named Tristan Montminy. Tristan is a university student somewhere outside of Paris who also works part-time in furniture construction, but you get the feeling what he does is not actually important. You've always been curious about how writers decide to craft their stories. Obviously not all information in a book is relevant to the story but where do authors decide to plant the clues about what really matters? Clues about where their tale is truly headed?

The book opens with Tristan at his workshop. He's in the middle of building an oblong kitchen table when his girlfriend, Emilia, shows up in a huff. She is pissed at him for something he doesn't even remember doing, but he doesn't appear to be too worried about it. He's been forgetting things lately anyway, presumably a result of all the marijuana he's been smoking. Trepanier then takes you on a two-page journey to Tuscany; a flashback to when Tristan and Emilia once took a trip together and came home with a wooden vegetable crate full of pot. After a brief and fruitless argument, Emilia exits just as abruptly as she entered. From there, Tristan continues his woodworking, now with the author inexplicably going into great detail about the grain and the color of the wood. There's nearly four pages of description here.

You look up from the book; the F-Train has stopped at 42nd Street/Bryant Park. Only four more stations until Roosevelt Island. The old man across from you is still smiling at nothing in particular. If only you could summon the bravado to ask him what kind of prescriptions he might be on because it's definitely not the same as what you're taking.

As the train starts off again, you continue reading. Tristan is on his way to class, though there's never any mention of what classes he's coming from or going to. Upon entering the lecture hall, Tristan stops. He suddenly recalls a dream he had one week before; a dream he did not remember until now. However, the reader is not privy to the details of this dream, which you find irksome. Tristan snaps out of his reverie when someone calls out to him:

> "Luca!" the voice shouted. "Hey Luca!" Tristan looked around and spotted a stout young man he did not recognize. This person appeared to be waving at him. "Luca! What are you doing here?" he asked.
>
> Tristan looked behind him but nobody was there. The man was definitely speaking to him. He waved politely at the stranger and sat on the far side of the lecture hall rather than in his usual corner. He hoped to see a recognizable face amongst the crowd but there were none to be found.

It takes your brain a few seconds to register hearing the announcement that the train just left the 21st Street/Queensbridge Station. *What?* How did you miss your stop? The old man is gone now too, probably having exited the train while your attention was caught between the pages of the book in your lap. The next stop is Jackson Heights, a fair extra distance from where you want to be, and you sit alone the entire way there. You fold the corner of the page you're at in *The Third* and watch as a darkened Astoria and Woodside pass by the window. The subway is so close to a few of the buildings that you can see the details of the lit apartments. Tiny slices of unknown lives flicker by, not unlike a film reel, almost animating the goings on inside. Mostly just televisions tuned to the same channel. The lonely blue lights are so hypnotic, you almost don't realize the train is slowing down. Slipping the copy of *The Third* into your rucksack, you exit the eastbound station and run the gauntlet over to the Manhattan-bound side, barely making it in time for the next F-Train. You scramble through the swarm of midnight commuters spewing from the train and find a spot, this time in the familiarity of the very last car.

There's some bug buzzing around the tip of your nose and when you try to brush it away, it hovers around your left ear, humming its maddening song just for you. Then over to your right ear. Swatting at the thing maniacally, you almost miss seeing the girl outside the window. She must have just gotten off the train as you went the other way. Even with the prosopagnosia, you know for sure it's the same girl you'd seen during the parade yesterday, still in the same clothes, still wearing the same sunglasses. You can clearly see a skull-and-crossbones pattern stitched onto her jacket. Her short, white hair barely flutters in the subway's presence, ignoring the blasts of air coming in through both ends of the tunnels. Although shrouded by the eyewear, you can tell she recognizes you, too. That, or she just might have a staring problem. It's the same look as the one from across the street the day before. You don't even have time to raise a hand or nod in mutual recognition before the F-Train clatters off and the girl disappears back into a primarily faceless crowd.

ooo

The van rattles across the Roosevelt Island Bridge, back over into Queens. There are handwritten signs taped to the inside of every window on the van which read: *NO Money. NO $$$. NO Valuables. LOTS of Boobie Traps.* Honestly, you're not sure what the difference between Money and $$$ is. Bester is sitting beside you; you're driving while he's rolling the marijuana you'd given him, totally ignoring the large bruise you're sporting on your face. There's something under the van, down below your feet, that's making a noise it shouldn't be making. Even you know enough to know that. It clangs and clatters a little louder with every pothole you hit. "What the hell did you do to this thing?" you ask him.

Bester's in the midst of a futile attempt at lighting the massive thing at the open window. "You definitely do *not* want to know," he says matter-of-factly. He holds the unlit joint in the palm of his hand for a moment as though he were summoning the willpower to try again. Maybe attempting some sort of pyrokinetic trick. The two of you sit without words a while longer before he continues. "But I'll tell ya, I'm gonna need to start buying some different pants if I'm gonna keep getting blowjobs in the company van."

"Jesus," you say, squirming. "Wouldn't most people have ended the conversation on the *You-don't-want-to-know* part?"

"Sorry. I figured you actually *did* want to know. I mean, why else would you have asked, right?"

You don't answer, hoping this is going to signal the end of the dialogue.

But Bester can't help himself. And honestly, he never can. "It's just that these friggin' jeans are too constrictive, you know? I can't get comfortable. I gotta pull them all the way down to my ankles, bro! That's not cool. What do you think? Do you think my cock's too big?" Unlit joint in his mouth, he claws at his crotch madly like he's trying to shoo a cat away.

"I think it's your balls."

"Aw shit. C'mon, bro. Nobody wants giant balls. Why you gotta go there?"

"Could we maybe not talk about the size of your genitalia right now?"

"Hey, come on. Whatever happened to living vicariously through me and all that shit? Weren't we just discussing this last week?"

"I said I felt like living vicariously through *someone*. I don't recall being so specific."

Finally, Bester succeeds in lighting the joint. "Well, you take what you can get, right?"

You twist through the streets of Brooklyn. Everything is brick and the summer heat still radiates from the crumbling, weed-infested sidewalks. Auto body shops and convenience stores, all with their awnings so faded you'd probably have no idea which was which until you stepped foot inside them. Shady characters patrolling the streets wearing heavy bomber jackets, oblivious to the evening temperature. The icky smoke from the factories along the East River forming the only cloud cover in the night sky.

Finally, you concede. Maybe you shouldn't be so quick to vilify the lives of others? "So, who was she?" you ask.

"Who's who?"

"The girl in the van." The putrid scent of other people's sex lingers in the seats, and you feel you already know her better than you want to.

"Just someone I met at The Salt Mine. A waitress or something."

"You mean you only met her tonight?"

"That's right."

"Sounds like you really took the time to get to know her."

"Who's got the time these days? She was on her smoke break."

"Seriously, Bester. Do you pick up girls from these restaurants all the time?"

"Sure I do. We *all* do."

"We?"

"Yeah. Everyone at work. Everyone who isn't *you*, that is." It might sound stupid, and you hate to admit it, but Armand Bester is without a doubt the coolest person you've ever known. Even when he's insulting you, he somehow still seems cool. He's handsome, with dreads pulled back in a ponytail. Any other dreadlocks you've ever seen have been so dusty and dirty; you don't know how Bester keeps his hair so clean. Suede blazers and vests and an expensive watch with a brand name you can't even pronounce. The four clanking pewter bracelets on his left wrist may or may not be assisting him with what he refers to as his Zen-mastery. It's the bold belt buckles, the complicated shoes, and the sparkling cufflinks that all add up to something which can only possibly be described as cool. It's the kind of cool you know you'll never attain. "Man, the stories these vans could tell," he says wistfully.

He's still a dog though.

You turn your head a little, and from your peripheral you spot the mountain of dirty laundry piled in the back of the van. Just imagining the activities that may or may not have taken place upon those bulging bags sends a shiver spiraling up your spine.

"You know, Epic, you're really not doing any better over there. When's the last time you got any?"

You don't even want to embarrass yourself with an answer, so you try not to think about the question. Instead, the image of the girl you spotted twice in the last two days suddenly pops into your head. You run your tongue along the top edge of your teeth before boldly lying to him. "Actually, I have been seeing someone lately." It's not really a lie, but it's not entirely the whole truth either. You have *seen* her, just not in the dating sense of the word.

Bester nearly spits out his joint. "No kidding? What's her deal?"

"I'll be honest; I don't really know her all that well yet." You don't want to sound like you've set yourself up for failure, so you just make up some crap for him to chew on. "She's from Colorado."

Bester's mouth puckers, like he just bit into a green banana, peel and all. "*Colorado*? Who the fuck's from Colorado? No offense, but this sounds like it's going to be one quick ride, bro."

"How do you know?"

"Trust me. A dude can just tell these things sometimes."

"Simply because she's from Colorado?"

"There's that. Not to mention the fact she's dating *you*."

"Thanks."

"But it doesn't diminish the fact that I'm happy for you. And fuck, *you* should be happy too."

"Don't I seem happy?"

"How long have I known you? Two years? I'm fairly certain I've *never* seen you happy. Not once. So, I know you *that* well, at least."

He knows you; you can certainly give him that much. It's like what Gideon said just yesterday: "*Better than you know yourself, is that how it goes?*"

Bester may be a sexually-charged oaf with a marijuana problem, but he's also extremely observant. Obviously, he does not dream of working for a simple laundry and linen delivery service for the rest of his life; Armand Bester is a writer through and through. His observational skills are probably what make him so good at it. Though his work has never left much of an impression on you. He has occasionally tossed short stories and poetry of his your way, but his writing has never really made sense. You blame yourself though; too much of a low-level thinker, perhaps. Bester attends university full time and it's not uncommon for you to catch him writing something whenever you meet, whether it's a poem, a play, or just jotting down ideas for some big novel he's got percolating in there.

Bester is passionate about his creative outlet, and could perhaps go down in history as the most ambitious pot-head ever. Maybe he's delusional? Or maybe that's you. Are you intimidated by the potential of others? Maybe if you never know the true extent of his talent you'll never have to feel like you should be jealous or sorry for him. Armand Bester has written many stage plays, his love for the theater shows in most of his off-work wardrobes. One time when the two of you went for drinks after work he wore an eye patch. Just for flair. Recently, he's had some play of his produced and it's finally debuting this week at some small hole-in-the-wall theater out in Bushwick.

You met him on his first graveyard shift at Brooklyn Whites; you were asked to show the new guy the ropes so someone with more authority wouldn't have to. The two of you just sort of clicked, even though you've got virtually nothing in common with one another. Right from the start, Bester jokingly referred to you as "Bestest," a nickname that's just stuck. Bester and Bestest. There's another guy at Brooklyn Whites you sometimes work with who you both refer to as "Worst." Of course, Worst has no idea you call him that behind his back.

"So, where did you meet her?" he asks you.

"Surf Avenue. I think she mistook me for someone else at first."

"That's not the best start. What's her name?"

You think about this for a moment before slyly stating, "Come on, Bester. You don't think I'm going to tell you everything at once, do you?" And it seems like he buys it.

"Nah, bro. I understand. It's just cool that you found *someone*. I mean finally. After all that Reya shit, right?"

"Right. The shit."

"You ever think of her anymore?"

How do you tell him she's all you think about still? You can't help yourself. You might feel like you're the world's biggest heartbroken loser, but you certainly don't want to promote yourself as such. "Sometimes," you say. "It's hard to get over someone who meant that much to you. Does anyone ever, really?"

Bester leans his head back on the seat, staring at the van's rusted ceiling. The marijuana joint dangling from his lips. With all the shaking and rattling, it's surprising to think he can actually concentrate so hard on whatever it is he's dwelling upon. You figure if he was planning on answering your question he would've had an answer by now. And all he eventually manages to say is, "Shit, it's hot out, innit?"

ooo

You pull up in front of an apartment complex somewhere in Sunnyside. There's a girl standing outside the building giving off a hooker vibe but even from this distance and the two A.M. moonlight you can tell she's far too pretty for it. She's talking to a tall man, oblivious to the fact you've just pulled up across the street and are watching the both of them. He's wearing a basketball jersey. 76'ers, maybe? The rumbling of the van makes it impossible to hear any of their conversation. This is where you and Bester will part company for the night. This is where you *always* part company, though you're fairly certain he doesn't live around here, and you know for a fact this is the first time there's ever been anyone else loitering outside the building.

Tonight though, he lingers beside you for a moment longer. He seems to have a lot more on his mind than the filth — of both laundry and sex — in the company van. Finally, he turns to you and smiles. One of those big white smiles you cannot help but love to be in the presence of. He says, "Why don't you bring this new girl to my premiere on Wednesday? I'm sure it would help."

"How would it help?"

"Mostly because I never met Reya and I just want to make sure this one actually exists."

"Ha, ha. You're very amusing."

"Come on, bro. This show is important to me. If it's big, it could be my ticket out of here."

"Out of here? Where would you go?"

"Going isn't about leaving. It's about *making it*. Putting your name on something that will stick around long after you do."

In your dreams, you're not prolific, but you are leaving something important behind.

The couple outside the apartment are still talking. You try to imagine what their conversation might be about but you've never been any good at knowing what people want from one another. The man abruptly walks away and takes only a few steps before turning back toward the woman. Bester watches them too.

"What's it about?" you ask him. "The play, I mean."

"If I tell you, you'll just find an excuse for why you can't come." He reaches into the inside pocket of his suede blazer and pulls out a piece of paper, folded in half. He hands you the playbill. *The Duality of Thee*, it's called. There's no image on the cover at all, just the title and Bester's name: *A Stage Play by Armand Bester*. "Just come. And bring the new girl."

With that, Bester opens the door and hops out of the van. You look past him and the other man has already disappeared somewhere. "Thanks again for the weed, bro."

"It's medicinal, remember."

"Nah. It's only medicinal when *you* take it." He sucks the last bit of fire out of the joint and flicks it right through a sewer grate at his feet. "See you Wednesday, Bestest!" He sashays over to the girl, holds her from behind, and seductively plants one on the nape of her neck. You watch as they embrace for a moment, sinking into the seat as though they don't know you're still here with the engine running. But they don't seem to care either way. The girl reaches behind her and runs her hand along the back of his neck, fingers entwined in his dreadlocks. His hands are quick to test the waters, first a little below her breasts and then just a little lower. He's bold, but she certainly doesn't mind. She turns now and Bester smacks both hands firmly on her rear. The two of them share a passionate kiss before disappearing up the front stoop and into the apartment.

To a passerby, you probably look like a massive pervert. Based on perception alone, you probably wouldn't blame them. You wonder what it is about some people's inhibitions when they can so easily suck face on the sidewalk while others can only sit in a parked van trying to figure it all out. You don't wish to be someone else, you never have; that's a dream reserved for those who want too much. But you must have missed out on some memo somewhere. What else have you missed by simply being you?

Holding up the playbill again for another look, you notice something as it falls out from within the folded paper: two tickets to the show on Wednesday night. You shift the van out of park and head back to the warehouse in Gowanus, the rattling below you continues the entire way.

ooo

The F-Train sounds worse than the van did, but nobody ever minds a shaking subway. You could prove it too, if there were anyone else riding the train at this hour. The closing doors almost took your foot off as you boarded; your focus is somewhere else tonight, too busy working through what has transpired in the last couple of days. From Griffin to Gideon to spotting that peculiar girl twice now. There's a big, black garbage bag on the seat across from you and you wonder if it's the same one you'd seen earlier. You can't recall if the old man across from you on the subway had taken it with him. You weren't paying attention to much else besides the book you found. You withdraw *The Third* from your rucksack and continue from where you left off.

Tristan Montminy had just been mistaken for someone else, someone named Luca. He doesn't think much of it, as Jean Trepanier writes:

> Everybody is mistaken for somebody else at some point. Identities from our pasts adjust to fit identities from our futures.

You don't know exactly what the author meant by this, but it sounds like something you'd be familiar with. Your prosopagnosia is quick to make strangers out of friends, but recognition — or lack thereof — is a constantly shifting thing.

Identity is not reality.

The chapter concludes with no more insight aside from the meal Tristan consumed at the university cafeteria. Two pages of the smell, color, temperature, taste, and texture of a plate of pork chops, corn, and gravy.

You continue reading into the next chapter where Tristan Montminy is at a Parisian fountain. He'd decided to skip classes today on a whim, and now here he is: surrounded by crowds and lost within a tidal wave of tourists. A couple approaches Tristan and asks if he might take their photo, handing a camera to him. He argues that he does not know how to work the expensive camera so of course, predictably, the reader is bombarded with three pages describing how a Russian Zorki 4K camera operates. Upon relenting, Tristan takes their picture and the couple finally leaves him alone, tossing some coins his way as payment for the kind gesture. Without thinking, Tristan lobs the money over his shoulder and into the fountain.

Just as he hears the water plopping, he also hears a voice speaking to him. You have no idea what is said here, because for some reason, this part of the French dialogue is not translated for the reader. Perhaps it is unimportant, but it's strange since the rest of the novel so far has been entirely in English. Nevertheless, Tristan turns and immediately recognizes the gentleman standing there. But not because he knows him: he recognizes the man because he is physically identical to himself. A mirror image, the author calls it, though you know Jean Trepanier must not have meant it literally since this description implies details like scars and moles and the part in his hair would be on the opposite side of this other man's body.

You are now introduced to Luca Desplante III, a locally-known rogue and troublemaker. Though the two have never met before, it is not surprising that they find themselves drawn to one another. Naturally, they want to explore the reasons behind their similarities. They are certainly not brothers, but they are without a doubt twins. Luca's hair is a bit longer and Tristan's hands are calloused from his years of woodworking, but they are otherwise identical.

When Tristan explains how lately he's had feelings of loneliness and how he questions the directions his life has been heading, Luca expresses the same. He makes Tristan a bold offer, and for the first time this story feels like it's actually heading somewhere:

"Let us make a switch."

"Trade lives?" Tristan asked.

"Of course! It would be so simple! You love your girlfriend no?"

Tristan did love Emilia but recently there had been a gap there. One that was becoming larger almost daily. "I do" he admitted.

"But still you wonder. Correct? What it must be like to have another? To feel the skin of another fruit? To taste the juice of a different harvest?" Luca dipped his fingertips into the fountain and licked the water from them tenderly.

Tristan confessed what Luca was proposing did seem like something familiar. How different can two different men truly be?

"Then let us go our separate ways" Luca insisted. "However dissimilar our paths were meant to be let us now follow the path of each other. Let us now live as another man. If only for a moment."

The dialogue here is so horribly unnatural, almost Shakespearean in its awkwardness. You don't really know though, since you've never once read Shakespeare. Again, you have to wonder if this is simply the French-to-English translation or if Trepanier is so truly untalented. So, after some further encouragement on Luca's part, the two men agree to switch lives but they also agree to meet back at the same fountain once a week. The same day and time as now. They hop over to a side street, and exchange clothes to complete the transformation. Jean Trepanier calls it a metamorphosis, but that doesn't sound right. Tristan and Luca swap addresses and then they're off, Luca riding away on the bike Tristan had brought to the fountain. For a moment, Tristan Montminy is left wondering about the pact he just agreed upon.

As you disembark the F-Train and begin your walk back home, you think about the rest of what you'd just read. What's most confounding is that it is clearly implied Luca is meant to look identical to Tristan, but Trepanier's descriptions of Luca in the book are constantly changing, and — to the reader, at least — he never really seems to look anything like his "twin." Luca is black; he's Chinese; a child; female; overweight; you name it. And yet nobody seems confused or bothered by this. In fact, the two characters don't even notice a discrepancy, nor is it ever really described in the book as being even the slightest bit odd. Tristan and Luca are simply seen as twins. And nothing more.

A few weeks have passed in the novel, and Tristan and Luca had both routinely met back at the fountain every Thursday afternoon. The twins were now working one another's jobs (both of which they were better at) and they were now having sex with one another's girlfriends (each of whom were both much more satisfied). His "new" girlfriend, Grace, asks Tristan at one point about his hands. They are so much more calloused and worn than she'd ever noticed before. Tristan just tells her they've always been that way. But Tristan is now finding it hard to be in a relationship with Luca's girlfriend. He misses Emilia too much. He wonders if Luca is having some of the same problems, or if maybe he's just seeing both of the girls. Grace certainly does leave their apartment on her own a lot. Tristan intended to ask Luca about this the next time they would meet. But Luca (who was last described as a pre-pubescent Inuit girl) does not show on the following Thursday. Tristan sits at the fountain in much the same way as he did weeks before, though he's beginning to consider whether or not he's actually lonelier now. As he ponders his predicament, another couple approaches him for another photograph, of which Tristan refuses outright.

This novel confuses you more with every chapter and every word. What's the point of it all, really? You're still not entirely sure. When you get home, you try and put it all out of your mind. But as fractured as your mind seems to feel lately, you know it won't be long before unwanted thoughts creep back in. Maybe some of these new prescriptions Gideon gave you will help?

After your first session yesterday, you went straight to the pharmacy and gave them the list of psychopharmaceuticals that will presumably begin to finally help you. You've been instructed to take three 25mg Effexor venlafaxine hydrochloride tablets a day (one with each meal), two sprays of Zolpimist zolpidem tartrate oral spray over your tongue (one in the morning, one at night), and one 20mg Celexa citalopram hydrobromide tablet daily, in addition to the 30mg of Vivactil protriptyline hydrochloride tablets you were already consuming. No more Lexapro. Goodbye, Pristiq. It's been a blast,

OxyContin.

This morning, you placed the 100-count bottle of Celexa on your bedside table, the Zolpimist spray bottle in the medicine cabinet, and the package of thirty Effexor tablets into your bag, along with one of your Vivactil bottles. Everything placed systematically where you will best remember to take them daily. Patterns and procedures and routines to form the habits you won't ever need to stop to think about. Your rucksack is always dumped beside the bedside table. The medicine cabinet is always left slightly ajar.

Removing the tickets and playbill Bester gave you, you barely even glance at them before chucking them onto the kitchen counter.

You think about how you'd felt lucky earlier this evening; riding the F-Train to Roosevelt Island. And it occurs to you now, that feeling had not surged through your body or crossed your mind at all during the ride back home. Maybe these tickets to the play would feel luckier if what you'd told Bester was actually the truth: that you really *did* meet someone new rather than feeling like you're simply digging a deeper and deeper hole dwelling on thoughts of Reya instead.

THE UNDINER

"What do you mean you met someone new? Do not give me this bullshit Luca!"

Of course Tristan wanted to tell her it was not bullshit. He wanted to tell Grace that the someone new was really a someone old. Someone who he had known long before the switch. He wanted to tell her that he missed Emilia more every day. Every week that passed was a reminder of everything he'd given up. But he could not find the courage. "I am sorry Grace" he said. "But things have become far too complicated lately. Sometimes I find myself forgetting even the details of who I am truly."

"I have no idea what you are saying anymore Luca. I know something in you has changed but I know not what that is. It is impossible. You are impossible!"

Grace turned around and disappeared from his sight faster than Tristan thought the girl could move. And then he was alone once again on that rain-soaked bench in the courtyard once again. The ivy vines on the brick walls reminded him just how twisted and confusing life can become if unmanaged properly. If Luca had not already stolen his identity surely Tristan would have had to consider leaving it behind in this place where it could do no further damages. He knew that he did not love Grace and yet he was finding it harder so harder to hurt her every time they met. Not unlike how it feels when one feels love for another. Perhaps though it was how Luca had meant for things to play out? Perhaps Tristan considered the most hurtful damages are always inflicted through a third party?

He tried to think of Emilia again but found her details a little more misplaced than they were the last time she had crossed his mind.

The sound of heavy, metallic clinking from back in the diner's kitchen breaks your concentration. Like a mountainous pile of cutlery is being dumped into a full sink. You lay the book face down on the Formica table, wondering how you've already read as much as you have. The translated English is atrocious, to the point where you're not certain the translator even knew English very well. The concept is mostly unbelievable, the characters are simply unlikable, and yet the story is still somehow gripping. The two identical men, Tristan and Luca, have switched lives, but Tristan is slowly beginning to regret the decision. He knows he doesn't love Grace, in fact he doesn't even enjoy her company, and he hasn't seen or spoken to Emilia or Luca for weeks now. He's returned to the fountain a few times to look for Luca with no luck. What can he do at this point? Tristan is stuck, trapped within a life he never really asked for. But at the same time, he's not entirely convinced that he's ready to return to his old one.

It feels like you, in a way. Like this is all just someone else's destiny. You keep trying to fool yourself into believing you're not actually stuck in this life, but who are you kidding? You opt instead to simply flag the waitress down for another cup of coffee. Save the fantasies for where they're meant.

Her name tag reads "Dorothy," though if in fact all the waitresses here actually used the same name tag you cannot be sure. No matter what time you visit this diner, Dorothy is the only one who's ever served you. With your prosopagnosia you'll never know the difference. Uniforms are a tricky one: the individuals need to have even more specific memory triggers in order for you to differentiate. Her details are not so specific; they're hard to pin down. A little too fluid, maybe? She takes orders in her head. She never touches that pen in her hair, lodged in like a superfluous twig in a nest. As few words as possible; not one for small talk. She pours the coffee. Serves the bran flakes. Refills the coffee. Every waitress here has only ever done the same. Still, she seems to know what she's doing, so you're assuming you've seen her here before.

They must, without a doubt, all know who *you* are, however.

In your dreams, you would never need a name tag to recognize Dorothy. Even though in your dreams, you know you've never once stepped foot in this diner. In your dreams, you make your own destiny; your life is your own.

In your dreams, you're fully aware of who it is you truly are.

In your dreams, you're the opposite of every decision you made along the way to where you are now.

Just as Dorothy refills the coffee, you realize you've already had too much. You don't need another cup; it's only going to make you all the more jittery and unfocused. But the chipped, yellow ceramic mug is full again, and you would only feel guilty if you left a full cup of cold coffee behind. There's a thick puddle of the stuff on the tabletop, pooled together within the crusty ring of coffee that's been there since the last time you sat in this booth. Attention to detail and proper restaurant hygiene seem to be things of the past here at The UnDiner.

That's right, The UnDiner. It's kind of the anti-diner; a restaurant that doesn't want to be, as the name implies. And it just might be right. Nowadays there aren't too many of these places where you can't find a hipster with a handlebar moustache or a mousy girl writing the next great American novel on her tablet, but you certainly won't find them here at The UnDiner. Its only customers seem to be single, middle-aged obese men in sweatpants, war veterans, and spinsters. And you. Just another member of this miserable lot filling up on burnt coffee and stale bran flakes, yet you continue to come here instead of finding something that might possibly make you happier.

In your dreams, you make your own destiny.

You notice the two of them as soon as they enter The UnDiner. The bell above the door jingles when they come in. The boys in blue. Two identical uniforms, though one man — the bigger one — walks with a slight limp and the other — the smaller one — is Hispanic and sweating profusely. They walk swiftly across the restaurant toward the counter where an unknown man who you hadn't noticed until now is simply trying to remain anonymous. Just like everyone, really. You can hear the start of their conversation, with generic cop talk and downplayed authoritative aggressiveness. But their dialogue becomes quieter, more private. Still, it's none of your business so you don't bother turning around.

No, The UnDiner is certainly not the place to be if you're looking to be seen. Best if you're just looking to vanish, to go unnoticed by the rest of the world. The walls are cracking, the over-abundant kitchen fires have permanently blackened the ceiling, and the whole building is in even worse condition than your father's apartment on Mermaid Avenue, which is just about one more complaint-to-the-city away from being condemned. You're pretty sure the pies behind the glass display are the same ones that were there the first night you came in. The coffee cups are all different colors and sizes and shapes, not in a quirky, intentional kind of way but more because it was just the way things ended up. The diner's only neighbor is a laundromat which never seems to have any laundry in the machines. As far as you can tell, the single redeeming quality of The UnDiner has to be the bacon. You make sure to also order the cheapest item on the menu — the child-sized bowl of bran flakes — as the lamest form of misdirection. But the bacon, it's cooked to a crisp and drizzled in honey and sticky brown sugar. How could you possibly eat anywhere else in this city?

"You've got the wrong guy!" the unknown man at the counter exclaims, interrupting your thoughts. He yells it so loud, it makes him seem that much guiltier. "I'm tellin' ya, you've got the wrong guy!"

You have no desire to turn around for fear of things escalating. You think any eye contact with any of these men would only be making trouble for yourself somewhere down the road. It must be this kind of foresight that makes you seem so aloof at times.

There's a scuffle, like hostile, pugnacious hands grabbing at clothing, skin slapping skin. And you try drowning out the horrible ruckus by turning an ear toward the whirring of the small, blue plastic fan behind your head. Before you know it, the cops are yanking the man from the counter and ushering him outside, taking their conversation elsewhere. So much for them.

But you have the opportunity to think only for a tiny moment more before you hear the voice behind you. "Excuse me?" she asks, as though waiting for a reply to a previously unheard question.

You turn slightly, just enough to instantly know everything you need to.

It's her.

Prosopagnosia be damned. You recognize the stark white hair with the pink stripe, the piercings, the olive-green army jacket, and the sunglasses still covering her eyes. You freeze. All you can do is wonder why she's here and what it is she wants from you.

"I said, do you have a napkin over there?" This girl. She lifts her sunglasses up over her forehead so they rest in the shallow nest of white. Her reddy-brown eyes are as dark as the Earth's deepest clay. You remember her clearly. You watched her from the window of Gideon's office and she had stood so terribly alone on the other side of the freak parade. Still, there's something oddly familiar about those eyes. In one swift motion, you pick up and hand her the entire napkin dispenser.

"Some people call them serviettes," she says. "Though I've never met anyone who calls them that." Without saying thanks, she turns back around and goes about her business of breakfast.

And you sit now with nothing left to wonder but what the hell just happened. You were certain the first time you'd spotted this girl — waving at you from across Surf Avenue, and again from the window of the F-Train — that she'd recognized you. Truthfully, you think it was a wave, but the more you try to remember it, the less it feels like one. The way she stopped to look at you, like seeing a beautiful storm in the far distance and not knowing if it's coming for you or not. Helplessly watching as the world slowly explodes around you. And yet now there is nothing; not even the faintest sign of it. But maybe you were just fooling yourself? Maybe the prosopagnosia was simply playing a trick on your memory? More than it usually will, that is. Perhaps this is not even the same girl. Perhaps she never was.

You turn back around but she's already lost in her world. Maybe you'd be better off doing the same. You open *The Third* back to the folded corner marking the page where you'd left off:

Emilia had once meant everything to him Tristan knew that much. But would he even recognize her now if they passed one another on the street? Would she recognize him? Would she want to?

Tristan sunk a little farther into the bench. The wet unvarnished wood would want to absorb all of him. It would take him inside if only the cracks were not so worn and rounded off. A fresh slit or nick in the wood is so much more alive. His hand caressed the wood but not in the same way Tristan would embrace his own furniture. Tristan had not made a new piece for so long now but he still could not forget that oak table and the intimacy of its touch. He could disappear into his own furniture so easily.

Tristan wished for nothing more than to disappear now but he no longer knew how.

You stop. Is it normal for the mind to break so easily? Are *you* normal? You can't help yourself from folding the same page corner back down and placing the book on the table again. You sneak one more peek behind you. You think it's the army jacket with the skull and crossbones design that tells you you're missing something here. What is the possibility she's just like you? Maybe she lacks the same facial recognition abilities you do? One person in every fifty has some form of developmental prosopagnosia, whether extreme or mild versions. What are the chances?

Ridiculous, you tell yourself. The chances are a ridiculous improbability.

Tristan tried as hard as he might but it was not going to happen. This is where he was. This courtyard in the rain was where he was meant to be for the now moment. Maybe a different bench in a different courtyard with vines twisted a different direction would have yielded happier results tonight. Who can know these things?

Let's be honest. It's not as though what you're feeling is a physical attraction, right? It's a mnemonic one. A triggered memory and nothing more. You shouldn't be afraid to get this girl's attention. Now Reya, she was a different story, wasn't she? You weren't afraid of her; you just saw her and you talked to her. You asked her what was wrong and she told you all about it and she didn't think you were a freak. There's something wrong with everyone. You're all damaged goods. With Reya, you should have been more scared than you were. But you weren't. And this should really be easier than that. This is nothing.

Who can really know these things?

You close the book once more and turn back around. If she's waiting for you to say something, this girl is doing a spectacular job at making it seem like she could actually care less. She collects syrup off the edge of the plate using scrambled eggs on the tip of her fork. But you don't care if she's ignoring you or not; you're too determined to go outside your comfort zone, just as Dr. Griffin had told you before he died and as Gideon had seriously suggested you not do.

With a fearless clearing of the throat you ask, "Do I know you?" hoping this is enough to get her attention.

She turns her head a little to the right and suspiciously raises an eyebrow, almost like she's sensing trouble from you. "God, I hate that line."

"I'm sorry, it's not a line. I'm just asking." She turns fully and stares blankly at you now, maybe not used to being spoken to so bluntly. You tell her, "I have prosopagnosia."

"I'll be honest with you, Rainbow. I have no clue what that means." She calls you *Rainbow* as though she's had the pet name for you forever.

"It means I don't recognize people very well. Even people I've maybe met hundreds of times before. That's why I was asking."

"All right," she replies like what you just said makes complete sense to her. The breeze from the fan behind you catches the stark white tips of her hair, and they tease the space above her like a cat might test a bowl of sour milk with its tongue. "Sure," she adds a little too late, but you follow along anyway.

You try to gulp down some coffee but it's too hot to taste any more than just a sip. You almost burn your lips. "I was only asking because I feel like I recognize you, even though I technically shouldn't."

Identity is not reality.

"I don't know what to tell you, Rainbow. We've either met or we haven't."

"What does that mean?"

"Maybe it means I'm not sure either." She collapses her head a little into her shoulder and seems to bite the inside of her cheek, maybe considering what to say next. But her next move is nothing more than turning back around; maybe glad she doesn't have to talk to the kook behind her any longer. She's got her napkins, or serviettes, or whatever she's going to call them. What more needs to be said?

You turn your attention away from the skulls on her jacket and back into *The Third*. Tristan remains on the bench in the rain and he's exploring his feelings toward Luca a bit more. Recollecting how, at first, he had enjoyed pretending to be someone else, but now he's clearly jealous and angry when thinking about someone out there pretending to be him. You're becoming more and more curious about this novel now, feeling for the plight of Tristan Montminy, but you can't deny the fact you find the girl behind you much more remarkable.

Your focus is scattered. You can sense her there like the heat from a furnace on a cold night. Her presence is the sort of comfort that is really noticed when it's *not* there. When it's lacking.

Holding your knife up to your face, you find her reflection inside of it. At least you know she's not a vampire. That's something. In your shaky hand, the stitched skulls on her jacket jump around the knife's rippled surface; they look more like obscure characters from some alien language. She's sitting still though, lumped over a bit with her face buried in her left hand. The waitress is asking her if she wants something more but the girl just shoos her away. It's so muggy you want to do the same, rather than expend any more energy asking for another refill, but when Dorothy comes over, you just slide the cup toward her and let it happen. You grunt a thank you and plunk the knife into the steaming liquid, letting the utensil's thin handle clink against the rim.

You place *The Third* down beside you on the seat cushion, out of the girl's view, and bite the bullet. "I'm sorry," you say, forgetting to turn around, but knowing exactly where you want your words to land. "Even with my condition I can't help but think I know you from somewhere."

"If you want your napkins back, just ask," she says. "You can cut it out with the foreplay and idle chit chat." You turn once again and she's looking right at you, arms crossed and elbows resting on the back of the peeling seat. Her eyes flicker from you to the fan and back again. "You mind if I sit with you so we can merrily share in this wild experience of simulated sea breeze? I'm not getting diddly-squat over here."

"Idle chit chat's not so bad now?" you say, relieved. "I don't mind. I could use the company."

She moves fast, like she fully expected you to say yes. She brings the napkin dispenser with her and plants herself across from you now, adjusting the small plastic fan to sit at a more generous angle. "I should have said I *am* getting diddly-squat, since diddly-squat means barely anything. Double negatives really piss me off. It's like I say: *double negatives are a no-no.* How come you didn't correct me? Not a word guy?"

"Is that the same as *doodly*-squat?"

With a slight frown, she whimpers a little "*Whatever*" to herself. She withdraws the knife from your cup of coffee and plants it on the tabletop. The heat it gives off is barely noticeable from the temperature sweat that's already glistening on the Formica table.

"So, you're telling me you don't recognize faces but you *do* recognize *me*? How is that?"

"I don't know," you say honestly. "But for some reason I do."

"I suppose no one else can leave as lasting an impression on you as I can. Maybe that's it?"

"Maybe."

"If we'd met before, that is."

"Yes. If."

"Would you recognize your own mother if she walked in here right now?"

"No. But my mother probably wouldn't be the best example."

She takes your coffee cup into her hand, not by the handle but by the top. "Why do you drink hot coffee when it's a hundred degrees outside?"

"Hot drinks are good for you in the heat and dry temperatures. They make you sweat more."

"And more sweat means you're cooling down. Am I remembering my eighth-grade science correctly?"

"That's right."

She takes a tentative sip and nearly chokes on it. "Too bad for you this has got to be the worst cup of coffee in the city."

"Undoubtedly. Though they've still got the *World's Best Coffee* sign on the front window."

"Ironic. So, what's your name?"

"Epic," you tell her. "Epic Small."

"That's ironic too," she says. But you're not a word guy so you don't really know if it is ironic or not. From what you know, people seem to misuse the word ironic all the time, so chances are pretty good this girl is wrong too. "My name's Abigail."

"Abigail. Can I call you Abby?"

"You can call me Abi instead."

"Uh, is there a difference?"

"Well, I know you're thinking A-B-B-Y. But I prefer A-B-I. I mean, where did that Y come from anyway? And the double B? Come on. A-B-I just makes more sense, doesn't it?"

"What does it matter how I *think* it's spelled? It's not like your nickname is on your birth certificate or driver's license or anything. It's still pronounced the same."

"It matters to *me*."

"Okay. Fine."

She pushes the coffee cup back toward you, obviously ticked, and pushes the subject a little more while she's at it. "I work in insurance; identity theft actually. I see firsthand how people deal with or struggle to deal with having something as important as their own identities being taken away from them. It's horrible. Probably the worst thing that could happen to a person." She runs the tip of a finger around the lip of the ashtray sitting on the table, almost out of reach. "So I don't take these things lightly."

It's so damn hot in here and she's making your brain hurt. You don't know what's worse. You think: Home theater systems. White lithium grease. Cloud computing. Table saws. The Shamwow.

When you finally regain your senses, she's got the coffee cup in her hands again. She takes tiny sips, waiting for you say something. "Sorry about that," you say. "Sometimes I check out when there's too much information to take in. It's a habit of mine." You dab your forehead with a crumpled, food-stained napkin.

She places the mug gently back on the table. "It's no problem. Trust me, I realize I don't always make the best first impressions." Generously, she repositions the fan toward you so you're getting a little more breeze. "So, what's with the bruise on your face? Girlfriend troubles?"

"Not really."

"Boyfriend?"

"I'd rather not get into it."

"What do you do for work then, Epic?"

"Laundry," you sigh. "Basically, I do laundry."

"Jeeze. Don't go and get too excited about it. I'd hate for you to black out on me again." She smiles with her eyes; those fantastic eyes that simply want to be auburn in color but are actually so much more. And then she asks, "Do you AIIB?" You don't have any idea what she's saying, but she pronounces the word like it was a name: *Abe.*

"*AIIB?*"

"Yeah, the online VR/MMORPG game."

That's a mouthful of letters. "I'm sure I wouldn't know where to start."

"I don't know. You'd probably like it better than the real world."

"What about you? You said you work in insurance. What else do you do?"

"Oh, you know."

"Not really, no."

"Mostly nothing. But I'm around." Abi glides her hand around her, through the air like it's a jet ski riding ocean waves. "I'm here and I'm there."

She almost hits Dorothy as the waitress approaches your table. "I see you've found a friend," Dorothy says to you, maybe with a hint of disbelief in her voice. "Can I get the two of you anything else?" *The two of you,* you think. That just sounds funny.

Abi slides a menu right out from under Dorothy's arm and opens it up to take a look. Your coffee is topped off again just as she makes her decision. "I think I'll just have an order of the bacon." She looks at you as though waiting for some kind of approval. Maybe she knows the bacon is the only reason to come here? Or maybe any menu items at this dive are simply worth questioning. You throw a reassuring smile her way and she confirms with a nod for Dorothy.

"I'm sorry, but we're all out of bacon."

"It's ten in the morning!" Abi proclaims. "How could you possibly be out of bacon at ten in the morning?"

"Some things you just can't explain. And it's actually 1:30 in the afternoon."

Abi slides the menu back to Dorothy and looks at the name on the front: *The UnDiner*. It's written in some strange font which makes it incredibly hard to read. She stares at the letters for a long moment before finally figuring them out. "What's that mean anyway? Does it mean you can't actually eat food here?"

"No," Dorothy answers, oblivious to any of the sarcasm. "I like to think of The UnDiner as kind of like the Undead of diners."

"I don't get it," Abi says.

"It's a joke. I tell it to all of my customers."

"Well, maybe it's lost some panache over time. Might be time for some new material."

Dorothy's smile goes suddenly straight. She points with her thumb over to the table Abi had been sitting at until a few minutes ago. "I sure hope you've left a tip today," she says bluntly and walks away.

With her hand Abi makes the *yak-yak-yak* gesture as Dorothy walks away, like she's performing with an invisible sock puppet. "I think your girlfriend's pissed at me now."

"She's not my girlfriend. I don't even know her name."

"Her nametag said Dorothy, genius."

"I've learned not to believe everything I read or hear. I'm better at picking up on memory triggers like facial tics and tells."

Abi studies you with her eyes, but it feels more like she just thinks you're a freak. "That's cool," she says finally. "So, do you *have* a girlfriend then? I feel like you've been dodging the question."

"I don't think you've been asking a question."

"Well, *do* you?"

"No."

"Shit. That was a fast answer. Been a while, huh? Well, what about the last girlfriend you had?"

"Her name was Reya."

"And—?"

"I really don't have much more to say than that."

"Sounds to me like you're going out of your way to forget about her."

You know that's not true but you don't know how to respond to the comment.

"Would you recognize this Reya person if she was in The UnDiner right now?"

You scan the restaurant slowly. Then you breathe in through your nose carefully, like trying to pick up the trail of a fading scent. "Without a doubt."

"So, is she dead?"

"What—? No."

"*Un*dead?"

"Come on."

"Well, when's the last time you talked to her?"

Again, you don't know how best to respond. You slump back in the booth, crossing your arms defensively.

"Fine. But we all go through bad breakups, Rainbow. That's how they're *supposed* to go."

"What about you?"

"In a nutshell, he cheated on me. And here I am."

"Here?"

"Coney Island."

"Nobody comes to Coney Island to fix a broken heart."

"Probably not." She shifts in her seat a little and turns her eyes away from you. Her delicate fingers pick at her jacket and you notice one sleeve is completely covered in what looks like fluffy, sand-colored cat hair.

You ask, "Do you have a cat?"

She stops her hands for a moment and scratches at the studs in her ear instead. "Funny thing," she says. "I was walking to the train this morning and a fucking cat jumped out of the alley, right on me. I had to punch the stupid jerk right in the whiskers to get it off my arm. Disgusting things." Her fingers move back to the sleeve of her jacket, and continue right where they left off. She peels a tiny clump of hair off and lets it go, watching as the fan blows it part way across the diner before dive-bombing to the dirty floor. "Actually, I'm really just in Coney Island to see my father."

"Oh. Your father lives around here?"

"Yeah. He told me to come to Coney Island to see him on my twentieth birthday and that he'd have a big surprise for me. This is the third time in two days I've gone to find him but he hasn't been there." Arbitrarily, she takes a napkin from the dispenser and crumples it into her fist. "Today's his last chance. Or mine. However you want to look at it."

"How are *you* looking at it?"

"I don't exactly know yet."

"Well, happy birthday anyway."

She tosses the balled-up napkin over your head onto the table where she was first sitting. It hits something and bounces off onto the floor next to the clump of cat hair. "Thanks."

You hear a strange sound through the blowing fan; it sounds like popping, almost like the manic popping of bubble wrap. It's faint though. Abi's hands are under the table. "Is that you?"

And then it stops. "Sorry. I crack my knuckles when I'm anxious."

"They're loud."

"Yeah. People have told me I have really loud knuckles. It's a peculiar thing to tell someone, don't you think? But it just helps to calm me down. Kind of like *your* weird thing."

"Am I weird?" you ask bravely.

"Yeah. But I think I like that about you." Under the table, she continues to crack her knuckles until they're all popped. Then she shakes her hands out and folds them nicely on the tabletop. "Hey. Would you like to come with me? To see my dad?"

You immediately recall what Gideon told you, about pleasure delaying and not jumping into new situations without really evaluating them first. Do you really do that? You almost said yes to Abi right away, so maybe you do. You think about it for another moment. "I'm not really comfortable with the idea," is what you tell her instead.

Abigail seems confused, but luckily Dorothy drops off your bill before you're obligated to say any more on the matter. You look the bill over, pretending it's not the same total it always is just so you don't have to look anywhere else right now. But you feel her staring at you, sizing you up.

"You're special, aren't you?"

"Not really. I'm just a regular guy."

She taps the bill with her finger, noting the bran flakes and multiple coffee refills. "Yeah, I can see that. You keep yourself real regular, don't you?"

"As much as I can, I suppose."

You try your best to avoid looking up, hoping she'll be on her way by the time you do. She's not though. Abi's just sitting there, scratching at her ear again and staring at you sideways. "Well, suit yourself," she finally says and rises from her seat. "It was nice talking to you, Epic Small. I'll be sure to say hi to my dad for you." And then she exits as abruptly as she'd jumped into the booth in the first place. Like an idiot, you don't even muster a goodbye. You're already starting to consider the mistakes you must have made this time around.

In your dreams, you're the opposite of every decision you made along the way to where you are now.

For certain, Abi wasn't what you would call relationship material, but she did seem like someone who might be a good friend. And who couldn't use another good friend? Or a single good friend, in your case.

Taking *The Third* back into your hands, you open it up on the table. One hundred and fifty-four pages in and you're wondering when things are ever going to start happening for poor Tristan Montminy.

Tristan wakes up in Grace's bed; she has already disappeared to wherever it is she goes every day. He can't believe he doesn't ask her for details like that, but at the same time he realizes if he were *actually* Luca he'd already know them. Tristan decides he needs to find out more about Grace. So, he starts snooping around her apartment, which predictably is another four pages of him looking through kitchen cupboards and digging his hands deep into the toes of all of her shoes and boots. You are even privy to the exact details of each pair of Grace's underwear in her bureau. Details as unnecessary as loose threads and faded stains.

Before Tristan finds anything of any consequence, a shadow crosses over you: Abi has returned. Again, you recognize her without fault. "Hey, did I leave my ring here? I had a ring and now I don't." She hops onto the booth, on all fours, looking around where she was sitting only minutes ago. "Sometimes I slide my rings on and off my fingers. I can't help it. Another nervous tic, probably?" She digs deep into the cracks of the cushions and looks under the table. "But I don't see it here. Maybe I wasn't even wearing it today? It wouldn't be the first time I'd have forgotten, you know."

"I'm sorry," is all you squeak out.

"It's not your fault. Hey, what are you reading?"

Marking your spot in the book with a finger, you close the cover so she can see. "It's called *The Third*," you say.

"Cool. What's it about?"

"Mistaken identity."

"Why's it called *The Third*?"

"I think it might have to do with this character's name: his name is Luca Desplante *the Third*." You don't even think to say the name with a French accent so it sounds pretty stupid when the words come out of your mouth.

"But honestly, I have no idea."

Abi stops looking for the missing ring and stands up, straightening her clothes with the palms of her hands. She scratches at her left ear again and you notice she's biting the inside of her mouth. Then she asks, "So you really don't want to tag along with me? You seem like you're maybe finishing up here."

"I think I'm just going to stay and keep reading," you say.

"Cool," she states again, a little under her breath. Her dialogue seems to shift inexplicably and without warning, like the inside of a lava lamp. This girl is either babbling in long, rambling sentences or she's just using short, simple words.

Your eyes lock for a moment; there's a feeling you're feeling that you cannot place, and you can tell Abigail can't put a finger on it either. The two of you are just trapped in this sliver of a moment. Stuck in time, but only for what seems like a microsecond. And then, just like a leaf in a windstorm, she's gone again.

It hits you as soon as Abigail vanishes. The realization that the feeling you shared was the feeling of all the things the both of you have ever missed out on in your lives coming back haunt you. Whether it was due to making a different decision or if it was simply being late, maybe by a minute or by ten thousand years. It sucks when you realize the amounts of things you cannot change.

You shake the rest of these thoughts out of your head. But you only have time enough to find the spot in your book where you left off before Abi's back and sitting right across from you once more.

"Me again," she says, before launching right into: "You know, if the two of us got married and I changed my last name to be all classic-woman and such, my name would be Abi Small. Get it? *Abysmal.* I just thought of that outside right now." You don't really know what to say in response to that. "I mean, that's fucked up, right?" Abigail leans forward, propping herself up on the table with her elbows and takes a look into your coffee cup, still more than half-full and waiting to be cleared away. "That coffee's not getting any better, is it?"

"No, not really." Before you lose the feeling completely you ask her, "What were you doing ten thousand years ago?"

"I don't know. Must have been doing something though."

"What makes you say that?"

"Reincarnation." She moves in even closer to you, choosing now to sit atop of the wobbly Formica table. "I believe when we die our souls are dispersed into multiple new bodies, which dilutes them somewhat every time. I mean, how else do you explain that connection you have with so many people? You hear about it more and more often lately, don't you? People having instant connections with strangers they've just met. It's because we're really all the same person."

"So, I'm *you*? Is that what you're saying?"

"Sure. You're me. I'm that waitress over there. Brad Pitt's the Pope. And all of us are each other. Think about how many atoms and particles you consume just breathing in every day. They were once parts of other bodies. I mean, really think about it. We're all just teeny tiny pieces of everything and everyone else."

"I've never thought about it like that before." You want to say it makes sense but you're not entirely sure if it does.

"Listen, Epic. I'm gonna have to admit I might actually need someone to accompany me to see my dad. I'm nervous. And the truth is I *didn't* try seeing him twice before this. I chickened out. Kind of like right now, and how I've been trying to leave this diner."

You don't care; you finish the last of your coffee in one gulp, wiping the drips from the creases of your mouth with the sleeve of your hoodie. "And you're picking *me*? Why?"

"Doesn't matter really, does it?"

"I suppose not."

She tugs at her earlobe decisively, as though attempting to open a plugged ear canal. "How about this," she says. "If you help me with *my* thing right now then I'll help you later with *your* thing."

"I have a thing?"

"Well, it's obvious to just about anyone that there's something up with you when you're sitting here drinking the city's worst coffee and eating a bowl of bran flakes."

"You really should try the bacon next time."

"Right. Next time."

You consider what Dr. Griffin had always told you: just go with your impulses. Do what feels right. Maybe take some chances in life. And then he went and killed himself.

You think about your conversation with Gideon just two days ago. He told you about pleasure delaying. Suggested you try slowing things down. You jumped right into your relationship with Reya. Like you said, you should have been more scared than you were but you weren't. And this Abi thing — whatever this Abi thing is exactly — this should really be easier than that.

This is nothing.

So you treat it like nothing. "Sure," you say finally and scoop up your things. "I could maybe use some air."

And she smiles. It's not one of her crooked smirks or something that's betraying her truths. She simply smiles and you walk toward the door together.

"What's your last name anyway?" you ask, still stuffing your copy of *The Third* back into your bag.

"It's Ayr. With a Y. Abigail Ayr." She holds the door open for you. "I guess you *could* use some air, hey Rainbow?"

And you walk out of The UnDiner together, back out into the afternoon heat.

DEMON OF THE SURF

You follow Abigail Ayr for nearly ten blocks along Surf Avenue. Piles of garbage remain strewn about the parade route. This city is always so quick to plan events like the Mermaid Parade yet, inevitably, will take its sweet time in cleaning up the mess that follows. Of course, clean Coney Island up as much you like, it will continue to remain the filthy armpit of Long Island.

After passing blocks of parking lots, condemned buildings, and shady ice cream shops, you're at the corner of Surf and Twelfth when Abi stops. Just a little farther east is Gideon's office, above the furniture store and directly below the subway tracks. You can see the windows clearly. It was only two days ago, but your first session with Gideon already feels like it never happened. You can recall the words he said, you can hear his voice in your head, but the actual, physical being there seems like nothing more than a dream now. The only part that resonates as reality is when you spotted Abi outside the window that afternoon. When she waved a tiny, crumpled hand at you, unsure of whether she should or not. And this is when you notice she's looking at the exact spot you are.

"What is that place?" she asks without turning her eyes away. An F-Train rumbles along past you, on its way to Manhattan.

"What do you mean?"

"I saw you the other day. In that window up there. You saw me too and neither of us knew what to do.”

You stare at her like an idiot. And you feel like one too, still incapable of comprehending the reasons why you can recall this girl so easily when you shouldn’t be able to.

And she makes note of the anomaly too. “I mean, with your condition. You shouldn’t have been able to recognize me, right? But I know you did. I could tell when we were at the diner. You remembered me back there, didn’t you?”

“I did remember you.”

“I remembered you, too. I was just going along with it, trying to play the same game I thought *you* were playing. So why would you lie to me?”

“Lie to you? About what?”

“About your condition, whatever you called it.”

“Prosopagnosia.”

“So, did you just make that word up?”

“I didn’t make it up. It’s a real thing, and I really do have it. Why would I lie to you?”

“That’s what I just asked you.”

You pause for a moment before simply answering her original question. You point up to the window with your thumb. “The truth is, I was seeing a therapist. That’s his office up there.” She doesn’t say anything in response though. You can’t tell if she thinks you’re a total nut-job or if you’re already far past that point. “But I don’t think I’ll be going back.”

“Why not?”

“Because he’s crazy.”

“Are you seeing *him* or is he seeing *you*? Isn’t it *your* role to be the crazy one?"

"I'm not crazy. I'm just depressed."

"Shit. We're *all* depressed, Rainbow. And we all need somebody. If you need the help, you should go back. I wouldn't let some bonehead doctor screw with who you are. I mean, there's a reason you started seeing this guy in the first place, right?"

"Actually, my regular therapist killed himself and I was sent here. I've only seen him the one time."

Abi considers your words for a moment. "Well, this world is mysterious," she states. Though the way Abi says *this world* makes it seem like she knows of others. "And so are the people in it who we meet. Sometimes we choose them, sometimes they're chosen for us." She looks at you now, with that same crooked smile you saw the first time. Like she's unsure of her own words herself but still wants to convince you of their truth. "If I were you, I wouldn't be so quick to move along."

The same advice Gideon himself would have doled out, you're certain. Maybe there's something in that? "Why do you keep calling me Rainbow?" you ask, finally.

"I don't know. Whenever I meet someone new I like to make up a unique nickname for them. Helps me to remember them if I can't recall their real name later. And sometimes the word just sticks. I mean, you're *totally* a Rainbow, you know?" She picks a bit more cat hair from her sleeve then crosses the road, heading south along Twelfth Avenue. "Now hurry up!"

You only make it as far as the sidewalk, where the colorful three-story building that houses the Sideshows by the Seashore attraction is situated. This is Coney Island's infamous freak show, a generally-misunderstood collection of human oddities. In all your twenty years, you've never once stepped foot in the Sideshow, but from what anyone's ever told you, there are no longer traditional "freaks" here but rather just a bunch of tattooed gypsies who like sticking swords down their throats and lying on beds of nails. The giant, bright painted posters along the outside of the building boast *Strange Men!* and *Weird Women!* and showcase a collection of cartoon characters: snake charmers, fire eaters, contortionists, four-legged women, dog-faced men, and the Blockhead — a guy who apparently enjoys hammering nails into his face.

It's all a little eerie due to the imagery and the lack of windows which shrouds the Sideshow's actual contents, but the disturbing nature of it all is somewhat downplayed by the laughter emanating from the Ferris wheel spinning just behind the fence in Luna Park and the old, wooden Cyclone coaster thundering in the distance.

Abigail waves you over to the Sideshow entrance. She's talking to a woman at the ticket window who could just as easily be working the stage at a burlesque show.

"We're meeting your dad in here?" you ask, following her inside reluctantly.

"This is his office, so to speak."

"What is he, the manager?"

"Not quite," she says, briskly walking a few steps ahead of you. "Come on, keep up."

The old walls inside are covered with posters that are much the same as the larger ones which adorned the outside of the building, all painted in that unsettling turn-of-the-century style which straddles the fine line between cartoony and creepy. Many of the characters depicted have intriguing names that really harken back to the days when the Sideshow was probably something to be taken more seriously: *Excello: the Great Escape Artist! Serpentina! Madame Twisto & Jelly Boy!*

Slinking farther inside, you start noticing things taking a slightly more morbid turn. Some of the artifacts are still fairly laughable, such as the taxidermy-gone-wrong bat/pig hybrids, eyeballs in cloudy jars, and a bottle of hair and teeth labelled as the last remnants of an electric chair victim. But somewhere between the coffins full of dirt and the jars of silver nails purportedly used to slay Mexican werewolves (who had once performed here until they allegedly began eating tourists), your nerves begin to get the better of you.

This is when you read signs detailing the existence of an alien baby. From what you gather, visitors can pay an extra charge to enter a secret area of the Sideshow and see this alien baby being kept alive in an incubator. You don't know what it is about this — alien subject matter has never really bothered you — but you're quick to track where Abi has gone and you shuffle back over to her side as fast as you can.

Abi leads you through some darkened hallways that lack any air conditioning whatsoever. It's mercilessly hot and sticky in here and the smell is a permanent fusion of sleaze and sweat. Eventually, you enter a larger room and discover the performers' stage. The audience is made up of maybe eight people, all seated upon old wooden bleachers. Onstage is a tattooed woman who currently has five swords shoved down her throat. She's looking up to the ceiling and slowly preparing to swallow a sixth blade. You're taken aback at first, but then notice the faces on the crowd: they seem remarkably uninterested. Probably desensitized from act after act of standard sideshow performances. Maybe she should have stopped after three swords? Still, you can't help but watch with partial awe, even as a couple from the audience get up from their seats. Her trick seems authentic, though you can't help but wonder if there's some bogus nature behind it. You remember having a toy knife as a child, one where the plastic blade could retract into the handle on a spring, and it would simulate the act of being stabbed. How fun is that? So great for kids. You were partially fascinated but mostly repulsed at first, watching your father stab himself in the neck before falling to the floor motionless. You hesitated the first few times you tried the toy on your own body; there was something uneasy about it all. Months later, when there was an unsolved stabbing in your apartment building, you discretely tossed the plastic knife into the garbage, just in case.

Abi's whisper-shouting snaps you out of your reverie. "Epic! This way!"

You apologize and catch up to her once again, following her through a door that leads to another short, darkened hallway. At the end of the hall you walk down a flight of stairs and you take note of the intricate detail on the hand railing. With the tips of your fingers, the design feels like swirling waves or seashells, but upon looking closer you can tell it's a complicated moon and star pattern. The deeper you go, the more this place reeks of the stale smell of sex and debauchery. Years upon years of sordid depravity must line the walls and floorboards of the Sideshow; filthy characters have been filling these halls for a hundred years, all of them castaways from a society that rejected their deformities and dark talents. All of them finding solace here with one another.

Downstairs, the cracks and dirt in the corridors are more evident. The walls are lined with old black and white photographs of performers from days gone by. Abigail runs her hand along one side, her fingernails scratch sharply across the glass of the framed photos. The sound seems to almost pierce your skin, scraping at your insides. The deeper you go within these halls, the farther the Sideshow's dark shadows spread, the more unsettled you become.

Finally, you reach the end, at a closed door with a gold star nailed to it crookedly. "Here we are," she says with a pessimistic air about her. She taps her finger inauspiciously on the last picture, placed purposefully beside the door. This is not a photograph but a poster, drawn in the style much like the ones you saw outside the Sideshow, back on Twelfth Avenue. At the top in bold letters are the words: *LOBSTERO! DEMON of the SURF!* There is a red-skinned man emerging from the ocean with giant lobster claws for hands. He looks like a 1940's comic book super villain, though the details of his face had been rubbed away long before this poster was set behind glass.

Abi knocks on the door hesitantly, as though there might be another option worth considering. You hear some shuffling inside; a chair or something bangs against the wall and someone sounds in a hurry to get dressed. You're startled a little when Abi grabs a hold of your arm, but you're not bothered. It's almost nice in a way.

The doorknob jiggles longer than you would expect it to, like a dog is on its hind legs and trying to open it with its mouth. Slowly, the door creaks away from the frame, and a man pokes his face through. He sees you first and couldn't be more wrong in assuming you're here for trouble, almost closing the door immediately. But then he notices Abi at your side, and concedes a smile. A tiny one, but it still counts for something.

"Abigail? Well, holy smokers. It's been a while, hasn't it?" He opens the door wider now, having dropped his guard a little. Abi's father is stout like a dwarf, though much taller than you might expect a dwarf to be. Not a little-person dwarf, but more of the Dungeons & Dragons variety. People have told you before that there's a difference. He is bald and has a chinstrap beard without the mustache; a tattoo of some kind marks the top of his head, but you cannot make out what it is. All he seems to be wearing is a bathrobe. The first thing you really notice about this man though, are his teeth. There are gaps between every single tooth, like they're too small for his mouth. Like the tiniest kernels at the tip of a cob of corn.

"Hi, Dad," Abi replies without answering her father's question. "How have you been?"

"Happy."

"You're always happy for some reason."

"Can't help it. Although I'd be happier if I saw my Pearl Girl more often, don't you think?"

Again, Abi simply ignores her father's question and makes her way into the room. You follow close behind her, and he makes more than enough room for you. Once inside, you can tell this is more like an actor's dressing room. A table at the far end is covered in a mess of mostly empty makeup containers and various articles of clothing; there is a mirror with large round light bulbs around it. The rest of the room is not much more than a couple of wooden chairs, some posters on the walls and a closet shut tight. Everything aside from the tabletop is just tidy enough that the closet feels like it must be stuffed with a hundred years of secrets. There's a thin shine of something from under the door, and you can't tell if it's metallic or liquid. Whatever it may be, there is a sheen to it of seemingly sinister portent.

This man still looks you over warily like you pose some kind of threat to him. "Who is your associate here?" he asks carefully. "Boyfriend?"

Abi leans back on the table with palms down. "No, Dad. Epic is just a friend-friend."

"Epic?" he confirms. "That *is* strange." He extends an arm to shake your hand and this is when you notice them.

You thought his teeth were off-putting at first but now you see what it is about the man that makes him a true member of the sideshow circus: both of his hands are nothing more than a thumb and a single finger, or more specifically, what seem to be two or three fingers fused together into one single, enlarged appendage. Sort of like a malformed, fleshy lobster claw with a giant fingernail at the end.

He just smiles with his hand still out. "But nothing is ever *too* strange around here, is it?"

You hesitate for a moment but he doesn't seem to notice, probably because this is the exact reaction he must get every time he meets someone new. But then you place your hand in his and you're aghast once more. His bumpy, cucumber-like digits feel unusually strange in your sweaty palm: both fleshy and bony at once. You're embarrassed to admit it, but the first sensation holding his hand reminds you of is grabbing your own erect penis. You let go quickly, but there is a peculiar urge to shake the man's hand once more, just to experience the oddness of it all again. You're pretty sure you're going to need an extra Celexa tablet tonight.

"You can call me Lobstero," he says and then snaps his thumbs and fingers together like an overzealous crab. "For obvious reasons."

"It's—nice to meet you," you stumble. Your attention is diverted a little by the posters, photos, and newspaper clippings around the room. All of them serving as a shrine to this Demon of the Surf.

"Have you seen my act?" he asks, tapping a malformed finger upon one Sideshow poster that has Lobstero front and center. Again, he is depicted as a monster; his hands are more claw-like and his skin much redder than what you see before you.

"I haven't. No. Sorry."

"No need to apologize, friend-friend. My best guess is most people haven't." It's subtle, but you catch the all-too-quick glare he throws Abi's way. You don't know if it's something more than just a look, but you feel like you need to bail her out.

You ask him, "What *is* your act?"

His eyes light up and he turns back to you quickly. "Oh, it's fantastic! They tie my hands together, lock me in a small cage and then lower it into a big pot of boiling water." He articulates wildly with his arms, making big gestures.

"And you have to escape before you're cooked, right? Like a real lobster?"

"That's right. But between you, me, and the wall, it's not really boiling water. We just dump a bunch of salt and other chemicals into the pot to make it bubble like that. It's all smoke and mirrors, Epic. It's hiding the truth in the darkness. Like everything else around here."

"You really don't have to be so dramatic, dad," Abi finally says after being silent for what has felt like forever.

Her father waves his hands gently through the air in front of him. "Do you think I have any other choice with these things?" He pulls his chair toward him and sinks into it, taking a seat at the makeup table. "When I first came to Coney Island, it was like my life had suddenly just begun. The deformity I'd always tried to hide actually *helped* me here. But we're a close-knit community at the Sideshow, and we like our secrets."

Abigail moves closer to you again, even as her father continues talking.

"Do you know what Coney Island means?" You want to answer him, to say *No* at the very least, so you might feel like you're a part of this dialogue, but he doesn't give you the opportunity. "It literally means *Rabbit Island*. When it was first settled, this part of Long Island was covered with rabbits which were eventually run out of town by resort developments. But the Indians who originally lived here—"

"*Native Americans*, Dad."

"Hey, they were happy being Indians back then. The Indians called this place *Narrioch*, which translates to *the Land Without Shadows*.

"Why was it called that?" you ask him.

"Let me tell you," he starts excitedly, like he's some sort of Coney Island history buff. "Because the beach is in direct sunlight all day long. Never a shadow to be seen. Except in here where we, the deformed freaks of nature reside. We're expected to simply hide in the dark of this sideshow monstrosity, aren't we?"

"Well, I don't think there was a freak show here back then, was there?"

"No. Just the Dutch, right?" he chuckles mostly to himself. "I can't deny I love it here though. But the name is still ironic, don't you think?"

"I suppose," is all you say. Maybe you still don't know exactly what irony means, but you *do* know you have no idea how anyone could be so happy with this life. Then again, you're the one who's in therapy. Still, after all of this, you manage to ask Lobstero, "Do you have any regrets about this life you've chosen?"

He looks away from you, where exactly you're not certain. You can see a thousand answers dialing through his head, like he's finding it difficult to simply pick one of them. "Plenty," Lobstero says somberly, and turns to his daughter. "Like your mother, for one."

Abi clutches your arm again with one hand and scratches at her left ear with the other. "My mother was a prostitute," she tells you bluntly. "And I doubt my father ever even knew her name."

"I did know it," he adds. "For a little while anyway."

Abi looks you right in the eyes now. "I'm just the daughter of a circus freak and a fifty-cent hooker. She died from a drug overdose before I'd ever truly met her." She doesn't appear sad or irritated that these memories have dug themselves up; it's more like she's thought about all of this too many times in her life to really be affected by any of it anymore. "Epic, listen. I know you're unhappy and depressed and all that, just please don't go thinking my life's been any better than yours. I mean, we're *all* secretly-damaged goods, aren't we? I chew the shit out of the inside of my lips. See?" She pulls the side of her mouth away so you can see inside. It's all just blood and scar tissue. "Don't know why, I just always have. But nobody can tell."

Lobstero leans in toward you. "She's a special girl. Always has been. Abigail's always had a special kind of intuition about her, always having lots of imaginary friends when she was little. *Ghosts*, I remember she used to call them."

"Maybe that's because my father was never there to be my best friend," she says to you while looking at him.

He adds, "And maybe it's because we're all just hiding in the Land Without Shadows?"

You want to tell Abigail Ayr you're sorry for whatever sorrows she may have experienced in her life, for a mother who never loved her, or for whichever boyfriend crushed her heart in his hands. But you cannot simply apologize for another person's suffering, can you?

"Whatever the case," her father continues. "You're lucky to have her. Whether you're really just a friend-friend or actually something more."

You almost say something about your own mother and how she left you, too. Sometimes when you think about her you catch yourself wishing she had left you and your father even sooner. Before you had the chance to remember anything about her at all. But you're not here to compare shitty family notes.

This is when the woman who you'd last seen onstage swallowing swords appears at the door. She says with a wink, "Lobstero! You're on in four, hon."

"Thank you, Deirdre." He reaches for a red piece of cloth from the table and stands up. "I'm sorry guys," he tells you. "But I've got an audience waiting with bated breath."

You think to yourself, All five of them? Of course, you don't have the guts to say it aloud.

He removes his bathrobe, revealing a taut, muscled body underneath wearing nothing more than sparkly swimming trunks with lobster claw patterns on them. He takes the bright red mask in his hand, like he's a Mexican wrestler, and slides it over his head. This is when you realize you never did get a good look at the tattoo on his scalp.

Lobstero quickly escorts the two of you out of his dressing room with him and closes the door. The gold star rattles upon the worn wood. He touches his daughter gently on the shoulder with a lumpy finger. "It was good to see you again, my Pearl Girl. But take off the jacket, will ya? It's a hundred degrees out there."

"It keeps the bugs away," Abi says in her best *don't-tell-me-what-to-do-dad* tone.

He shrugs as if to say *Fair enough*, then turns to you. "Friend-friend here's got the same idea, doesn't he?" Lobstero tugs at the sleeve of your hoodie. "Them bugs are really biting in this heat." And with that, he takes off down the corridor.

"I'll pick up some bug spray just in case," you say, knowing full well you never will.

"Won't do you any good!" he calls back, already halfway up the stairwell.

After confirming neither of you wished to stay and watch her father's act, you and Abi slowly begin walking back through the Sideshow and outside to Twelfth Avenue. It certainly feels much hotter out here than it did before you entered.

You walk down Twelfth toward the beach but you're not really headed anywhere in particular. You know you're not yet ready to say goodbye to Abi, partly because there are still questions you have no answers for. Why do you continue to recognize her? What just happened back there in her father's dressing room? You wish she'd have asked you something about your own family since it doesn't seem fair that you were allowed to be witness to so much of hers in so little time.

And so, you simply launch into it as you walk. You tell her about your mother's strange and lasting words for you and of what little you can remember of the man who came to visit her so often. You tell her about your father's business, the shoe store that was destroyed by those two idiot friends of yours. You tell her your father lost a little bit of himself that day, lost some of his grip on his own identity and never fully recovered. Now he has recently been diagnosed with brain cancer and is sitting in a hospital bed wondering why his son hasn't visited him for weeks.

You tell her more about the book you're reading. And about how you don't feel like you belong here and that you think your dreams are trying to convince you to be somewhere else. You tell her about the light you saw when you were born and how you sat in the van last night and watched your friend Bester as he made out with some girl. You tell her you were beaten up outside the Starfish Room in Brighton Beach after pretending to be much braver than you are. You ask if she's ever heard of the band Whitesnake, and you describe the *Lovehunter* album cover on the wall in Gideon's office.

Of course, pretty much the only thing you don't tell her about is Reya, even though you want to.

This is everything you tell her so things will seem fair and balanced. But now she's looking at you like you're crazier than she'd ever have guessed. But you don't care. You think you'd look just as stupefied if someone you'd only met had poured their insides out in front of you.

You cross the old wooden Boardwalk together and Abi sits down on an empty bench facing the ocean. The tide is really in today and there are only a few beach blanket lengths before the water laps at the sand. The smell of fish and salt water permeates so much of the Coney Island neighborhood, that you almost don't notice it anymore. Sometimes you forget how close you are to the ocean. It's a shame that the only land mass you can see in the distance has to be New Jersey.

You sit down beside her. Abi's knees are tucked in tight under her chin. "Thanks for telling me all that," she mumbles finally, still staring out at the water. From her tone, you can't tell if she's genuine or if she's being sarcastic. Maybe something in between. "I guess nobody's family life is perfect, huh?"

"That's for sure. Was that story about your mom really true?"

She turns her head slowly toward you and rests one cheek on her knee. "Why would I make that up? What reason do I have to lie to you?"

"I'm sorry. It just seemed strange, is all."

"Stranger than knowing my father's got lobster hands and works in a circus sideshow? I guess it's all how you perceive things." Abi turns back to the ocean and leans back into the bench. "That's only the *start* though," she adds, but then goes quiet. Like she's struggling with what to say next.

"It's not exactly another *in-a-nutshell* story, is it?"

"Not exactly, no." She looks up into the sun, squinting and cracking her knuckles again. For some reason, she kicks her boots off and places them on her lap, one on top of the other. Her bare toes wiggle about, surely grateful for the fresh ocean breeze.

You think about how in stories the ocean is supposed to act as symbolism. You've heard that somewhere before but don't have any idea at all what the symbolism is supposed to be. Is it up to the writer? The reader?

"Well," she finally starts. "I grew up outside of Denver in a small town called Memorial. It was the kind of town that really didn't deserve to even make it onto a map, and it probably didn't on some. I grew up on Main Street, which was ironic because it was the only street in town that wasn't paved. Nobody ever took care of that street. One time when a tree fell down in a lightning storm, it blocked traffic for months. The bright side was that things were always pretty quiet. I lived with an adopted family — I never knew that growing up, of course. All I really knew was that I was sad and I didn't want to talk to anybody."

"Sounds a lot like me, actually. Did you have any friends?"

"Imaginary ones mostly. But they were only ever good for coming to my funerals."

"I'm sorry? Your funerals?"

"I used to have funerals for myself. I'd stage them in my bedroom, maybe every few days. Is that normal?"

Yikes. How do you say anything is not normal considering the crap she must have seen in her life? Instead you tell her, "When nothing in this world makes a whole lot of sense there's no use in seeing things as normal or not."

"That's a good point." Abi wipes the sweat from her brow. Still, she refuses to take off the jacket. "But that was how I played when I was a little girl, pretending I was small enough and dead enough to fill a shoebox. And I would place that shoebox at one end of my bed like a cardboard coffin and I would sit on the other end and I would give my eulogy. I would talk about myself in front of everyone who wasn't there and I would say awful things about 'her' and make up horrible stories about how 'she' died. Hit by a train. Eaten by birds. Trampled by unicorns. It was never by suicide, even though that's what I always wanted to say. But even in front of imaginary friends I couldn't so much as mouth the words."

"Sounds familiar too," you say. There's a bit of a breeze coming off the ocean, not enough to feel cold but you hold your arms tight to your body anyway.

"I would always conclude the service by saying how much I'd miss her though. How much I'd miss myself. And then I'd put the shoebox back up on the highest shelf in my closet and shut the door tight and try my hardest to *become* somebody else. Maybe I could like myself more? Maybe someone else would too? Inevitably though, I would only end up pulling the shoebox back out again."

A couple of shirtless, over-muscled dudes are walking toward you along the Boardwalk and they both take extended looks as they pass by. They're sweating profusely; their whole bodies glistening in the hot afternoon sun. You're not sure what it is they think they're staring at, but whatever it might be it is certainly none of their business. They make you a bit uncomfortable, but you've never been comfortable when you feel strangers sizing you up. Thankfully, they just keep going.

You ask Abi, "Was your town big enough to make any *real* friends?"

She's still watching the two men out of the corner of her eye; she leers at them until they're half a block away from you. "I guess my best friends were the triplets who lived next door to us. Those girls were weird, always carrying their birth certificates around with them for some reason. Like they had trouble remembering their names or something. I don't know; maybe they couldn't tell themselves apart? I'm sure they had other qualities, but we tend to only remember the oddest things about people." She swats ineffectively at a fly or mosquito or something that buzzes around between you. "When I asked my parents one day about my own birth certificate, they told me they didn't have it. They explained how my birth certificate and pretty much all of their other important documents were lost in a house fire when I was just a baby. I never believed them though, since I knew that was the only house we'd ever lived in and I was smart enough to be able to tell there was never any significant fire damage. One day when they weren't home I began searching around the house. I looked everywhere, even in the most ridiculous places like behind the refrigerator and inside the chimney. Eventually though, I found them: my adoption records. They were under my parents' bed mattress like some dirty porno mags. This is when I finally realized they weren't really my parents."

"Did you say anything to them?"

"Nope. After that, I ran away from home like a coward. I think I was only twelve years old. My real father's name was written in the adoption papers and I eventually found him in New York. Here in Coney Island. He explained to me how my actual mother was a prostitute and she died from a drug overdose basically five minutes after I was born. And there he was, with his Star Wars Space Slug hands and living with a bunch of other freaks of nature. My father had chosen these people to be his family — the Mexican wolfmen and fat ladies who like setting themselves on fire — instead of his *real* daughter. It was so fucking sad to me. The truth of it all was nothing like I thought it would be. I realized then that the adopted family I had back in Memorial was actually better for me so I decided to go home. My dad paid for my bus ticket though, and before I left he told me to come back here on my twentieth birthday and he'd have a special surprise for me. I said I would and I hadn't seen him again until today. Can't believe he actually recognized me right away."

She hangs on this last thought for a moment longer than what might seem necessary. Almost like she's digging deeper into her past than she initially intended to go. There's a complex expression on her face. "As I was leaving Coney Island, I saw a tattoo parlor and decided on a whim to get one."

"When you were *twelve*?"

"I could've been thirteen. But either way, I always looked old for my age. I got a tattoo of my birth certificate on my right shoulder blade so I would always have my real identity with me wherever I went." She pats her arm with her left hand for emphasis. "You wouldn't believe how difficult that makes it to sneak into bars underage on hot summer nights."

"Identity seems to be a big thing with you."

"Tell me about it. And after my bad breakup with my shitty boyfriend I decided I should leave Colorado and come see my father again, conveniently just in time for my twentieth birthday. I took a little time off work, and now here I am."

"I noticed your father didn't mention anything about your birthday."

She scratches at her ear again. "You think *I* hadn't noticed?" Abi goes quiet now, which is sort of jarring considering the long story she just prattled off.

She watches some speedboats in the far distance as they zip through Lower Bay. After the strange meeting with Lobstero and hearing Abigail's story about family, something hits you. You sink a little into the Boardwalk bench when you realize the truth behind your relationship with your own father. He never did anything but be a good father to you and you've never done anything but pretend he was as gone as your mother. How is that fair? How is it fair that Leo Small is sitting in a cancer ward and you're watching speedboats? The boats are not so far away that they can't be seen, but too far to hear the smacking of their hulls on the waves as they go. Just little grey specks on the horizon.

Whatever Abi is thinking right now is completely lost on you. Maybe she's considering when she'll be holding her next funeral for herself? "Come on," she says finally and rises from the bench with boots in hand. "Let's get out of here."

But you stay right where you are. "You go on," you say. "I think I'll stick around here for a while." You know it's been far too long since you've seen your dad and it's time you did something about it.

Abi's caught in a moment, focused on tying the laces from her two boots together. Finally, she succeeds, and flings them over her shoulder. "Suit yourself, Rainbow. But how about we agree to meet up again? Instead of having more of these chance encounters on subways and parade routes."

You wouldn't say you and Abigail Ayr feel *wrong* together, but there is certainly something that doesn't feel completely right about it either. "That sounds good," you say.

She says she'll add you on Facebook as soon as she gets the chance, but when you tell her you're not on Facebook she pulls out a pen instead. "Well, let's do this the old-fashioned way then." She grabs your arm and writes her phone number on the inside of your wrist. "There. Now you've got an official Coney Island tattoo, too."

After only a few steps, she turns back to you and thanks you for coming with her to see her father. "For what it was worth," she adds.

You hold your limp wave pathetically as another mosquito bites the back of your neck.

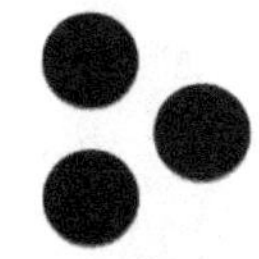

SMALL SHOES

"I'm sorry, Mister Small." There's a receptionist at the Maimonides Cancer Center you do not recognize. You question what it is she's saying, but you're really just not listening. In your head, all you can think about is your last visit to Dr. Griffin's office; it was three days ago when you had expected to see him but were instead informed of his death. Remember? It was suicide you were told. And now here you are, finally paying your father a visit and instead being apologized to again. "I'm sorry," she repeats glumly.

In your head, what you're hearing is: "*I'm sorry, but unfortunately you cannot see your father today.*"

"What are you talking about?" you ask her.

She says something else, but what you're hearing is: "*I'm sorry, but your father is dead.*"

"I don't understand," you say.

Her mouth opens and closes some more. She looks like a fish, really. The actual words don't matter. In your head, you're hearing: "*I'm sorry, but your father killed himself this morning.*"

"Don't you people monitor things like this?"

"I'm sorry?" she says again, though this time posed as a question rather than as an apology.

"Weren't there any signs? I mean, aren't you monitoring him?"

You're obviously frazzled, confused, and coming apart at the seams right here in the hospital waiting room. Yesterday, after your time with Abigail Ayr, you worked a double shift until this morning. You thought of your father all night, finally deciding you would visit him as soon as your shift was done. You haven't slept or showered and you've shown up at the Maimonides Cancer Center more fatigued than you're comfortable with.

A security guard who's never once moved from his post — he's never even so much as blinked — comes over and helps you to the absolute nearest seat. "Sit, sir," he commands. "You're going to need to calm down."

The first thought that crosses your mind is: *Did I take my Lexapro this morning?* You always take a 10mg Lexapro from the medicine cabinet just before leaving your apartment. Right after you take the 100mg Pristiq from your computer desk and two 10mg OxyContins from the bottle in your rucksack. But Gideon changed some of your prescriptions, didn't he? And you've already confused your routine now; all it took was three days without Dr. Griffin.

"Take a deep breath," he says.

You stop. Focus, you tell yourself. You think about Periscopes. Kayaks. Carburetors. Garburators. Basketball sneakers.

You turn to the guard, who you now recognize because he's still as can be. Staring directly into your eyes with his hands on your shoulders, but as still as a statue. Aside from the uniform, this is the first memory trigger you have for this particular hospital security guard. Right before you check for the missing lobe on his right ear, and how his hair is parted right down the middle. The way he rests his hands on his belt is another trigger you'll use for him: most security guards seem to relax with their thumbs inside their belts, but this guy — and you notice now that his nametag reads Errol — he prefers keeping his index fingers in his belt at all times. This is how you recognize the man who would otherwise be lost to you in a crowd.

"Are you better, sir?" he asks. It feels strange to be called sir, like you're not old enough to have earned the title.

Calming down, you realize what the receptionist told you was that your father is no longer here because he's been moved to another treatment center. The words echo in your head slowly. "Yes. Thank you, Errol." you say. Your father always reminded you to call someone by their name if you knew it, especially if you did not know them that well. According to him, it helps form better relationships, particularly with strangers.

You rise back to your feet and approach the receptionist again, this time with your senses better collected. "Can you tell me where my father is?" She's not wearing a nametag but you're not certain you'd say her name even if she was.

"He's been moved to a hospice in Manhattan. Here, I'll pull up that information for you." She clacks away at the keyboard, her little microphone headpiece thingy bobbing up and down as she goes. "Leo Small was transferred almost a week ago. When's the last time you spoke with your father anyway?"

Who is she to throw such judgements your way? You look over at Errol in the hopes he'll have your back here, but he's returned to staring at his favorite spot on the opposing wall. "I've been busy," you tell her.

She writes the address and phone number for the hospice down on a yellow notepad, then tears it off and hands it to you. "Here you are. You can collect the rest of your father's things from his room. I'm sure he'd appreciate them." She says *appreciate* like she's really saying, "*If you can spare the energy to think about your sick father from time to time. The poor man's dying, for fuck's sake."*

"Thanks," you say derisively. You fold the note into your pocket and walk down the corridor that leads toward your father's old room.

ooo

The door no longer has your father's name on it. In fact, the old guy who shared a room with him doesn't have his name there anymore either. There's only one name, K. GACK, on the wall outside the closed door. You slowly push it open and it creaks and echoes like you're in the bowels of an old wooden ship.

There is a sickly man — presumably K. GACK — in the bed your father once occupied. You cannot tell if he is barely conscious, asleep, or dead. You presume the intermediate beeping from the machinery can only mean he's still alive, though you don't pretend to know anything about this equipment. For all you know it could be monitoring to see if he comes *back* to life. Are there machines that do that? This man has only scattered, thin patches of hair left on his head and his skin looks to be dry as a rock in the sun beat desert. His skinny arms lay flat over pressed white sheets and tubes connect to him from various blinking equipment, stuck into his nose and wrist and the inside of his elbow. His arms remind you of the painted cover of *The Third*, with wrists exposed to the world.

The unoccupied bed in the room has a cardboard box beside the pillow. It's a Costco-sized cracker box of Stoned Wheat Thins, you're guessing from a bulk order at the hospital cafeteria. There is a strip of masking tape on the side of the box with "Small" scribbled in black marker. If you knew your father better, you could probably tell whether or not this was his handwriting, but you can't say for sure. You drop your bag on the bed, sit down, and place the box in your lap so you can take a look inside.

The contents are a jumbled mess, and include a toothbrush and toothpaste sealed in a plastic sandwich bag; four pairs of clean, white (well, yellowed) Fruit-of-the-Loom underpants; a long piece — maybe three feet in total? — of twisted up black wire; a note torn off from a novelty Big Apple souvenir notepad that has four phone numbers (one of which is the number you share with your father) written on it, but with no names attached to any of them; a couple of pages torn from magazines and folded into perfect squares; a ratty comic book — called "Mutant X" — published by Marvel Comics in 2001; a shoehorn; and a tiny, worn metallic box containing only a few screws, nails, and one-dollar and ninety-three cents in loose change. You place the yellow note from the receptionist, the note with your father's current whereabouts written on it, into this small metal box.

There is a faded floral print on the metal box that adorns the lid and sides. You recognize this object immediately: it was a favorite item of your father's when you were growing up. Its contents were constantly shifting, but you know the container always held items that were very important to him. It was kept at his shoe store in a prominent spot above his workbench in the back. There was never anything of monetary value — certainly never two-dollars in change — but he simply liked to know it was there. As far as you knew, he'd lost the box with everything else in the fire but you can tell from its blackened sides that this is the same one. Chalk it up to being just another thing your father had done that you were unaware of. It seems his life has been one surprise after another. Quite simply, the man did not tell you anything, not even the tiniest of details.

So, you were left to piece it together as best you could.

Leo Small was raised in Brighton Beach by his parents; the grandparents of yours who died before you were born. The other set, your mother's parents, were just as gone as she was. Your father began working at the family business — a dilapidated shoe repair store on Fifteenth and Neptune — while he was in junior high. Small Shoes was not much to look at but it had its fair share of loyal customers.

You don't remember many stories your mother told you before she left, but you do recall her telling you how she'd met your father. Her name was Wilma Dradtstl. As her story goes, the senior prom was in two nights and young Wilma had broken the heel on one of her shoes after chucking it at her on-again, off-again boyfriend. She panicked, and her mother — Mrs. Dradtstl, who had seen her share of shoes repaired — sent her to Small Shoes. As luck would have it, Leo Small was working alone that afternoon; his father had been driving around the city looking for shoe polish or extra thin laces or some such. Wilma and Leo had known one another from school, though only just barely. She begged him to fix her shoe. He asked her who she was going to the prom with. She told him Sam Cleffton. Or Bam Cleffton, as everyone else called him due to his propensity to knock over anything that moved on the football field. Wilma asked Leo about his own date. He told her he hadn't asked anyone because he wasn't going. She told him he was an idiot; nobody had ever missed the senior prom before! He told her he didn't believe that statement. She called him an idiot again. And he fixed her shoe anyway.

But just as Wilma was leaving Small Shoes, Leo's father came running in. He was exasperated, claiming a young man had run in front of his car. "Bam!" he exclaimed. "Right into me!" Yes, it was Bam Cleffton all right, trying to catch an errant football right out there in the middle of Neptune Avenue. As it turned out he couldn't attend the prom with a shattered hip, so, left without any other option, Wilma Dradtstl asked Leo Small. And he agreed. They were married a year later and Sam Cleffton never had any idea what hit him.

Before his father died, Leo took over the family business and you were born sometime after that. Ten thousand years too late, depending on who's telling the story. Roughly five years later, Wilma Small disappeared and you and your father barely mentioned her in conversation again. Unless it was a passing comment to remind you just how batshit crazy she was. Honestly, you don't even remember what she looked like. Your father kept a crumpled old photograph on his workbench at Small Shoes; it was a faded black-and-white picture of a woman posing in a garden, smiling shiftily like the Mona Lisa. In the photo, the morning breeze had trapped the rising hemline of her white dress forever in time. You have no idea if she was your mother, your father's mother or some other woman altogether. But it doesn't really matter now, you suppose.

You worked at the shoe store when you were growing up, just like your father did before you. But the store wasn't around long enough for you to make it to your high school graduation. You don't know if you could have fixed a broken heel from a shoe belonging to a classmate of yours, or if your father might have run over her boyfriend, prompting another fairy tale prom story. Chances are slim, but history seems to have a funny way of repeating itself, doesn't it? You didn't go to your high school prom, you know that much. You didn't hate working there, sweeping the floor and helping your dad glue and stitch shoe soles, but you think it was the beginning of the loss of your sense of belonging. You knew the shoe store was not where you wished to spend your life, and yet, you had no idea of where else you might have wanted to be instead.

But then you never actually had a choice in the matter. When you were thirteen, Small Shoes was destroyed in that fateful fire on the day of the Mermaid Parade. The very fire that was started by your two idiot friends after you told them to just grow up already. Barton and Reilly were never caught, and you never told your father you'd known who was responsible. You just pretended you had nothing to do with it and watched as he filed for bankruptcy.

After that, your father worked a lot of odd jobs, never seeming to be anywhere nor doing anything for any longer than a few months at a time. He sold vacuum cleaners door to door; he worked at a gummy worm factory; he wrapped meat in an unlicensed butcher shop; he changed billboard advertisements; he cleaned all the garbage out of Jamaica Bay. Leo Small was the only adult you've known to have his own lemonade stand. As a result of all of the dozens of jobs he worked, your father began to lose a sense of his own identity, never getting back to where he was before he'd lost the family business in that fire. Eventually, all he did with his time was pull weeds from the cracks in the sidewalk that lined the apartments around your block. By the time he finished he'd end up where he started and the weeds had already grown back. So, he just kept on going.

As he became more and more distant, the two of you talked less and less.

You never did find the right opportunity to tell your father you were depressed. You grew up with depression and never wanted to talk about it out of fear of being judged. Knowing that something is wrong with you but being too young or too naive to do anything about it is so very difficult. You never told him agonizing loneliness and aching melancholy were basically all you'd ever felt. All you'd ever known. But maybe he felt the same way? Maybe he could have helped you feel like you belonged somewhere here, when all you ever wanted was to be somewhere else. You never told your father you'd been in therapy with Dr. Griffin for two years and that you've been on some pretty heavy prescription medications. You regret never having talks about girls with him in high school or telling him about your relationship with Reya. You don't really know what he might have said anyway. What advice he might have had.

Maybe if Leo Small had been a more present father you wouldn't have had to piece his life together for yourself. But if you hadn't been such a distant son, maybe the two of you could have dealt with your grief as a pair, rather than on your own.

The last time you spoke with your father was five weeks ago when he phoned you at work to say he had just been diagnosed with a brain tumor. The doctors didn't yet know if the tumor was benign or malignant, which didn't really mean anything to you. Try as you might, you simply could not get those table cloths clean enough that night. When you returned home the next morning, he was already in the hospital. You've been to the Maimonides Cancer Center a few times since, though you've only ever seen him sleeping. He's looked thinner every time, like his body is trying to find some way to slip away from the world. You wouldn't go in that room though; choosing to simply sit chewing your nails in the waiting room, or you'd pace back and forth behind his door before chickening out and slyly sneaking off the premises. His relocation to some hospice in the city can only mean one thing: he's not getting better. Soon there won't be anything left of him.

A vivid memory flashes through your mind as you sit on this hospital bed. You were maybe seven or eight years old and freezing in the backseat of your father's rusty old car. The windshield wipers barely worked anymore and the snow on the window was piling up faster than it was being brushed away. The leather seats inside were cracked and hardened from age and neglect. It felt more like sitting on a bench made of beef jerky. The seat belts were frayed to nearly nothing, or were missing altogether. Basically every instrument on the dashboard was busted. You don't remember where it was you were going or where you were coming from. The only other part of the memory you have is listening to him sing. Leo Small couldn't carry a tune; he couldn't whistle or hum to save his life. Maybe he thought you were asleep. Or maybe he was actually singing just for you. You don't know what difference it would have made. You still remember pieces of that song but you never did learn what it was; all you know for sure was that it was the saddest song you'd ever heard. But to you — sitting back there, wishing you were somebody else, and wondering where it might be that you *really* belonged — it was the perfect soundtrack to your solitude.

Just as you begin to place all the items back into the cracker box, the beeping from the machine across the room intensifies. The old man is stirring, and he coughs up something disgusting onto the sheets. You figure this is as good a time as any to make your exit. As you walk past him the man grabs onto your arm, but his grip feels about as strong as tissue paper. Still, it's enough to momentarily stop you in your tracks.

"Where are you going, Janice?" the sickly man asks, presumably to you.

"I'm sorry. I was just on my way."

"We haven't finished though," he wheezes. "You were saying something about Amsterdam?" His hand loosens and he straightens the creases from the sheet covering his legs.

You don't know what to say; you only want to get out of here. You tell him, "Only that it's lovely this time of year. That's all I said."

He smiles, though you're utterly unsure why. "That's my girl," he says.

You feel like a character right out of *The Third*. This misunderstanding of who you are is not unlike Luca Desplante III; even though he is Tristan Montminy's identical twin, the description of Luca's appearance never seems to match up. Luca is Tristan but he appears Nigerian. Luca is Tristan but he looks like Colonel Sanders. You're Cepik Small but you're mistaken for Janice.

Identity is not reality.

"I'll take you there as soon as you're better," you say.

"We both know that's hardly true anymore. I'm not getting better."

You have no more words; you can only stand there and let him hit you with some more of his own. With a crooked pinky finger, he points to the other bed across the room, the one you were just sitting on. Where your father's old roommate used to be.

"Just like that fellow over there. He knew it was coming, said he felt like he'd been waiting for the end forever. And then yesterday? Poof."

Of course, you have no idea who Janice is, but you can probably guess.

Nurse? Wife? Sister? You don't know for certain, but you say it anyway: you tell him, "You'll be fine, Dad."

And then you leave.

When you return to the front desk, you ask the receptionist who Janice is.

"Janice? You mean Kermit's daughter?"

"Kermit Gack?"

She nods a little, wondering why you'd ever care to be asking her such things.

"I think you'd better give her a call. Her dad doesn't have long left." The cracker box rattles with the sounds of your father's discarded junk as you exit the hospital.

ooo

Another memory starts playing in your mind as you wait for the next N-Train to Coney Island. The last time you'd come to see your father you were asked to first sit down with one of the doctors from the cancer center. This man — with his airy lisp and claw-like carpal tunnel fingers — explained how your father's brain tumor was a very rare form called *sarcoma*.

"You may have noticed," he said, "some of the following symptoms: dizziness, loss of memory and/or concentration, numbness on his left side."

"Not really," you told him. But seeing as how little you'd recently seen your father — even when you lived together — you could hardly have been considered an expert on his current health.

"Our next steps," he continued without your asking, "would be to perform surgery on the brain as soon as possible, then to follow immediately thereafter with radiation and chemotherapy. This might keep the tumor under control for a while."

"How long is a while?"

"Months? Days? If even a few brain cancer cells are left behind they could grow back again. Maybe even worse than before. I'll be honest with you: there's more than a really good chance things will get worse. I'm talking about trouble with speaking or understanding conversations. Extreme mood changes. The inability to form new memories. Facial recognition problems. Don't be surprised if your father simply does not recognize you. A lot of people find that to be the hardest part."

ooo

Before walking home from the station, you take a slight detour up to Neptune and Fifteenth to a place you like to refer to as "The Bleakest Corner in the USA." This one, single intersection offers up a mishmash of convenience stores, beauty salons, laundromats, vacant lots of abandoned cars, insurance offices that appear as though you'd need insurance just to enter them, and crumbling apartments with rickety balconies holding impressive collections of plastic lawn chairs, dead barbecues, and stacks of worn tires. If they knew about this location, aspiring filmmakers hoping to shoot post-apocalyptic zombie wasteland flicks on the cheap would be swarming down to Neptune and Fifteenth in waves. It's dismal, but this is also exactly where Small Shoes used to be. A slew of withering storefronts all within mere steps of one another.

You look into the yellowed window of the now-dying bagelry and imagine Leo Small and Wilma Dradtstl speaking to one another for the first time.

Your meticulous memory of the shoe store conjures the familiar scents of mink oils, glycerin bars, and saddle soaps. The tinny jingle of the miniature bell above the door still reverberates in your mind. You can't shake the recollection of the metallic screech of the bent cash register drawer in its attempts to slide open and closed. The dust motes of the sweaty workshop forged a soft, translucent shield from the harsh world outside. You envision yourself, behind a counter that is no longer there, lost in callow thoughts; wondering why everyone at school seemed to be pairing up with someone else while you were just a blubbering idiot around girls. You see Barton and Reilly with gasoline and matches. Flames licking the window's backside, the view warped forevermore by the extreme heat.

Behind you in the window's reflection, you spot someone approaching. You turn quickly to discover a kid — probably fourteen or fifteen — holding a camera. He's not dressed like he belongs in the neighborhood; he's far too proper to be here. Perhaps the preppie son of a Park Avenue lawyer who's come to Coney Island to bear witness to and catalogue the last dregs of a society he could never possibly understand simply by Googling it.

"Smile," he says, raising the camera.

"What for?"

"We're on a scavenger hunt." You notice two other kids the same age standing upon the opposing sidewalk. They're eating hot dogs and drinking coffee. "We just snapped a photo of a dead bird. Next on our list is taking a picture of the saddest person we can find."

"You came to the right place," you say. You don't know how on earth this scavenger hunt might work or what brought them to this corner at the very same time you've found yourself lost in unhappy memories. Maybe they followed you off the train? Maybe all the way from the hospital? But you smile as candid a smile as you can muster before you all part company.

You imagine this photograph: the guy with the still-bruised face standing outside his family's long-forgotten shoe repair business that's now a decrepit bagelry on the Bleakest Corner in the USA and holding a cracker box full of nothing but scattered pieces of a dying man. You don't even know if it's sweat or tears you feel streaming down your face. That photo will be *exactly* what those kids were looking for. The buzzing of mosquitoes picks up again the closer you get to your apartment building.

ooo

You plunk your rucksack and the cracker box on the kitchen counter. It feels like it's been forever since you were home. The heat punches you in the face but everything in the apartment is still where it should be. This is when you realize that because you weren't home, you missed some of your medication. To make up for the gaff, you take 20mg of Lexapro from the medicine cabinet before taking 200mg of Pristiq off the computer desk and 40mg of OxyContin from the bottle you keep in your bag. You turn on the air conditioner and sit at the computer.

Once the computer warms up, you find three unread messages which bleep happily in the mailbox. There is another email from the same Massive Multiplayer Online Role-Playing Game, though this time you notice it is from AIIB, the same one Abi had talked about yesterday. There is an image attached to the email; all it is, is a shadowy man sitting on a rooftop and watching the sun rise or set behind darkened skyscrapers. On the image are the words:

SIGN UP. DON'T JUST PLAY NOW — LIVE NOW!

You hit delete and the entire internet application suddenly closes. Usually it takes a few seconds for your computer to respond to any commands, but this is instantaneous. You click open another window and return to your mail, taking note that the online gaming invite is no longer in your inbox. Aside from the vanishing email there doesn't seem to be anything else amiss. The next message is from an "Assistant at the Working Office of Gideon Flat." You can only assume Gideon Flat is his full name. That's one mystery solved. It says "Assistant" but you can tell it is obviously still him. He is requesting you come in for another session tomorrow:

> Gideon Flat prefers to not wait a week between appointments with new patients. Studies have shown that one week leaves too much time for an unfamiliar patient to kill himself.
> Please contact our office as soon as possible to confirm your status.

Yes, this is actually what it says. You're unsure that if by status he is questioning whether you are currently alive or dead. It's all too weird to dwell too heavily upon. What you really want to do is email the Working Office of Gideon Flat to tell him you do not intend to keep seeing him. But then you remember what it was Abi told you yesterday: *"We're all depressed,"* she said. *"And we all need somebody. If you need the help, you should go back."*

So instead, you email Gideon back, telling him that no, you're not quite dead yet and that you'll see him tomorrow.

Finally, you stare at that single unread email from your father that's been sitting for nearly three weeks now. It sits in your inbox like a Trojan horse that has been wheeled past the drawbridge and into the courtyard; the secret inside having yet to reveal itself.

You click it open.

The email tells you how your father's health has been deteriorating more quickly every day.

He writes, "This life is slipping through my thinning fingers. I'm looking at the backs of my hands as I type this letter now and I barely recognize them. All the cragged lines I see are like historical records of my every mistake."

He writes, "It's troublesome, and I'm feeling angrier every day."

He writes, "The only words I have left are for you, my son."

He writes, "I think they'll be moving me to a hospice in the city."

He writes, "I don't have much longer on this world." Just like that, in those exact words: this world. As though there were any other. You think Abi had also said something along those same lines yesterday.

He even writes, "Your mother is still a raving lunatic."

As awful as his words are, the truth is, it is not until the last paragraph when you really start to worry about your father. He writes, "I pray you will come see me soon. I have something very important to give to you. And some things to tell you. I pray you will come."

Your father was never a religious man but you've heard it said that dying can often do strange things to people. Though you wonder now if perhaps your father had not been a stranger to prayer all his life. Had Leo Small prayed for Wilma Dradtstl to walk into the shoe store that afternoon? Maybe he prayed for *you*? Maybe even for the fire that took your father's entire life away or at least altered it enough to force him into making a change he was never strong enough to make on his own.

It's nearly impossible to fathom just how much he must have needed to hear from you these last few weeks. You've tried to find a reason for why you almost seem to prefer the distance between your father and you, but you just can't put a finger on it. It hurts though, whatever it might be. You take two more of the round, white 10mg OxyContin tablets to try and dull the pain.

You decide to update your journal before shutting the computer down for the night. The last two entries briefly discuss your first session with Gideon on Saturday and finding the copy of *The Third* on Sunday night. This was when you were on the subway, on your way to meeting up with Bester. You mention seeing the girl across Surf Avenue and again at Jackson Heights. Now you write about meeting Abigail Ayr officially at The UnDiner, where you usually choose to go to be ignored. And how she somehow convinced you to accompany her to see her father at the Sideshows by the Seashore. Lobstero, his name was. You write about how she opened up to you about fairly intimate details of her past. And your visit this morning to the Maimonides Cancer Center, hoping to see your father.

And you write about more of the wonderful dreams you've been having:

In my dreams, I'm in a grassy field, on my back and watching the clouds. Clouds so big and puffy and white you'd think they were from a children's storybook.

In my dreams, I'm counting the rungs on a ladder. I think there's twenty-four, but that doesn't seem right so I count again. I'm drinking a root beer float in a bright pink and blue diner. There's a large neon sign outside with a sleeping sheep on it which makes the diner actually look like it should be a mattress store instead. The sheep looks not unlike one of those fluffy white clouds.

In my dreams, I'm actually filling out the entire New York Times crossword and not just staring at a mostly-empty puzzle. At a bus stop, a man asks me for change and I give him a dollar bill. He couldn't be happier.

Finally, you lay on your bed in the hopes that sleep will take you. It never does. Another OxyContin might do the trick, but it usually doesn't. You don't care though and take one anyway. Too many synapses are firing in your head at once. The buzzing intensifies, and you don't know if it's another mosquito in your apartment, or the street light outside, or if your head really is about to explode. The light bulb's chain hanging from the ceiling seems to be dancing by itself. The four walls are waving softly. Your father's closed bedroom door breathes worryingly within the cracked frame.

You slowly wobble your way to the bathroom medicine cabinet for another hit of Zolpimist oral spray. It says on the bottle that the clear, colorless solution is cherry flavored but it doesn't really remind you of cherries. If it can help your insomnia you really wouldn't care if it tasted like expired foot cream.

From the kitchen counter, you retrieve the book from your bag, and then crash back onto the bed. When you last left Tristan, he was digging through Grace's personal belongings, looking for some sort of evidence of who she really is and where she goes in the day. Your eyes are having a hard time adjusting. The words are skittering upon the page, and they pulsate between being blurry and incredibly crisp. Finally though, things calm down and you find the spot where you last left off.

Tristan locks up the apartment and walks to the fruit market. He is going there to buy ingredients for a surprise dessert he's making for Grace, presumably because he feels guilty for having rooted through her stuff. Suddenly, a Vespa rattles by and somebody in the sidecar chucks a heavy baguette at Tristan.

Tristan collected the bread from the street gutter. Dusted it off on his shirt sleeve. Took a bite. A little stale but it was hard to beat the authenticity of a true French loaf. Why would anyone toss a baguette at a simple passerby? Though maybe the proper question should be why not?

Tristan combed his hair back into place with his free hand and entered the marketplace. Fresh fruit smells wafted around him. Digging through the clementine the prune and the nectarin he found the dessert components. To taste the fruit before purchase is not suggested commonplace though Tristan bit surreptitiously into the skin of one single nectarin. He found it most pleasing and was happy to discover there were still moments of childlike joy to be found in his days.

But just as he savored a second bite Tristan was approached by someone he did not yet know. "Luca! There you are." It was a police officer. Not of impressive stature but certainly having the size of power about him. "Where have you been?"

"Around" Tristan cautiously replied. It was difficult to think just how odd it was only weeks ago to be addressed as his twin. Now though he thought he might find it uncomfortable to be called Tristan in conversation. "I have been around."

The officer stepped in closer. "Have you got it?" he asked in a hushed tone.

"Have I got what?"

The eyes darted back and forth looking around on guard. "Come now Luca. Must you always play such games? Keep you promises and I will keep mine."

With his own hands Tristan patted himself down with hopes that he could play along with the unidentified charade. The officer grew noticeably impatient with the cheap act. He grabbed Tristan by the collar of his shirt and pulled him into an alleyway just outside the market. Tristan wanted to break free but he could not.

The policeman seemed much bigger than he did initially and Tristan could not tell if in fact he was also foaming at the mouth. From a place unseen the officer released his baton with a quick hand and stuck Tristan in the ribcage before raising the weapon up under his chin. Tristan could hardly swallow.

"The fucking drugs Luca! Where are they?"

There is a sudden burst of sound from across the room, like a muffled pop of something electric on the fritz. You see the tail-end of a sliver of smoke from the air conditioner and it immediately hits you that everything has gone deathly quiet. Wonderful. One-hundred-degree weather and now the AC calls it quits.

Folding the corner of the page, you place *The Third* beside the bed and take a closer look at the metal box on the windowsill. The air conditioner is certainly dead, you know this much. Obviously, you have no idea what to do about it so you do nothing more than gaze out the window. This humidity is certain to be the death of you tonight. There is still plenty of activity on the street corner below; the usual assortment of women and the aroma of fried chicken. There's a car sitting parked with its wheels right up on the curb.

You swat at the cloud of insects, trying to keep as many of them as possible outside of your apartment. You still hear them after closing the window. The heat is not likely to get any worse and you'd prefer to not be eaten alive by mosquitoes and who knows what else tonight.

You finish the chapter in bed before finally closing your eyes. You know it isn't going to take long to fall asleep. You're so tired, it doesn't trouble you at all when Tristan decided to get out of town after his encounter with the cop at the fruit market. In that moment, he chose to escape not only from the aggressive police officer, but also from Grace and Luca's lives. He chose to return to his own. You're so tired, it doesn't shake you in the least when you read about how Tristan returned to his actual apartment for the first time in weeks. And it doesn't rattle your nerves, not even in the slightest, when Tristan opened his door to discover Emilia dead on the floor and then he turned to see the cop had followed him all the way to this horribly gruesome crime scene.

None of it bothers you in the least.

You simply hold your arms tight, sing your father's sad song in your head, and you're out.

BILDUNGSROMAN

Reya had a way about her. It was the way she'd try to sneak up behind you, but only if you already knew she was there. The way she'd shush you in the movie theater and then curse like a trucker while riding public transit. The way in which she might attract friends and lovers but how she'd pique the interests of strangers even more. How she put so much thought into a Halloween costume but then ended up going as a ghost every time. Every time. She'd actually throw on the old white bedsheet with two eye holes cut out haphazardly with the sharpest key off her key ring. She even had pictures to prove it. Pictures from the last six or seven Halloweens stuck onto her radiator with Pablo Picasso magnets. She hated Picasso with a passion but friends kept giving her Picasso-themed gifts because she couldn't stop herself from displaying them. *"Oh, you must love the works of Picasso. Here's another."*

Her voice was like something you'd heard in the air. The first time she spoke — that night outside the subway station — it was like you knew it already, didn't you? So familiar were her voice's reverbs and resonations.

The freezing cold also has a way of reminding you of Reya. For what it's worth, you still think of her when the temperature's boiling too. It's so hot out this morning, you seriously consider not moving from your bed. Better to just lie here and sweat. You stare at the ceiling and try to find the mosquito that had been buzzing around your face all night, but it must be gone by now or too tiny to spot. You're going to be scratching at fresh bites all day.

They said today is going to be the hottest one yet.

You have your next session with Gideon Flat this morning. The follow-up appointment you booked so he'd know you weren't dead. You know he's going to ask about Reya some more, but you've convinced yourself that it will be good for you. You know talking about something is really the only way to make it any better. But it's hard to open up to someone new. They're quicker to judge. A new confidant will have less information to go on, so any perceived negatives will only seem much more amplified. That much worse.

You peel yourself from the bed and drag yourself to your appointment.

Not surprisingly, Gideon Flat is unrecognizable to you but there are just enough memory triggers to know this is the same man: the futility shown in the way he attempts to brush the wavy hair back behind his ears; the long, pointed nose; the finger lodged deep within said nose; the key attached to the rubber band on his left wrist; the familiar lilac-colored journal in his hands. "You're Gideon, right?" you ask as soon as he appears out from behind his office door. It helps that he's still the only person who seems to work anywhere close to this office. Today he's wearing a bright pink t-shirt with a palm tree logo and the words, "No Bad Days."

"Yes, of course." He looks at you sideways. "What was that thing of yours called again?"

"Prosopagnosia."

"That's right. I should have written that one down, hey? Sit down, Epic."

You seriously reconsidered doing this. It took enough awful events in your life for you to decide to start seeing Dr. Griffin in the first place. Why would you wish to relive any of that? But it wasn't until five minutes ago, standing outside Gideon's office on Surf Avenue — your hand quivering no more than an inch away from the unlocked door — when you really had to stop. And it was Abi's words of wisdom that popped into your head. It was what she told you when the two of you stared up at this very office from Mermaid Avenue that urged you on. She said everyone's depressed and they all need somebody. She said the world works in mysterious ways and sometimes it chooses the right people for you. And that was good enough. So, you sit down. The office window is open again today, though it's much quieter than it was the other day during the Mermaid Parade.

"So, your name is?" Gideon asks.

"Uh, Small. Epic Small. Did you not write that down either?"

"No, no. This is how I would like you to begin each of our sessions. You say: *My name is Cepik Small—*"

"Epic," you say, interrupting.

"Right. Yes." He makes another note in the journal. But he seems distracted, like the thought he'd just written down was an item he needed to pick up from the store on his way home: A carton of soy milk. Some Toilet Duck. He places his pen back down, carefully lining it up perpendicular with the edge of his notebook. "So, I want you to say, *My name is Cepik Small,* and then let me in a little further. Maybe by explaining something new about yourself."

"Something new?"

"Right. Anything I don't already know. For example, you might tell me something that's occurred since you were last here. Any sort of change in your life. Maybe you switched toothpaste brands? Or went to a dog show?"

You don't know why, but you feel like there's a hidden camera watching you. Recording this conversation. "And *why* do I have to do this?"

"Well, every time I see you I should know *more* about you. And you should know more about yourself, too." He catches you glancing down at his journal and then reels it in closer to himself, crossing his arms over the top of it. "So, go on."

"Okay. My name is Cepik Small." Do you tell him about your father? The sarcoma that's quickly killing him? Or your surreal encounters with Abigail Ayr? How about meeting her father at the Sideshow? Somehow those don't feel right. You're not ready for any of that yet. "I found a book on the F-Train the other day. And I started reading it."

"That's a good start. Tell me about that. What's the premise of the book?"

"It's about twins. But they don't seem to share any relation." You try your best to tell him every detail of what you've read so far: how Tristan Montminy meets Luca Desplante III; how the two men switched identities and girlfriends and apartments; how Tristan quickly becomes bored of Luca's girlfriend, Grace; how he's approached and followed by the shifty police officer looking for drugs; and how Tristan decides to stop the charade and return to his previous life, only to find his girlfriend, Emilia, dead in his old apartment. "It's pretty complicated," you say, summing it up.

"It's French, right?"

"I'm sorry?"

"The book. It sounds familiar. I think I've read it before."

"Um, yes. It was originally written in French. Though the copy I found was an English translation. And a very poor translation at that."

"Yes, right. I remember. It was called…" he trails off, trying to recall the title.

"It's called *The Third.*"

"Yes! Yes, I *have* read that. It was a very long time ago, however." He wistfully thinks back to what must have been a much better time. "Boy, I barely remember."

"You remember the characters though, right? The twins? Tristan and Luca."

"Sure. And the third one."

"The third one? What do you mean?"

"A third twin. Well, a triplet I suppose technically."

"Maybe I haven't gotten up to that part yet."

"You must have. I remember—the three of them all met at a fountain in Paris. Tristan, Luca, and The Third."

"You don't remember his name?"

"That *was* his name. His name in the novel was *The Third.* He wasn't as successful as the other two. He didn't have a girlfriend or an apartment, I don't recall. And when they all agreed to swap lives, he only ended up screwing up everything they had. He tried to eliminate them, like they were different sides of him; dark sides he didn't like. And then Tristan and Luca have to join forces. They band together to stop The Third from destroying everything."

You can't believe what you're hearing. None of this sounds like what you've been reading. It might, however, explain the title a bit better. "That version sounds pretty stupid, actually. A third twin? Perhaps you're remembering the book wrong."

"I'm positive."

"Is it possible that I just missed something?" Pulling at your bag, you open it up to find your ragged copy of the book. You hold up the cover for Gideon to see. The image of the two left forearms.

He recognizes the book immediately. "Yes! That's the one. It's been a long time since I read it. Maybe twenty years? I think I still have a copy at home somewhere too." Gideon closes the journal on his desk now. He takes the book from your hand and leafs through; the worn, flimsy pages barely touch his fingertips as they flip effortlessly past his wide eyes. He mumbles under his breath, as though trying to dredge up certain memories relating to having read the words years before. He flips back and forth between a few sections, including a stop at where you've folded the corner of the page down, before finally just opening the novel to the last page, dissatisfied by what he finds there. "This is very puzzling."

"What is it?"

"Far be it from me to ruin the ending of a book for anyone, but I can say with confidence that this is quite dissimilar from what I can recall reading in my youth."

"Are you sure about that?"

"Oh, without a doubt. But saying more might spoil the ending. And I'm not one to spoil the ending for anybody." Gideon peruses the front matter now, running a finger down the page and stopping half way. "This translation was published twenty years ago. This is the same year you were born, isn't it?" He holds the page for you to see and then hands the book back, which you take cautiously as though it's really some ancient, dusty tome full of dark magic and written with the blood of virgins. "Again, I don't want to ruin the end for you."

You look at the date now yourself: it *is* the same year you were born. Ten thousand years too late. You place *The Third* back inside your rucksack. "What would account for the variances then?"

"Variances?" He pauses for a short moment before prodding any further. "You're thinking divergent copies, maybe? Tell me Cepik, do you believe in conspiracy theories?"

"I believe people are capable of theorizing conspiracies. Is that the same thing?"

"If that's where you truly stand then the big picture doesn't matter much, does it?"

"I don't think anyone's out to get me, if that's what you're asking."

He leans back in his chair; the look on Gideon's face tells you he's a little shocked by your answers. He blinks his eyes rapidly a few times. "Listen carefully, Cepik. There are conspiracies *everywhere*. And I'm talking about a whole lot more than just the perfect lightbulb."

"The perfect lightbulb?"

"Yes," he says. And then he rises from his chair and closes the window behind him, shutting you out from the world outside. Maybe shutting the world out from the two of you. With his back turned, you stare at the closed journal on his desk. On the spine, there is a printed label you hadn't noticed before. It reads:

Small, Cepik

"They've invented a lightbulb that can never die. You've never seen one but obviously this has already happened; companies just don't want this to be public knowledge. The might of the all-American dollar, right? But I'm not talking about that. And this doesn't quite fall into the same category as 9-11 or JFK or KFC either."

This is only your second visit with Gideon but you already feel more like you're here to act as a sounding board rather than for the purpose of getting to the root of your *own* issues.

Gideon sits back down. "The information they want us to have is constantly being beamed into our heads. Even now. The world we *want* to know is a total secret to us and the world we *think* we know is a fraud. They're turning cameras into microphones, recovering conversations from sound vibrations seen in objects. They've got genetically modified ladybugs that have been programmed to kill us as a form of population control. A single one of these could wipe out all of Manhattan."

"I don't believe that."

On Monday, the last thing Abi's father told you was that bug spray wouldn't do you any good. Did Lobstero know something else? Does everybody know something you don't?

"What the hell do you think is happening in Louisiana right now?"

"I have no idea what's happening in Louisiana."

"It doesn't matter what you believe though. All that matters is what's real and what isn't."

"Sorry, but am I paying for this time right now?"

For a moment, Gideon glares at you disappointedly, but soon corrects himself. "Excuse me. You're right." Opening his journal and keeping his pen at the ready, he asks, "The new prescriptions I gave you; have there been any noticeable changes or challenges so far?"

You're unsure of what you should tell him. You want to say: *"What do you expect when I suddenly stop popping back 250mg of prescription meds on a daily basis and start taking 100mg of new ones?"* That's what you want to say. Of course, you're afraid of appearing more irritable than you used to be. But he's still staring right through you so you've got to respond with something.

You say, "I've heard the first things to go with new medication are the dreams. But my dreams haven't been going anywhere. If anything, they seem to be intensifying."

Gideon writes this, or something, down into the journal. "Have you been adhering to the suggested prescription quantities? Not taking any Tylenol or aspirin on the side?"

"No," you lie. "No extras. I'm sticking with what you've given me." You had three more aspirin right before you stepped foot in here today.

There are some further heavy pen strokes across the page now, either underlining or crossing out of information. Then he suggests, "How about we go into a bit more detail about this girl. Ray, was it?"

"Reya."

"Reya. Yes, that's the one." He pauses and looks over your shoulder for only a moment. Like someone had just popped their head in the door. "Not a common name, is it?"

"I suppose not."

"The last time we spoke, you told me she was gone. How about elaborating?"

"She's still gone."

"Why don't you tell me how the two of you met?"

You explain the details of that night. How you'd spotted her outside the subway station. She'd just been mugged and you were the only one there to help her. "When I first saw her, I knew I would need to compile a detailed list of memory triggers because I knew for certain I wanted to see her again after that night. They would be the only way I could instantly recognize her."

"Right. Because of the prosopagnosia." He gets it right this time. "Tell me about those memory triggers."

"It was how she relaxed her hands. When Reya wasn't focused on something she kept her fingertips together like they were delicately tying shoelaces. Or carrying really tiny shopping bags. The way she paused momentarily before saying anything. Barely perceptible, but it was a definite pause. She always held her chin unusually high, as though peering over a fence that was just a sliver too tall."

"And do you always make such meticulous lists?"

"Not always, no. Usually just enough so that I don't forget someone during a single conversation. Things like hair and eye color. Basic facial structure and shape. But for someone I plan on seeing again it requires more comprehensive triggers."

"Fascinating," he mumbles to himself as he jots some more notes down. "Have you made a list of triggers for me, too?"

"Of course I have."

"Simply fascinating," he repeats. "But let's stay on topic. What were some of the things you talked about with Reya when you met?"

For a moment, you pretend to be thinking back in time, even though you don't need to. Memories of Reya are always right there on your mind. "There were words she said to me after our first night together. I remember them so clearly. I had my arms around her and she said: 'Please *don't hold me like that. Not if you're thinking of letting go later.'* I had absolutely no intention of ever letting her go, and I only held onto her that much tighter. We saw more of one another. Almost every day. We had something real. At least it felt real to me. We'd do nothing for days at a time. Nothing at all. We would watch people at train stations, trying to pair up who was waiting for whom. She made me happy and she made me want to dream bigger. She told me her secrets. I mean, isn't that a decent indication that we must have meant something to one another? Sharing secrets?"

"That doesn't mean anything," Gideon points out dismissively. "Anyone can tell you a secret but it doesn't necessarily make it real. I could tell you I've been hired by the government to kill you. How would you ever know whether that was the truth or not?"

Did he just say that? If you told anyone you were legitimately afraid of your therapist they'd tell you to get out of this relationship. But who would you tell anyway? And *would* you? You're only one session in but you already feel like you're committed here. "Some things you can just tell," you say to him.

"Like I said earlier, it doesn't matter what you believe. All that matters is what's real and what isn't."

Identity is not reality.

There's an awkward pause between the two of you now, as neither side is entirely sure where to tread next. You slouch back into the sofa. Gideon brushes his hair a little, tucking some unruly curls back behind the crests of his ears. Then he asks, "So, who finally let go of whom then?"

You don't answer. You don't want to remember anymore.

He waits for a response for a few more seconds before giving up. "Have you met anyone since Reya?"

You look over at the window to where you'd first spotted Abigail Ayr four days ago. "I have."

"That's good. Who is she?"

"She's—odd."

"Odd? Odd is a peculiar word choice for describing someone you're in a relationship with."

"She's just unusual. In an interesting sort of way. But this isn't a relationship."

"Do you want it to be?"

"Me? I don't think so."

"And her?"

You don't have an answer for his question. An honest answer would only sound much too ambiguous. Too vague. You say, "I'd seen her a couple of times before we ever spoke. We just kept spotting one another from a distance. In a city this big, we continued to cross paths. And then before I knew it, we were sitting together at The UnDiner one afternoon, just chatting. Mostly small talk."

"The UnDiner?"

"Yeah. Do you know that restaurant down Surf Avenue?" You nod your head in the general direction.

"Never heard of it."

"Just as well, probably." You explain to Gideon the things you and Abi talked about. It actually feels good to open up, even if all it is, is simply you describing all of her peculiarities. Like her childhood funerals and the way she chews up the inside of her mouth and her cat hair-covered jacket with the skull stitching on the back and her freakshow father with his crazy penis hands. "She gave me her number but I don't really know what to do with it."

"Maybe you should ask her out somewhere? Somewhere other than that shitty coffee shop or the Coney Island Sideshow. That's what couples do. I'm sure it would help you with getting over Reya too. Move that much further in a positive direction rather than in a negative one."

"But I told you already. We aren't a couple."

"Not yet, no. But isn't that why we're talking about her right now?"

You're trying to be rational but you're really not so sure about anything. "So where would we go then?"

"Surely you must know *somewhere*. Take her to the beach. How about the aquarium? Or get her out of this goddamn heat and go to a movie or a show."

You remember the two tickets Armand Bester handed to you the other night. His play, *The Duality of Thee*, is tonight. Before you'd ever spoken to Abigail Ayr, Bester told you to bring her to the show. Now, remarkably, you have met her. And whether you can admit it aloud or not, she fascinates you. You remove the tickets from your bag now, they were resting within an inside pocket, pinned beneath your copy of *The Third* and next to the bottles of Vivactil and Effexor tablets. Without much enthusiasm, you toss the tickets onto Gideon's desktop.

"A friend of mine gave me these," you explain briefly. "But I wasn't really planning on going."

Gideon takes one ticket into his hand, inspecting it closely and carefully. "Interesting," he comments to himself, reading the information printed on both the front and back. Then he tosses it back down beside its mate. He says, "Maybe you should?"

"Take her to the play?"

"Of course."

"What about pleasure delaying? Weren't you suggesting last time that I try slowing things down?"

"Well it's not a hard and fast rule. Besides, I simply asked you to consider your actions a bit more before jumping in. To talk about things first, which is what we're doing right now, correct?"

You can't disagree with him. "But this girl. She's—well, I just don't know."

"Does she have a boyfriend?"

Abi told you she broke up with her boyfriend, but who's to say she hasn't met someone else. "I don't think so."

"Is she clinically insane?"

A little erratic. Overly impulsive, maybe. But insane? "She doesn't appear to be insane."

"Well, would you rather keep making out with other dudes' girlfriends at Brighton Beach dive bars? Your face is looking much better, by the way."

Your jaw still hurts. "Thanks."

Gideon leans back in his seat and exhales just long enough that it's obvious he's digging around inside for something more. Finally, he says, "There's a German word for novels like *The Third*. A literary term. It's called a *bildungsroman*."

"What does that mean?"

"A bildungsroman is a type of coming-of-age novel. Treat this moment in your life as your own bildungsroman. Go and make some changes, Cepik.

Sure, there'll probably be some more mistakes as well, but this is a key moment for you. Take the girl to the play. You never know how it might end."

"The play or the relationship?"

"Either."

"Just don't be afraid, right?"

"That's right. You know, you can't unscramble an egg or take the paint off a wall and put it back in the can. Once it's done it's done. But these things are not ruined. They're just not as they once were. They're different. And sometimes they're worth taking a chance on."

Without looking you feel the inside of your wrist, where Abi had written her number before you parted ways on the boardwalk.

"I say call her as soon as you walk out of here. And when you come back here on Saturday for our next session we'll know exactly where to start, won't we?"

You take the two tickets back and return them to the recesses of your bag. *Bildungsroman*, you repeat to yourself. "Coming of age" doesn't quite feel like the right term, you think. You've already lived for twenty years. Are you still not yet an adult? You've experienced adolescence and sexual awakenings. If you wanted to, you could vote and give blood and drive a car. But maybe there's something else you're not yet aware of that's waiting in the wings? Maybe some other event or some particular change is destined to occur? Do you seek it out or let it come to you? Does destiny care about the journey or will it happen anyway?

In your dreams, you make your own destiny.

And yet, even with hopeful storybook thoughts like this, the darkness —

your darkness — still controls the light. What if there is no happy ending? So many of your days feel like those moments in relationships when you know it's nearly at an end. Usually lying in the dark with your partner after yet one more lamentable argument. You hold her, but you know it's only a matter of days — a matter of moments, maybe? — that one of you will have to end it.

THE DULLAHAN

You won't find this theater in any New York City guidebooks. Surely no one in Bushwick has ever recommended the Dullahan Theater to anyone else outside of Bushwick, and perhaps not even to those within Bushwick's humble boundaries. But that's the nature of community theater.

It's certainly not much to look at from the sidewalk. There's a noticeable lack of promotional posters outside for *The Duality of Thee* and the empty box office tells you this must be a very exclusive event. That, or you've found yourself at the wrong place.

You followed Armand Bester's chaotic directions (scribbled on a napkin of the finest linen, stolen from a Zagat-rated Midtown brasserie) as best you could, and when you found the corresponding address, the first detail you noticed was the doors. One might pass by the Dullahan Theater entirely if it weren't for its thick copper doors. You were struck by the detailed imagery embossed on their exterior. They appeared to be angels, though you do not profess to know for certain. Those circles above their heads could just as well have been hula hoops or Frisbees, rather than halos. Still, this was definitely not a cathedral or any sort of place of holy worship. Perhaps you're merely jaded, but your first assumption is that the heavy doors were pilfered from someplace else, and transplanted onto the front entrance of this theater.

Surprisingly, the theater is beautifully grandiose inside. Hot as the flames of Hell itself, but still beautiful. There are rows of plush, red seats and a couple of balconies flanking either side of the old stage with warm lighting and deep velvet curtains. A painted mural adorns the cornice above the stage; some sort of garden scene with a bunch of bearded men standing around talking and wearing a lot of drapery. Again, you're not versed enough to recognize this as a portrayal of some religious occurrence, but there are enough robes, palms clasped together, and a lack of women to suggest so.

Upon the stage is what must be the set for *The Duality of Thee*. It's a fairly scarce set: a single room apartment, complete with bed, dresser, desk, and chair. You surmise these were all constructed backstage since there's something about the furniture — the angles are a little bit off — which makes you assume they are not authentic. There's a tiny kitchen in the corner and three closed doors. An open window looks out to the city below. The buildings in the distance appear more detailed than the rest of the props, with glowing lights and a hazy blue skyline. The whole design reminds you of your own apartment on Mermaid Avenue. And it's just as empty. Your father hasn't been home for more than a month now. You get a weird feeling like you're watching your real apartment from afar, like everything you own is nothing more than simple props made from wood and paint. It really looks just like any generic set piece but are the similarities only a peculiar coincidence? You're fully aware that Bester has visited your place a few times before, but you can only assume he was far too baked to note the layout. You remember your father liked him a lot, too.

You called Abi this morning from the rusted payphone behind Gideon's office, just as soon as your therapy session was over. You'd already memorized the phone number she'd written on your wrist before washing it off in the shower. At first, you assumed she'd given a fake number since when you called there was nothing. No busy signal or recorded message. Nothing but ringing.

Ringing.

Ringing.

You crumpled yourself up inside the phone booth and you tried to visualize the digits that Abigail had written. Maybe you remembered them wrong? Maybe the numbers were in the wrong order? But maybe they were never right in the first place?

Maybe Abigail Ayr had already passed through your life, and she is just as gone as everyone else?

And in that moment when you decided the only reasonable conclusion would be to simply move along, the payphone rang. It was a staticky kind of ringing, like the archaic phone booth was trying to let someone know it still had more left within itself. You picked up the receiver and knew instantly what you would say:

"Hey," you said. Yeah, real smooth.

It was Abigail Ayr all right and you simply asked her if she wished to come with you tonight to see Bester's play. No big deal. Gideon suggested you do it and you did it. Turns out she had other plans tonight, but they had been canceled just before you called. No, you don't know if you believed her or not, but the end result is the two of you are now at the Dullahan together. And it came as no surprise when you recognized her immediately. A lighthouse beacon amid the faceless sea. You took your seats amongst the other patrons, the few of them who could be bothered to come out tonight.

You wonder if this place will end up being even half full. Or half empty, depending on how you want to look at it. Abi's bag is on the seat next to you; she's been in the bathroom for maybe fifteen minutes now. Here you go again, questioning whether or not she's given you the slip. Why do you do this to yourself?

Finally, Abi glides down the aisle and returns to her seat. "What took you so long?" you ask her.

"Just wasting time," she says. "They're serving wine out there in the hall, you know? This is one classy event. I was going to get you a glass, but I wasn't sure if you drank or not."

"I don't, really. Not unless I'm thinking about making some more mistakes in my life."

"Yeah," she agrees. "Booze is certainly good for that. It's how I met my last boyfriend."

Of course, you don't have any idea whether she's joking or not. The silence lingers between the two of you, resting uncomfortably upon the armrest-for-one. She's taking a good look around; her head darting in circular patterns like a tiny bird.

"God, I hate being in places like this. So full of people. I can't help but imagine once the lights go down, one of them is going to go ballistic and shoot the place up. It happens all the time."

You glance at her with a worried look but she doesn't pay any attention.

"I see the backs of heads and wonder which one it'll be. Like a hidden mine in Minesweeper. Just waiting to blow."

"I don't even know what that is."

"You're sweet with all your innocence, you know that? You've never heard of Minesweeper?" You give her a blank look. "It's just a stupid video game."

"What's the point of it?"

"Well, you have this grid and within it are all these bombs and you work your way around trying to avoid setting them off."

"What happens if you set them off?"

"They blow up and you die."

"What happens if you avoid them all?"

"You live. Well, you beat the game. You win."

"Why'd you change your response from living to winning?"

"Well it's not like you were ever going to die. So, it's not really living then either, is it?"

"Sounds like life to me. You go through your whole life just trying to avoid all the shit that can ruin it for you. One mistake and boom."

"Yeah, but when you beat Minesweeper it's just over. There's never really any point to it. No consequences. It's nothing more than a time waster."

"Still sounds like life to me."

"Fuck, you're an epic downer, Rainbow." More silence. But then Abi nudges your elbow slightly with her own. "Hey," she says, speaking more quietly than she needs to. "Thanks for asking me to come to this with you. I think by the time the night is over I'll realize I really needed it."

"Does that mean you're not completely sure about it right now? Like it might still be a mistake on your part?"

"Or maybe a mistake on *yours*," she says sneakily.

"Well," you start before realizing you've got nothing on Abigail Ayr when it comes to witty repartee. "You're welcome."

With that, the lights come down a little and Armand Bester walks onto the stage. He wears a top hat and a cape and carries a cane for show, but he still walks with a certain confidence you can't help but envy. He absolutely owns that stage. Bester welcomes the audience, gratefully thanking everyone for coming out tonight.

Abi asks, "Is that your friend?"

"That's him."

"He's cute."

"He's all right."

"He sure is. And there's a kind of confidence about him. It's powerful."

"*Powerful*? I don't know about powerful."

"No, it is." Abi scans the theater for a short moment before suddenly rising from her seat. "Come on," she says. Like lightning, she darts a few rows closer to the stage and seats herself in a previously unoccupied spot. She waves her arm at you to follow and you do, only having to excuse yourself past two other people. You feel like a drunken fan at a baseball game, sneaking closer to the field to nab the more expensive seat. Abi leans in closer to the stage, wide-eyed with tiny fists keeping her chin aloft.

Concluding his introduction, Bester asks that everyone please enjoy his play, *The Duality of Three.*

THREE? You were sure the ticket read *The Duality of THEE.* Removing the playbill and ticket stubs from your rucksack, you see you had originally read it wrong; the title is indeed *The Duality of Three.*

He bows dramatically, removing his top hat as he does so, and exits the stage. His cape billows dramatically behind him and then the lights go black.

You hear a door unlocking, creaking open, and then shutting. The sound of the closing door is the kind of hollow echo that makes it obvious there is no ceiling or load-bearing walls like a real apartment would have. It's all just a prop. Heavy footsteps cross the stage, and when the lights return, there is a man standing there. He wears a faded blue three-piece suit and his hair is short but disheveled. His face is a little hard to make out, like maybe the actor isn't wearing proper stage makeup. Whatever the reason, the unrecognizable quality of it only serves to remind you of your prosopagnosia. Across the room, on the other side of the bed, there is a body on the floor. It's a woman's body lying motionless on stage. Consulting the program, you assume the man's name is Christopher since he gets top billing. You also notice a character named simply 'Dead Girl' and you wonder how that's even a role. Christopher doesn't yet notice the body; instead, he sits upon the end of the bed. He removes a folded-up letter from his coat pocket, opens it and sighs deeply. Then he speaks to the audience:

"Who is Jude Cascade?" he asks aloud. He shakes his head, confused. "I can't believe I want to waste your time asking a question you cannot possibly answer. But it's been nagging me for hours now; *days* even, gnawing at my memory. And yet, I know the answer is out there somewhere." He holds the letter up high, as if searching for a place in the air in which it might fit. "Caught like the thinning shopping bag that's been snagged for years on the barbed wire entwined along a chain link fence. But I don't want to reach for it in the chance I might lose my hand." Christopher stands up now and walks slowly across the stage, still paying no attention at all to the body on his floor. "It's been almost ten years now since that night I woke up in a sweat. I'm sorry, but I cannot recall if it was a hot sweat or a cold sweat — and I'm really not interested in the hypothetical, theoretical, metaphorical, or logical reasonings or differences behind either of the two — even though I'm more than certain there is a significant cause for waking in one state or the other. Only that there was sweat. *That* is what I chose to remember. There was a dream too. Perhaps it was a nightmare? Though I didn't find it frightening. If you wish to define a nightmare in such a way, that's entirely up to you. I woke — staring into the midnight void, highlighted only by the luminescence of the flickering neon blue cross of an all-night animal hospital out the window — next to a girl I can't place, listening to the off-putting city din: an unusual muffled static instead of the stream of ambulance and squad car blaring I'm far more accustomed to. Lying in an apartment that had no business in not being condemned. This is when I sat up and called out the name." Christopher raises his fists high and shouts dramatically, "*Jude Cascade!*"

Abigail is still on the edge of her seat; her chin remains atop tiny balled-up fists. The theater feels quieter than it should for a short moment, until Christopher sits back on the bed. He lies down on his side and feels the empty half of the bed with the palm of his hand, pretending there is still a body next to him. "And even through my shouting, the girl next to me remained unconscious, the only sign she still yet contemplated the idea of living was the flittering of hair matted over closed eyes in an REM state." Christopher sits up again, rubs the back of his neck as he continues his monologue. "Though the instant after I called out I had already forgotten my reason for my doing so. The only dreams we ever want to hold on to are the ones which instantly disappear upon the lucidity of reality." Again, he stands and begins pacing back and forth across the stage. "And my life from that point on basically went like this: I asked myself, '*Who is Jude Cascade?*' and then I fell back asleep, puttered along for an entire decade, and accomplished nothing more than a drinking problem. Until *today*. Today, when I finally discovered a single, folded piece of paper in the middle of the street." He holds the letter out to the audience as proof. "I don't know why I was drawn to it, but I picked it up anyway. I opened the paper. It was a hand-written letter. And the signature at the bottom told me everything I needed to know: it was Jude Cascade who had written it. I knew I had to find her."

The opening monologue ends, and audience members clap in unison. Neither you nor Abi were aware that you should clap at this point — perhaps you just don't appreciate performance art on the same level as the rest of this crowd — but you both join in anyway.

You're confused by pretty much everything that's going on.

It's so muggy in here.

Your back is slick with sweat.

After this, Christopher finally discovers the dead body on his floor. It turns out this is — or *was* — his girlfriend. There are obvious signs of a struggle but he doesn't know who might have been responsible for the act. Without much more time to think about it, there's a knock at the door. Christopher stops, maybe hoping whoever it is will go away. But the knocking intensifies.

You stop. This is where things begin to get weird. The man behind the door identifies himself as a police officer and is soon let in. The cop behaves much like the French cop in *The Third*, and he even asks Christopher for drugs, just like in the novel. The rest of the play kind of idles along; at parts, you honestly cannot tell if it is supposed to be a comedy or a drama. A light farce or some kind of puzzling mindfuck, requiring actual mental fortitude.

There are similarities to Alfred Hitchcock's *Rope* as well (you recall watching it with your father one night last year), as Christopher attempts to hide the body (even while the cop is still there) and then when his roommate, Samuel, later shows up, the two of them decide to hold a dinner party in the apartment while the dead girl remains stuffed under the table upon which the bowl of punch rests. Christopher and Samuel are even mistaken for one another by a couple of party-goers, though they are decidedly not twins.

The Duality of Three ends without any resolution of the dead girlfriend in the apartment. And it could be that you simply missed it, but there was no further reference to the Jude Cascade character either. Was *she* the dead girlfriend? What was the point of that letter Christopher clutched so tightly at the beginning? The opening monologue seemed like it was part of a different play entirely. Again, maybe it's just that you simply don't get theater. But you fake it by clapping along with everyone else once more.

You turn to Abi who is apparently just as in the dark as yourself. "What was *that* all about?" you ask her.

She's already standing up from her seat. "Beats me."

"I mean, did that make *any* sense at all to you?"

"I don't know if it was supposed to." Abi is looking around the dim theater now, as if trying to find someone. "But sometimes ambiguity is best, don't you think?"

"I suppose. As long as it's intended to be that way." You're not sure if you have enough artistic faith in Armand Bester to believe there was ever meant to be some deeper meaning in what it was you just witnessed. A couple of shrugged shoulders are all Abi is still willing to contribute to the remainder of this discussion, however.

The clapping continues as the actors return to the stage for curtain call. Some of them you vaguely recognize, while others you've already lost track of. Bester stands between the two roommates, Christopher and Samuel. He's ditched the top hat and is wearing one of those ridiculous Cat in the Hat hats now. You can't really take the glorification of their egos any longer — their bowing and clapping for one another — and you stand up to leave.

Abi's definitely got other ideas. "Where do you think he'll be after this?"

"Who? Bester?"

"Yeah. We should go congratulate him."

"He's probably got more important people to be with."

"Pshaw!" she says, slinging her bag over her shoulder. Abi makes her way down the aisle, toward the stage rather than in the opposite direction, not waiting for any further response from you.

Gazing around the theater briefly, you catch a familiar form. You think it's Gideon Flat who you spot through the crowd. You catch the long, pointed nose for a moment before his head turns away, leaving only the wavy hair for you to work with. Unfortunately, the man disappears quickly, lost in the relative sea of people and you can't manage a second look.

Why would Gideon be here? You recall how he held and looked at the tickets for the play in his office earlier. Is he stalking you, or did he simply have nothing better to do tonight? Maybe he lives around the corner anyway? Or perhaps it wasn't him at all?

Identity is not reality.

"Epic!" Abi calls from a distance. She's down at the front row, right next to the stage.

You put any thoughts of your therapist out of your head for now and head on over, just as Abi is hopping onstage.

"What are you doing?" you ask her. "You can't just climb up there."

"Why not?"

There's nothing for you to say. You don't really have an answer; you just assumed there must be an unwritten rule somewhere about not helping oneself to the actors' performance space.

"No one assumes that anybody is ever going to just climb up onstage. Which is why there's no one here to stop us from doing just that. Come on."

You hesitate for another moment before pulling yourself up beside her. It's weird onstage; the seats out there all look so small. Though you can't imagine having to try and ignore everyone in the audience, to pretend like there's nobody out there and just focus on remembering your lines and choreography. There's no way you could ever do something like this.

It's also particularly odd to essentially be in your apartment, or at least a relative facsimile of your apartment. You're at home but you're not. The bed, the desk and the window out to the city street are all so similar, but they're merely props. Their false duality made evident by the rough construction on the sides opposite from the audience. Pencil marks and frayed edges sliced by handsaws and blades remain exposed and unpainted. Your life as a prop. You do like the rug under the bed however. It's a nice touch.

You stick your head out the window. Those buildings in the distance which had seemed so realistic from your seat are nothing more than a single piece of plywood with some Christmas tree lights glued messily and sporadically.

"How's the view?" Abi asks.

"Better than my own place, actually."

Abi's looking high above, staring straight up to the rows of lights which are unseen by the audience. She runs her tiny hand along the top of the table, the prop where the body of the dead girl was hidden under the majority of the show. There's a lot more room inside than you'd first thought.

"It's funny," she mumbles. "How in a lot of ways this shallow, made-up world is actually better than the ugly truth of reality. Don't you think?"

And just as you're about to agree with her, she makes a move toward the curtains and disappears somewhere backstage. You take one last look back toward the theater seats, but everyone has left. No audience or ushers or janitors or enigmatic therapists. Quickly, you follow Abi to wherever she's gone.

You catch up and the two of you make your way from the near-pitch black backstage, through a door, and into a dim corridor. There's nowhere else to go from here but down a short staircase, and you cannot help but think this theater's layout feels very similar to that of the decrepit Sideshows by the Seashore building back in Coney Island. The walls seem to emit the same stale pungency too, but perhaps it's just the summer heat. You place your palm on the stair rail, and feel exactly what you were hoping *not* to find: the same star and moon pattern you took note of at the Sideshow is carved into the wood here too. It's exactly the same.

And at the bottom of the stairs, the hallway beneath the Dullahan Theater is also similarly adorned with framed photographs, each depicting the various casts and shows of the past. Some promotional posters from plays-gone-by hang desolately. Their artwork comparable to those of the Sideshow's various freak posters. The photos go all the way to the end of the hall where you find a closed door upon which hangs a warped, wobbly golden star. It says "The Best" on it.

You still feel uneasy about barging in like this. Like maybe you're not wanted here. "Don't you think he's got better things to do? I mean, I'm sure Bester's got better ways to celebrate than hanging out with the two of us."

"He'll be happy."

"How do you know? You don't even know him."

"Maybe it's because he actually considers you to be a friend, Epic? Not the kind of person you seem to think you are."

This old theater is creepy and uncomfortable and you simply don't like it. Even the crooked star on the door makes you uneasy. There's a lump in your throat. Making sure you have your bases covered, you tell Abi, "Just so you're aware, I may have mentioned to Bester that we were dating, you and I. But I wasn't serious."

"Whatever," she says, almost as if she didn't hear a word you just said. "This has got to be it," Abigail proudly declares, tapping the shiny star with a fingernail. You don't know if she's noticed the same similarities as you have — nor do you know if the similarities are unusual enough to even warrant any apprehension — but Abi makes no mention of any of it.

Bester's not surprised to see the two of you outside the dressing room, almost like he was expecting the visit. He opens the door wide to welcome you inside, still wearing the long black cape. There's someone else, a girl, in the room. She sits atop the makeup table with her back to you, gazing into the mirror and removing makeup from her face.

"Bestest!" he exclaims. "You're the man! Did you bring me anything?"

By anything you know he means marijuana, which you didn't. "Sorry."

Turning to Abi now, he sidesteps. "Hey, hey. I see you brought a different kind of treat though. And you are?"

"Abigail Ayr," she says.

He turns and questions you. "The girl from Colorado?"

You'd forgotten until now how you had made up a short backstory for Bester when the two of you sat in the company van that night. You told him the girl you were "seeing" was from Colorado. And by sheer fluke, Abi explained to you how she'd grown up there. She gives you a look out of the corner of her eye, maybe wondering what else you might have mentioned to Bester.

Still, she feels the need to clarify. "Memorial, actually."

"Never heard of it."

"You're lucky. If you'd heard of it that'd mean you probably lived there which I wouldn't wish upon anyone."

"Well," Bester says anyway. "It's nice to meet you." They shake hands and he plants one on the inside of her wrist. You don't think Abi is the blushing type but you turn away too quickly anyway to find out.

The girl on the makeup table is still focused on the mirror, but she looks at your reflection now, and you lock eyes. You don't recognize her, though in the tiny moments when her eyes blink it feels like a sort of memory trigger. Still, you can't quite place it.

"Don't worry about him," she says to you, throwing a nod over her shoulder toward Bester and Abi. "Armand is really just a harmless flirt. He's more scared of girls than he thinks he is." You just shrug. "I'm Margo," she adds before focusing her attention back to her own face. Margo's features might best be described as Mediterranean: wavy jet-black hair, a straight brow, dark eyes, olive skin, and a granite face. Those aren't very helpful descriptors but there's no denying she's very striking.

The rest of the dressing room holds a few hats here and there but not much else. The closet door is open and you spot Bester's stage cane standing upright inside. There's a large gemstone on the one end it rests upon, making it seem more like a wizard's magical staff than perhaps a walking cane. The bright lights around the mirror dazzle off it.

From Margo to the walking cane, Bester snaps you out of your trance-like state. "So, what did you guys think of the show?"

"Oh, it was *fabulous!*" Abi proclaims, sounding more like a boy band groupie than the girl you thought you knew.

He's still holding onto her wrist. In the mirror, Margo pretends to gag on a finger.

You say, "It was—different." You hate it when people use the word *different* to describe something they don't understand, but you don't know if it's any worse than saying you simply don't understand theater. "There seemed to be a lot of empty seats out there. Maybe a poster outside would've attracted a bigger audience?"

Bester dismisses your remark with a swish of his arm through the air. "There was *exactly* the number of people out there I wanted. It was *perfect*. Any more and they wouldn't have appreciated it." He flashes a big toothy smile.

"I guess," you say without really catching his drift. "What's wrong with your mouth? Your tongue's all pink."

He sticks his thick tongue out as far as he can, trying to get a look at it with his own eyes. "Cream soda Slurpee. There's a 7-11 behind the theater.

And right now, it just might be the best place to stay cool in this city."

At that, Abi's eyebrows perk up higher than you've yet seen. You don't know if she's got such a childlike fondness for slushies or if her infatuation with Armand Bester has heightened to eye rolling levels. Before you know it, the four of you, Margo included, are on your way to the 7-11. Bester leads the way and Margo quietly shuffles along behind.

"What's the deal with that chick?" Abi asks you, motioning over her shoulder toward Margo. "She's a strange one, don't you think?"

"I'm having a hard time placing her," you say, your memory still muddles every time she blinks.

"Epic, she was the actress — and I use that term loosely — from the play."

"Which one?"

"The dead girl. How could you not remember? We just saw—I'm sorry. I guess she wasn't being herself, was she? Only playing a part. Man, your head thing really throws me for a loop, you know?"

You don't bother asking her to imagine how your prosopagnosia — your *head thing* — makes *you* feel. But you recall the name in the program now:

Dead Girl.................................Margo Asus

The 7-11 really is right behind the theater as Bester explained. Upon opening the back door of the Dullahan, you're in the convenience store's small back alley parking lot. Entering inside, the temperature is almost frigid, with air conditioners and freezer units blasting out cold air like they were trying to win a prize. There's a couple of small tables inside too, though why anyone would want to sit around a 7-11 eating Jujyfruits and day-old taquitos is a mystery to you. Of course, it's a nice interlude from the heat wave which is currently making the streets ache outside. The freezer aisle is void of pretty much anything behind its glass doors; wet from condensation. It feels like you're in some sort of zombie apocalypse and all of the food has already been seized for survival. You sit around one of the tables and guzzle your giant-sized frozen drinks. You don't know why you opted for the cola flavor. It's horrible. The table wobbles like it's supposed to have more than three legs.

Margo sits up on Bester's lap and he doesn't seem to even notice her there. And truthfully, you don't think she's said a word since telling you her name back in the dressing room. Bester had bought a giant box of Nerds candy, those little artificially-colored sugar nuggets; they rattled around in their box like it was your bottle of Vivactil tablets. He proceeded to empty the contents of the candy box into your plastic cups which only makes your drink that much worse. Still, Bester, Abigail, and Margo all happily suck them up through straws. Abi continues to throw flirty congratulations his way, praising Bester for every aspect of his show. The accolades do not really interest him however, and he suggests instead that you move your gathering of four to Margo's place.

So, you're off again, this time headed north to Knickerbocker Avenue. Hopping on the M-Train, you ride it west into Manhattan. Abigail sits beside Bester while you're on the opposite side of the car. Margo swings gently and trivially from the metal bar between you all like the world's laziest pole dancer. You overhear Abi asking Bester if he's ever seen *Donnie Darko* or *Big Man Japan*, though you're pretty sure he doesn't answer her questions before boasting about his own ideas for a movie he wants to make someday.

"It's like Blaxploitation set in a fantasy world. I'm thinking of this Shaftlike dude who's transported from his world to another. And he's there for like fifty years, all the while he's conquering cities and slaying dragons and bumping uglies with princesses and having a wild time with a bunch of wacko, otherworldly drugs he could never experience in his own world. All in the name of good, of course."

"Of course," you all agree.

"And when this brother finally returns home, not a moment has passed since he left. He's still working at the video store and everything."

"So, it was all just a dream then?" Abigail asks.

"No, he really did experience all of it."

"So, was it simply his mind that went to the other world, while his body remained here?"

Bester seems confused by the question. "No, he was actually, physically transported away. But then he was transported back after everything."

"But he lived for fifty years in the other world. How does he de-age?"

"It's magic."

Abi's face puckers. "You know what really bothers me about movies like that? How does he live for so long in this alternate world and eat meals — I'm presuming three meals a day? — and not return home with a full stomach? If no time has passed and he's consumed a lifetime of meals within that time frame, wouldn't he simply explode? There's *no way* he could digest all of that food instantly."

Bester is clearly annoyed; irritated that anyone might think to question such an idea that's been done successfully for years. "Don't worry about it," he says. "It's magic."

Abi looks at you now, maybe for the first time since you boarded the train. "Magic. That's a pretty convenient solution, isn't it?"

You just shrug. His film concept doesn't sound any worse than anything else these days.

Eventually you're exiting from Lafayette Station and you make your way downtown, south along Mulberry. Margo's family are European transplants with money, the typical Manhattanites. Her father and step-mom set her up with a modern steel and glass condo cut into the heart of what was once a block of brick and mortar. The front door is flanked by two concrete planters which are taller than you. Her security card gets you all inside the building and you ride the deathly quiet elevator up a few floors. The icy cold temperature of the hallway hits you as soon as the doors silently glide open and before you know it, you're in a swank loft overlooking the hazy, indifferent lights of the Lower East Side.

Margo tells you all to have a seat and you do, on her massive sectional that's been keeping cool under the two large ceiling fans. Bester is still yammering on about some big budget spy movie he'd recently seen and Abigail lies between the two of you. It's becoming increasingly clear that your friend is on something, something other than the usual marijuana you supply him with. He's been acting odd all night. Not helping the matter is Margo, who has now returned from somewhere with a bulging bag of weed. Without any caution, she dumps the contents onto the coffee table and begins rolling joints like a pro.

"Oh shit, yeah." Bester shrewdly proclaims. "Those are some right jumbo fatties, Margo!" Margo Asus shrugs like it's no big deal but Bester can't help from slapping his thighs like a kid on Christmas. He turns to you and says, "Bestest, this is *THE* stuff, bro. I know this shit isn't *your* world, but come on over to *our* world tonight, will ya?" He holds out the first joint for you to take. "This is *unparalleled.*"

A look into the history of anyone will reveal a jaw-droppingly large number of poor decisions made over a lifetime. Sure, there will always be a lot of good ones too, but the only decisions anyone seems to ever remember are the ones that also come with the most regret. Now, you don't usually bend to peer pressure — you've gone most of your life being your own person, for what it's gotten you — but here you are again. You should never have thrown eggs from the Mermaid Parade floats with Barton and Reilly, yet it still happened. Maybe you shouldn't have continued the cannabinoid prescriptions with Dr. Griffin for the sole reason of giving your friend his fix? Comparatively, you're certain Armand Bester, Abigail Ayr, and — even though you barely know her — Margo Asus have all amassed a handful of regrets throughout their own lives. Some perhaps based solely upon the pressures of others. Who knows what you might regret if you smoke this tonight?

The stoic hand of Bester still lingers before you. You look up and see an air vent on the wall, close to the ceiling. For a new building there sure seems to be a lot of dust and dead flies around the vent. You shrug your shoulders and reach for the burning joint but Abi snatches it away before you can take it. Like a pro, she takes a drag and then passes it back over to you with a smile. The two girls fall back giggling, each on one of Bester's shoulders.

You sit and stare at the thing in your hand. Maybe long enough for it to seem weird, but the three of them don't appear to notice. Reya once told you that if you ever started smoking weed then you could kiss what you had goodbye. She said the same about buying a motorcycle or firearms or a condo in the city, didn't she? All you could tell her was the chances of any of those happening were pretty slim, especially since you didn't want her going anywhere. Still, look what happened. Sometimes even the most well-intentioned decisions blow up in your face. Sometimes you have to say, *Why not?*

Your jaw is still a little sore from being sucker punched outside the Starfish Room a few nights ago, and instantly you know there's no way this joint in your hand could possibly be a worse decision than that.

So, you plug it into your mouth and allow the night — and your life — to unfold.

ooo

This is bad. You really need some air. All of you have been lazing around smoking high-grade marijuana and giggling for hours now. But then you had to tell them, didn't you? You couldn't help yourself. Not after Bester had finished explaining his theory about many of the world's leaders actually being other-planetary lizard people who have secretly been beaming thoughts into your heads for hundreds of years now, and Abigail had talked your ears off about her favorite online RPG, and Margo danced Swan Lake across her concrete floors. You couldn't help yourself. You told them your therapist had killed himself because he didn't want to see you anymore. You tried your best to explain how crazy Gideon Flat is. You summarized the list of antidepressants he's got you on.

And then you talked about Reya.

With an aching heart, you described the way a flickering flame would calm in her presence. How she might find a bird's feather on the sidewalk and be mesmerized by it for hours. The fantastic sound the air on her teeth would make when pronouncing J-words.

Abi just stared at you, impossibly confused with her mouth hanging open.

When you get up and look at the time, you realize you've only been here for maybe a half hour. How did you just open up and spew your guts like that in such a short amount of time? You don't share any of your intimacies well, especially not the embarrassing stuff. That's just not you. Again: this is bad. You need some air.

Navigating through the thin cloud of smoke inside, you step out onto the balcony and slide the door closed. The city, though growing ever-darker tonight, is still burning from the heatwave. From here, you spy rooftop greenhouses and tennis court bubbles all lit up, like some giant illuminated organs keeping the city alive. Just barely though, as the heat wants to make them wither like month-old balloons. There's a potted plant out here on Margo's tiny balcony, something small with seven large red petals. An eighth one lies on the ground beneath it, like she had been playing *He loves me/He loves me not*, but stopped after the first *He loves me*.

Before long, the balcony door opens and your self-imposed exile comes to an end. The prosopagnosia does the math for you: this isn't Bester or Abi, so it's simply a matter of process of elimination. It's Margo Asus, the Dead Girl herself.

"You look like you're waiting for the end of the world out here," she says discerningly. In truth, you're not sure how right or wrong she just might be. She closes the door behind her.

"Aren't we all, though?"

"I guess, maybe." She takes in a deep breath and exhales slowly, out across the Lower East Side. "I mean, we all know there's an end coming at some point, don't we? But rather than simply waiting for it, isn't it better to live as much as you can until it comes?" She's locked her view onto something; the nearly undetectable flickering of her eyes gives her away.

"That's ironic. Coming from the dead girl," you say. Margo turns to you, a tiny grin barely concealed within her thin lips. Her eyes sparkle in the moonlight. "I'm sorry. Did I use the word 'ironic' wrong?"

"No, no. I just hadn't made that connection myself until now. You're very astute, Epic. Very intuitive. I can see why Armand likes having you around."

"He likes me because I can supply him with weed."

"I really doubt that. I've got some too and to be frank, mine's *much* better." She laughs a little again, though you can tell she is legitimate; these are definitely not any pot-induced giggles.

"What is it?"

"It's just funny how I praised your perceptiveness just now, and then you go and say something stupid like that." You want to apologize, but you know it would only serve to make you seem that much more oblivious. "So, how about that Reya girl, huh?"

"You mean the one I wouldn't shut up about back inside?"

"Yeah. What happened there?"

"I guess what always happens. Someone falls in love with someone else until one of the someones is afraid they can't do it anymore."

"Which someone were *you*?"

You look back inside the apartment and spot Bester and Abi through the hazy fumes. They're still on the couch laughing. But you can't muster an answer for Margo. Your head is fuzzy and her features jump around, making it impossible for you to tell if she's actually waiting for an answer to her question or if she was just asking for the sake of saying anything at all like people tend to do.

"We're all afraid of something," she says. "And usually it's more than just one thing. If I had to make a list of my own fears, I'd probably run out of paper. Is it possible to be afraid of *everything*?"

You cross your arms, holding your elbows tight. "What about dying?"

"Death's not so bad. I mean, all I have to go by is from laying on that stage for two hours. But it's kind of nice, actually."

"You seem like a very positive person, Margo."

"Hey, there's really only three types of people, aren't there? Those who cry after the shit happens, and those who cry over the shit that hasn't happened yet. The milk all over the floor, or the milk that hasn't yet spilled."

"Who are the third?"

She catches you by surprise and spits off the balcony, out somewhere on Mulberry Street. "We're the ones who don't cry about anything."

You look back inside her apartment to see Abi. She's holding her belly she's laughing so hard. Bester's hopping around on the floor, doing some sort of T-Rex impression.

"She's not a bad girl," Margo says. "You're lucky."

"Abigail?"

"Is that her name?"

"Yeah. But really, we're not dating or anything."

"Not anything at all?"

"No."

"Do you *want* to be?"

You both let out a deep sigh at the same time. You say, "I don't think so. What about you and Bester though?"

"That man would never label us like that. And neither would I." Very abruptly she places her hand on your shoulder and turns your body so you're facing the street. "Do you see that rooftop down there?" She's directing your attention to a four or five-story building below you. There are some words written on a water tower, the stark white paint on old weathered wood can clearly be read even in the night sky. It says: "the meaning of life is love."

You read it aloud, though your voice is swallowed up instantly by the city's din. "Is that true?" you ask. "Is there truth in those words?"

"I don't believe them," she says, shrugging her shoulders. "But sometimes they're a good reminder." Margo turns back to her sofa. "She likes *you* though."

"It sure seems like she couldn't care less right now," you say.

"Some things are obvious. Call it women's intuition or whatever, but I can tell there's something there."

ooo

Your conversation on the balcony with Margo seems so surreal already. When you finally went back inside the apartment, Abigail was fast asleep on the couch, her feet propped up in Bester's lap. You were ready to leave and thought about waking them but you knew any attempt would have been futile. Margo offered for you to stay the night but you said no thanks and simply left on your own. Your head was still spinning from the pot and you wobbled back outside to the station, riding the D-Train back to Mermaid

Avenue where you collapsed onto your bed without taking any medication.

A PARTING OF THE SENSORY

In the beginning, there is darkness. It's just a big, black nothing. This is more than the pitch-black fear children know, hiding in their closets at night with the lights off. This is really, truly nothing. If you could scream, you know you wouldn't hear yourself. But it's not scary, you know that much. It just *is*.

Somewhere along the way everything shifts from *being* nothing to more of a *feeling* of nothing. And because there's no sense of time here you cannot tell if you've been experiencing this for merely a slice of a second or maybe days. Months. Years, even. Then there is a cloudy shine in the distance, like the dark glimmer of onyx behind a thin, veiled curtain. Or the hint of something under a door. You want to step closer but it's impossible to pinpoint the direction. Anyway, you cannot move; you're paralyzed. You can only watch helplessly. If watching is truly the right word for what it is you're doing right now.

The shine intensifies. Slowly, is it? Or in the blink of an eye? It's only a dot, a weak, grey pinpoint at first, then the light spreads wider. It spins through the color spectrum until pure white encompasses the totality of your vision. It's all you can see. It is the opposite of how this all started: nothing but white now, and again, you cannot be sure for how long.

Impossible as it seems, this white nothing intensifies ever brighter. Now it is far more than just light, and you can feel it physically too. Your body quivers. Your bones feel cold. Your blood thickens and scratches your insides. Teeth chatter. Fingernails split. Hair grows in, instead of out. Eyes burn and water up. Strong winds smack you in the face. Tears stream across your cheeks and down your neck, trickling over your shoulders and along your naked back. You cannot tell if you're even *seeing* anymore or if that is a sense you no longer require. The same goes for your hearing, smell, taste, and touch. All of your senses have either abandoned you or been rendered inert.

But it gets worse before it gets better. Better before it gets worse. You still can't quite tell which is which. Whatever this is, it slowly filters from your body and moves into the Earth itself. You're certain that is what's happening. As this occurs, you're one and the same; the totality of the entire planet and your single, tiny, insignificant body. You are next to nothing. You are epically small. The feeling is astounding; it is the one part of this event you want *more* of. You want more time in this unity, but it passes so quickly.

And then, right before it's all over, you see it.

Instead of the white nothing of everything, you see a life form. Just a fetus at first, but then you blink.

A baby now.

Blink.

It's you. There you are. Cepik Small. It's not like a mirror though, more like an out-of-body experience.

You blink again and see a pair of shoes. Sneakers, actually. Not a pair though, but identical. Two left feet.

Then two identical arms.

Blink.

A familiar pool of blood.

You blink one final time and it's done.

You're awake in your apartment and completely covered in a sheen of cold sweat. Your body still feels inert; you're on the bed and unable to move. Or more like you're afraid to, as though moving would only send you right back into wherever it was you just were. You know the summer night's heat is still pouring in through the open window but you're freezing nevertheless. You're shaking. God, how you wish your father was here right now.

Finally, slowly, like emerging from a coma after all of your twenty years, you stagger to the bathroom and turn the shower on, cranking the hot water up as far as it will go.

And as you brace yourself in the shower, your forehead pressing hard into the tile grout until sore, all you can think is: *What is happening to me? What the fuck was that?*

In your dreams, you're in control. In your dreams, you make your own destiny. In your dreams, you fell in love, didn't you? In your dreams, you're everything your mother and father really wanted you to be.

This was definitely not one of your dreams.

ooo

You told yourself you had to get out. That's how you found yourself here. It's four in the morning and you desperately need nothing more than to *not* be home right now. Even if it's just down here in the dirty restaurant below your apartment devouring fried chicken with a warm beer.

You know you're out of place here, but feeling out of place is nothing new for you. You mull over the crazy night you just had. The one thing that fully comes to mind is the pot you smoked earlier this evening with Bester, Abi, and Margo Asus. Where did Margo get that stuff? You wonder how it might compare to the fictional marijuana Tristan Montminy and Emilia had purchased in Tuscany. Maybe you're understanding that book a little better now?

As you sip the bitter beer, you think of Abi, too. You consider exactly what your feelings for her might be, obviously without reaching any conclusions whatsoever. That girl perplexes you so.

You think of your father and wonder about the places where some people choose to search for hope when the end of everything is so close at hand. You suppose one of those places must be with the company of others. Perhaps that company is total strangers in a 24-hour fried chicken dive. Or maybe it's just seeing your son again.

You recall what Abigail Ayr said when you were sharing the booth in The UnDiner and she'd asked you to come with her to see her father. She said: "*If you help me with my thing right now then I'll help you later with your thing.*" And you guess she owes you one, so you decide to cash in on that promise. And with freezing, jittery fingers you give her another call.

BUZZ KILL

Three days ago, when you agreed to tag along with Abigail to visit her father you didn't know the "thing" she'd help you with later — what she categorized as *compensation* — was actually going to be the same. This morning you asked her if she'd come with you to see *your* father, and before she even agreed, Abigail Ayr was already on her way to meet you there.

You're riding the subway downtown with the cracker box full of your father's stuff on your lap. He's been moved to some hospice in Lower Manhattan. If you'd taken Margo's offer to crash at her place last night you'd be there already. But instead, you're trying to find some breathing room on the J-Train amongst all the suits on their exodus to Wall Street.

It's a faceless army of black, grey, and pinstripes with bold pops of color in neckties and dress socks. The bowtie and suspender crowd seem to take up the back of the train like some overly serious clowns, but make no mistake: each and every one of them clutches a briefcase here. Their own personal financial assignments; shots at accumulating ever more money and watching it continue to just pile up. They all want it. They all think they'll get it. Because they all think they deserve it. You can't tell any of them apart; not the ones who will succeed and not those who'll fail. Some will retire young. Some will have a career change. Some will fall victim to jealousy, revenge, or suicide. Some will wake up one morning and simply wonder what the point of it all was. Will it matter if you have no idea if you'd ever even known them? Probably not, but you try in vain to place them anyway. Slicked-back hair, stubbled chins, overwhelming body spray. More and more mystery men board the train. You feel your anxiety level rising a little higher at every stop.

You disembark at Broad Street and they follow you out, presumably heading toward their six-digit day jobs, but you can't shake the feeling of something sinister hanging in the air. Two of them are right behind you, both on their cell phones. Clutching the cracker box tighter under your arm, you turn onto New Street only to see more men coming your way. You don't know downtown well enough to escape unseen, but the hospice must be close. Another one passes by on your left; you have no idea if you've seen him already or if this is someone new. Financial towers and the Canyon of Heroes surround you. Along with the persistent heat, it's making you feel like this is some dark recess of Hell.

Memories of the dream you had last night flash in your head. Never mind the temperature today, you still can't stop from shivering.

When you were much younger you'd created your own personalized numerical system. Honestly, it wasn't much more complicated than Roman numerals but you never liked Roman numerals. Too many straight lines. Yours was all circles and dots. Big ones, little ones, combinations of the two. Single dots. Double dots. Triple dots. You name it. One tiny dot for a number one, a big circle for the number ten. You can admit now it was stupid and didn't make much sense to anyone else, except when you were eight there was the need to create something all your own. An *Epic System*, you called it. But when one looked at the Epic System it was overwhelming, illogical, without enough difference between each unique number.

This must be similar to what these men in suits feel like some days, staring at their screens filled with strings of numbers. And you feel just as numb right now as they flood all around you, suffocating your attempts to find a safe path out of here.

You pick up speed and try to lose them, running almost two full city blocks before finally bracing yourself on a large placard outside a soup and sandwich shop. Shifting yourself in behind it as best you can, you catch your breath, close your eyes tight, and quiver alone as the black and grey masses slowly dissipate and eventually go their own way.

When you open your eyes again, you're alone outside a crypt of a building. Alone, that is, aside from loitering pedestrians, dozens of taxis, a graffiti-covered delivery truck, and a few road workers jackhammering the asphalt to pieces. Never truly alone in Manhattan. The suits are gone though. You double check the address on the yellow note which the receptionist at the Maimonides Cancer Center gave you. Astoundingly, you're exactly where you should be.

Abi promised she'd meet you here but she's nowhere to be found. She's not outside the coffee shop or poking her head in the window of the art gallery. She's not hiding in the shady patch beneath a limp and listless flag. After waiting for another fifteen minutes, someone eventually tosses some loose change at you and your sad cracker box. You give up and head inside.

You decline the first three available elevators, opting to wait for one that's empty, and you ride it straight up eight stories to the hospice's reception. You give your information to the man at the front desk and he asks you to please take a seat for a few minutes. He whispers it too, like your waiting to be called is meant to be some clandestine event. You're the only person here. The building smells like any hospital: the laminate floors shine with fresh wax and cleaning products. But this isn't exactly a hospital, more like a holding pen for the terminally ill. There is no hope in here, even if you're certain hope is something discussed often within these walls. There's a line of sparkling green Christmas tinsel hanging from one wall. Maybe that's hope? A stack of brochures lies on the table next to you and you take one and flip through it. It informs you that the team of healthcare professionals here are providing maximized comfort for their patients while reducing pain as well as addressing spiritual needs. Hope, hope, and more hope. Patients here are not just dying from cancer, the brochure tells you; some may have heart disease, dementia, or chronic obstructive pulmonary disease, whatever the hell that's supposed to be. You keep seeing the words "Six Months or Less" printed in a slightly lighter and gentler font.

Hope is so fleeting, if it had ever existed anywhere at all in the first place. Why try and dress it up or camouflage it?

While you're still lost in thought, the elevator dings and the doors open. Abigail Ayr announces her arrival. "There you are," she says, bounding across the room to sit beside you. "Why weren't you outside?"

The man at the desk blows a polite "Shhh" across the reception area.

"Why weren't *you*?" you whisper. "I was waiting out there a half hour ago."

"Sorry," she apologizes. "I was AIIB'ing all morning and then I couldn't find any change for the train."

You don't know if Abi stayed the entire night at Margo Asus' apartment or if she went back to wherever it is she stays in Brooklyn. When you called her this morning everything on her end was very quiet. But you don't bother asking either. You choose instead to distract your thoughts the only way you know how:

E-books. Tripods. Flightless birds. Invisible ink. Bell curves.

She nudges you in the ribs as you zone out. "Huh?" is all you manage to say.

"I said, what's up with the crackers?" With a tiny fist, she knocks on the box in your lap. "Breakfast?"

"Just some of my father's stuff."

"Okay, sure. My dad likes crackers, too."

Soon, a nurse with a clipboard enters the waiting room and lets you know you're allowed to go in and see your father. You place the brochure back on the table and rub your palms together nervously. Abi rises from her seat before you and you make your way in. As you pass the nurse she says, "Welcome back."

"I'm sorry?"

"I said, welcome back." Then she senses your confusion. "Weren't you just in here Monday morning?"

You'd spent most of your Monday morning and afternoon with Abi; sitting with her for the first time at The UnDiner and then meeting her own father. "I don't think so. You must have mistaken me for someone else."

Identity is not reality.

The nurse crooks her head into her neck, obviously still confused. "No, I'm sorry. There was someone else here on Monday visiting Leo Small."

"Are you sure?"

She looks back and forth between you and Abi, then down at her clipboard and back up again. "I could be mistaken, I suppose. It happens." At that, the nurse directs you down the hall, claiming Room 817 is where you want to go.

Abi asks, "What was all that? You're certain you've never been here before?"

"I'm sure."

"So why do you think she recognized you? Maybe with your prosopagnosia thing you just don't remember."

"That's only with people, not actual places," you say. "I know I've never been inside this building before today."

"Well then, that's really weird," she adds. "Don't you think that's weird?"

You just shrug your shoulders.

The door to Room 817 is right under the only burnt out light in the entire hallway. There's a scuffed-up welcome mat on the floor and a tiny garbage can full of latex gloves and Styrofoam drinking cups. Another bit of seasonal décor — this time a paper ghost — is taped to the door above its tiny window. With your hand on the door handle, you hesitate.

"What's wrong?" Abi asks, even though she must have a pretty good idea already.

"I'm trying to decide if I want you to walk through this door with me or if this is something I need to do on my own." You want to peek in the window but you don't.

Thankfully she's not offended by your conundrum and instead tries to help you decide. "I needed you with me when we saw my dad."

"You didn't even know me though."

"And do you really know me so well?"

"Not yet, I suppose." You look at the window; just not close enough to see what's on the other side. You notice the bottom edge of the window is orange and the door has since been painted over with a cool, pale blue. But the edge here was missed. "Truthfully, I don't know *him* so well either."

Abi doesn't push you any further, instead she looks at you in a way that tells you whatever you decide is okay with her. All in one little look. This time you peer through the glass and you see your father, a shell of the man you used to know, lying in bed. Even from this vantage point and the bad lighting it's easy to tell he's already so much thinner than he was six weeks ago.

You open the door slowly and reluctantly enter alone.

The room is dark but calming. There's a definite serenity inside, with a cooling breeze and soft pan flute music playing on the speakers. The window offers a view of Lower Manhattan that is nothing short of breathtaking, especially at this time of day.

Leo Small is hooked up to all sorts of equipment. You know this is your father even if he no longer possesses the memory triggers you used to rely upon. There are tubes in his arms and in his nose and his hair is gone. It's clear his head has been sewn back together after having been operated on, probably weeks ago. There are dark, heavy bags under his eyes and his lips are dried and cracked. Even to you and your naïveté, it's heartbreakingly obvious how much time your father has left; just like he wrote in his email: "I don't have much longer on this world."

You sit on the single chair beside the bed and lean your head in closer while trying to keep your body as far away as possible. He's conscious, both the thin slits between his eyelids and the dying glimmer in his eyes tell you so, though just barely.

Guardedly you ask, "Dad?" And you take a deep gulp. "Can you hear me?"

His lips try to part, some of the skin taking longer to peel away from itself, and his mouth quivers.

"Can you speak?"

He closes his eyes in what feels like slow motion. Tears seep out from the corners.

You look around the room, hoping to find something that might make this easier. Through the window into the hall, Abigail is nowhere to be found. The distant pan flutes have been replaced by what sounds like a rainforest. There are monks humming somewhere. Your father's eyes are open again, and although he stares at nothing in particular, you do catch a quick twinkle within.

That twinkle instantly takes you back in time. You're ten years old again and your right hand is in a cast. You'd broken your hand when you were with your friends, Barton and Reilly; you were goofing off on your bikes in the stairwell of a condemned building behind the middle school. Your father was helping you re-learn how to throw a baseball with your left arm instead. You were in the alley outside the shoe store and he'd lined up half-broken soda bottles along the top of a dumpster. When you threw that ball — when you smashed the first bottle into tiny shards — your father had the very same twinkle in his eye. You seriously doubt he's as proud of you right now as he was back then at that moment, but it's something. And maybe it's not something to be measured anyway.

You place the cracker box onto the floor and reach into your rucksack, pulling out the book. Holding the cover of *The Third* up for him to see, you ask, "Would you like me to read to you?"

The right side of his mouth rises. Bubbles flow faster through the tube from his nose. You fan through the pages of the novel until you reach the one with the folded corner, maybe two-thirds of the way through. The last you'd read, Tristan Montminy had just returned to his apartment to find his girlfriend, Emilia, dead. The French cop had followed him there and Luca Desplante III is nowhere to be found.

Somehow, inexplicably, Tristan escapes from the apartment and tries to elude the cop through the streets and alleys and parks that he knows so well. This is where you begin reading to your dying father: this bizarre chase scene, where seemingly everywhere Tristan runs, every corner he turns, leads to more and more policemen. He can't tell one from another and before too long he almost feels guilty just for running. Tristan decides he'll head to his workshop, which is where you stop reading, upon realizing the author is about to kick off another lengthy introspective describing the smells of the shop: the whiff of fresh-cut wood as well as the lacquers, polishes, and varnishes. You skip three pages and continue reading:

> But this cannot be the end can it? Tristan thought his whole identity was now compromised. He may never be the same person he was before. He may not become the person he once tried to become. Could he become Luca Desplante III instead? Or was this impossible too? Tristan thought it was like himself did no longer exist. And Luca? Did Luca ever exist himself? Was any of it real? Was this what it felt like to be dead? Tristan had all time imaginationed that death might not be so bad. Whenever death chose to come for him Tristan believed it would might feel right. Something is as it should always be. He

wondered if this is true.

But if this really was death he was not ready for it. Not at all.

Your father's hand has latched onto your arm; you have no idea when that happened. You ask him, "Do you want me to continue?"

He clutches tighter and his mouth opens again. This time though, you hear him speak. "You—" he says. Your father's voice, just as your memory preserved it, only as a whisper.

You try to say something, but you have no response.

"You are—you're like a shadow." His voice, once identified by the doctors to be no more, is back. "Cepik," he continues. His breathing more labored with every word. "You are like a shadow," he repeats, and chokes down some more air. "I don't know when you'll fade away."

"Dad, that's not me," you say meekly, belying the statement. The sense you get is that your father is talking about himself, not you. He's watching helplessly as he fades slowly from the world around him.

"Your mother. She was right." You think, My lunatic mother? When did your dad ever tell you she was right about anything? Then his eyes widen. "I just want—" His grip on your arm tightens. "I want to see my son."

It's like he doesn't recognize you. Does he even realize you're here? "I'm here, Dad. I'm right here."

Identity is not reality.

Your father's eyes close again, his grip loosens and his hand falls to his side. You tremble powerlessly at first before realizing he's merely fallen asleep. If this really is death, then you're not ready for it. And neither is Leo Small.

"I'm sorry, Dad," you say even though you recognize the words are futile and far too late. You want to tell him you're sorry Mom ever left the both of you, but that sounds like a stupid thing to apologize for. You want to say you're sorry for not visiting him more often, but what would the point have been, really? It could not have possibly changed anything.

You failingly try to smack another buzzing bug away from your ear. Your only accomplishment is banging a knuckle on the metal bedrail behind your head.

As you rise from your seat, you notice a tiny envelope on the far bedside table. You walk around and take the paper into your hand. The side that had laid face-down is clearly marked *CEPIK* in shaky printing. Again, you recall your father's words in his email: "*I have something very important to give to you. And some things to tell you. I pray you will come.*" You contemplate the envelope for a moment before deciding to leave it unopened; you slide it into the still-open copy of *The Third* and close the book tight. You leave your father's box of mementos behind on the table.

A wolf howls in the distance of the playing music as you turn out the light and exit the room. Abi is still outside in the hall, propped against the wall and typing something into her phone. No words are said as you walk back toward the elevator.

Your hands touch as both of you go for the same button in the elevator. "Sorry," she says first. "Listen Rainbow, I just want to say—I understand now why you've always looked so sad."

"Sad? I'm not sad."

"Well, *distant* then."

"Why's that?"

"Because of your dad. And how far away from you he is right now. How close he is to the end, right?"

"It's not because of my father, Abi. I guess it's just that I feel so lost. Like this life is so meaningless. Hopeless."

"It's not though. You just have to make the best of it. This is the only life we get, Epic."

"What about your reincarnation theory?" you ask, recalling what she said to you that first day at The UnDiner.

"What? You didn't really believe that, did you?"

ooo

The heat sticks to you all the way to Rector Station, where you're catching the R-Train to work your afternoon shift. Abi tells you she's got to run back up to Margo's apartment because she left her socks there last night. Sure. Okay. You go your separate ways with the promise to meet for breakfast at The UnDiner tomorrow morning. You should have thanked her before saying goodbye but you didn't.

ooo

It's past midnight when you finally return home from work, and collapse into bed. You try to sleep, but something's preventing you from doing so. Are you afraid of repeating the dreams you experienced last night? Is it your father? Abi? Where have all your dreams of Reya and corn fields vanished to lately? The mundane dreams where you're drinking root beer or rolling a marble in the palm of your hand.

You're still shivering, even in this heat. A couple of times tonight you had to stop what you were supposed to be doing and just sit quietly for a moment in a dark corner of the warehouse. Cold sweat envelopes your body and you try to go numb to it all by cocooning yourself in the bedsheets. It's no use.

You take a couple of 20mg Celexa citalopram hydrobromide tablets from the bedside table. Then you grab your rucksack from the foot of the bed, removing your copy of *The Third* and the pack of Effexor tablets. After popping out two of the peach-colored 25mg venlafaxine hydrochloride tablets from the package, you swallow them all and open the book to the find the envelope from your father. Holding it up to the window, you try to garner a clue to its contents under the light of the moon. Again, you think about opening the seal, but decide against it. You're not prepared for whatever message it contains. But there's a feeling about it, like this object with your name on it is not actually meant for you. It's stupid, but this is the feeling you have. Your own fault really, having pretended for so long now that your father barely existed. And then to see him in that state this morning, like he wasn't the same man you'd remembered.

Just as you nearly succumb to the feelings of guilt, regret, and remorse, through your melancholy, you hear it.

The buzzing.

It's the same fucking insect that's been driving you crazy for the past few days.

This bug has to die.

Though the apartment is only lit by the moon and the red and blue of squad car lights from the street below, you still notice the insect stuck to the ceiling. Creeping closer, you take a swing with your bare hand but only connect with the dangling chain from the lightbulb. It buzzes off. You track the sound closely until spotting it once more. You're not sure what it is —

whether a mosquito, a fly, or even a ladybug — but it's on the wall, just above the bathroom door. From the kitchen counter, you take a plastic blue cup in your left hand and you focus. Your father's voice echoes in your head again; the same memory from when you were ten years old. He explained to you how, when throwing a baseball, there were three phases: the stance phase (hands together against your chest), the velocity phase (using your fingers to add extra power upon the release), and the accuracy phase (keeping your head on the target, throwing with elbow up and arm straight). If you could master each of these throwing mechanics, he explained, then you would have the best arm on the field. That last part didn't matter much since you never made any of the teams you tried out for, but your dad made you work on your throwing all the time, hitting bottles lined up along the dumpster behind the shoe store.

You remember your father's words clearly as you bring not a baseball, but the cup to your chest and you throw it as hard and as accurately as you can against the wall, smashing the plastic cup into tiny shards. You tear off two squares of toilet paper and collect the dead bug, dropping it and the broken cup into the kitchen garbage.

And with that, you're back on the bed and falling into a deep, deep sleep.

ooo

Sometimes when you wake suddenly from an intense dream, there's still some retention of it; a heavy, lingering memory of things experienced. Even when woken prematurely, something is likely to remain. Perhaps the last image before your eyes burst open, back to the world where you never felt a part of. But the banging on the door right now is so severe, there is no fading memory. In fact, you feel as though you don't yet know if this is reality or if you're still sleeping. What's worse, you do not know if you're alive or dead. You wonder, *How much more frightening can things become?*

The pounding slows but intensifies in power, almost like the bottom of a boot instead of the flailing of fists. You hear shouting from behind the door, but you can't make out the words. Of course, information such as that does little good when you're getting your fucking door kicked open. The hinges tear off the frame, their screws burst in every direction like candy from a piñata, before rattling along the floorboards, and a lone silhouette walks forward; at first stepping across the door which now lies on your floor, cracking it in half, and then lumbering closer toward you.

This is when you try to wake yourself, when you get a good look at the interloper. The sneakers and khakis are not so strange, but this man is clearly wearing a houndstooth trench coat over his shirt and a horrifying animal mask on his head. In your panic, you cannot tell for sure if it's a raccoon or a grizzly bear or a cross of something somewhere in between, but you can have a free pass here — a man has just broken into your apartment in a Halloween mask. You can be forgiven for some of the details that may get overlooked.

"Where is it?" he yells at you, his voice muffled a little inside the furry mask. You're too terrified to question what he's talking about. "What have you done with it?"

You have no idea. You cower in your bed with the sheet pulled up around you, as helpless as an old woman in a boxing ring. This man moves to the open window and looks out, then down toward the street. "Jesus *FUCK*, man!" he yells before turning to face you, a gloved finger waving as a warning. "You better watch yourself. Don't mess with shit you don't understand. You understand?"

Your jaw hangs open in disbelief of everything that is happening. Maybe it's because you *don't* answer him that he takes the book from the bedside table and chucks it at your forehead. The spine hits you so hard it breaks the skin. How's that for velocity and accuracy? A throw any dad would have been proud of. "Jesus fuck!" he howls again. You're wiping blood with the bedsheet as he hastily exits the apartment, shouting more indiscernible threats down the stairs.

Understandably, you do not sleep the rest of the night. In fact, you barely move at all.

What the hell is happening to you?

ooo

The morning haze reminds you of your dreams. You're still trying to piece together what must have actually happened last night. You kept one of your father's old t-shirts on your head wound for an hour or so until the bleeding stopped and left the splintered apartment door propped against the frame with a brief note stuck to Stanley's — your landlord's — door letting him know what happened ("*door busted = home invasion = I'm fine = thank you*"). You made the astute decision to leave out the details of the man in the badger mask.

When you step outside onto Mermaid Avenue, you're struck by the sky. It is powder blue; void of any clouds whatsoever aside from a fading pink line cutting through along the horizon, resembling a crocodile spine or a tear in cheap fabric. You only note this because it feels more like an evening sky, the pink cloud reminiscent of a typical summer sunset over Coney Island.

You check over your shoulder as you make your way to The UnDiner, but there are no men in suits or fuzzy masks and houndstooth coats to be seen. No fictional French cops trailing you for their next drug hit. Finally, you arrive at the restaurant and thankfully — mercifully — Abigail Ayr is already waiting there for you. You brace yourself on the tabletop and wobble slowly into your regular seat.

Seeing your fresh head wound she asks bluntly, "What the fuck happened to you?" The girl pulls no punches. After ordering a coffee and a plate of bacon, you explain it all as best you can. She scratches her head, probably wondering how the hell she ever got mixed up with someone as crazy as you in the first place. But instead of questioning your sanity, she blows it off. "Sounds like just a load of bad luck to me. You sure do seem to get hit in the face a lot though."

"Bad luck? How can you dismiss all of this so easily? There's been a lot of really scary things happening to me. And I feel like I'm drowning; grasping to stay afloat when there's nothing to reach for."

"Come on, Rainbow. It can't be as horrible as you're making it out to be. Just remember that a bit of bad luck is still better than no luck at all."

Is that all this is? Bad luck? You wish you could put a little faith into the words Abi tries to comfort you with.

Then she asks, "What else can you tell me? Did this guy say anything else to you?"

You shake your head. "It's like it was a dream. And the details are already fading away."

"Well, maybe it *was* a dream?"

"How do you explain this gash on my forehead?"

"You wouldn't believe the injuries I've woken up with before," she says. In spite of her competitive jest, Abi seems noticeably shaken by your story. In midstride, Dorothy lurches by and plunks your order of bacon in front of you. The plate spins a little on its bottom edge, stopping only when Abi reaches over to snatch a still-sizzling strip. "You said it was a wolverine mask? Like the superhero?"

"No, the animal. Though it could have been a lemur or a jackal. I wasn't really trying to nail down the specifics of the whole event."

She takes a bite of the crispy, sticky bacon and her eyebrows jump. "Oh. My. God."

"What is it?"

"You were right. This really is the best bacon ever."

"Occasionally I'm right." You take a gulp of black coffee from the large, grey ceramic elephant mug; the thick trunk acting as the handle. Abi's coffee cup has a photo image of someone's grandmother on it. She appears to be in a greenhouse and smelling a rose or something. "I really don't know what to think of this whole situation though. Am I losing my mind?"

"Sometimes when nothing seems to make any sense it helps to witness something else that's even *more* preposterous. Even more spectacular."

"What is it you're suggesting? It sounds like you have something specific in mind."

Licking her fingers clean of the bacon's maple and brown sugar coating, she leans in toward you and asks in a hushed voice, "Do you believe in ghosts?"

"Ghosts?" You remember her father saying something in his dressing room about Abigail's childhood imaginary friends. Ghosts, he definitely called them. "Why? Do *you*?"

"I know there's *something* out there. What they are exactly, I'm not so certain. Ghosts are the best I've come up with so far."

"Out where?"

"There's a spot I've been to, some place in Brooklyn. I couldn't tell you where exactly, but I do know how to find it. It's a small park. I've seen it a few times, the first by pure accident. After that, I just wanted to see it again. But I can't really explain what it is. Like it's haunted."

You sit back in your seat and dismiss her crazy talk. "I don't believe you. A haunted park? You can't be serious."

"Does it sound any more viable than a well-dressed man in an animal mask kicking down your apartment door in the middle of the night and throwing flimsy threats your way?"

You open your rucksack and place the Vivactil and Effexor tablets onto the table. "Did I tell you my therapist switched a bunch of my medications?" Gesturing at the meds you say, "I was taking all of *this* shit and now I'm taking *this*. Just like that. That can't be good for me, can it?"

"Hey, I'm on *your* side here, Epic. Don't go starting up with any more of your crazed conspiracy theories."

You think of your last session with Gideon and his talk of the perfect lightbulb, hidden cameras, and other hyper-analyzed conspiracy theories. Does Gideon Flat have secret motives? Is this all part of his plan? Are you being played the fool? You swallow the tablets with some coffee — unsure if you even counted out the right amount — and close your eyes tight.

You think: Blenders. Seahorses. Angler fish. The Bat Signal. Political parties.

Abi snaps a finger in your face. "Hey! Epic! Come back to the real world here."

"Sorry," you say rubbing your eyes with your palms. "I haven't had the best of sleep lately." You dump the drugs back into the bag.

"Listen, why don't you come with me?"

"To see the ghosts?"

"Yeah."

"I have to work. Bester's got his second showing tonight so I'm double-shifting and covering for him."

"Meet me later then. It's probably better at night anyway. What time are you off?"

"I can meet you back here around ten. Is that too late?"

"It's never too late, Rainbow."

"I guess it isn't," you say. Even though it only ever feels the opposite.

OUR WORST GHOSTS

The fading smell of lawn clippings and barbecues is unfamiliar to you, but strangely nostalgic. It's a sort of nostalgia for the things you've never known. Anyway, it feels *something* like that.

You'd taken the F and C-Trains across Brooklyn before finally arriving somewhere in Woodhaven. Outside the station, Abigail sweet-talked a man into giving you a ride closer to the park. You got the feeling she'd done that sort of thing before. But she was quick to jump into the backseat, leaving you to ride shotgun next to the man who smelled and looked like a pirate. The "Treasure Island" kind, not the Somali variety. Nobody said a word either, which made you more than a little uncomfortable. You were dropped off in a quiet, suburban neighborhood and Abi guided you through unknown streets that felt more dreamlike than lifelike in their allure.

You're still unsure where you are going to end up but you can't help being excited; a feeling you haven't had course through you for quite some time now. And just as the summer sun finally sets behind an unseen Manhattan, after treading along dim lit streets with names like Peony and Periwinkle, past laughing kids on bikes and scooters, Abi says: "We're here."

It's a small patch of green grass, a local park with a modest playground right in the middle. The park — you notice the unscathed wooden sign labels it "Penelope Park" — is literally surrounded by suburban homes, their backyards all facing you. The only entrance to the park seems to be through this narrow fenced-in walkway running between warm houses. If you could describe the feeling of standing in Penelope Park right now it would be akin to a warm hug from your mother. Well, not *your* mother, but one you'd never known. Though maybe you're simply comparing this feeling to the rest of your life. Still, you could step in dog shit right now and it wouldn't be all that bad.

As you walk closer to the playground, you slowly get the sense it's the one black spot here. Its rust and general neglect help put you at ease a little. The rest of this idyllic *Leave It to Beaver* fantasy landscape could only end up making you more apprehensive in its whimsical serenity. Your footsteps go from the soft padding of dead grass to the crunch of dry gravel.

"What are we doing here?" you ask Abi, running your palm along the rusted chain on a swing set. The seat, hanging from only a single chain, has carved a circle in the dirt and pebbles below it. The second chain has been looped around the crossbeam high above you so tightly you can't reach it. There are weeds growing out from the gravel, overrunning the playground equipment, but mostly just dead from the dry summer air.

"I've been to this park a few times before, usually when life gets confusing." She keeps her distance from the playground equipment, still standing on the grass surrounding the patch of rocks. "Sometimes it feels like there are too many things spinning out of control. Like it's impossible to ever piece any of it together. I just come here so I don't have to figure any of that other stuff out."

"I'm not sure I follow."

"There are—*things* here. Things I've seen that don't make any sense at all." She waves for you to come closer to her. "Come on. I'll show you."

You follow her toward the houses surrounding Penelope Park. Most of their lights are on inside, like each house is the point on a star; each part of the same thing but as far away from one another as possible. You can see that one of the yards has a treehouse, half of it hanging over the fence. This is where Abi is headed.

"I like to watch from up there," she says.

You want to press for answers, but you know you'd only receive none. She lifts herself onto the top of the fence with all the grace of a house cat; moving quickly and without thought, as though she's done this a thousand times. The old fence wobbles a little, but she ignores it and effortlessly grabs a hold of a tree branch at chin level, climbing on up. You follow unsteadily, and she coaches you along the sturdiest branches, the easiest route into the treehouse.

Abi ducks, but you catch a mouthful of spider webs as you enter. This shelter doesn't appear to have been used for years. It stinks, too. Musty, falling somewhere between sex and roadkill. Maybe a bit of both. There isn't enough room to stand upright, but you can crouch fairly comfortably. Each of you finds your own dusty wooden apple crate to sit on. There are signs of children having been here, but not for a long while now. Some rusted toy cars. Plastic machine guns with their triggers broken off and busted. Smashed flashlights and batteries strewn about. Faded posters of Spider-Man and Conan the Barbarian are cracked and peeling from the walls.

You wonder where those kids are now. Are they still living at home? Did they grow up and move out years ago, finding careers and families of their own? Do they ever think of this treehouse anymore? Are they happy?

Miserable? Dead? All of these questions make sitting in here that much more difficult. You should find easier ways to disconnect yourself from your thoughts sometimes. You want to zone out and think about Dress socks, Frittatas, and Unlisted phone numbers instead, but you don't.

Abi is staring out a small open window, out toward the park. You join in, and the two of you watch in silence for a while. It feels like you're waiting for something to happen, but you don't know what in the world it might be. You're partly afraid she's going to try and kiss you here. Is that a normal fear? But you don't have those kinds of feelings for her — at least you don't *think* you do — and you're pretty sure she doesn't share them either.

Still, you catch yourself looking at her anyway. Her chin sits atop her knees, her hands resting uneasily below them. The summer twilight warps her face beautifully. You're fascinated by the way she's chewing up the inside of her mouth: voracious, like a wild dog on fresh meat.

You don't want to break the silence first, but you do anyway. You ask, "So, what is it we're waiting for, exactly?"

"I'm waiting for a lot of things," she says ambiguously. "Have you ever had someone tell you, *You'll know it when you see it*?"

"I'm not sure."

"Well, you wouldn't think so, but it's true."

You look at her with no more words, but your face says it all.

"What are *you* waiting for, Epic?"

"I don't know if I'm waiting for anything, really."

"So, everything's just as you want it to be then?"

"That's not what I meant." From somewhere, a cricket chirps for you.

"So, what is it?"

"I just—I *miss* things. More than anything else, I miss certain things."

Abi makes a noise like a little laugh. Like a laugh someone might make when they can't believe someone else would say something that they did. Like she's disappointed in you. She asks, "Is this about that Reya girl?"

You realize at first how you'd already mentioned Reya to her a few days ago when you shared the table in The UnDiner. But then you remember your melodramatic outburst at Margo's the other night too. Reya. Reya. Always Reya, isn't it?

"Usually."

"Do you remember that ex-boyfriend of mine I was telling you about?"

"Sure."

"He was a gamer. Online games. That was pretty much all he ever did. Actually, when we were together, that was all the *both* of us ever seemed to do. AIIB was *my* thing. He liked *War of the World-Makers*."

"Is there a difference?"

"One's awesome and the other's shit." You think she was hoping for a laugh from you here, but continues her story instead when she doesn't receive one. "AIIB is the *real* world, that's what makes it cool."

You search around the inside of the treehouse with your eyes. "Isn't *this* the real world?"

"Well, technically, I guess. But World-Makers is stupid. It's all Dungeons & Dragons, you know? With elves and goblins and magical talking swords."

That does sound kind of stupid, you think.

"I tried it once," she says. "I made up a character and everything. I think I was a kobold or something? Didn't matter. I was dead before I even left my cave dwelling. Some Level-30 asshole thief slit my throat and jacked all my stuff. My boyfriend convinced me to give it another try. He was a Level-42 warrior dwarf and was leader of his own guild."

"What's a guild?"

"It's a group of World-Makers who band together as a team. You know, strength in numbers."

"Did you join his guild?"

"Are you kidding? They'd never let some newbie tag along with them. I'd only be a liability. Dead weight." You shrug your shoulders hoping Abi can tell you're already lost. "But I caved in and gave it another chance. I created another avatar. Now I was a human warrior! You know, something that could put up a fight. How awesome is that, right? But then some nerd lured me into a tavern where he and his wizard groupies zapped me and transmogrified me into a pile of dirt. After that, I told my boyfriend he could keep playing his stupid game but I'd be sticking with AIIB."

"How is that better?"

"AIIB's not about killing everyone else on a power-hungry quest for glory. There's no rage. It's all about being happy. You can go to that special place where you've always dreamed about going. You can say the things you can't say here. Look how you want to look. Or watch the sun rise and set from any rooftop in the world. The real gamer nerds don't care about the little things like this; happiness to them is destruction and conquering over everyone else."

You look at the Conan poster peeling off the wall. The barbarian is standing upon a pile of bones and bodies, his thick muscular arm triumphantly raised above his head and holding a massive, bloodied sword.

"So, what about your boyfriend then? What happened between you two?"

"His guild had a meeting in Houston."

"There's a place called Houston in War of the World-Makers?"

"No, the *real* Houston. Texas. Sometimes guild members will plan real-world meetings where they dress up like their avatars and talk about the game at a TGI Friday's."

"Really?"

"Sure. This is the real hardcore players I'm talking about. You know, in most cases the other members of their guild are their only friends."

"Is this when you broke up?"

"Yeah. He texted me from Houston to tell me as much. Turned out he was cheating on me with one of his party members."

"In the game or in real life?"

"I think both. And I don't know what's more disturbing: finding out he was cheating, or that he was a dwarf and she was an orc. I mean, how does that even work, right?"

You try to avoid any unnecessary images in your head. "Dumped for an orc? That's pretty bad."

"Tell me about it." She cranes her neck a little, watching something outside in the park. You can tell by how she slumps back down that it was nothing. Like she only *thought* she'd seen something.

You hear the screeching sounds of a garage band playing way off in the distance somewhere. "But how are you doing now?"

"I'm good," she answers, almost instinctively. But then Abi actually thinks about it. Dissecting the real truth within her words. "No, fuck that. I'm not good. I'm hurt and I'm pissed off at him and I feel ugly. Nobody's good after a breakup. Why does everybody always say they're good? After he dumped me, the first thing I wanted to do was log on to AIIB and go crazy. Like those guys who put on body armor and shoot up elementary schools. I wanted to run around with a chainsaw or a machete and just start laying into other people's avatars. Turn the whole virtual world into my own personal War of the World-Makers. But I knew that wouldn't make me happy."

She lays on her back now, her tiny body almost spanning the length of the floor. Abigail closes her eyes and lets out a long, heavy sigh. "I'll tell you what the best part of any break up is though. It's what I like to call the *Non-Judgmental Mourning Period*. This is the time when you can sit around feeling sorry for yourself and questioning everything you've just been through and nobody has the right to judge you. In fact, most people will sort of envy you." Abigail kicks her boots off. She scrunches her toes together, cracking tiny knuckles.

From the corner of your eye you see a light out in the field. Maybe it's more like a soft glow or a shimmering or a flickering candle? Whatever it was though, it's gone by the time you actually look over.

Abi continues whatever she was going on about. "You know what I mean?"

You snap back to reality, having been distracted for only a fraction of a second. "I think I do," you say. Whatever it was out there, had momentarily stolen your attention; it had you in some ethereal grip. Like you were momentarily pulled right out of this treehouse. An out-of-body experience, maybe.

"Yeah, I know, right?" She's still on the floor with her eyes closed, oblivious to anything you might have seen just now. "At some point in our lives we've all wanted nothing more than to wake up at ten a.m., eat bowl after bowl of no-name brand marshmallow cereal, and watch *The Price is Right* followed by some *Maury Povich*. I guarantee you anybody who hasn't been there has wanted to be. It's just a moment that lasts a bit longer for some than it does for others. For me, it was approximately five months. Seriously, that was about as ambitious as I got then. And nobody judged. Not one person."

"And that's when you came to New York? To see your dad?"

"That about sums it up, Rainbow." She sits up and takes another defeated look outside. Then she turns to you, eyes wide open like warm, glassy pools. "So, you want to tell me more about Reya now?"

"Not particularly."

Suddenly she takes on an entirely new demeanor, like she's just missed her chance at something. Those big reddy-brown eyes want to dig further. You're already trying to figure out the whole Reya thing with Gideon, what's the point in talking about her here, too? You keep closing the same door on Abi so she might as well try opening another. "What else then?"

"What else do you want to know?"

"If you don't want to spill the details about your *last* girl how about your *first* one?"

It's your turn to look back out to Penelope Park now. The air is so dry outside you think the dust must still be settling over by the swing set. The mosquitoes buzz around outside, like they can't figure out how to find the two of you here in the shelter of the treehouse. You owe her something though, right? "My first time—" You think back. Back before all this. "My first time was with a girl named Liisa. With two i's."

Abi spells it out: "L-I-I-S-A?"

"That's right."

"What the fuck is *that*? Who would ever want to go through life constantly adding, *That's with two I's* to the end of every introduction? Every time someone asked for your name?"

"You got me."

"So, when was this?"

"I was sixteen." It feels like such a long, long time ago now. You explain to Abigail about how, in high school, you'd reconnected with two idiot kids named Barton and Reilly. The same two boys you caused all kinds of trouble with in your neighborhood growing up. After they set fire to your father's store, you made the logical decision to stop hanging out with the two of them. Though high school has a tendency to change a lot of things about people, doesn't it? Barton and Reilly still weren't popular or cool, but they certainly weren't sitting on the last rung of the social ladder either. That was you, of course. Until they took you back under their wings, that is. They smoked behind the school a lot, in a charming area known as the Smoke Pit. In the Smoke Pit, no one was an outcast. Even the new kid who got pulled in. Everyone was an equal, sharing one another's cigarettes. Everyone breathing in what everyone else was breathing out. You tried smoking a couple of times but you couldn't stand it. They allowed you to stay anyway.

You and Barton and Reilly never spoke about your father's shoe store or what any of you had been up to over the last few years. You'd heard stories about them. They'd probably not heard a thing about you. But again, that's high school, really. They weren't bad guys; they just wanted that image. Barton had a swastika tattoo now, but what most people didn't know was that he drew it on every morning with a blue Bic pen. He was getting really good at it too. Very precise line work. He had his head shaved like some Hitler youth, though the popular theory was that his mom gave him a bad haircut so he just took the rest off himself with the blade she used to shave her armpits. Reilly wasn't doing much better. You were pretty sure he still had that enormous collection of plastic dinosaurs hidden around his bedroom somewhere.

"Anyway," you continue. "One day, the boys and I are in the Smoke Pit and we're approached by this girl named Liisa. She's a grade younger than us but she's much hotter than any of the girls our own age. Reilly gave her a smoke and he and Barton got all giddy when she left. They turned to me and asked if I was interested. I said, *Interested in what*?" even though I knew what the *what* was. They told me Liisa Lonzo had been around, which I knew. They told me she screwed around with college dudes, which I definitely *didn't* know. How did someone from here even meet university students? It seemed unfathomable, but there was a lot I was oblivious to as a kid."

Abi brings her knees up; her chin returns to its familiar resting place. "So, what did you do?" She seems genuinely interested in all of this.

"Well, nothing right then. But one night, a few weeks later, the three of us went to some house party in Queens that none of us were invited to. But everyone was going. Some kid's parents were vacationing in Florida. You probably know how these things go."

"We didn't have house parties in Memorial, Colorado."

"Trust me. You're not missing out on anything." You remember approaching the house and hearing tired speakers blasting something undiscernible through the streets. You were drinking Mountain Dew out of a

Big Gulp cup, but you told everyone it was booze. Not anything specific of course; just booze. Nobody prodded anyway and the truth was no one probably even cared. It was weird being at a party in some other kid's house, with pictures of his parents and his sister and their dog all over the place. Seeing his mom's CD collection right there in plain sight. Some wooden key holder mounted on the wall that he must have made for his dad in the second grade. You remember it said *Dad's Keys* in big, orange bubble letters. Whoever he was, there were all these signs everywhere that he had such a nice, normal family life but his number one priority was waiting until the house was empty so he could invite everyone from school over to trash the place.

"I was feeling out of place, not really wanting to be there, and Barton and Reilly had already ditched me so I felt a little more lost than usual. I was taking a closer look at the list of chores his mother had left for him, stuck to the fridge with a Daisy Duck magnet when I noticed this girl standing beside me smiling. It was Liisa. She looked drunk and smelled drunk and then she very bluntly said to me, "*I'm drunk.*" I don't remember many more details of that conversation but it was pretty brief and before I really knew what I was experiencing, I was making out with Liisa Lonzo in the den. The family dog was on the floor watching us, probably out of sorts considering all the beer he'd had poured on him all night.

"Then Liisa unzipped my pants and slid them down to my ankles. I remember thinking about how she'd slept with all those other guys and that in her drunken state she was probably just going through the motions, not even aware of the loser I really was. She was so hot though that I couldn't stop it all from happening, especially considering raging teenage hormones and my complete inexperience with situations like this. She grabbed at me; I was repulsed because it felt like an assault, but I was also excited, the blood quickly flowing from one part of me to another. I was still so shocked though, that I basically laid there and let it happen. For a while, I regretted not being a better participant. I wished I'd grabbed at her too; pulled her thin t-shirt up over her head; felt her breasts. Embraced her tightly. But I didn't. Liisa Lonzo pinned me down with impossibly-strong arms and she did all the work herself."

Abi smiles. "You lucky boy, you."

"Yeah. Until the door to the den burst open and Barton and Reilly and a few other partygoers caught us in the act."

"Ugh. Been *there*."

"The rest of that night is mostly a blur. Whether I blocked it out from the embarrassment of it all, or if someone actually slipped something into my Mountain Dew, I don't really know. Mostly though, I can't recall what Liisa said to me after that. If she acknowledged me or slipped out of the house without another word."

"And that was that?"

"No. Not at all. The worst part—"

"There's a *worse* part?"

"Yeah. The worst part was on Monday morning. I returned to the Smoke Pit not because I wanted to but because I thought I'd left one of my textbooks there on Friday. Reilly was there all by himself. I'd hoped against all odds that everyone might have forgotten everything about the weekend. No such luck. Reilly came right out and told me. He said that he and Barton had paid Liisa Lonzo to have sex with me at the party. Some others chipped in too — I think there may have been a bet going on — even if not everyone knew who Epic Small was."

"And no one acknowledged the fact that this basically made Liisa a prostitute?"

"Like I said, there was a lot we were oblivious to back then. High school is a paradox on many different levels."

"That is mortifying."

"Yeah. It was. But I figure everybody's first time is something they probably don't look back on too fondly. Mine is just another story. Part of my identity."

Identity is not reality.

She asks, "How long was your Non-Judgmental Mourning Period?"

"I don't know if I've ever spent too long mourning anything. Sometimes I wondered though, why it seemed as though crap like that was always happening to me."

"Hey, the way I see it, is even the sexiest undies get farted on."

"Uh. I guess that's one way of looking at things."

"My point is, it doesn't matter, Epic. I used to always think back to when I was happiest. Way, way back it feels like sometimes. But you know those thoughts, the ones that are basically your childhood? Lying on the grass and staring up at the clouds, waiting for them to pass right by but they just keep coming; wave after endless wave of puffy white dreams. I think back to reading Murakami in class instead of that trite dribble we were supposed to be reading. Or maybe it's just going to the corner store and buying candy bracelets? Whatever it was, it's gone now. Now it all just sucks. Growing up sucks. I could disappear forever tomorrow and barely a soul would notice or care. But someone makes a bad Superman movie and the world goes to shit. No one, nobody in my entire lifetime, will ever care as much about me as much as millions of people will care about some fictional character."

"That's because Superman is a simplified version. He's not as complicated as you or me. And people hate complicated. They run away from it."

Abi stares at you, like you just had a fantastic breakthrough. "Still, it's not *real* happiness. Happiness is when you meet someone special. And happiness is even when you're allowing them into your life and you know at the same time that you're also giving them permission to rip your soul in half and smash your heart to pieces when they choose to eventually leave you."

"I don't ever remember being happy. I only ever wanted to be somewhere else." In your dreams, you see that fence in the countryside again.

"Like where?"

You see the coarse hair from a horse's tail snagged on a loose nail in the fence and it quivers a little in the gentle breeze. "I never knew where. I'm still trying to figure that one out. And I've never read Murakami either. What's he like?"

"Weird. But I adore it." Just like at The UnDiner, she picks at some more cat hair from her jacket and releases a clump out the treehouse window. "How's that book of yours coming along? What was it called? *Three's A Crowd?*"

Three's a crowd was how you felt at the Dullahan two nights ago. But you don't dare tell Abi that. You don't tell her about the book's eerie similarities to Bester's play either. "*The Third,*" you say instead.

"Is it making any sense yet?"

The last chapter you read was when you were at the hospice, reading to your father. "The main character, Tristan Montminy, has just realized his identity has been compromised. He doesn't know if he can ever be the same person he was before."

"Before what?"

"Before the *switch*. He and this other guy switched lives because they looked the same. Now he's unsure if he should just suck it up and become Luca completely, or if he'll fight for his old life. But it's like he doesn't exist anymore. I don't know, like he's nothing more than a shadow maybe?"

"You're like a shadow," your father said to you. *"And I don't know when you'll fade away."*

Abi scratches her ear, thinking about it. You open your rucksack to pull out your copy of *The Third* but it's not in there.

"What's wrong?"

You dig a little deeper but all that's in the bag are some prescription bottles and your workplace ID. "My book. It's not in my bag." Did you lose it? The last time you know for sure you had it was at your apartment, and— *shit.* The unopened letter from your father. That was inside the book too. Your ancillary bookmark.

"Where could it have gone? Retrace your steps."

Fear wells up inside you again. "That man who entered my apartment last night — did he take it?"

"Wait, there actually *was* a man in your apartment last night?"

"I told you there was!"

"I thought it was a dream. Or a joke."

"Why would I—? That's not the point here!" You chuck your bag across the treehouse. Pill bottles fall out and rattle across the wooden floorboards. You don't mean to show an angry side of yourself, but you're not thinking straight. And then you show a different side.

A worse side. Jealousy.

Out of nowhere you ask Abi, "Do you have feelings for Bester?" You don't even know how it could possibly make a difference to you right now.

It's barely perceptible, but Abi moves away from you slightly. "That's preposterous." You want to apologize but you can't seem to find the words. Turns out you don't have to. "Anyway," she says. "I was only pretending."

"Why would you do that?"

Everything's quiet. This is that pause that always happens in movies right before the main character is hit with important information. And then Abi hits you with it: "Because I like *you*, Epic."

Now you worry again about the possibility of a kiss. You knew from the start — from the time four days ago when you shared the table at The UnDiner — that Abigail Ayr was not relationship material. But there is something here. If there wasn't, you surely would not have felt what you felt when you first spotted her across Surf Avenue. "But I get the feeling there's more to it, isn't there?"

"Yeah."

You know how this goes. "You're about to say it's complicated, right?"

"Complicated? No. Complicated implies I have some vague conception of the many levels and layers of it all. I'd simply call it *confusing*, because that's what it actually is." She reaches for the Vivactil and Effexor bottles, puts them back in your bag and hands it to you. "I mean, what I feel is—I feel like I *should* love you, but I don't. It's dumb, I know. And I also know it doesn't make any sense at all but that's the best I can do. That's the closest I can get when I think about what's happening here."

There it is again: the slight shimmer of some luminescent presence by the slide. Maybe it's just the stars and the moon far above the playground. But it's gone by the time you turn your head. "So why did you bring me here again?"

"I've seen things here. I say *things* but only because I'm pretty sure I don't believe in ghosts. If I did believe in ghosts that's what I'd call them." Abi peers back out toward the playground, resting her little chin on the edge of the window.

Her eyes flutter, as though hoping to catch some sight of whatever it is. But maybe the lights are just meant for you tonight? Then her head turns to you quickly and she asks, "You saw something though, didn't you?"

You don't give her an answer because you don't know if she'll be disappointed or resentful or just happy for you.

So, she puts her boots back on instead. "Come on," she says, a little bit dour. "Let's get out of here."

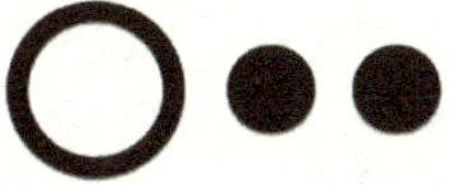

SOMEWHERE WE BOTH BELONG

Everything is the same here except for the hole. A tiny void. The framed *Lovehunter* album cover is, inexplicably, gone somewhere and in its place remains an empty wall; empty but for the unusual hole in it. This hole seems too big to be from a bullet, though you're not ruling out this building ever playing host to illicit, criminal activity. It's too high up to have been used for cable access. You highly doubt the potential for a peep hole, as the reception desk in Gideon's office is directly behind the wall; an indiscreet location for spying on someone. Maybe the hole has always been there? Maybe it was added only recently? Maybe it's nothing, and the naked woman on the snake was simply covering up the blemish? But maybe it's everything, and the removal of the album cover directly coincides with it.

Of course, the possibility remains that simply being in this office makes one prone to collecting conspiracy theories at an astounding rate and frequency.

It's Saturday morning. You haven't been here since Wednesday when Gideon suggested you take Abigail to the play in Bushwick. Obviously, quite a lot has transpired since then. You haven't slept since Thursday night, what little sleep you enjoyed before having your apartment door kicked in, that is. You think through all the events of the past three days, hoping to find the right story to share with him when Gideon returns from the bathroom.

Today's session has only just started, and he wasted no time in excusing himself to use the bathroom adjoining his office.

He's been in there for a while now, leaving you alone, seemingly, to contemplate nothing more than the hole in his wall.

But the mind has a terrible habit of treading unexpectedly to places previously unthought of. Gideon has only been absent for less than a minute, when the notion of snooping around his desk comes to you. No, you tell yourself. That wouldn't be right. And you certainly don't want to get busted. What then? You might be sent to see a therapist even less qualified than Gideon Flat, if that's at all possible.

Then a couple more minutes go by and you think that if you'd taken a look around when you first wanted to, you would have been fine. There would have been more than enough time to find something, anything, to satiate an ounce of your curiosity. But now, well, he'll be back at any moment, won't he?

Another five minutes go by and all you can think about are all the things you could have investigated.

Where does he keep the journal he seems so overly-protective of? You didn't notice if he'd taken it into the bathroom with him. Is it in his desk? Are the drawers locked? He has that desk key tied to a rubber band around his wrist but maybe he never locked the drawer before leaving? What information is on his computer screen? You could at least look out the window, couldn't you? Out onto Surf Avenue where you first spotted Abigail Ayr before all of this had even had a chance to start happening.

And then, of course, there's that hole in the wall. The longer you stare at it, the more you think you're seeing it move. It pulsates. Maybe this is just the heat though, or perhaps more apparitions carrying over from last night. Perhaps once you think you've seen a ghost for the first time the feeling just starts to snowball.

You wait another minute and still no sign of Gideon. Certainly, you ascertain, the sound of the toilet flushing or the blasting air from the hand dryer would be enough of a warning for you. So, you rise slowly from the sofa and move closer to the wall to investigate, creeping along like you're stepping through a den of sleeping wolves. As you near the dark hole, you know there's something off; you can feel it in your soul. But before your curiosity is appeased you spot something else from the corner of your eye: across the wall on the top shelf of the tall bookcase are four or five different-colored journals similar to the one Gideon insists on keeping within his grasp. These other ones also have names on their spines, presumably all printed from the same label maker. Likely other patients of his. You're fairly certain that Kerrigan, Dr. Griffin's secretary, told you Gideon Flat was new in the neighborhood and looking for patients so it's fair to assume this small number might be the entirety of his clientele. There's a gap between two of them where your own personal notebook was probably pulled from. The label on one of these — a journal that's mustard-yellow in color — is already peeling off at the top and dangling in a sad candy cane shape. You reach up and flatten it back into place with your thumb.

Like another sucker punch to the face, the name hits you unexpectedly:

Graves, Reya

Your heart sinks. Reya Graves. Your Reya. You wobble a little and an image of her electric green eyes flashes through you. How could she—? You reach for the book and wonder what you might find.

ooo

"Is there something you're looking for?" Gideon's voice snaps you back up straight.

"There's just, ah—I was just looking at that hole up there." You point to the wall with a shaky finger. "Why is there a hole there?"

Gideon looks up now too. He eyeballs the spot on the wall where the *Lovehunter* album used to reside and his eyes dart around to the bookcase and back to you. You can't tell if he knows what your attention actually was focused upon or if the readjusted label on the journal's spine is already enough of a dead giveaway. Either way, he directs you back toward the desk with a reassuring hand on your shoulder.

"Do have a seat, Cepik."

You do, and you watch him carefully as he rests the lilac journal on the desktop. He doesn't open the book, but he does have his pen ready to go. "My apologies for being in the bathroom for so long. I'm on some new medication that's not exactly agreeing with me."

That makes two of you. "I guess if nobody was taking drugs we'd all be fine, right?"

"Sure. Except for the pharmaceutical companies." He winks like this is all one big joke, but then quickly holds an open palm out to you. "Why don't we get started then? Go ahead."

"Well, okay then. My name is Cepik Small. I think I saw a ghost last night. An actual ghost. And I smoked some pretty high-grade marijuana for the first time."

"How certain are you that the two events aren't connected?" Winking again, then laughing, he says, "I mean, a ghost? Come on. Really?"

You don't answer him because you don't think you have a fair answer. He continues without one anyway. "This marijuana. Where'd you get it? It wasn't your prescription cannabinoids, right?"

"What makes you think that?"

"Because it's never for the guy who it's prescribed to, that's why."

"It was from someone we were with."

"We?"

"Abigail. And a friend of mine from work."

"Abb-ee-gail..." he drones, jotting the name down in his journal. "Or Abi, I guess, for short. Is that with an I or a Y?"

You just shrug your shoulders in response.

"So, is this the girl you met at the restaurant? The girl I suggested you take to your friend's play?"

You must not have mentioned Abigail's name to Gideon the last time you were here. Perhaps yet another detail that slipped away from you? "The same."

"How'd that work out?"

You release a heavy sigh from somewhere deep within. So much has happened in the last few days: the strange play followed by the night at Margo's; that horribly lucid dream of yours; seeing your father in the hospice; the man in the houndstooth jacket who broke into your apartment; the trip to Woodhaven last night. But still, Abigail Ayr's presence throughout all of these things has been comforting.

"Good," you mumble. "It's been good."

"Excellent!" Gideon gives a *hang loose* sign with his hand. "And the play? How was it?"

"Confusing." It's hard to fathom that the least-perplexing thing in the past few days might have been the bizarre connection between *The Third* and *The Duality of Three*. Like it's been lost in it all. And now the book is missing too. "I, um—I thought I saw *you* there, actually. At the play."

"*Me*?"

"Yeah. Were you there? Was that you?"

"Nope. Wasn't me. I must have a twin. Or maybe even a triplet, right?"

"Right," you say, not wanting to remain on the subject any longer. Instead, you explain to Gideon how you all went to Margo Asus' apartment after the play and how you smoked that supernatural pot of hers. How Abigail seemed far more interested in Bester than in you. "I thought maybe I'd made a mistake in bringing the two of them together like that. But then she tried to clear everything up at the park last night."

"And did that help?"

"Hardly," you say. Last night, Abi explained how her feelings for you were not complicated, but confusing. Right now, you're not sure if you're comfortable delving into this with Gideon, but you do dwell on it for a moment longer. What else could you tell him? You could tell him about the dream you had or the man in your apartment. Or you could tell him about the things you saw last night in Penelope Park.

How you're quite possibly losing your mind.

Gideon breaks your train of thought. "What else are you thinking?" he asks. "I can tell there's something more going on in that head of yours. Anything to do with the gash on your forehead?"

You think about asking him to elaborate a little more upon those government-created and controlled insects he told you about; conspiracy theories and bioengineered killing machines. About how you think maybe, just maybe, there's the possibility you're being followed too. The memory of the army of men wearing three-piece suits and flooding Wall Street comes back to you.

But the part of you that really wants the help is the same part that's worried Gideon Flat will try to finagle his way out of these therapy sessions. Paranoid that he'll become the next therapist who contemplates killing himself just to avoid you. Surf Avenue sounds even quieter this morning, like the streets have been completely evacuated.

Gideon breaks the silence; he directs the discussion for you. "What about this ghost then? What can you tell me about that?"

"Abigail and I trekked out to Woodhaven last night. We sat in a treehouse and talked for a while. It was surprising, even though she'd told me beforehand to expect something weird."

"She knew then?"

"Yeah. She'd seen them before."

"The ghosts?"

"Honestly? I don't know if *ghost* is the right word for what it was I saw."

Gideon scribbles some more in the journal. Finally, after a long moment, he continues. "Why don't you try to describe it then? What *did* you see last night?"

The right words elude you, but it's easy to remember what you saw. You close your eyes and try to explain. "It was the shimmer of something off the children's slide in the middle of the playground. A reflection, but I felt it was more like from a shadow than from a light. A soft glow that seemed to be missing any feeling of warmth. A flicker here, then over there. The way I felt momentarily misplaced."

When you open your eyes again you half expect to see Gideon writing this down in the journal, but instead he is staring incredulously at you. Like you're making it all up. Like he doesn't know what kind of problem he has on his hands now. "Like a *shadow*, you said?"

"I don't know."

His tongue prods around inside his mouth; in the pocket space below his gums. He puckers his lips a little before asking, "How far are you in the book? *The Third*?"

"Half-way, maybe." Tristan had just run away from the cop and he hid in his old workshop. His identity was in flux, unstable. He was no longer Tristan Montminy but he wasn't entirely Luca Desplante III yet either. He didn't know where he belonged or which identity might actually belong to him. Tristan felt like he didn't exist anymore. He was just a flicker in space. A sliver in reality. A ghost. Or a shadow. "Perhaps more like two-thirds. But I lost the book," you say to Gideon. "I wanted to show it to Abi, but it wasn't where I thought I'd left it."

"Well," he starts slowly. "One of the concepts Jean Trepanier wrote about in *The Third* is ghosts. But he didn't call them that; he called them *shadows*. I remember it clearly. And his description matches that of what you told me you saw in the park. A reflection that is more from a shadow than from light. A glow that lacks warmth. Feelings of misplacement."

"I didn't read that part," you admit to Gideon. "But perhaps it wasn't in my version of the book? Another one of those variances, maybe?"

"Maybe." Gideon pauses. "Or maybe it's me who's starting to forget the details now?"

With his choice of words and incantation of them, you can't tell if Gideon is joking with you or intimating something more. But you laugh anyway; a laugh that's more like just blowing some air out of the side of your mouth.

"You haven't told me anything about your father yet." He clatters his pen between his teeth, his version of a rattlesnake intimidating its prey. "Would you like to talk about him now?"

Your father told you, "*You are like a shadow.*" He said, "*I don't know when you'll fade away.*" Two days ago, when you sat beside his dying shell, Leo Small said to you: "*I just want to see my son.*"

And while your father lays out there somewhere hanging on to what's left of his life, you find it hard to put a finger on how it is you feel. Do you begrudge him? Is it jealousy?

"He's dying," you tell Gideon. "Brain cancer."

"And this makes you feel—*what*, exactly?"

You crouch forward in the sofa and hold your arms tight, mulling your feelings over for a minute, trying to find just the right one. "Impatient."

He looks you over carefully, eyes scanning up and down. Gideon repeats your answer to himself and writes it down slowly like the word is much, much longer than the nine letters you thought it was. "Do you have ways of distracting yourself from thoughts of your father?"

You don't tell him that *not* thinking about your father is really not so difficult of a thing for you. Instead, you ask: "Like what?"

"There are a number of activities I often suggest to my patients. Positive activities that are particularly good distractors: painting, indoor rock climbing, or just watching the ocean. Even exploring virtual worlds."

"Virtual worlds, you say?"

"Yes, online games and other such things of that ilk. Some of my clients utilize them and find them extremely therapeutic."

You don't turn around, but you can't stop yourself from thinking about the mustard-colored journal on the bookshelf behind you. The one with *Graves, Reya* on the spine.

"Activities like these may help you in dealing with your concerns for your father. Death is a touchy subject for some," he says.

You remain in your defensive position, but you do not answer Gideon.

"Epic, you and I are vastly different, aren't we? I'd venture a guess that we've lived totally opposite lives. But death is somewhere we both belong. It's not something you should be afraid to speak about. In death, we are all the same."

"But we're not, really. What we are in death is how we are remembered by the living."

"Okay. So how will *you* be remembered?"

"I don't feel like I will be."

"That's your problem right there. If you're afraid you won't be remembered — that you're leaving nothing behind worth remembering — then you should probably want to do something about it, shouldn't you?"

"But I don't. The thing is, I'm not concerned about trying to leave something behind. I'm not trying to get it in under the wire before I'm done here. I'm not afraid of dying."

"Even now with this Abigail Ayr in your life?"

"Abi doesn't change anything."

"Everyone says they're unafraid of moving on until the moment is there; then, inevitably, there's nothing but dread." You don't know how many people Gideon Flat might have watched die in his lifetime, probably more than you, but you can't help feeling like he could never understand. "Tell me," he says. "How do you really feel about Abigail?"

It would be so easy to say the words: *I don't know.* It's true; you really don't know why you can recognize Abi when your prosopagnosia prevents you from identifying anyone else you've ever met in your life. And your confusion certainly isn't helped by the feelings she admitted to last night when you were together in the treehouse: "*I feel like I should love you but I don't,*" she told you.

"It's confusing," you say instead. It's not complicated, it's confusing.

"Confusing? How so?"

"I guess I wonder why books and movies can't be more like real life. Most of the time, in a made-up story, we know which characters are inevitably going to hook up. Which of them are predetermined to fall in love. And sometimes we already know ahead of time what the outcome will be, but we go ahead and commit to it anyway. In life, you never know when you'll meet someone new and, even once it happens, you really have no idea what's to come of it."

Gideon looks confused. "Don't you mean you wish our lives were like books instead? I think you're trying to say it would be nice to know everything when you meet someone for the first time."

"No, I'm not stupid enough to believe you can change how life works. I just don't like it when the real world is so egregiously misrepresented. It's like we're being lied to. Or fooled into believing things actually work in some preset way. There's something to be said about the thrill of a stranger; that unknowable percentage in life." That's how things were with Reya: she was a complete unknown. You'd only wanted to help her out that night, but it quickly became more than that, didn't it?

"The thrill of a stranger, you say? I think I see where you're coming from. The thing about strangers is that they're always more interesting at first because we don't yet know what purpose they'll serve."

And yet, with your prosopagnosia, even a good friend can be a stranger sometimes. "Still, I'd love to read a book like that, if that makes any sense."

"I don't know if books like that exist." Gideon places his pen flat on his desk and leans back in his chair, with hands clasped together behind his head. He takes a deep breath in and exhales slowly, in no rush. "You know, when I read *The Third*, the book was given to me by a girl. I met her at an arcade. You know, one of those places full of big video game machines you plop quarters into?"

"I know what an arcade is."

"Most people don't these days. She showed me how to punch holes in quarters and tie strings through them so you can pull them back out of the machines. Unlimited lives, you know? Anyway, we went out for a while, a few months I think it must have been. One day, out of the blue, she gave me this book and told me to read it. Back then I didn't read books. '*What was the point?*' I thought. But when a girl you really like insists you do something, you usually do it. Because that's how relationships work when we're young. Of course, eventually this girl turned out to be someone I didn't think she was. It ended badly. I questioned *everything*. She hated me pretty quickly. And when you came in here the other day talking about the very same book, I instantly remembered all of the details. All of the ways she broke my stupid little heart. When I think about that book, that's what I'm reminded of. And when I think about *her*, about our relationship and how it all ended, that book is still one of the first things that comes to mind. Sometimes I can't remember if I only enjoyed the story because I thought I was in love."

"You could read it again. Didn't you say you had your copy still?"

"If I read it again it would only remind me of her. And I don't want to go back there. Perceptions and memories are complicated things, Cepik."

Identity is not reality.

"It seems that way."

And then, almost out of left field, he asks you: "Do you think you can trust Abi?"

"Why wouldn't I?"

"Why wouldn't you, or why *shouldn't* you?"

ooo

You take a longer route home after your session with Gideon Flat; going up along Neptune Avenue (past The Bleakest Corner in the USA) and walking west all the way to 37th Street. You can't shake from your head the last question Gideon had for you. And by the time you get back to the apartment you're still asking yourself: *Why shouldn't I trust Abigail Ayr?*

The door to your apartment is still off its hinges and leaning against its empty frame. You've barely the time to start up your computer before you need to head back out to work tonight, but when you finally do check your email there's another message from AIIB: Don't Just Play Now — LIVE Now!

After hitting delete once again, you have a brief moment of reluctance. You click into your Deleted Messages folder, open the most recent one in there, and without any further hesitation, you click on the SIGN-UP NOW button. The only thing that happens is the appearance of a pop-up window that reads:

Please await further instruction

That's it? No credit card information necessary?

Whatever, you think. You shut the computer down, turn your light off, and leave for work, limping past the empty door frame like a ghost through a wall.

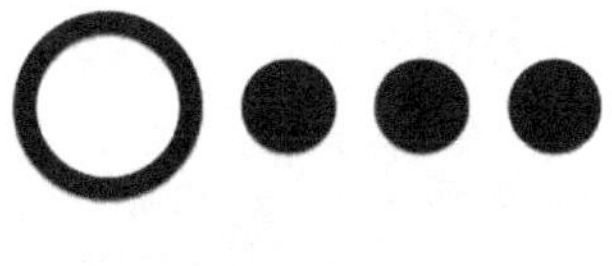

EPOCH

Sunday morning. It's cooled off slightly though it feels less like the heat coming to an end and merely more of a brief respite. Like things are about to get worse. Still, you'll take the break while it presents itself. There's an ocean breeze finding its way along Surf Avenue and it seems to carry you all the way to the cracked and peeling door of The UnDiner.

You worked all night and have yet to return home, choosing instead to come directly here for breakfast. Has it been two full days now with no sleep?

You're feeling off; a little woozy and a tad agitated.

Someone named Dorothy greets you as you enter. You dismiss her with a wave and almost sit at your regular booth when you notice a man is already there. His most distinguishable features are a thin, grey beard and some scratch marks on the backs of his hands. He wears a light brown suit with a matching fedora sitting beside him on the tabletop. The small fan blows generously in his direction. He's eating a big breakfast: fried eggs, potato hash, sausage links, and pancakes. All stacked together on one plate and doused in maple syrup. A big pile of food, glistening golden brown. You sit down at the next booth over.

"You may sit here if you'd like," the man says, though it takes you a long moment to register that he's actually speaking to you. "I don't mind." You assume he must have noticed you contemplating your seating options before making the decision you did.

You wave him away too, preferring to simply mind your own business. Dorothy comes by and places an empty coffee mug on the table. It's a tall, slender, pink mug, though the ceramic is very thick. She fills the mug almost to the rim. You ask her if anyone by any chance might have found a ratty old book over there, gesturing behind you to the only other occupied table in the diner.

"Sorry," she says, not asking for any more details about the book. You suppose there are not enough novels washing up around here that the missing artifact in question would require any further clarification.

"It's called *The Third*," you say drearily, not ready to give up just yet.

"I can give you a Coney Island tourist map if you just want something to look at." Thanks, Dorothy. Big help there.

For the third time in less than five minutes, you wave your hand, signaling the end of the conversation. You must appear more ornery than usual, if anyone around here is logging away their own memory triggers, that is. There's an oily swirl on top of your coffee and you stare at it until you can no longer tell in which direction it spins.

That's when you notice the man with the grey beard and brown suit standing beside you. You almost don't recognize him as the same man you had only just approached, but the scratch marks on his hands give him away. "Do you mind if I sit here then?" His accent is odd, and if you had a more acute awareness of European linguistics you might be able to put your finger on it. He plunks himself down in the seat across from you, placing the fedora and the plate of food on the Formica tabletop.

You ask, "Do you want something from me?"

He fits a forkful of egg and potato into his mouth; his jaw bones reshaping his beard with every bite. There is another sort of familiarity here you cannot place. Not an uncommon feeling for you to have, and if this man is someone you've met before it shouldn't be long before you nail it down.

Upon swallowing the food, he wipes the excess syrup from the corners of his mouth with a napkin and then scratches at his beard. "We've met before," he says, not unexpectedly. The question is: will you recall who he is before he cuts it out with all the sly talk? "Don't you remember?"

There's a feeling you get, like when you're playing Whack-A-Mole. Mallet in hand, you watch over the board as the little plastic beasts pop in and out of their holes, hoping for a pattern to emerge. Or, failing that, you keep a steady eye on a single dark hole, waiting for the moment when the tip of the mole's head begins to surface.

Then the man says everything you need him to. He says, "Epoch."

And your eyes lock instantly. Whack!

When you were a boy and your father was working, your mother would sit alone in the kitchen. As for you, you would be in the living room, maybe watching *The Jetsons* or *Scooby Doo* or practicing your cursive if the only shows that were on were the ones you'd already grown overly tired of. Your mother sat alone blowing smoke from a thin cigarette out the open window. And she'd sit until there was a knock at the door, at which point she'd let the man in. Then there were two of them in the kitchen, and your mother would put the cigarettes away and you would remain in your favorite spot in front of the television oblivious to whoever he was and whatever he wanted from her. The only thing you do recall is that when this man left he would say goodbye to you. And instead of Epic or Cepik he would call you "Epoch." It's a name you'd only ever been called by this one person, so long ago that you'd forgotten all about it.

Until now.

And just like the mole: Whack!

This man shovels another heap of breakfast into his mouth. He chomps away and you don't know what you're supposed to feel right now, if you're meant to be feeling anything at all.

Finally, in his funny accent, he asks, "Do you know what an epoch is?"

Like you told Abi, "I'm not really a word guy."

"Well," he says. Then he licks the food from off his fork. For a moment, his tongue seems to hang off the utensil like a sloth would hang off a branch. Then he reels it back in. "There are a few meanings for the word. A particular moment in time for one. As a reference point signifying the beginning or the end of an era of importance. On the geologic time scale an epoch is a length of time, generally considered to be smaller than a *period* and larger than an *age*. Astronomers use the term to note moments in time that relate to planets and their orbiting moons and satellites." Now he inspects the fork, making sure he's gotten every last bit from it, and then puts it down on his plate. It clinks heavier than it seems like it should. "Me? I refer to an epoch as a key moment in time. An important phase in the development of our universe; how we perceive it to be and what we really know about it."

"But you called *me* epoch. Why?"

He sits back in the booth now and takes a deep breath; sucking in more air than it seems he could possibly let out again. His fingernails dig into his beard a little more, then at the scratch marks on the backs of his hands.

"What do you know about black holes?"

"I'd say about as little as anyone could know. That is, basically nothing."

"Well," he starts again. "Centuries ago, there was a black hole. It was light years away from us. It had all the characteristics black holes were *supposed* to have: the event horizon, the photon sphere, gravitational time dilation, infinite space-time curvature, and so on. But then it died."

"Died? How does a black hole die?"

"There are many ways, really. But in this case, our black hole collapsed in on itself. And when this happened, all that was left was pure cosmic energy. Because the physics of space and time demand energy go somewhere, it did: it burst outward, like an explosion. At least that's where we *think* the energy came from. It definitely came from *somewhere* though, and the popular theory is that it was once a black hole."

"So where did this cosmic energy go?"

"Well, everywhere really. But mostly — most importantly — it came *here*. It took a few thousand years, but eventually this energy wave hit our planet. My team was tracking its unique signature. This specific cosmic energy was nearly undetectable. Imperceptible by anyone else. We saw it a couple of years before it hit the earth."

"How did no one else see it coming? What makes you so special?"

"Kid, there's billions — *kajillions* of different energy frequencies out there, and we happened to key in on just the right one at exactly the right moment. It all boils down to luck, really."

"And then what?"

"Well, then you were born. Though that's just simplifying things. What I mean is, the two events are connected but not wholly dependent upon one another." He runs a piece of toast through the puddle of syrup on his plate and delicately folds the piece into his mouth. "My team was in Switzerland," he continues with a mouthful of bread. His accent — German, you presume — is less noticeable now. "We were tracking the cosmic energy from a small city called Neuchâtel. For two years, we studied its properties as best we could, and we had dozens of theories regarding what it might be capable of. It was an exciting time for science. And then, when the energy finally did hit the earth, absolutely nothing happened."

"Nothing?"

"Well, we didn't experience anything special or sense anything different aside from a few reports of computers and electrical equipment shorting out. Like a small electromagnetic pulse. I imagine if it had occurred today, the way technology has advanced, more people would have caught it. Little slivers of cosmic ripples in space-time. And then just like that, the cosmic energy was gone, already a million miles away. We thought we'd failed to accomplish anything. All those years of time and research wasted. But we continued to search for some trace of what had been left behind. And a few months later, we got lucky: we found something. There was a tiny blip of that same cosmic energy in New York. It was another sliver. We didn't hesitate; we packed up our equipment right away and came to America, traveling all the way here to Coney Island. Right to the home of Leo and Wilma Small." With his knife and fork he cuts the pancake stack on his plate. A perfect triangle of three pancakes is removed from the stack and stuffed into his mouth. "And this is where we really began putting the right pieces together."

"I still don't understand. What does all of this have to do with my family?"

He finishes chewing before answering you. "I spoke with your mother. Many times. She claimed that when you were born she felt very strange. I remember her dispiriting words clearly. The joylessness of it all. How she told me she felt some loss of vitality; of ebullience. That she was so dizzy she nearly fell out of her bed. But it was when your mother looked me in the eye and spoke, '*Nobody believed a word I said*,' that I really had to stop. We knew the lights in the hospital had gone out at the same time and some of the equipment went haywire, but the doctors and nurses assumed things were fine. And as for this strangeness that she felt, well, the nurses had only told her that everyone experiences giving birth a little differently. But when she gave birth to *you* she knew something was wrong. To her, something unnatural had occurred."

"What was it?"

"According to Leo Small, nothing at all. The first time I spoke to your father he told me to turn around and go back to Switzerland. He labeled Wilma Dradtstl-Small — his own wife — as an irrational, spaced-out hippy and had never put much stock into her supernatural claims. In fact, no one was entirely sure what we were dealing with exactly. But I still had my suspicions."

"Which were?"

He scratches the back of one hand again. Then the other. "I'm sorry, but I think I neglected to introduce myself to you. My name is Zoltan Lintzel." He signals Dorothy now, offering up his breakfast plate before asking her for a cup of hot water. "Well," he continues. "Your father was irrelevant anyway. And as it turned out, your mother was too."

"What happened to my mother? I'd always assumed she left us for you. Where is she now?"

"Epic, your mother is dead."

Dorothy returns with the hot water in the ceramic elephant mug; the same one you drank from a couple of days ago, the morning after the apartment break in. Zoltan thanks her, and nonchalantly shakes the tiniest bit of salt from the shaker into the mug, like he hadn't just told someone their mother died. He blows gently at the steaming liquid in his hands. "I'm sorry," he offers.

"So, my mother *didn't* leave us?"

"Well, she did. Just not in the way you've imagined. Wilma was getting worse and worse. She was losing her sanity. She just couldn't take it anymore. And she killed herself. I wasn't there when it happened, but I could see it coming. I mean, this event had only served to compact the horrible memories of her previous pregnancy. It brought the earlier tragedy to surface once more."

"Earlier tragedy? What pregnancy are you talking about?"

"Your siblings?"

"I thought I was an only child."

This man's eyes roll back into his head, digging for the right memory fluttering around in there somewhere. "Your father never told you, did he?"

"I'm sure there's plenty my father never told me."

"I wouldn't worry about it. Like I said, your father was mostly irrelevant. Your mother confided a number of things in me during my visits, one of which was that her first two children, the twins, died in utero. But as it turns out, they are not of any particular consequence either, are they? It was all about *you*. And I have to say, your timing was impeccable."

You are twenty years old and this stranger knows more about you and your family than you ever have. You're not even sure what part of this conversation you want to resolve first. All that comes out of your mouth is, "Why wouldn't you tell anyone? You said you could see my mother's death coming. So why couldn't you even warn her own family?"

"Let's just say details like that weren't going to change anything for us. They were inconsequential. I was only visiting your mother so I could keep an eye on you."

"But once my mother was gone I never saw you again."

"Tell me, Epoch: how good is your memory?" You can't tell if it's an intentionally cruel joke on his part, but you stare at him like an idiot, your jaw hanging open. "Trust me when I say we've had plenty of other ways of monitoring you." With that, and quite abruptly, the man politely excuses himself from the table to use the bathroom, claiming his hot water could use a few more minutes to cool down anyway. He walks slowly, carefully yet purposefully toward the washrooms.

And you're left wondering about the situation you've now found yourself in. Is Zoltan Lintzel for real? More specifically, is the guy a total whack job or did you imagine him altogether? Did any of this just happen? The steaming water in the elephant mug is the only indication that anything at all might have occurred here.

You have a difficult time believing what you've just been told, but you sense a tiny schism within you suggesting Zoltan's narrative is true. Unless your childhood was all a dream, this is unquestionably the same man who visited your apartment years ago.

How worried should you be? If what you've been told is not true, Zoltan is clearly deluded enough that he believes what he's saying. Is Zoltan actually coming back? Is he — or worse, are *they* — watching you right now? Your knees are shaking. Should you leave the restaurant, escape while you still have the chance?

But you don't move. You're still in the same spot when Zoltan returns to the table. He sits himself back down across from you, but you cannot even make eye contact; instead you stare into the steaming water. He picks it up and takes a sip and you're left gaping at the circle of heat on the tabletop, watching it dissipate until it is gone entirely. "Perfect," he says contentedly. And then, "What, you cannot look at me?"

Without wavering you say, "No."

"So where are you looking then?"

"Sorry? I don't understand."

"You're very observant. I can tell as much." Zoltan softly places the mug back down on the table. "Listen, have you ever caught something out of the corner of your eye? You think you see something there but when you turn, it's gone?"

Instantly, you recall the lights you'd seen in the park. They were just as he describes: you thought you'd seen something moving, something shimmering. A shadowy glow, but as soon as you turned toward it, the light was no longer there.

"What that is, is the sliver of an alternate reality. Just a slice of an opening for only a fraction of a second, and always when you're not fully paying attention."

"An alternate reality? This is just what I was saying to my therapist: I really am losing my mind."

"You most definitely are not. Just listen closely to what I'm telling you. Alternate universes and parallel worlds are *real*. There's too much evidence to suggest otherwise. Just how many of them, I cannot be sure, but there is at least one. And it is all connected to the black hole that died ten thousand years ago."

Ten. Thousand. Years.

"But even though this other world and ours are technically separate planes, free to act independently from one another, they do still share a common level."

"Which is?"

"Well, that's where it starts to get interesting. Like I said, it all boils down to frequencies, really. Here—" he reaches behind him over to the next table and removes the ash tray, placing it on your table right next to the other one. "Let me explain." Zoltan braces a palm above each of the ash trays. "These are our two earths. For argument's sake, let's refer to them as *Earth-A* — with us and everything we know on it — and *Earth-B*. Neither one is technologically superior to the other. If you think about concepts such as gravity or weather patterns or the internet, both of these worlds would use the same rules and have the same constraints." Now he removes a napkin from the dispenser and holds it firmly. "So, let's pretend this serviette is the *internet*. You would consider this as one thing, correct? One concept? A single idea?"

"Sure, I guess."

"But—" Zoltan places the napkin on top of one of the ash trays and then places the second ash tray on top of that. "—now things have changed, haven't they?" He talks to you like some bad junior high science teacher would explain colored dye in water. "The internet is still a single thing, but only half of it is accessible to each ash tray, to each world. We only interact with half of the serviette. But think about what it is. It's porous, isn't it? Under the right conditions, what exists on one side of the serviette can potentially find its way to the other."

Strangely, you find yourself actually following along. You don't have to think of things like Reflecting pools or MP3s or secret handshakes or Morse code. "So what kind of conditions are you talking about?"

"Again, it's all about frequencies. We've found a frequency which can potentially be used to make contact with this parallel earth. It's the same frequency we were tracking thirty years ago until it hit the earth. And it's that very same frequency that makes up these slivers — the tears in reality — that arbitrarily appear in space-time. They say parallel lines can never meet, but that's simply untrue. There's always a way to accomplish something. Anything is possible."

"So, let me see if I'm following you here. These things I've seen, they are actually windows into other dimensions?"

"Not windows, no. They're more like doorways."

"Is that what you mean by tears in space-time? It's literally an opening from here to another world?"

"That's right," he says. Like it's no big deal.

"So, what is your purpose here? And what makes *me* so special?"

"These slivers — we like to call them slivers — they appear all over the world, but seemingly in very different places at completely different times. We're still trying to nail down the specifics of them. A real pattern has yet to be discovered. I haven't even seen one with my own eyes yet. But the idea is that if the right place and time are known for where and when a sliver would appear, we could activate a pre-planted device to "capture" it and keep the gate open in space-time long enough."

"Long enough? For what?"

"To enter, of course."

"What is this device you would use?"

Zoltan reaches into his pocket and takes out an iPhone. Without thinking, he taps on it a few times with a fingertip before passing it to you. You reach across the table and take a look. There's a picture of some sort of shoebox-shaped mechanical contraption sitting atop a well-lit table. It's not much to look at; mostly a jumble of wires, exposed circuitry, and missing buttons. "My team has developed this prototype technology that would potentially capture one of these slivers in reality, keeping it open for someone to cross through and, hopefully, back again."

Unimpressed, you slide the phone back to him. "What would you call something like this?"

"Uncreatively, we're calling it the Proto-Tech for the time being. It stands for prototype technology. And we think we're at the point now where it might actually work."

"You don't sound too convinced."

"We've been running as many tests and simulations that we can think of, trying to account for every potential risk. All sorts of things could go wrong here. Gravity from our own universe could leak into a parallel world creating an imbalance. Details like that, something that sounds so insignificant, could be disastrous. Do you understand?"

This man, this Zoltan Lintzel, has talked your ear off long enough now, you're at the point where you actually believe the outrageous ideas that are being presented to you. Up to this point in your life, you could never really comprehend most things, even the simplest of ideas, like the working mechanics of a doorknob, but for some reason you find yourself understanding all of this. It makes logical sense. "I guess what I'm still grappling with is this: why are you telling me all of these things? What do you actually *want* from me?"

"Remember that blip of energy we found in Coney Island? It was *you*. For some reason, you share the exact same energy signature as that cosmic light wave that passed through the earth twenty years ago. Cepik, I think maybe you are the *key* to getting to the other earth."

Zoltan takes one more sip of hot water. He seems to hold the liquid in his mouth longer than necessary, like he's trying to delay his next thought.

Finally, he swallows and says, "One hundred centuries ago, a black hole collapsed. A cosmic light wave hit the earth ten thousand years later; in the same instant, a baby boy was born."

ooo

Zoltan Lintzel left The UnDiner an hour ago and you've barely moved since he said goodbye. He offered to take you to his laboratory to see the device for yourself. *"Just give it a chance,"* he said. *"See if anything I've explained to you makes any sense at all. What's the harm?"* You declined, but he wrote the address down on a napkin — the "internet napkin" you'll call it — and reminded you to think about it again before leaving you alone with your thoughts.

You don't look at the napkin he left on the table until now. The mysterious laboratory is located somewhere in Queens; Zoltan has scribbled a five-digit address for you and he's noted: *GO TO BASEMENT*.

If you'd had any sleep at all in the last two days would any of this make any more sense?

On the back of the napkin is something else though; some other notes he'd scribbled. You don't know if this information is connected in any way or if he'd maybe just jotted down some ideas in his head as the two of you spoke. There are two phrases, neither of which makes much sense to you. He's written: *EPOCH-A* and *thisneverhappened*.

It feels like it would be impossible right now to be more confused than you were a minute ago, but there it is.

You officially have no idea what's going on.

WELCOME TO THE AIIB EXPERIENCE

Your landlord, Stanley, is waiting for you at the top of the first flight of stairs. Stanley's door is right there, and you're certain the man can tell who is coming simply by the pressure of the stair creaks and the swiftness of the footsteps. "Small!" He calls you Small because he's incapable of pronouncing your first name. "I gots a package for you. Big one. Been waiting all morning here."

You can't place his ethnicity, never could. Is Stanley Puerto Rican? Middle Eastern? Native American? Honestly, it's impossible to tell. Almond skin, squinty eyes, and curly hair growing from his head, neck, and shoulders. Like he's wearing some weird sort of fuzzy, hooded cape. He's easy to recognize since the only place you've ever seen him is at the top of these stairs. Sometimes he comes up to your floor if he's looking for the rent, but he's only ever wearing that yellowed wife beater. And through your door's peephole you can quickly identify the tattoo just under his clavicle: a crooked blue crown with one of the three points broken off. Maybe he comes from some obscure European royalty?

"A package? What's it look like?"

"Big one, I said. Very suspicious."

"Suspicious? I don't want a suspicious package."

"Small! You take it then figure it out. I no want it outside my door."

You see the box obscured behind him now; it is big. The delivery label on the side says something about AIIB. "Can you help me carry it upstairs?"

"I help you, yes. As long as no outside *my* door."

You've never been able to tell if his accent is really that thick and his English so poor, or if Stanley's just faking it. Because really, who talks like this outside of budget cop films?

ooo

Your apartment door is still not fixed. It remains how you left it: leaning up against the door frame with the large crack splintered down the middle. Stanley says to not worry; he'll get to it soon. He helps you set the large box down in your apartment before quickly heading back to play gargoyle at the top of the stairs, though your landlord has left part of himself behind in the form of dark sweat stains on the heavy cardboard. Your name and address are typed onto a label stuck to the top of the box and you wonder how they knew where to deliver the package when all you ever did was click the SIGN-UP NOW button online. Running your fingernail across the tape, you open the box and look inside.

The contents are covered with a thin layer of Styrofoam peanuts but it's not enough to keep things from bumping around. Inside are a bunch of computer parts and a photocopied instruction manual, about eight pages in total, stapled in the corner and with hand-drawn diagrams. Very carefully, you remove the equipment from the box, matching the components up with their labeled diagrams: Monitor; CPU Tower; Camera/Scanner; VR Headset with Goggles; Motion-Control Gloves and Boots; Control Pad; Power and Ethernet Cables. Each and every piece has the AIIB logo on it.

Why are you receiving all of this equipment? All you did was click the button. Maybe you *did* somehow pay for all of this and just don't remember?

Taped to the monitor is a handwritten note, informing you all setup instructions will be provided as soon as the screen and tower have been plugged in.

You lift the Murphy bed up into the wall to make more room and then plug in the CPU tower and monitor, as well as connecting the control pad, which is kind of a cross between a mouse and a joystick from an old 1980's gaming system. It takes a minute for everything to start happening and you watch with bated breath.

The black screen suddenly flickers with multicolored bars, then they turn grey and finally stark white before a video recording begins playing. A man's face and shoulders slowly materialize. You don't recognize him, but he is probably around fifty and has thinning hair and glasses. His front teeth remind you of a chipmunk, as do his puffy cheeks. You can see he's wearing a sport jacket and tie, but the image is cut off below his shoulders.

He speaks now, though his eyes are looking a little off to one side, probably staring at the recording device. "Congratulations on signing up and welcome to the AIIB experience! Please allow me to be your guide and I'll assist you in getting started. First things first, you'll need to sign up. AIIB is the world's first truly real MMORPG experience so you won't want to wait to get started."

An AIIB login window appears with an onscreen keyboard below it. The voice continues, "To log in to your account for the first time, please enter the username and password provided to you. Keep in mind, these are case-sensitive."

Were you given a username or password? Not as far as you can recall. You think back to when you signed up; it was yesterday morning after your session with Gideon. You clicked the button and went to work. But are you missing something? What else happened? You search the box — inside and out — for some sort of code, but there's nothing at all that jumps out at you.

You wonder if maybe an email with the information had been sent to you. Booting up your computer, you wait a few long minutes before clicking into your inbox and finding nothing.

What could it be? You pace to the window and back again, hands in your pockets, trying to figure it out. From your pocket, you pull out the napkin Zoltan Lintzel handed you and you take another look. There's the address for his laboratory in Queens and written on the back is what didn't make any sense to you before:

EPOCH-A

thisneverhappened

Could that be a username and password? Zoltan never told you he was connected to AIIB but it's just strange enough to feel like you're on to something. With the onscreen keypad, you carefully type these into the two fields.

The voice says, "Welcome, Epic Small."

The login window dissolves into the AIIB logo — this time spelled "A-ii-B" — with the familiar slogan below it: Don't Just Play Now — LIVE Now!

The man's voice returns, though it feels more natural this time, rather than some pre-programmed introduction; as if he's right in the apartment. The company of the man's voice makes you miss your father a little less.

"Okay, so all you've got left to do is finish setting up the components that have been provided. Don't worry Epic, I'll keep walking you through it. Just follow my instructions."

After only a few minutes, you have all of the equipment set up; the camera is attached to the monitor and you're wearing the virtual reality headset (basically headphones attached to large yellow plastic goggles and a tiny microphone that sits above your lip, just under your nose) and the motion control gloves and boots (which aren't so much boots as they are socks, made from some thin, synthetic material). The goggles display exactly what's on the monitor no matter which way you turn your head. At the top, it tells you this is called your *Vis-Screen*. And the gloves perform the same functions as the control pad so you're no longer tied down to anything.

"Now you are ready to create your avatar," the voice informs you. It's pretty simple actually, as the computer's camera scans your face and head by rotating 360 degrees around you on a long extender. Your avatar looks just like you, and you customize it with jeans, white sneakers, and a short-sleeved t-shirt. You're given the option of adding a logo to the front of the shirt. There are a million image options to search through but you eventually type in *lovehunter* and the all-too-familiar Whitesnake album cover appears; the one which hung on the wall in Gideon's office. You select the image of the naked girl on the snake and decide you're satisfied enough with the look of your avatar.

You tap the LIVE NOW! button at the bottom of the screen with one glove. Everything dissolves again and you wait for whatever's loading to finish.

You wait. You stare up at the single light bulb on the ceiling, the length of chain hanging lifelessly. And you wait.

Nothing else is happening. But just when you think the computer isn't doing anything at all, you realize what you're seeing. This *is* the game. This is your apartment, but it's not.

Some of the details are wrong: the Murphy bed is pulled down again when you know for certain you'd just lifted it into the wall a few minutes ago; the Sinequan bottle is not on your bedside table where you always leave it; there's a tall floor lamp in the corner of the room and an area rug below you; the bathroom door is open when you're always in the habit of keeping it closed. Your apartment door is no longer broken and is back on its hinges. The smell is off too, which is when you realize the microphone device under your nose must also somehow create scent for the user, or more like the sense of scents somehow. The smell of fried chicken outside your window is gone, replaced now by what seems to be coconuts and the ocean.

You almost fall over because of the realism of it all. You're there, but you're not. You're really here, though it's all the same. Not everything is completely realistic though; upon investigating, you find objects like the refrigerator door and kitchen cupboards don't open at all.

At the top of the Vis-Screen is a small menu. There are options such as MESSAGE, HOME, PLACER, FINDER, and SAVE, though you're not sure what any of these might do exactly.

It takes some getting used to, but your avatar doesn't require you to walk or turn around in order to move; you simply use the gloves to guide yourself. The boots seem to be used strictly for actions like jumping and kicking. Making your way outside the virtual apartment and into the hall, you take note of the details as you go; most of your surroundings are accurately representing their real-world equivalents but some things continue to be a little off. Some of the details have been altered: the hand rail on the stairs — the one *you're* familiar with — has been worn down and scratched up from use, while here it feels as smooth as can be when you slide the palm of your hand along it. The front door to the building is now bright white. There are some trees along Mermaid Avenue which shouldn't be here. The fried chicken restaurant below your window is definitely gone; in its place is a nail salon called Cutie's.

There are some other people milling about, not as many folks as you're likely to see on a normal day, but enough that you don't feel as though you're experiencing this world by yourself. These must be other users. There's a woman across Mermaid Avenue who catches your eye. She sits on the stoop of a building; her head turns from one side to the other and back again. Over and over, like she's watching cars drive past that aren't actually there. You cross the street for a closer look, something you know you would never do in the real world. This woman is older, the lines on her weathered face give her years away, her lips are thin, and her eyes are wide. The dark mascara makes them appear even larger. Her hands are folded neatly in her lap. She raises one to acknowledge your presence, though does not look your way. There's something unusual about this person, but you cannot quite place what it might be. Another woman walks past, wrapped in a heavy mink coat with a big, furry headband sitting atop her head, like something one would wear in the dead of winter's cold. Or maybe in Siberia. On the other side of the street is a boy, maybe twelve years old, who opens the front door to one building and takes a look inside before moving along to the next one, now opening that door too. And he keeps going, making his way down Mermaid Avenue and around the corner onto 29th Street.

You look again at the onscreen menu and decide to tap the HOME button. A menu pops up asking: Do You Wish To Mark This As Home? You click YES and there's a happy little ping! sound. You try the PLACER button next and a dropdown menu appears with a list of about thirty different locations.

This must be some kind of quick travel mode used to access a variety of sites within the AIIB world. You click on one: Wall, South Dakota.

After what appears to be a bright flash of light, you are standing in some closed off yard, in front of a large wooden booth with an animatronic gorilla playing what sounds like *Pop Goes the Weasel* on a dusty piano. Its broomstick arms scrape gracelessly up and down along the keyboard. Behind you is a miniature Mount Rushmore and you spot another animatronic, this time a dancing jackalope. Weird.

You pull up the PLACER menu again and this time you try Neuchâtel, Switzerland. When you see the name, you recognize it from your discussion in The UnDiner this morning with Zoltan: this was the city he claimed to be from. You tap the button and after another burst of white light, you're now on a cobblestone street outside some quaint European shops and restaurants. There are gondolas running on wires high above you, and, just beyond the rooftops, you can see a funicular escalating up the side of a mountain.

Scrolling through the PLACER options again, you notice one for Versailles, Kentucky. In your dreams, you live in the country. Someplace like Kentucky sounds about right. You select this one and everything around you quickly fades to white again before you reappear in a field of grass. A dilapidated fence and an old barn are only footsteps away, and you recognize them instantly. You breathe in deeply and taste something sweet in the air: corn; grass clippings; the afternoon breeze. There are horses in the distance and a big sky as blue as blue can be. Exactly like in your dreams. It's perfect here. This is perfect.

God, you think. You don't ever want to be anywhere else. This is what Abi was trying to tell you about, wasn't it? *"It's all about being happy,"* she said.

You take a minute to feel the tall grass with your fingertips. You lay yourself down, spread your arms out wide and watch the textbook white, puffy clouds roll by. You breathe in deeper than you've ever breathed before. And you don't want to get up.

You know you're really just lying on the floor of your apartment right now, but you never want to get up.

This is when your serenity is interrupted by a tiny noise. The virtual world alerts you with a *bee-dee-deep*, letting you know you have a message. You tap the glowing MESSAGE window and the voice returns.

"So now that you've explored a few of the pre-selected locales, why not try the Finder Box and begin searching even further into the world of AIIB?"

The FINDER icon glows now and you tap it, opening up a search window with a blinking cursor. After considering your options for a moment, you begin typing:

dullahan theater bushwick new york|

You hit ENTER and the next thing you know you're standing outside the theater, immediately recognizing its thick copper doors. You see the same angel designs embossed into the metal, but the imagery appears less detailed, more simplified. Flatter. There is still no poster for the *Duality of Three* outside the theater. Trying the handle, you find the door doesn't budge at all. It doesn't feel like it's locked however, more like it is simply one solid construct, just like your kitchen drawers.

Tapping the FINDER once more you type in:

memorial coloradoI

ENTER. There is no white light. You're still on the same street in Bushwick. Nothing happens. The FINDER box reads:

search results = 0

You type the words again, slower this time to be certain you're spelling it correctly:

memorial coloradoI

ENTER. Still no results. The cursor continues to blink contemptuously at you. You tap the HOME button and are instantly back outside your apartment on Mermaid Avenue. Across the street, the same woman from before continues to sit on the stoop, her head still turning back and forth watching invisible cars go by. Again, her hand rises to acknowledge you. And then it hits you: the stark realization that here in this virtual Coney Island, your prosopagnosia is gone. The memory triggers you'd logged away — the slight hunch in how she sits, the lines on her face, and her wide eyes with the dark mascara — are not significant. They are simply superfluous details, unnecessary in your recognition. It's like your condition, the cognitive disorder you've endured your entire life and grown as accustomed to as a sort of sixth sense, does not apply here. To put it bluntly: you *remember* her. Just as anyone might remember anyone else.

Perhaps it's because the real world and the online world of AIIB are not the same things. These are not real faces but avatars digitally created by their users. It's almost like the AIIB system really *does* make life easier for you. And maybe that's the whole point of it all. AIIB is all about being happy. Staring at the building that is and isn't your apartment building, you consider the ramifications of everything AIIB might be suggesting. Suddenly, the MESSAGE button on your Vis-Screen flares. You click it and a message appears:

Florian_V requests a private chat. Accept? |

Hesitantly, you type YES and you're immediately approached from behind by another avatar. This one is spectacularly over-the-top: a shining gold suit of space armor beneath a dark hooded cloak. He has large red-tinted goggles on and some sort of mouthpiece so it's difficult to decipher what he looks like exactly. He towers above you in giant golden boots too, maybe standing seven-feet tall. "I think the two of us need to have a chat," he says. His words are tinny and echo a little, but you can tell right away this is the same voice as the one you heard when you first logged on to AIIB; the same one that has sporadically been walking you through this world.

"Zoltan Lintzel? Is that you?"

The mysterious golden space knight doesn't flinch. His speech is otherworldly, and he staggers his sentences oddly. "Though I do know Zoltan Lintzel, we are not the same. Zoltan doesn't know his way around the

AIIB system like I do."

"So, who am I speaking with?"

"You can call me Florian-Five. I am AIIB's creator. I've worked with Zoltan Lintzel for years now. We've known one another since Switzerland."

"The virtual world Switzerland?"

"Not at all. We go back much further than AIIB."

"Did you know my mother too?"

He pauses. "No. That was never my part in this." Florian-Five reaches out toward you and wraps a heavy metal arm around your miniscule shoulders. "Come. Let us walk."

You were perfectly happy where you'd been standing, but you now find yourself moving against your will. If Florian-Five really is the creator of this world, then surely he must have some extraordinary, demigod-like powers here. He seems content however, at least for now, to simply lead you around the block. "As I was saying, your mother and I never met. She was Zoltan's responsibility. My responsibility is with all the tech stuff: designing the tracking devices, scanners, drones, and other various, highly experimental gadgetry you may have seen. As well as the idea for an exploratory multi-universal virtual platform." He spreads his big arms wide, gesturing toward the world around you. "Which was the impetus for all of *this* you now see."

You turn a corner and there is something noticeably amiss in your field of vision. You're looking down Surf Avenue and the horizon line has changed. There are multiple buildings missing: large fifteen-story apartments you never thought you'd been paying attention to when they were right there every day. But as soon as they're gone you can't help but notice the variance. "So, you designed this world?"

"It's not so much designed as mostly just bringing life to my drone scans. But I can't take all the credit. Florian-Four obviously had a hand in this too." He says this with a noticeable amount of curiosity, like even he doesn't have quite all the answers he wants.

"Obviously," you repeat, though you're utterly unsure why this is in any way evident. "So, are you going to tell me what this place is really? I mean, what am I supposed to be doing here?"

"Do you like what you've seen so far? Are you happy?"

You think back to the grassy field of Versailles. You can almost smell the husks of corn still. Abi's voice echoes in your head once more; the simple answer she gave you when you asked what the whole point AIIB was. *It's all about being happy.* You look up into Florian-Five's red goggles and see your avatar's face looking back at you. It's an unusual sensation to recognize yourself in such a way. You nod in approval of it all.

"Isn't that enough then?"

"But why do I feel this way here? No video game should be able to make me feel how I'm feeling."

"Video game?" He exhales a short, derisive laugh like he's surprised you don't comprehend everything so far. "I told you, this is an exploratory multi-universal virtual platform. Only a select few people have ever been inside AIIB. The only users are the ones we've personally invited."

This is not what Abi made it out to be. She made no mention of exclusivity.

He says, "I understand you and Zoltan had quite the conversation this morning. But there was one very important piece of information he did *not* share with you."

"Which is?"

"The *truth*, of course"

"I feel like I'm being given all the hints about what the truth is, but so far the truth, the *actual* truth, is being withheld from me."

Florian-Five places a weighty palm on your shoulder once again. With his free hand, he pulls the hood off and lifts the goggles, though it doesn't do you much good since underneath the costume, his avatar has some weird, emotionless C-3PO droid head. "First, let me say that I've never actually had to explain any of this to anyone before so it might come out funny. To be honest with you, there's a very good chance it will just sound stupid." He pauses. "Zoltan Lintzel suspected that you, Cepik Small, the son of Leo and Wilma Small, are actually from another world. A parallel world to our own."

"You're kidding, right?"

"I'm not."

"That *does* sound stupid. Is this why Zoltan kept talking about alternate realities?"

"That's right. And he told your mother as much too. He told your mother everything, when he probably shouldn't have. But she fascinated him so much he couldn't help himself. He gets like that when something uber-sciency is presented to him. But it was *this* idea — the idea that Wilma had given birth to something not of this world — that she couldn't take anymore. It's what drove her completely mad."

You try to chew the words up before they come out, but you can't do it. You ask, "Can you tell me more about my mother?"

"I'm not sure what it is you might wish to hear." He remains extraordinarily motionless as he speaks. "Though it must be a troublesome thing to be responsible for bringing something into this world when it was only ever meant for a different one. I don't know what that might do a person. I don't imagine it would be very pleasant to carry this knowledge with you. You might always be wondering, *Is there something else inside me?* You might feel uncomfortable just thinking about it, to the point where you can't *stop* thinking about it. Like an itch you're only trying to ignore. Wilma Small couldn't ignore that itch any longer. It was the reason why your mother eventually decided to end her life. Though her death was inconsequential."

"That's just what Zoltan Lintzel told me."

"Well, sadly, it's true. The breach in reality is the thing that *really* mattered to us. It was why we came to New York twenty years ago. Our suspicions proved to be correct, and we've been tracking you closely ever since."

"So, if I am from another world like you say I am, how did I get to *this* one?"

"I imagine Zoltan told you all about that cosmic energy wave?"

"The one that was created ten thousand years ago when the black hole died?"

"You were paying attention."

"I'm not sure Zoltan really ever explained to me what its purpose was."

"To simplify his words, it duplicated everything it touched. Basically, when this cosmic energy was born it created an entire parallel universe at the same time. Though there will always be some differences along the way."

"How do you mean?"

"Well, like *you*." Even through the mask, it's obvious Florian-Five can tell you're not entirely following the path he's attempting to lay out before you. "Think of it this way: imagine the earth is like a printing press. And the newspapers or books are being spewed out one after another. *Chuckety-chuckety-chuck.* Suppose that ten thousand years after the collapse of our black hole, the resulting wave of cosmic energy hit this printing press. The pages that are printed at the precise moment the variance occurs would not be the same as the others; certain aspects of the story might be altered in different and very unique ways. You are that one unique book."

You're trying not to take all of this at face value, convincing yourself none of this is really happening, but the scary truth of it all is that it's actually making more and more sense to you. And the questions that continue to pop into your head seem to be multiplying by the second, like a wave of cosmic energy keeps hitting your brain. "But if I was meant to be born into this other world then who or what was meant for this one?"

"Well, the *easy* answer is you, of course. The *other* you, that is."

"Another me?"

"Tell me, what do you think the word 'parallel' means? What do you think could have possibly occurred when this invisible wave of energy struck our planet the exact same moment your mother gave birth?"

"I don't know."

"The you from here was born over there. And the you from there was born here."

You try to follow his words, making indistinguishable connections in your head. You hadn't really thought of it like that before now. How could you have possibly ever thought to? "Who else is aware of all of this?"

"As far as we knew there was no one else. But then your father said something interesting to you a few days ago, didn't he?"

Your father knew. In the hospice, amidst the haunting sounds of nature CDs and the buzzing of insects, he told you as much. He spoke to you in what was probably an exceptional moment of lucidity, just teetering on the edge of what was reality and what wasn't: "*I just want to see my son.*"

You are like a shadow. And you don't know when you'll fade away.

"Some things a father just knows," Florian-Five continues. "Of course, lies and truths are not physical things. There is no limit to the number of people who might hold them."

Identity is not reality.

You take a moment to break your concentration free from this barrage of jumbled information. This is when you notice you are floating high above Mermaid Avenue. Florian-Five is keeping you both aloft. You can see it all for what feels like the first time: your apartment; Luna Park; the office of Gideon Flat. There's a giant wooden elephant by the park entrance, obviously another of AIIB's variances. This one though, probably close to eight stories, is not as insignificant of an alteration. You look out toward Bushwick and Woodhaven. Back to Manhattan where one of the original World Trade Center towers still stands.

"Think of all of this as the world you were *meant* for. Some of it better than you know, some of it worse."

"But how am I supposed to get there?"

"You've seen the answer yourself."

The lights, you think. "Zoltan told me they were doors."

"That's right. And maybe you know of a special place where you've seen these doors? A place where both you and your alternate self would know where to go. That's where the best one would be. Which is why I'm telling you this."

You dwell upon it. *Sliver* is the term Zoltan was throwing around in the diner this morning. Obviously, the first place you think of is the park in Woodhaven. But these scientist guys say they've been keeping their eyes on you your whole life. They can see everything, can't they? Just like you now, in your current virtual vantage point above Coney Island. So why wouldn't they also know about your field trip with Abi to the park the other night? Maybe it has something to do with the break-in at your apartment? It happened just before you and Abigail went to Penelope Park.

"You're very observant," Zoltan praised of you. *"You think you see something out of the corner of your eye, but you turn and it's gone."* You saw the lights in the park. Lights that were really more like shadows. *"Just a slice of an opening to an alternate reality but only for a fraction of a second, and always when you're not fully paying attention."*

You're trying to pay attention now. But there's almost too much to consider. Not only what's right and what's wrong, but also what's real and what's not.

Florian-Five keeps going, "And if *you* know, then your *other you* will know too. Like I said, this is the world you were meant for. And if it's a world you want, then the decision is yours. Imagine you could simply make this decision. You could leave everything behind and begin anew like it was all just a dream. Just like this never happened. There isn't one single path, or even the right path. There is only *your* path."

You didn't notice the landscape shifting as he spoke, but once he's finished you realize you're back on the sidewalk in front of your virtual apartment building. He tells you to go to the basement in Queens — the same place Zoltan Lintzel had begged you to visit — to see the Proto-Tech for yourself. To ensure you know what you're looking for, a hologram image like something out of *Star Wars* appears in the palm of his hand: it's the same device Zoltan had shown you on his iPhone in The UnDiner. He assures you that once you see the apparatus, it will be enough to convince you. And then, Florian-Five's enigmatic golden avatar disappears from sight, presumably having logged out from the world of AIIB.

The woman on the stoop across Mermaid Avenue continues to swivel her head back and forth, watching the invisible traffic go by. *Alternate worlds*, you think. *What are the possibilities, truly?* You think back to when you were in Versailles, lying on the grass and watching the clouds roll by. It was like being in a dream. Specifically, just like being in your *own* dreams. Everything was so peaceful there, like it was where you were really, truly meant to be. You'd never really felt quite so content before. And you wonder if you'd ever been there with Reya. You feel like maybe you had been.

This is when it occurs to you that your other-Earth self must also feel the exact same way about somewhere specific. Is he unhappy too? Where would he choose to come if he were given the proper chance?

If he was you and you were him, where would you *both* be happy? Did Luca Desplante III have the right idea when he proposed the switch to Tristan Montminy?

"Let us go our separate ways," Luca insisted. "However dissimilar our paths were meant to be, let us now follow the path of each other. Let us now live as another man. If only for a moment."

ooo

Your avatar's footsteps feel heavy as you slowly plod up the stairwell. The door to your apartment is back on of course, since it had never been broken in the AIIB world. You feel like you should have a sense of being repaired yourself, but you don't. You feel less confused for some reason, if that makes any sense, but still far from being complete.

You turn the handle carefully and open the door. The rusty creak of the hinges you've grown used to over the years is not there; the door swings open silently. There's somebody else here now. At first you think it's a mirror you see in front of the window across the room. Another addition that's missing in the real world. But the reflection does not move as you do. Bewildered and a little frightened to see someone in your apartment, you stop for a moment before slowly moving closer.

You hope it's your father, but you know it's not.

He continues to stand there, this reflection of yours. This burning, luminous shadow. The details of his avatar are the same as yours, even wearing the *Lovehunter* t-shirt. His features are identical. You know now why there had been close to four pages of description in *The Third* when Tristan Montminy met Luca Desplante III for the very first time. You're not so good with words, but you feel like you could write ten pages describing this moment.

The truth suddenly pours into you.

It's you. And finally, because you have no idea what to say, he says: "We all have a shadow, don't we?"

You want to be gone. You tap the EXIT button on your Vis-Screen as quickly as you can. It's too jarring to see someone in your apartment, reminding you of how violated you felt when that man in the houndstooth coat and furry mask broke in. You're asked: Do You Really Want To Leave AIIB? and you confirm even faster: YES

Yes, you do.

And you're gone. You're out. You pull the headset and goggles off, and immediately confirm there isn't actually someone inside your real apartment.

No one but you. Or, no one but *this* you, to be more accurate. The door is off its hinges again; the bed is back up in the wall. There's the humming of the AIIB equipment still running and you pull the cord from the socket forcefully.

In spite of everything, you can't shake the feeling that you're still being watched. But there must have been a short time when you obviously weren't. Two nights ago: on Friday night, you and Abigail Ayr went to the park in Woodhaven and saw something. Ghosts. Slivers. Shadows. Whatever they wish to be categorized as.

You close the window and with your AIIB gloves still on, you go into the kitchen and open the garbage can.

ooo

You called Abigail and asked her to come meet you at your usual table at The UnDiner as soon as she could. She came even sooner than you thought she might.

When she sits down, you waste no time in unfurling the toilet paper you'd tossed into your kitchen garbage a few nights ago. You show her your discovery.

She looks at the contents with disappointment. "It's a dead bug. So what?"

"This isn't a *real* bug. Take a closer look. It's metal and plastic. It has tiny bits of circuitry. It's mechanical."

She stares closer. "Some sort of—*what*, then?"

"I think it's a spy drone. And I'm pretty sure it's been watching me." She squirms a little in her seat, maybe afraid you're not who she thought you were. Like a terrorist or some sort of fugitive war criminal. Someone she definitely does not wish to be involved with. "Listen, a lot has happened to me since you took me to that park." You explain to her how you've started playing AIIB. She seems happy for you. Or happy for herself. You can't quite tell. You tell her they sent you an email; how you clicked on the sign-up button and that was it. You were in. "It was weird though. How the computer and all the equipment and instructions just showed up on my doorstep."

"It *is* strange," she says. You can't tell from Abi's reaction whether it happened the same way with her or if the furtive, special delivery was simply unique to your own circumstances.

"But that's hardly the weirdest part of it all." Next, you tell Abigail everything about the scientists, how Zoltan Lintzel spoke with you here at The UnDiner. And how the game's actual designer contacted you inside the virtual world.

You're gesturing madly, just realizing now that you're still wearing the AIIB gloves and probably spitting all over the insect drone in front of you.

"You look tired. When did you last sleep?"

"Honestly, I've lost track of my normal routine." You ask her, "What do you know about parallel worlds?"

"Like in a video game?"

"This isn't about video games, Abi."

"But you said that AIIB—"

"Listen to me. AIIB was never designed to be escapism as virtual reality fantasies—" You stop.

This moment here. This is the moment when someone is about to explain everything about just how incredible something is by first stating what it isn't. And in this moment, the other person has no questions because they're simply waiting within the moment for the explanation to come. And in this paused moment you can't help but look at the doe-eyed Abigail Ayr and compare all of the things she isn't currently aware of with your ability to coherently explain them to her. There's no turning back the clock after what is about to come, after you open your mouth and finish your thought. There is no way this girl can feasibly remain the same person she is now. She will be forever changed. Her reality will be altered. You almost feel sorry for her because of what you're about to say. For all the ways in which you might potentially ruin her. And when this moment comes to its conclusion you say: "AIIB's purpose is to make contact with people from another world. A *parallel* world." And you tell her as honestly as you can: "These people are telling me I'm from that world."

So, then it's done. It's said. You've said it.

Abi continues to stare at you, like she knew something somewhere was amiss somehow and she's finally, unwaveringly, placing her finger on it.

"I knew you were special," she says, recalling her words from the first time you spoke. It was only a week ago on this world, but you're starting to get the feeling like it might have been much longer somewhere else. Why else would you have recognized her so easily every time your paths crossed? "But honestly, I really don't have any idea at all about what it is you're telling me right now."

You reach behind you for the glass ashtray on the next table. With the AIIB gloves on, the ashtray feels lighter, softer than it should. Placing it next to the other ashtray on the table you try your best to explain this as Zoltan did before you.

"Let's call these Earth-A and Earth-B." You rotate them around one another then stack them one on top of the other before remembering Zoltan had also said something about a napkin too. What was the deal with the napkin? He called it a serviette, you do remember that much. Abi continues to stare at you like you're totally nuts. "Ah, never mind."

So then finally she says, "Two earths, huh? Maybe I can start piecing all of this together, but you've got to help me out a bit more, man."

"Tell me what would help."

"Well. So—okay. You say you were born on another world, right?"

"No, I was born *here*." You hold one of the ashtrays up, flipping it over from side to side. "But I should have been born *here*. On this parallel earth instead."

"How'd the mix up happen?"

One hundred centuries ago a black hole collapsed. A cosmic light wave hit the earth ten thousand years later; in the same instant, a baby boy named Cepik Small found himself born in the wrong place.

As Zoltan Lintzel ambiguously informed you: Your timing was impeccable.

"Frequencies," you tell her simply, just as Zoltan had said.

"And AIIB? You said its purpose was for making contact with other worlds?"

"I think so. But not plural. Just one world: *my world*." You stack the two ashtrays upon one another again, trying to remember everything that has been explained to you in the last twenty-four hours. But you stop when you catch the logo on the backs of the motion-control gloves as you whirl them around in front of you. A-ii-B. And then it occurs to you. "Abi, it's not AIIB."

"What's not AIIB?"

"It's not pronounced AIIB. That's a Roman numeral. Two i's for the number two." From your rucksack, you take out a pen and you write out the name on a napkin:

A II B

"It sounds like *A-two-B*. But the number two is acting as the word *TO*: as an expression of movement in a particular direction or place. A *to* B. Like the ashtrays. Zoltan referred to them as *Earth-A* and *Earth-B*. The truth about AIIB has been there the whole time. Earth A to Earth B!"

She thinks about it for a moment. The evening heat in the diner is starting to intensify. "So, the in-game world is actually a real-life parallel world? That is fucked."

"I'm pretty sure it's more like a meeting place for those of us on *both* worlds."

"Well, that's kinda fucked too, Epic. It still doesn't make a whole lot of sense to me. So, I'm talking to an avatar of someone from a different reality. Then what? What are you supposed to do with that?"

You tell Abi about the ghosts she's seen in Penelope Park. And about the shadows and the slivers and how they're really all just the same thing: doorways to this other world. To your world.

And then without really considering any longer — maybe because she simply doesn't want to consider *anything* anymore — Abigail says, "Well, let's get back to the park, Rainbow."

"Right now?"

"Yep. Right now. Before I realize I'm a total idiot for believing any of this could possibly be real."

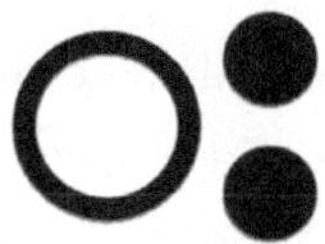

THE IN-BETWEENS

You've been staring out this window for an hour now and nothing so far. The only sign that anything at all had been inside this treehouse since you were last here is the fresh spider webs you swallowed on your way in. Again, you and Abi rode the F and C-Trains before begging another passerby to give the two of you a lift closer to the park. At least this time Abigail sat in the front beside the driver. He was a chatty one, questioning the both of you about books you've read. Apparently, he worked as a graphic artist, designing covers for second-print runs of novels nobody had ever read the first time around. You asked if he'd ever heard of *The Third* by Jean Trepanier but he had no clue whatsoever.

This time when you emerged from the same narrow walkway and entered Penelope Park, Abi described how she felt like a gladiator in the Roman Coliseum; how the surrounding houses might contain emperors and rich merchants who sneered at you as you entered and were waiting for nothing more than for you to die. Hoping you'd be slain upon their battlefield. *Let the dead, brown grass run red with the blood of these two!* You only commented on how you still felt warm and fuzzy here.

The rain is almost upon you now, you can smell it in the air. The last time it rained in New York was the same night you were punched in the face outside the Starfish Room. That was a pretty low point but you can admit now just how unaware you were of the extent to which things could get worse. Abi has kicked her boots off again, but she leaves her army jacket on. There's still that cat hair on her sleeve.

"Do you want to go out there?" Abi asks, gesturing her head out toward the playground.

"Not really," you admit. The lack of slivers or shadows or doorways or whatever makes you uneasy. Like everything you thought you'd just learned was a dream. Just like it never happened. You think if you saw something right now, one of those same shadowy flickers you'd seen two nights ago, you'd have more adrenaline coursing through you. Maybe the new drugs you're on — or the lack of old drugs — are making you feel like you can't even trust yourself anymore? You ask her, "You kind of dodged the question the first time, but can you tell me now what it was you've seen out here?"

"I told you already. *Things.*"

"But only because you don't believe in ghosts, right?"

She cracks her knuckles as discreetly as she can. Her fingers, her toes. "Sure." Her eyes flitter about, hoping to see something.

You recall the light you thought you'd seen in the field the other night. The shadowy, candlelight glow. A strange inverted haze. A miasma, neither hard nor soft. The presence that was gone just as soon as you'd felt it materialize.

"Maybe we're looking too hard," she suggests. "Didn't that scientist tell you it happens when you're not paying attention?"

That is exactly what Zoltan Lintzel had told you in The UnDiner. If he was ever actually there in the first place, that is. Instead of answering Abi's question, you propose this idea to her: "But what if I never was talking to a scientist in the restaurant? I mean, I could be that crazy person who's always talking to himself, couldn't I? The guy people go out of their way to avoid. I mean, there's hardly ever anyone but me in The UnDiner."

"That's because it sucks. Trust me, I've been to bad diners before and that one takes the shit cake."

"It's not that bad."

"It is, Epic. But maybe you *are* crazy. I'm certainly not the best judge." She grabs her boots and tugs at the sleeve of your hoodie. "Come on. Let's get a little bit closer."

You give in and venture down from the treehouse, back over the fence, and out toward the playground. The dry gravel crunches under your weight, but again Abigail refuses to cross the playground's perimeter; she stops and stands barefoot, scrunching her tiny toes into the wild, unkempt grass.

Still you sense nothing.

You wait. You turn and lock eyes, really taking in one another for perhaps the very first time. There is only this short distance between you, though you're just far enough apart that you're comfortable sharing the moment. Any farther or any closer and it would be unnerving. All at once she's beautiful and undesirable; delicate and unwavering; guarded and vulnerable. And there's something else deep inside Abigail Ayr. You feel it. Some dark, sinewy thing is twisting within her slight frame. You can sense it, but you are also ignorant toward its origins and intentions.

She watches you with matching intensity. You worry a little about what she might be sensing, whether she can pick up on your flaws, mistakes, and secrets, however insignificant any of them might be. And Abi's lip quivers now, as if detecting something inside you, but for only a microsecond before something else catches her attention.

This is what you were waiting for, right? Something out of the corner of your eye, but only when you're least expecting it. And always when you're not paying full attention.

There's fear in her reaction. She whispers, "Epic, what is that?" Abigail points a shaking finger behind where you're standing.

You turn to see only the dull glimmer of the playground slide. But then you cock your head only marginally and there's suddenly, and most certainly, something else there.

"I saw something move," she says apprehensively. "There was something there."

Taking one cautious step closer, there's a rustling as soon as your foot touches back down on the gravel. You see a furry striped tail. It's a raccoon, darting through the playground, already halfway across the park.

Abi doesn't want to admit she was actually frightened and she laughs a stupid laugh. "I'm sorry," she says. "Let's refocus." She takes your hands into her own and the two of you begin your dance anew. It's a dance which requires as little movement as possible so you're not preoccupied by whatever might exist around you, but you're also simultaneously cognizant of it all.

There's a feeling. It's happening again, you can sense it. Abigail can too. You both know as soon as you turn it will be gone so you silently agree to keep concentrating on one another instead. This thing — to you, a shadow — flickers to your left, but you don't break away.

Then there is another, this time to your right. Still, you don't lose your concentration on the girl before you. Then another. And another. You feel these shadows flickering all around you now. You know Abi feels them too because her gaze loosens; she quivers. Stay with me, you say to her with your eyes. She steps back just a little, seemingly unintentionally, maybe afraid of what it is you're both experiencing right now.

Identity is not reality.

But then you're the one who goes and breaks first.

And you're astonished. You see it there in the night sky. Just over Abi's perfectly sweat-streaked brow and her red-brown eyes. You crane your neck only half an inch, and look past her.

Mere yards away, between this girl and treehouse, you see it.

At first, it's just a ripple. Like a clear, flimsy screen blowing in the wind. Or like the surface of a nearly-still pond. But upon staring for only seconds at the anomaly, you see it more as a shadowy shimmer, stitched into nothing but the air.

This tiny patch of sky shudders and wavers a little more than everything surrounding it.

Images within begin to dance gently. Now, where the treehouse should be, there is nothing there. In fact, the entire tree is missing. The house is still in its place, but it is different too. A little less worn. A fresher coat of paint. A warmer light inside.

And within this sliver, you hear the raindrops patter and trickle off leaves. You can smell the peeling tree bark. You know what it is you're experiencing: this sliver is the same thing — the same piece of reality — but in an alternate world.

It is partly what should be there but also what shouldn't. Everything within this patch is sort of in-between your reality. Noticeable, but only in tiny ways. And though the in-betweens are not your world, you think they just might be. You think they *could* be.

But then her voice throws you off a little. "Epic—" Lost in all of this, even if she's been right in front of you, you'd forgotten all about Abigail Ayr.

But you don't look at her. Instead, you step right past her. You don't want to miss whatever it is that might be happening here. Even the rolling thunder in the distance won't distract you. Is the thunder from your own world or this other?

Behind you now, Abi continues to vie for your attention. "Epic, this is—"

"What?" you whisper, stepping even closer to the variance. "What is it?" But Abi doesn't answer. You take another step beyond her. It's nearly imperceptible, but the vision before you flickers like a staticky image on the television. "Abi? What is it?"

Still no response.

You stretch your hand out now. So close you feel it: bracing yourself on the edge of one reality while reaching for another. You could cross through right now, you know you could do it.

But then what?

You hesitate, only for a moment, and only to witness the sliver fade away instantly. Swallowed up by this reality so absolutely, you can hardly believe it was ever there. The shock of seeing this utter phenomenon implode in on itself is almost too much. The reality of what should be is quickly revealed: the treehouse has returned; the lights in the home are off once more; the sounds of rain have fallen into a deathly silence.

The storm is still coming, however.

Finally, you turn to find Abigail on the grass, crumpled in a fetal position. She's crying with her face in her tiny hands. You run over and ask her what happened, placing your hand on her shoulder in some vague attempt to somehow heal her.

"It was you," she says, wiping tears from her face. "Epic, I saw you in there."

"Me? What do you mean?"

"You turned away from me and all of a sudden there was an opening in the sky. The details were shaky, like they were almost vibrating. But for a moment, it stabilized and I got a good look. You were standing there watching me. And I knew everything instantly. It was you, but it wasn't. It was the you I've seen before in my dreams."

"You've seen me in your dreams?"

"It's why I recognized you the first time we met. When I waved at you from the other side of the Mermaid Parade; I waved because I *knew* you."

This is the moment when the rains decide to fall in your world. Another rumble of thunder. It begins quickly and comes down hard. This storm knows what it's doing, like it had been rehearsing for ten thousand years, just for this moment.

Abi still trembles beneath the palm of your hand. Trembles beneath the truth of it all. Like she just said: *I knew everything instantly.* Like in the world of AIIB when you saw yourself in your apartment. The truth has just been poured into Abigail Ayr. She knows why *this* you is the *wrong* you for her.

"It's why I feel like I should love you, but I don't." Burying her tears in her hands again, she can't even look at you now. Sobbing, weeping. *Over me?* you think. "But now it's gone, Epic." Abigail reaches out with a wet hand, hoping to touch some remnant of what was just there. "How do I make what I saw come back?"

You look around now and they're all gone. Luminous shadows replaced by this dark reality.

"Make him come back." She looks at you like you're responsible for whatever it was that just happened. Like you personally did something. And you could somehow do it again.

You explain to her, "What just happened here — whatever it was you just saw — was not because of anything *I* did. At least I don't think so."

"Just try it again, Epic," she persists. "Can you try again right now?" Abi points to the spot where she had just been. "Try standing right there."

It's useless to argue with her. So you don't. You walk to where Abigail directs you and you wait. But nothing special happens. In fact, there is a noticeable lack of anything at all around you. Like the more you want it, the less likely something supernatural is going manifest again. You know for certain it's futile, and you might as well pack it in for the night. You know this. The sudden downpour knows it. The entire moment has passed; the door has closed.

Without turning back to face her, you deliver the news: "It's not going to work," you say. The rain is so intense and you're already forgetting how much this city needed it. "But—" you start, and you think about what both Zoltan Lintzel and Florian-Five had said to you. They told you about their so-called Proto-Tech, the device that would be necessary to capture the portal, to hold it in place and keep it open long enough to pass through. They urged you to visit their laboratory, even giving you directions and insisting you come on by and see it for yourself. "—but there might be *another* way," you suggest to Abigail and you turn around to see her hunched over on the slide and soaking from the rain.

"I don't care," she tells you angrily. She's not having any of it. She doesn't want to wait. "Why wouldn't you go? I know you could have. You were even thinking about it! How could you do this to me?"

"What's the matter with you?"

"What's the matter with *me*? Why would you stay when it's not fair to everyone else? It's not right! Face it Epic, you don't belong here!" Abi takes her jacket off and covers her head to keep the rain off her face.

And you just stand and watch her because you have no words right now. You don't know what you could say that would possibly make enough difference for her anyway.

"Forget it," she says, exasperated. Abi rises from the wet slide and slowly begins to walk away, stopping at the broken swing set. "Let's call it a night. I just want to go home. I think it's time I went home."

"Home? What, are you going to go back to Colorado?" Now it's Abi's turn to keep quiet. She doesn't say anything, but there's some detail here that's off; something suspicious you're having difficulty placing. "When are you leaving? Tonight? Right now?"

And then you notice it. When she first mentioned it to you, your prosopagnosia logged the details away as you would with anyone. A memory trigger to identify her even though there was never any mistaking Abigail Ayr in the first place. You'd recognize her anywhere. But the tattoo she described, the birth certificate inked onto her right shoulder blade so she would never forget her identity, is not there. Her arm is disturbingly bare. It's like you don't recognize her now.

You ask her, "You don't live in Colorado, do you?" She still doesn't say a word to you. You recall now typing Memorial, Colorado into the AIIB system and you received no results whatsoever. "And Memorial?"

"I made it up," she says, defeated. "I made it all up."

"All of it?"

"My triplet neighbors. The boyfriend who dumped me for an orc. I don't know anything at all about identity theft. I work at a bookstore in Forest Hills and spend most of my free time playing video games. It wasn't my birthday on Monday either. Fuck, I even have three cats when I told you I hated the things."

"And your dad? Is he really the Demon of the Surf?"

"Unfortunately. My dad is one of the only details of my life I told you that *is* true. But I was only visiting the fucker so I could steal a few bucks from him. There was an envelope stuffed with cash on the table in his dressing room. I swiped it while he was blabbering to you about his circus act."

"I can't believe you'd steal money from your father. What else?"

"What else, *what*?"

"You said it was only *one* of the truths you told me. What's another one?"

She pauses. "How I felt about you. But now I realize that was actually a lie too. A lie I told myself, maybe. You're not the you I thought you were." She sits down on the one good swing and she doesn't even squirm when she realizes her ass is in a puddle of water.

"But why did you lie to me?"

"Because I lie about *everything*. To everyone. It's all so seamless when it's not the truth. Sometimes it feels like there'd be so many more details to keep track of if I was actually being honest. Like the truth is so much more complicated."

The truth is, you know she still isn't being completely honest with you. You know it for sure. When you were in AIIB, Florian-Five explained how only a select few people have ever experienced the game, and how the only users are those who are specifically chosen by them. So how does Abigail Ayr fit into it? You ask her, "How did you find out about AIIB?"

A longer pause. "There was an invite in my email. Just like the one they sent you. I already played so many different Massive Multiplayer games I didn't hesitate. I knew I had to sign up for this one too, whatever it was."

"And they sent you the equipment too? It just showed up on your doorstep, didn't it?"

"That's right. It was delivered that same night. I created an avatar and before I knew what was happening I was immersed in it. Experiencing the most realistic virtual world I'd ever seen. After I explored AIIB for a while I was contacted in-game by somebody I didn't know. He wore this crazy golden armor and talked real funny. Like a robot or something. And he asked me to find *you*."

"What for?"

"He asked me to tell you all about AIIB. I think he wanted you to see it for yourself. I don't know. At the time, I had zero idea who this Cepik Small person was but I was promised some sweet avatar upgrades if I agreed to go to this place called The UnDiner and talk to him. So, I did."

"And that was the first time we spoke. When you leaned over my table and asked for a napkin?"

"Head meet nail. You got it, Rainbow. He told me you'd be at the restaurant that morning and when I finally found the place, guess what?

There you were. But when I found you at The UnDiner, I had no idea I would actually *recognize* you. Because I'd seen you before across Surf Avenue and then again at the train station."

"So, you work for them? Like a secret agent or something?"

"Not exactly. Mostly I had no idea what it was I was supposed to be doing. Or how the golden avatar guy knew you'd be where you were."

They knew where you were because they'd been following you all this time. They've been following you for your entire life. "It's because they were watching me the whole time, that's why. They knew I was at The UnDiner that morning. That insect I killed in my apartment, it had probably been following me everywhere."

"I didn't know any of that. Honestly."

"So, all of this was really just part of one big lie? All you've been doing is leading me on so you could get some bullshit avatar upgrades?"

"At first, yeah. But my decision to keep seeing you was purely my own. I was legitimately drawn to you I just didn't know why. Until now."

"When you saw me — or, the reflection of me — in the air over there. Is that right?"

She's quiet. You know she learned the truth when she witnessed the phenomenon, but you wonder just how much of the truth did she understand? "I'm sorry. I fucked up. I realize if you really *had* developed serious feelings for me you'd be broken right now. But you had the chance just now to leave this world. That's what you should've done because that's how things are *supposed* to be."

Unless your being here was not a cosmic accident. Does destiny care about the journey or will it happen anyway? "I'm just not sure that's a decision I'm ready to make. Think about it: it's a massive commitment."

"It's selfish, is what it is. You know it would be the *right* thing to do, but you're contemplating not doing it because you're *afraid*."

By definition, if it was the right thing to do, then what Abigail is really telling you is that your being here is wrong. You, and everything about you, are wrong for this world. How might things have been different? Maybe your mother and Dr. Griffin would still be alive? Your father's business might never have been destroyed in the fire.

But you also might not have ever met Reya; never loved her. That's what you're thinking, isn't it? You would have missed out on everything about her. You think about the first time you met and the mornings you awoke holding one another tightly. The times you'd sneak into the loading bay outside Lincoln Center and listen to the mellifluous sounds of the orchestra from within. On a whim, you'd gone clamming in Peconic Bay, hadn't you? And then, of course, there was the night you sat atop that skyscraper overlooking the city. Would you be leaving these memories behind? If you left, would you even remember any of it?

"I need some time to think everything over," you say.

"That's not good enough for me."

"That's too bad," you tell her. "This is the way is *has* to be for now. There are some things I'm not ready to let go of."

You and Reya had been mistakenly asked to a party. You remember she had received the invitation in the mail by accident. You decided to go anyway because the party was at the tallest building in Lenox Hill and you thought there might be some good food. There wasn't, unless you'd been into fish roe and artisanal pickles. So instead, you decided since you were there you might as well sneak up to the rooftop for a view. You're pretty sure it was one of the last nights you'd ever spent together. Or was it?

Abi spits at you with her words. "You *are* a fucking rainbow, aren't you? I'm looking right at you, even though you don't really exist, do you? You're an illusion. A trick of the light. If I slugged you right now it wouldn't even matter."

It *would* matter. You *do* matter. Your *being here* matters.

Not wishing to argue about it any longer, you and Abi decide to turn away from one another and huff in unison.

But then, through the patter of the rainstorm, you decide instead to share your thoughts. You describe to Abigail the details of that one night with Reya. You were leaning against each other on the rooftop ledge, looking out across the city. The Empire State Building was lit blue, orange, and green that night for some reason you were completely unaware of. She wore a cocktail dress from a second-hand shop in the East Village. Reya told you how she was growing tired of New York, didn't she? She said she wanted to see the stars, but the city's constant light prevented that far too often. You asked her what the alternative was. "*Leaving*," she said simply. You remember the feeling of your heart sinking right then and there because you had initially thought she meant she was leaving *you*. But she asked you instead to come with her to the country. No, wait. She didn't say the country, she said Kentucky, didn't she? And you agreed to go with her.

You stop. In your head, you recall saying that to her, but you don't feel like you ever did.

And you remember now that you *did* go. You packed all of the belongings you wanted to keep into two suitcases and went to Kentucky together.

Specifically, you took a train to Versailles. But it doesn't feel like you ever truly experienced such a thing.

As you continue to question what's really happened and what you may have imagined or dreamed instead, you turn to Abigail for some sort of reinforcement.

But she's gone too. Only some wet cat hair remains in a puddle beneath the swaying swing.

THE DUALITY OF THEE

From Penelope Park, you traveled directly to Gowanus, straight to the Brooklyn Whites warehouse. With everything falling apart around you right now, you really don't think you need the added problem of worrying about doing your job too. You walked right into Esad's office and told your boss as much. He didn't even look up when you informed him you were quitting. Maybe he did as you were leaving though, just to make sure he knew who was officially off the payroll.

Now you're sitting outside the back door of the warehouse and hoping to catch Armand Bester when he eventually comes out here for a smoke break. You pull the sleeves of your hoodie down around your shaking hands. It's still hot out tonight, but you continue to shiver nonetheless. Everything is shining wet from the evening's passing storm; rain-filled potholes in the back lot look more like dark, oily patches. Like shadowy doors that might lead into other, much brighter worlds.

Finally, Bester comes out from the warehouse. You know it's him without even turning around: the specific, confident resonance his work boots make as he takes a step; the way he likes to clear his throat whenever approaching someone so as not to scare them accidentally; the acrid stink of his cheap cologne.

"Bestest! Where have you been? People have been worried about you."

He sits down beside you on the wheelchair access ramp, resting his hands upon the wet railing. You've never once seen anyone here in a wheelchair.

"Which people?"

"Well, I shouldn't say worried. It's more like, *Where the fuck is that guy?*"

"I'm quitting, Bester. I've got too much going on right now. I just told Esad as much."

"Quitting? Good for you!" Bester slings an arm around your shoulders, with bracelets jangling as his grip tightens. His other arm gestures out toward anywhere but here. "Now you can get out there and live your fucking life, right?"

You're not sure where you'd start. "Something like that. Tell me, if you had this sudden freedom what would be the very first thing you'd do with it?"

"Drink. Fight. Hit some whorehouses. I don't know; just go where the blood in my dingis leads me." He grabs his crotch with the same hand that was just around your shoulder, helpfully indicating what a dingis is supposed to be.

"*Whorehouses*? Do they still have those? Sounds kind of antiquated."

"The point is I'm a *man*, Epic. And you are too. You shouldn't have to worry about bosses like Esad, or ex-girlfriends, or having to pay the rent."

"I don't pay rent. I live with my dad."

"Just go out there and be a man. What else is there to fuss about?"

You look at him and hope he might intuitively pick up on exactly what it is you have to fuss about.

"Shit. You look tired, bro."

You grab the wet railing now too, bracing yourself uneasily. "I *am* tired, Armand."

"I told you never to call me that unless it was serious." He looks a little further into your eyes and this time you know he gets it. "You got some secrets, huh? Well, this is the place for dirty laundry, isn't it? So, go for it. Lay it on me."

You close your eyes tight and you tell him about the fight you just had with Abi. Was it a fight? Just a disagreement? You don't know what it was exactly. But whatever. "This is about so much more than Abigail Ayr," you say. "Or Reya Graves. It's about my mother and my father, but still not really."

"So, *what* then?" he pushes.

And then you let him have it: the Swiss scientists, the insect drones, and the apartment break-in. How you haven't slept in three days now. Or is it four? You honestly can't tell anymore. And then you decide you don't care: you go on and tell him about the parallel worlds. About Earth-A and Earth-B. About the death of a black hole, the AIIB virtual reality system, and your out-of-body experience in Versailles, Kentucky. And then there's the strange lights in the park, the Proto-Tech, and seeing yourself in your apartment. Sure, it was your virtual apartment maybe, but it's still fucked up, isn't it? It's everything you've been wrapped up in for the last week of your life. Every misleading detail and every incorrect fact. It's every lie you've been told that contradicts every truth you've been wrong about anyway.

Finally, you open your eyes — the eyes that only want to remain shut — and you turn back to Bester and ask, "So, what do I do? Should I find a way to that other world? Leave everything behind? Do I forget about Abi and

Reya and everyone here?"

He looks at you as though you're fully crazy, but talks to you like you're totally not. "It's like I told you, bro. It can be applied to any scenario: just go where the blood in your dingis tells you to go. You'll know where that is."

"I don't know if that helps, Best. But thanks."

He smiles one of those smiles you can't help but be envious of, and he gives you a wink. "I swear though, if you're holding out on me — if you're getting better weed from somewhere else — you'd best tell me about it. Cause what you're saying to me right now? Alternate universes and robot bugs? That is some good shit talking right there." Finally, Bester concludes by standing up. He stretches his arms like he's been sitting in one spot for an hour or so, and really, you don't know how long you've been out here talking anyway. "So, what's our next move? What are we planning on doing about all of this?"

"*We?*"

"Sure. I'm on the clock right now, but I've got the van. May as well put her to good use, right? Go pick up some girls?"

You roll your eyes. "My dingis is telling me the answer lies with the scientists and that prototype technology of theirs. I could use it to keep the door open long enough to leave here."

"What, you wanna go swipe it from them?"

You weren't thinking that, no. But how else could you get your hands on it, really? You still don't know what the motives of these guys are exactly. Maybe this whole discussion was spurred on by the fact you and Abi parted on bad terms, but you really just want a way out of all of this. And it might be better for her, too.

"Come on then," he says dangling keys between his fingers. And there's that smile again. "Let's go for a ride."

ooo

You don't know where you are now. Somewhere in Queens, you know that much, but Queens is a pretty big place once you actually start driving around. You gave Bester the address to the warehouse, the one you still had stuffed in your bag and written on the restaurant napkin. Somehow, even without GPS, he knew where to go and you just kind of blanked out along the way. You hope you fell asleep, but you don't know for certain. You're not sure if the drive was ten minutes or an hour or more. You really haven't been managing or monitoring your time very well lately. The clock display on the van's dashboard has never worked and is only ever a bunch of randomly blinking red horizontal and vertical dashes. Like the bottom of an almost-empty box of pick-up sticks. You jolt upright as the van's engine jumps under the hood before slowly sputtering into silence.

Across the street are a half-dozen parked cars sitting in puddles bigger than any you'd seen between Woodhaven and Gowanus. Must have been even more rain out this way. You recognize the five-digit address from the napkin, right on the front of a shoe repair shop called "S.O.S. SHOE REPAIR."

"Save Our Soles," Bester laughs. "As in shoe soles, get it?"

You didn't get it, but you weren't really putting much thought into it beyond the obvious coincidence.

"Didn't you say your dad owned a shoe store?" You nod, not remembering ever telling Bester that information, but assuming you must have at some point. "So, what do we do now?" he asks.

"Can we just wait for a bit?"

"I s'pose." A minute or so of silence passes before Bester asks, "Can we at least talk about something while we wait?"

"What do you want to talk about?"

"Did you enjoy the play?" It hasn't yet been a week since you watched *The Duality of Three* and you've already nearly forgotten about it. "Someone from the New Yorker came to the second show and interviewed me afterwards. It's been pretty well-received."

"That's good. I mean, I'm happy for you."

"But you didn't say if you enjoyed it or not."

"I guess. I mean, it was sort of—well, I didn't really understand what the point of the dead girl was."

Bester blows a short laugh out of the side of his mouth. "Margo wasn't a dead girl! That was Christopher's *soul* on the floor. What, you didn't get that?"

"Maybe I was confused because it said *Dead Girl* in the playbill." You look out across the street but everything is just as eerily silent as it was when you pulled up here. "What about the lack of a third act? Aren't plays supposed to have three acts?"

He makes some ambiguous comment about how third acts in stage plays are not always necessities. Meanwhile, you can't help from thinking about his play's similarities to *The Third* and how you lost the book after having only read two-thirds of it. "I guess I'm not smart enough for theater," you surrender.

"Man, she was right to call you weird."

"She? Abi?"

"Yeah. She told me there was something off with you. *Distant*, I think was the word she used."

"But not weird?"

"No, maybe not that exact word."

"She likes *you* though," you tell Bester, even if Abi confessed it was all just an act. Like the rest of her, apparently.

"She doesn't. Not really. We got along that night, that's all."

"*Got along?*"

"As much as anybody really gets along with anybody else. We all just put up with everyone's shit enough to be comfortable, right?"

"So, you think I'm distant too?"

"In some ways, sure I do. But if this alternate world stuff turns out to be true, I'll have a better idea about it all."

"What else did she say?"

"She told me she liked my play. Though, I'm not sure if she really understood it either."

"About *me*, I meant. What else did she say about me that night at Margo's place? You guys must have talked after I left?"

Bester flicks at the air freshener dangling from the rearview mirror. The sun-bleached green tree that once smelled of pine. Also, you're not sure why this van has a rearview mirror since there's no back window. "She was pretty high. But she told me she felt like she *should* love you, although she knew for sure that she *didn't*. She said the same thing about her cats, too."

Just as you're remembering why you came here in the first place, you notice two men on the sidewalk outside the shoe repair shop. "Wait. Look over there."

Bester follows your finger. "Who are those guys?"

They're pushing something large on a dolly, navigating it slowly across the large cracks along the neighborhood's neglected sidewalk. It appears to be a box partially covered with a sheet of some sort. The box looks comparable in size to the one that was delivered to your apartment after you clicked the SIGN-UP NOW button.

It's dark out tonight; the black rain clouds hang above you and the streetlights here seem to be nearly burnt out, but you don't require much light in order to recognize Zoltan Lintzel. You can identify him from his movements; his slow, purposeful walk and the way he scratches his beard and the backs of his hands are enough giveaways for your prosopagnosia.

"That's him. That's the guy I met at the restaurant."

Craning his neck and squinting Bester asks, "What? That old pimp with the beard? He's Swiss?"

"That's what he told me. He had an accent."

"Accents can be faked, Bestest."

"Why would he make that up? Of all the stuff he told me, why would he pretend to be from Switzerland?"

"Why did Abi tell you she was from Colorado?"

"Because she's a pathological liar, that's why."

Bester shrugs his shoulders and arcs his eyebrows, looking at you like you're no better than her. Like he's definitively made his point. You just peer back out the window and across the street. The two men have pulled the dolly up behind a parked van and are loading the heavy box inside. The second of the two has removed what you thought was a sheet covering the box and you can tell now it's a coat. A houndstooth trench coat, to be more specific. He puts it on with his large hands and you gasp. "That's the guy who broke into my apartment the other night!"

"You said he had an animal mask on?"

"He did. But he was also wearing that coat. No one else would wear a coat like that in this heat." Because of the flickering street light and the position of their van, you still cannot get a clear look at his face, only enough to tell he has a big, round head and he's got glasses on. So, is Florian-Five also the same man who burst into your apartment? The man who threatened you and threw the book at your head? They toss the dolly into the van now too before slamming the back doors shut and hopping into the front. Zoltan starts the engine and they drive off around the corner somewhere, maybe making another special delivery.

"We done waiting, bro?"

You nod and open up the passenger door. "Let's go check out that building."

But Bester abruptly places his hand on your thigh, preventing you from getting out. "Wait, we're not leaving the van here, are we?"

"Why not?"

He points to the parking restriction sign directly beside you. "Can't park here. I don't want a ticket, bro. I'm gonna be in enough trouble with Esad as it is without getting a damn parking ticket too."

For the first time ever, you manage to convince Bester otherwise. You lie and you tell him you won't even be ten minutes; you tell him you know *exactly* what you're doing here, when really the truth is the total opposite.

You step out onto the lifeless street and cross over to the other side.

Peering inside the darkened S.O.S. Shoe Repair, it's apparent this is nothing more than what it advertises. This place could even pass as your father's former business as the details within are much the same. Not surprisingly, the door is locked tight and you decide to walk around back to inspect further.

The alley is darker than you'd have imagined possible and you can clearly hear something scratching and scurrying around in the shadows. You're stepping in puddles of something, hoping it's nothing more than the evening's rain water. Luckily, Bester's always got his trusty lighter in his pocket which helps you find your way to the back of the shoe repair shop in no time. The same five-digit address is posted at the back door.

You almost try the door, but stop yourself before you do. There's a flicker of light that isn't yours. From the corner of your eye, you see it and you turn, but it's gone. Bester's staring at you; his eyes as large as a pair of quarters and shining like them too. At first you assume he's questioning your sanity again, but then you sense something different.

You ask him, "You saw that too, didn't you?"

He nods cautiously. "I thought there was a woman standing there just now. I could swear it." Bester shines the flame from his lighter around you and reaches out his free hand, trying to feel something that's not there. "Was that one of those funky-ass lights you were telling me about? The ones you and Abi had seen at the playground?"

You nod like it's no big deal, but the truth is, it still freaks you out as much as the first time. You reach for the door again, but this time, Bester stops you. His hand grips your forearm, but your fingers are still anchored to the door handle.

"What if this is a trap, bro? Think about it. Why would these guys give you this address and specifically tell you their secret lab is in the basement? Instead of just asking you to knock on the front door? It's like they're luring us down there." He looks back and forth, his movements all chaotic jitters. "They probably just drove around the corner and are watching us right now from the other end of this alley."

Obviously, it all makes fairly good sense. You still don't know what their motives truly are. These strange men you've only just met couldn't possibly be so benevolent and selfless, could they? But you dismiss Bester's concerns as boldly as you can. "So what? I mean, even if this *was* a trap, what could they actually do to us? An old dude and a gamer nerd in a fancy coat. What threat is there, really? And it's not likely they've just gone and left this door open for us, is it?"

You twist the handle and the heavy door clicks open. Just like that. Well, whatever. "Let's just check it out," you say. "We got this far, didn't we? We can't stop now."

No alarm rings. No lights go on. You close the metal door behind you and enter a workroom; again, much like the one your father used to have. It smells like it too. There's an old banker's lamp on the workbench, and you flick it on. Bester puts the lighter back in his jeans pocket. If this shoe repair store is really just a staged prop for these scientists to secretly conduct their research, they've gone to a lot of trouble to create such a realistic deception.

The workbench is loaded with supplies: mink oil, saddle soap, insoles, strips of leather, wooden and metal shoe trees, grips, aglets, and laces in dozens of colors. It stinks like someone has been sweating back here for fifty years. Maybe these guys actually repair shoes full-time? It *is* possible that pursuing dead black holes and parallel universes could simply be a hobby. What's more likely, is maybe they simply rent the basement? You have no idea, really.

There is another door in this room that is slightly ajar, with a dim, murky light emanating from the basement below.

You try to move as silently as possible, but your feet clang and echo off the metal staircase. Bester's bracelets scrape along the handrail. Only a couple of steps down and you can tell just how cold it is down here; even colder than the office of Gideon Flat. There's a constant beeping from somewhere, like a microwave timer has finished. A few soft, green-tinted overhead lights make it feel like you're underwater.

This is certainly not some fantastically immense laboratory with an army of scientists working around the clock inventing machines to change the world. This is a dark, smelly basement crowded with half-invented contraptions and it doesn't appear as though there are any more than the two men involved. There is a tidy desk near the stairs with nothing but a sleek, stark-white computer, a clean tea cup, and a small stack of factory-sealed packages of seaweed.

One corner houses two long rows of computer servers with fans blasting on full to keep things from overheating. Above the sound of the fans, there's the persistent beeping that seems to only be getting louder and increasing in frequency as you move around.

You realize now why Zoltan hadn't simply abducted you years ago. Why they didn't run you off into their research facility for countless tests. These guys are not some clandestine government operation, power hungry and fighting for mankind's future. They're just two guys in a basement in

Queens. Where would they have even kept you? The darkest corner of the room appears to be no more than a thick mess of cables and dusty devices.

"What is all this?" Bester asks, rummaging through a pile of cracked motherboards on a large table.

You let him keep digging and discover another messy work desk a few feet away. There are half-empty bags of cheese puffs and bottles of cola all over, on the desk and underneath. Filthy crumbs everywhere. The lingering smell of farts.

Set up on the desktop is the same equipment that showed up on your doorstep earlier: monitor, CPU tower, scanner, headset, gloves, boots, and control pad. The only difference is these all seem to have had a lot of use and the AIIB logo is nowhere to be found, like this is the original unit. You're guessing this to be Florian-Five's work station and his identity is that much more cemented now when you also spot the strange animal mask — the same one you'd seen in your apartment that night — stuffed within the cup holder on the giant, showy office chair. Taking it in your hand, you still cannot decipher what sort of creature this is supposed to represent, only that the vacuous eye holes are creeping you out even more than when they had woken you up in your apartment a few nights ago.

Thankfully, Bester unintentionally snaps you out of it. "Oh, shit balls," he says eloquently.

"What is it?"

He turns to you with something hidden in his hand. "I guess I gotta respect the fact at least *some* of your crazy story is turning out to be true." Bester's hand opens and his palm is full with the miniscule bits and pieces of various insects. Robotic ones. "These the same bugs you been telling me about? The things are all over the place. And there's a pile of books back here too."

"Let me see those." You take one of a dozen small, handwritten journals and flip through it. It appears to be a log of dates and times. You see the name *C.SMALL* all over the pages. They've definitely been monitoring you for a while, if not your whole life. This one you're holding, in all probability the most recent, seems to correspond with places you had been during very specific times:

SATURDAY, JUNE 21. 01:32 follows C.SMALL into brighton beach starfish room ... 02:09 C.SMALL beaten by male patron outside bar ... 02:13 C.SMALL converses with waitress at curbside ...

SATURDAY, JUNE 21. 14:10 follows C.SMALL into office on surf avenue ... 14:21 psychiatrist identified as G.FLAT ... 14:40 C.SMALL refuses to talk about mother WILMA ... 15:02 C.SMALL acknowledges unknown girl outside window* ... [*confirm identity of girl]

SUNDAY, JUNE 22. 23:38 C.SMALL reading book on subway ... 23:50 encounters same girl* from yesterday while changing trains ... [*contact made]

MONDAY, JUNE 23. 12:46 C.SMALL reading book in undiner ... 13:14 AA begins conversation, requesting serviette from C.SMALL ... 13:26 AA initiates discussion of a-ii-b ... 14:18 follows C.SMALL into coney island sideshows ... 15:12 C.SMALL sits with AA at beachside bench ... 15:27 C.SMALL obtains AA contact info ...

As you're reading this, you slowly become aware that the beeping in the room is now racing faster. Some sort of monitor beside you is definitely the source of the noise. There's a rudimentary map of the city on the screen and a little red blip somewhere in Queens. At the top of the screen and in some pixelated 1980's video game font are the letters C.SMALL.

"They're tracking you," Bester chirps up.

"No shit," you say and turn the monitor off, finally ceasing the mind-numbing noise. "And they've been at it for a good while."

On the tabletop beside the screen is a small stack of printouts. Photos snapped unbeknownst to their subjects, and all taken from the other side of windows and from various other unusual angles: there is an image of you lying on the couch in the late Dr. Griffin's office; sitting with your father in the Manhattan hospice; at your locker at work with your uniform half on; a grainy image of you standing wistfully on Margo Asus' balcony; and one of Abi behind a bookstore cash register with a nametag which clearly reads *ABBY*. After removing the picture of Abigail from the pile, you toss the rest to the floor. Some of them drift under the desk but you don't care. You fold up the paper photo in your hand and slide it into your pocket.

"This whole place is like some secret sanctum, some bizarre temple dedicated to studying me."

"You're like their god, I suppose."

"Am I though? Or are they using me for their own reasons as you suggested?"

Bester tosses the handful of dismantled drones onto the floor behind him like grains of rice at a wedding and he slumps deep into the big desk chair of

Florian-Five. "What did these guys really tell you about this alternate world, Bestest? Do you feel like their claims are substantial? Do you actually believe in the authenticity of it all?"

Without hesitation, you say, "I do." You tell Bester that yes, you believe right now on Earth-B, somewhere across the universe or wherever it might exist, your other self is also discovering the secret technologies of the other scientists. The other Zoltan and the other Florian must have also created a device that can hold a sliver open. A sliver that would lead them *here*.

Bester shakes his head. "But think about it, okay? So, let's suppose they're telling you the truth when they say they were tracking this energy for years before it hit our planet. But if the alternate earth didn't exist until it hit, then what were the alternate earth scientists doing the whole time? Obviously, they couldn't have been tracking it too because they didn't exist yet."

"Uh, I don't know. I haven't really thought about it like that." There's a part of you that wants to go along with whatever theories Bester has, since, compared to you anyway, he is the alternate world expert, having dreamt up and written so many fictional stories.

"Isn't this a little suspicious? There's holes in their story. Big ones!" Then he feels the furry mask in the cup holder and looks more closely at it before finally chucking this across the room too. He thinks a bit more about what it was he was trying so hard to determine. "Unless when an alternate world is formed, all the past is created along with it? That's why there'd be bones in the dirt and rings inside tree trunks."

"Well, I mean, there's so much even they don't know."

"And who's to say that only a single alternate reality was ever created?

Why couldn't there be more? Like, if every decision we're ever faced within our lives can result in a hundred different outcomes, couldn't each of those outcomes create an alternate branching reality? Just right now, when I was holding that mask, maybe an alternate world Bester decided to put it back where he found it while another Bester chose to put it on his head. And yet another Bester had maybe never picked it up in the first place. I mean, just what is the extent to which we're dealing with here?"

You don't know what to say, only that the way Zoltan Lintzel explained things to you — and Florian-Five after that — all made perfect sense. You tell Bester as much, and hope that's good enough for him too.

"Yeah," he agrees half-heartedly. "But I just don't wanna be played, bro. I ain't getting played here."

"You won't be," you reassure him. Though you're not entirely sure you believe your own words until you happen to spot a plug in the wall, and you follow the cord that's snaked along the dusty floor until it leads you to the reason you've come here. It's their prototype technology. You recognize it from the hologram image Florian-Five had shown you while you shared a moment in the AIIB world. It's a rectangular metallic box with a thin slit on the top, like a box of tissue, and it's just sitting there on the floor. Wires stick out all over the thing, and a few more generators are helping to keep it alive. It chugs along under a dome of dim light, some kind of sparkling, crackling energy. You direct Bester's attention toward the so-called Proto-Tech. "Maybe this will help settle your nerves," you say.

"That looks just like one of those ghost trap thingies from Ghostbusters," Bester comments.

"I've never seen Ghostbusters."

"I'm talking about the *original* one." His arms sink when he realizes you wouldn't know the difference. "How have you never seen Ghostbusters?"

"That's really not the point here, Best." You crouch in front of the device for a closer inspection, though it's obvious you're both a little afraid, waiting for the other one to touch it first.

Bester reaches in closer; his palms feeling for heat like the two of you are sitting around a campfire. "So, if this thing is the key to getting to an alternate world — holy shit, I can't believe I'm even saying something so stupid — then what are we supposed to actually *do* with it?"

In your dreams, you really are sitting in front of a campfire. But it's not with Armand Bester; you're with Reya, aren't you? You're holding each other closely discussing how much you both hate marshmallows, roasted or otherwise. "I guess we listen to our dreams."

"The sex ones?"

"Not every dream is about sex, Best."

"Whatever. But if you can tell me you're not fantasizing about sex all the time, I'm not gonna believe you."

In your dreams, you're tossing hay bales into the back of a rusty old pickup truck. You're wiping the sweat from your brow with a dirty cloth you keep in your back pocket. There's a girl next to you again and you're almost certain it's Reya but you can't see her clearly in the beautiful darkness. You're sitting with her in a gazebo under the twilight, listening to the croaking frogs and the soft buzz of dragonflies. You can hear water lapping along the lake shore. These are your fantasies. "So, what was the last dream *you* had about?"

"It was about sex."

You try to explain your dreams to Bester. In them, you're not doing much more than simply existing. The nature of your dreams is very specific and they seem to be getting only more detailed. They used to be more intermittent. Sporadic. Your memory of what your dreams once were is a little patchy. But they've definitely increased in frequency lately, you know this much. Yes, your dreams might be mundane and, quite frankly, very routine, but no one can help what they dream.

In your dreams, you are definitely a participant. In your dreams, you fell in love. In your dreams, you are everything your mother and father really wanted you to be.

The only exceptional variance in your dreams occurred a few nights ago, when you smoked that pot and proceeded to dream about your senses hyper-accelerating, swelling in capacity. When you felt like you were experiencing the entire universe at once just before the totality of it all was purged from you. And then you saw the blood again. And it was done.

You don't tell Bester about the blood.

The last dream you had was interrupted by the intruder in your apartment. You've only been barely awake since then, but right now you feel more alert than you've ever been.

He swings back and forth in a semicircle in the big chair. Metal on metal screeches in piercing hiccups, in desperate need of some lubricant. He asks, "You say your dreams don't go very far back into your childhood?" Suddenly Armand Bester makes you feel like you're in yet another therapist's office.

You think about it, wanting to be as right as you can be. "It's like dreams never used to happen at all. Or maybe I just didn't remember any of them. But then slowly they began to build and build to the point where I can't escape them. I experience them all the time."

"Even when you're awake?"

"Yes. But I *am* on a lot of prescription medication."

"Do you think," he starts before stopping himself mid-thought. Bester caresses his strong jaw with a firm hand.

"What?"

He steeples his fingers together. "What might the chances be that what you are dreaming is what the other you is actually *experiencing*? Dreams as windows into parallel worlds." His eyes grow bigger the more he speculates. "Your childhoods probably didn't differ too much. But whenever a new factor was brought into the equation for one of you, it spawned multiple new divergences in your life, making it that much more different than the other's."

"That's absurd."

"Even after everything you've experienced in the last few days? Everything you told me tonight?" You wouldn't have thought Armand Bester capable of postulating any more clearly than either of the scientists. "Just because the other Earth has been classified as a *parallel* Earth, doesn't mean everything is the *same*. How is it possible that every decision you've made here lines up with the decisions your other self is making over there? Not to mention the influence that the decisions made by billions of other people must have. Of *course* you're going to have different experiences and meet different people and dream different dreams." But he's making a solid case. There's certainly much more to consider here than what you've been presented with. "Is that still so absurd?" he asks, in a tone more serious than he's ever asked you before.

You reflect upon everything. Fast forwarding through all your twenty years. As the low-lights of your life flash before your eyes you ask, "Why would he agree to this?"

"He?"

"Cepik. The other me. Why would he possibly want what I have?"

"Why *wouldn't* he?"

"My life is miserable. *I'm* miserable. I always have been. The only part of my life I've never wanted to forget was Reya. I miss her Bester, I truly do. If everything good I'm dreaming is really my other self's experiences, then it's safe to say he's probably suffering through mine. Why would he ever want this? He's got it great over there. How could he ever possibly agree to make the switch?"

"Maybe you're not getting the whole story? Could be, things aren't all roses and rainbows over there. Maybe your other self is just as unhappy as you are and he dreams about all the positives in your life."

"The positives? Like what? I don't see any positives."

"Maybe you need to look a little harder?"

He's right. But the point is you're not searching for answers because you're unhappy. It's because you really, truthfully do not belong here and you want to make things right. To fix a stupid, unfair mistake the universe made ten thousand years ago. Still, you cannot help from dwelling upon the things you've seen and done and feeling sorry for the other you who's probably had to endure all of it in his own dreams.

"Come on, Bestest. Don't be so hard on yourself."

The duality of his statement certainly does not elude you. Hard on yourself. Apprehensively, you unzip the hoodie you're wearing and slide it off, dumping it on the table. You do the same with your t-shirt, after pulling it off over your head. And you share your darkest secret with Armand Bester: the horrible, heavy scars on the insides of both of your arms. The dual, jagged purple mountain ranges that run from armpits to wrists. Every time you look at them you experience the pain of what you did to yourself that night. Every single time. The permanence of the torment you performed will never cease. When the dollar store steak knife you'd pierced deep into your right arm tore through flesh, muscle, and tendons; splitting veins and scraping along bone. The sheer disbelief that so much blood could possibly pour out from you was the only thing that kept you conscious. You remember feeling too astounded to want to miss it. And it was enough to make you continue on to your left arm, in exactly the same fashion. Inspecting the mutilation many times since, you still can hardly believe the near-symmetry of your injuries. You remember someone in the trauma and emergency room saying the same thing, but who that person ever was you can't be sure. It's possible you dreamed the voice too. Sometimes identity is not always reality.

The first person you do remember post-hospital release was Reya. You met for the first time shortly after all of that, didn't you? Outside the subway station, the night she was mugged. The night you couldn't possibly stand by and see someone in pain. Nowhere near the level of pain you knew, but suffering and in need of help just the same. God, that smile of hers.

Bester's gone as white as he possibly can. "Holy fuck."

There is no believing what he's seeing. Some people don't want your secrets. He rises from the seat but steps no closer.

"I did this to myself," you finally admit to him. "I don't even know why anymore. I can barely remember when." Your father happened to find you and most certainly saved your life. You never saw that apartment again; the memories of that night would have been too much. The stains would probably never be erased completely. You told Gideon you had only ever *contemplated* suicide, never having the guts to actually go through with it. The truth is, the only thing holding you back from trying again was the thought that you might fail a second time. You feel your wounds again with your fingertips. You don't know why because they only ever serve as a reminder that you're still here. "The point I'm making is that, I wonder—I mean, do you think my other self has ever dreamed anything so awful? Just like you said: *dreams as windows into parallel worlds.*"

Bester apologizes to you for something there's no way he should feel guilty for. You think other people like to say they're sorry as a way of hoping to remove the pain someone else is feeling. Like it's their fault, when it never is.

"It's okay," you say reflexively. "Do you still think you're right, though? That things could be just as bad in the other world?"

Finally, he reaches over and hands you your shirt back. "You never know, bro. Maybe though, what you need to do is make sure things are as decent as they can be over here."

You slide the shirt back over your head and work your arms back in. They can still feel a little numb, sort of frozen at times. "What do you mean?"

"You need to find Abi and apologize to her. Do it for yourself."

"I know."

"And don't worry about the job. I'll tell Esad you never meant to quit. I got this. I got your back, bro."

ooo

The chill of the basement is forgotten as soon as you walk back up into the shoe repair shop. You and Bester unplugged the Proto-Tech from the wall outlet, but there's a small generator attached to it, keeping it alive; its bizarre energy continues to pop and crackle quietly. Still, the entire device fits comfortably wrapped up inside your hoodie.

Bester finally asks, "Where are we taking this thing, anyway?"

Your whole plan tonight was to find this mysterious apparatus and bring it back to Woodhaven. You explain to Bester that during your conversation in The UnDiner, Zoltan Lintzel told you it would be possible to capture a sliver with the Proto-Tech and keep the gate open long enough to pass through. You just needed to know the right place and time. While in the AIIB system, Florian-Five hinted that if you knew of a special place where you'd seen the doors, then that's where the best one would be. Penelope Park is obviously where you should be heading.

"Don't you think that's exactly what these bozos *want* you to do? Why else would they just leave it out in the open for you? Why not protect it a bit more?"

You say, "It's not like anything else down there was protected any better. Plus, we did break into their laboratory."

"But then why show you what it looks like so you'd know how to find it? What's in it for them?"

Again, what's in it for them? The question keeps repeating itself, returning to the back of your thoughts like an unwanted dog that just doesn't get it, but too many other events have been happening lately to keep track of all the chronic questions. You open the back door again and step out into the alley.

Bester asks, "You said you met yourself in the computer game?"

"Briefly. Then I panicked and disappeared."

"I got ya. I think I'd shit myself too if that happened. But maybe you should try and contact him again?"

"In the AIIB system?"

"Right. But maybe suggest another place to meet? Another place to make the switch."

The Switch, you think. Just like Luca and Tristan did in *The Third*. That was exactly what the author had called it. "Maybe the fountain in Paris? How would I even get to Paris?"

"*Fountain in Paris*? What the hell are you talking about, bro? Maybe nothing so exotic. Perhaps there's another place that means something to you?"

You carefully tiptoe around the corner, back out toward the street where the van is parked. No sign of the scientists or their vehicle. The sun is beginning to rise in the East, a sliver of orange on the horizon. Bester's over the moon to find no parking ticket folded and waiting for him under the wipers. He opens the passenger door and holds your concealed prize for you as you climb in, perhaps subconsciously seeing you as though you were now handicapped; your scarred limbs having actually been amputated instead.

You sleep in the van again on the ride back, the moving vehicle lulls you into unconsciousness as though you were a baby. Your dreams are not so much dreams as they are realizations now. Realizations that you're effectively living two lives at once, in two bodies that remain identical. Your name is Cepik Small. But are you *more* than that? Are you also Tristan Montminy? Are you Luca Desplante the Third? Are you living any of this at all or are you confusing reality and your dreams? Just what is real and what isn't? In your dreams, you doubt all of it. Are there things you *think* you've dreamt that you've actually experienced, and vice versa?

Identity is not reality, you try telling yourself. You wake up saying the words out loud, oblivious to the fact you're still in the Brooklyn Whites van.

"Identity is not reality," you say. Bester doesn't hear you, but there's an unexpected part of yourself that does.

Like a heavy knock on thin glass you hear it: the drumming of an answer you've been looking for without knowing it; the undiscovered truth behind questions you never asked yourself before. Something in the rattling of the van over unattended roadways must have jarred it loose from your soul. You haven't realized until now, of all the thoughts you've ever had about Reya — of all the memories you keep reliving — you've never once thought about one very important detail: how your relationship *ended*.

Because maybe, just maybe, it never did.

Did you dream her too?

ooo

Bester drops you off on Neptune Avenue and you run three blocks under the warmth of dawn to your apartment, entering through the back door only because that's the door you never use. Once upstairs, you're not surprised at all to find your broken door still off its hinges. You place the still-wrapped Proto-Tech on your kitchen counter and try opening a drawer beside the sink just to make sure you're where you should be. The drawer opens smoothly, unsorted cutlery rattles around inside. Your bed is still turned up into the wall, a reminder of just how long it's been since you've slept. The AIIB system starts up much faster this time, maybe due to having logged on once already. Who knows? But before long, you're back in your virtual apartment and selecting the MESSAGE button from the top menu on the Vis-Screen. In the SEARCH FOR USER bar you type: *EPOCH-I*.

USER FOUND > PLEASE ENTER MESSAGE |

Without any hesitation, you type: *will you meet me in versailles?*

MESSAGE SENT |

You stare at the blinking cursor and contemplate the parallels between Tristan Montminy and Luca Desplante III swapping girlfriends in *The Third*, and Epoch-A and Epoch-I being with the wrong partners in your own worlds.

MESSAGE RECEIVED |

Reya Graves and Abigail Ayr. The fictional Emilia and Grace. All playing unknown parts in bizarre events that had no right in ever coming to be. Blurring the lines between fiction and non.

EPOCH-I TYPING RESPONSE ... |

Until finally:

YES.

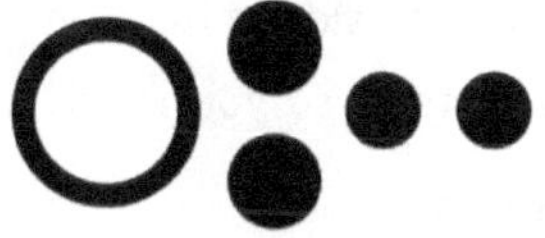

CONTEMPLATING KENTUCKY

Luna Park is not open to the public on this Monday morning but this doesn't seem to be an hours-of-operation issue as much as maybe the goings-on of something much more criminal within. There are three squad cars parked up on the curb outside the entrance gate; four or five cops meandering about on radios looking generally confused. The public has already been diverted elsewhere, though a group of them still loiter around; arms and legs flapping inquisitively across yellow police tape.

The Ferris wheel is not spinning. The Parachute Jump remains as lifeless as a bad photograph. The Cyclone is not moving either; its incessant click-clacking wail appropriated by nothing more than the screeching of seagulls. This absence of the usual background clamor is disturbing. When something you're so used to is suddenly not there, it's unnerving to say the least.

Almost as unnerving as seeing a receptionist behind the front desk in Gideon's office. It's a man. He reminds you of somebody, but you cannot place him. Probably someone you'd encountered merely in passing before, maybe a clerk at a store or a commuter on the subway. An individual who you'd only logged away enough memory triggers to remember in that one specific moment, with no intention of ever seeing again. His forehead bears a complex network of freckles that you whimsically make out in the pattern of a tentacled sea monster. The desk lamp exposes the slight indication of pubescent acne scars on the right side of his chin. There is no nameplate on the desk to help you any further, so you make the decision to not worry about it.

"I'm here to see Gideon," you tell him.

"I should hope so," he says, apparently joking about the lack of anyone else in the building. He makes perfect eye contact: his focus is on you and you alone. "But he likes to be called Dr. Flat."

The first time you met, Gideon had mentioned he wasn't actually a doctor. You still have no idea what he meant by that.

"At least," this man continues, "that's what he asked *me* to call him."

There are stacks of file folders all over his desktop. He catches you watching him try to make sense of them all. "Organized chaos," he laughs uncomfortably. "Evidently some other therapist just died and all of his patients are slowly being transferred to this office."

"May I speak with him?"

"The dead guy?"

"Gideon."

"Do you have an appointment?"

"Not today."

"Dr. Flat is with a patient right now."

"I know," you say and the man gives you an odd sideways glare.

The last time you were here, you'd spotted the mustard-colored journal on the bookshelf in Gideon's office, didn't you? The one with *Graves, Reya* on the spine. You reached for the book apprehensively and had only enough time to flip through some of its pages while waiting for him to finish up his business in the bathroom. It was apparent by the number of blank pages that she'd only had one or two more sessions with Gideon than you, and all had been at the same time and day of the week: Nine o'clock on Monday mornings. On the last written page and in his handwriting, Gideon had noted asking Reya Graves about you. *"No recollection about the man named Cepik Small,"* he wrote. This was followed by: *"She denies having any knowledge whatsoever. Like this person has been deleted from Reya's memory. I believe her, but it might be worth prodding a bit deeper."*

When you heard the toilet flush, you managed to shut the journal and slip it back into its spot on the bookshelf right before Gideon Flat returned.

The receptionist directs you to the chairs against the wall. "If you'd like to wait here, please take a seat until he's finished."

You look at the clock on the wall. It's 9:45. "I'll wait," you say. Can't be much longer. You sit down and flip disinterestedly through a boating magazine from the table beside you. There's a feeling that comes over you: that wonderful feeling of being somewhere and knowing for certain it is for the very last time. The date on the cover of the magazine reads: May 1993. You can't believe how many cigarette ads used to be in magazines. You look up at the Bill Clinton campaign poster and its *People First* slogan. You have no idea what that means or what might have come second. Maybe there was no second. Maybe that was the point. All the while you keep a corner of an eye on the door to Gideon's office.

ooo

You snap yourself back to attention when the door finally opens. Gideon Flat enters the reception area and he almost trips over his feet when he sees you. Pausing warily, Gideon closes his office door behind him before you get the chance to see who else is in there.

"Epic, hello. What brings you here this morning?"

You stand up straight and give yourself enough time to decide how to best answer him. You didn't exactly plan what you were coming here to say to this man. "I've decided I'm leaving." He scans you up and down, not showing the least bit of concern but merely wondering why you'd need to show up here and tell him this right now. "A road trip," you add, hoping in vain to clear things up a little bit.

"Where to?"

"Kentucky."

"Kentucky. Very good." Gideon says this in a way that makes it sound like it was a test and he's proud of you for picking the correct answer.

You stare at one another for a long moment; he seems to be waiting for more, but you, you're only here because you wanted to see Reya with your own eyes.

Gideon asks, "Why are you telling me this?"

"Well, do you remember in *The Third* when Tristan Montminy leaves the university on a whim one day? He just up and left and went to Paris for no apparent reason at all."

"Any reason has to be apparent to someone."

"Maybe. Consider my going away to be like that."

"Yes, but then Tristan met his twins and they all switched lives. Is that what you're planning?"

How can you possibly admit to him that's about as close to the truth as you can get without sounding like a complete nutcase? How could the truth ever come close to making any more sense? Maybe Abigail was on to something when she began masking the truth about everything behind lies and charades?

"The truth—" you start, choking back emotion. "The truth is, I'm going to Kentucky so I can return to where I was *meant* to be."

"Return?" he questions. "Can you return to a place you've never been to before?"

"I've been there in my dreams. Does that count?" You hold up your rucksack and tell Gideon the device hidden within is all you need to make it happen. The collection of pill bottles rattles around inside the bag, muffled by the additional presence of the Proto-Tech wrapped in one of your hoodies.

"I see. And what about The Third? Will he be there in your version?" Now you cannot tell if he's mocking you or not.

"In my version, I *am* The Third. That's what Zoltan Lintzel told me."

Gideon purses his lips now and gauges you with his eyes before looking over to the reception desk for the briefest of moments; just long enough to give the man at the desk a barely perceptible nod. You almost don't notice it yourself. When he turns back to you, he gives you a different look. You've seen this same look on the faces of others, usually when you don't recognize them and they assume you do. It's like they're thinking: *Who is this bat-shit crazy head case?*

He sits down now and motions for you to sit beside him. Being seated side by side in the reception is so totally unlike being in his office with a large desk between the two of you. It's as if you're just having a friendly chat. But it's also sort of like he's actually more concerned for you this way.

"Cepik, are you observing the prescribed medication intake? You're not still taking any of those old prescriptions, are you?"

"Of course. I mean, no. I'm not. I mean, I'm taking exactly what you told me to take."

"I don't have my notes here but I'm fairly certain you've never mentioned anyone named Zoltan Lintzel before now."

There is a pause here, enough time for you to say something, anything. But you can tell Gideon was never really expecting to get an answer from you anyway. "Tell me," he starts cautiously. "Do you recall in our first session when I'd asked you if you knew what a griffin was?"

"I do. You said it was a mythological creature."

"That's right."

Pause. "And—?"

"To be honest with you, I find that when I'm working with an individual who expresses low-to-mid-levels of onset dementia, the symptoms there are typically very simple. They're very easy to analyze and anticipate."

"Did you just say *dementia*? What are you suggesting?"

"Please. Allow me to finish. I was going to say that with *you*, right from the very start, I could sense I was dealing with something more serious. There are signs."

"What signs?"

"Hallucinations, for example."

"You're not serious, are you?" Can you afford to tell him the truth at this point? He's probably already got the insanity police waiting outside, straightjacket prepped and all ready to toss you into their padded room. Do they still do that?

"I had another patient, not so very long ago. He had an extremely rare case of dementia, known as—" he pulls his phone out from his shirt pocket and scrolls through some pages on it before finally finding what it is he wanted. "Yes, known as *Creutzfeldt-Jakob* disease. It's a degenerative neurological disorder that can very quickly lead to particulars such as hallucinations, memory loss, and fluctuations in personality." He very calmly places the phone in his lap. "This man — he's dead now; suicide of course — exhibited all of these symptoms. And his hallucinations were decidedly very specific: he believed he was seeing mythological beings everywhere he went. Leprechauns. Mermaids. Christmas elves. Hercules. You name it."

"But what you're insinuating—I mean, Dr. Griffin was a *real* person."

"And Margo Asus?"

"The actress from the play?"

"Yes."

"What does she have to do with anything?"

"You know of course that Margo is a short form for Margaret."

"I guess so."

"And another nickname for Margaret is Peggy. Or just Peg." He types something into some application on his phone and then holds the screen up for you to see: PEG-ASUS

"Pegasus? You can't be serious, can you?"

"The theater you went to was called the Dullahan, which is another name for the creature known as the Headless Horseman. Even this restaurant you frequent. The UnDiner? If you don't know, an *undine* is an underwater sea faerie from ancient Greece. A seahorse with a human face."

"That's stupid." You never realized any of this. Gideon Flat sounds like the insane one here, not you. "These are all incredibly outrageous coincidences. Nothing more."

"You claimed to have spoken to a lobster man too."

"He was a circus freak! Lobstero is Abi's father."

"That's what you told me before. And what about this Abigail Ayr person? How are things going with her?"

"You say her name like she's a fictional character. Like I made her up."

"Well?"

"We had an argument."

"And so you're escaping?"

"I didn't say I was escaping."

"You said you were going to Kentucky. To me, this sounds like a man who's trying to escape from something."

That's not what you're doing at all, you think. "If that's how you want to see it, fine. But escaping is certainly not how I perceive it." You have a choice now. You can sit here and continue to take this assault on both your integrity and your sanity, or you can give him the truth. "Abigail is meant to be with somebody else. Just like I am meant to be with someone else, some*where* else."

"Reya Graves?"

Of course, Reya Graves. Who else have you been talking about all this time? You glance over at his office door, still closed tight.

He says, "I have something for you." Gideon directs you toward his office, opening the door. "Follow me."

ooo

You step inside. There's no one else in here. He closes the door behind you and asks you to sit in your usual place on the couch. You notice the *Lovehunter* album is back on the wall. Whatever furtive holes that had momentarily been exposed are concealed once more. The mustard-colored journal of Reya Graves is on his desk beside an open laptop and he places his cell phone facedown next to it. The Lilac journal labeled *Small, Cepik* is nestled back in its own spot on the bookshelf.

Gideon unlocks the desk drawer with the key around his wrist and pulls something out. He then shows you a book: it's a copy of *The Third*. At first you think this is your missing copy but you notice the cover is not vandalized like the one you found on the subway. "I want you to have this," he says to you.

"Why?"

"You know, Cepik, the irony of it all is not lost on me."

"I don't understand irony."

"Well, *dramatic* irony in this case. Think about that book again and what you've read of it so far. Tristan and Luca traded lives and, in the process, they also swapped lovers: Emilia and Grace. Just as you are suggesting right now." He looks at the book in his hands with a certain melancholy you can't quite place. "Sometimes readers will love certain books so much they start to believe they're actually living in that fictional world. They become a character; find themselves trapped within their own mind's eye. Identity, reality, and fiction all blur together into one singularity."

He holds out his copy of *The Third* and you take it with some trepidation. There's a wooden bookmark sticking out about two-thirds of the way through the novel. You don't know what Jean Trepanier meant when he wrote his puzzling opus or why it seems to be oddly scripting the direction of your own life, but it's all a coincidence, is it not? It has to be.

Gideon picks up the mustard journal on his desk now and presents the spine so you can read it. You gulp. "My last appointment was rescheduled as a Skype session. She told my receptionist she was too nervous to come in, and had asked to do things this way instead. She later explained to me that she felt like she was being watched. That someone might have been following her." He places the journal in his lap now, under the desk, like if you can't see her name she'll be out of your mind. "But this is common for patients with a lot of anxiety. Still."

Still? What does he mean by Still? To quote the man in the houndstooth coat and bandicoot mask who broke into your apartment the other night: *Jesus fuck*. You *ARE* losing your mind, aren't you?

"You seem to think that if you go to Kentucky, you'll be fixing everything. But consider the harm you might be inflicting here. The irreparable damage you'd be leaving behind. There are others involved, Cepik. This life of ours is all one big, sensitive machine. *Kentucky—*" and here he gives air quotations with his fingers, "—may not be the answer for you."

The way he says the word Kentucky; it's like he really means something else. Like it's some kind of allegory. "You think I'm going to kill myself, don't you?"

"Am I wrong to assume such thoughts? Isn't '*Going to Kentucky*' your way of saying as much? Like a code?"

Is it you who's a total wacko, or is it this guy?

The cellphone on his desk buzzes and he turns it over and glances at the number. "I'm sorry, but I have to take this. It's my daughter." With his eyes,

Gideon directs you to the door.

Your head is still in a fog but you feel you should tell him something else before you go. "You may or may not see me again," you say, turning to leave. You slide the copy of *The Third* into your bag.

"I realize that."

"Well, this is a bit different of a situation."

"Everybody's situation is different, Cepik. It's what you choose to do with your situation that matters. Remember what Jean Trepanier wrote: '*We all have a shadow, but we must remember shadows can only exist with light.*'"

You don't remember that line at all. But maybe you will. "Thank you for the book," you say, with your back turned to him and already out the door.

ooo

There are still officers wandering aimlessly about outside. They don't seem to know any more about anything than you do. One guy gives you a dirty look as you try your best to slink away; he reminds you of exactly what the French cop in *The Third* might have looked like. Behind the entrance gate to Luna Park, you spot two bodies on gurneys, covered in white sheets. Twins. The less you know the better.

Outside the crumbling Sideshows by the Seashore building, you sit on the curb and open the book Gideon gave you. You slide the wooden bookmark out and inspect it. It is handmade; some tiny, faded paintings of seagulls adorn one side. There is a quarter on a string attached to it as well, a hole drilled into the center of the worn coin. On the back of the bookmark and written in red marker is a message from someone named Julie-Ann:

"Gids, There's always one more life."

THIS NEVER HAPPENED

This is it. This is exactly where you were meant to be. Just as you'd seen in your dreams. Just as you'd experienced online. You've returned to the field in Versailles, back for the first time. The details of this field of grass are far richer than what you'd known while inside the AIIB system, but you get the same feeling nevertheless. The sun is already setting on the horizon; the sky a brilliant orange. The ramshackle barn exists here, the ancient fence stretching for miles does too. There is a smell upon the gentle breeze you can't quite place but it doesn't fail in making you feel welcome here. Happy. *"It's all about being happy,"* Abigail said to you.

You packed nothing before buying a return ticket from Penn Station to Versailles and hopping on the train. During the ride, you had more than enough time to finish *The Third*. This was the copy Gideon Flat handed you this morning and you read it from cover to cover. There were definitely some inconsistencies from what you'd originally read, some divergences in the story; the most obvious of them being the inclusion of the extra character, The Third. Turns out it was all pretty stupid and never really made much sense. Maybe to a younger, wider-eyed, more malleable and impressionable man in love for the first time, but the point of it all was certainly lost on you.

You wonder though, just what the ending would have been like in the copy you'd lost. Maybe you can find another copy of the novel when you reach your destination? Maybe you'll be satisfied with how the story ends there? With how *your* story ends.

You left *The Third* behind on your seat in the train when you disembarked in Kentucky, the personalized bookmark with its defaced coin still tucked within.

It didn't take you long to find the right spot in this field. You knew for certain you'd recognize it when you found it. That's how dreams work sometimes. Sometimes it's a familiar voice, other times it's a specific place.

When you returned to your apartment on Mermaid Avenue after your brief talk with Gideon, you were happy to discover both your front door and bathroom mirror fixed. Thankfully, you still had your keys on you. You had only a couple of things to take care of before leaving again though, and you knew you'd never really get the chance to appreciate the upgrades or even thank Stanley for replacing them.

First, you wrote a brief letter for yourself and left it on the kitchen counter. Next, you contemplated unplugging the AIIB system from the wall, maybe even destroying it outright. But it felt like that would only be creating more problems. It would also only serve to slow you down, so you left the equipment as is.

You removed the Proto-Tech from your rucksack. The device was still wrapped in your hoodie and almost burned to the touch. Its generator continued to chug along and you suddenly realized you should have considered some better ventilation for the thing. But just as you castigated yourself, you also came to the conclusion that you hadn't slept in more than three days aside from the brief nap last night in the company van. Some things should be easily forgiven. You poked around your father's room and dug inside his dresser drawers until you found one of his old coats folded up in the back and you decided to conceal the device in that instead. Being in your father's bedroom actually brought a nervous smile to your face.

And for whatever reason, the apartment seemed a little cheerier when you peered back in one last time before locking the door behind you.

Now you're unwrapping the Proto-Tech from the dusty coat and you very carefully place it on the ground. The sharp blades of grass tickle your shaky fingertips. There's the feeling of someone around you. The hint of a shadowy light in your peripheral.

Before heading into Manhattan, you first took a train to Forest Hills. The payphone behind Gideon Flat's office was the only place you knew where you could find a phonebook, so after the earlier discussion with your therapist, you looked up the address for the bookstore. In the picture of Abigail you had in your pocket — the one you swiped from the basement lab in Queens — her name tag read JUST BOOKS! right above the ABBY.

You finally entered Just Books! after getting lost a couple of times. The only time you'd ever been to Forest Hills was when you were ten and you and your father attended a funeral for some distant cousin of his. All you remember about it was the roast beef sandwiches and cocktail wieners.

Abi wasn't wearing her army jacket this time, though you still had your own arms covered. She did have the same name tag on as in the photo: ABBY. You watched her shelving books for a few moments, recalling the feeling you first had when you realized you actually recognized her. No memory triggers necessary; your prosopagnosia momentarily fading away, making you feel almost normal. It was a great feeling.

Not as much as what you think falling in love must actually feel like, but still wonderful. You and Abi spoke for a while, long enough for her boss to get mad at her. Jokingly, you promised that if she got fired she could count on Bester to talk to her boss for her, too. It didn't take long for the two of you to settle your differences; the blow-up from the night before was already like it had never happened. You told her you now had another way to fix things; you explained your whole plan to her. You were so excited when you covertly unwrapped your father's coat and showed her the Proto-Tech, that for some reason you even asked her to come with you, even if you knew better. It wouldn't be fair to her but you also did not wish to deny her such an opportunity.

"I can't, Epic," Abi said. "I can't go. You know that." Carefully, she placed a hand on the otherworldly device. Her red-brown eyes lit up.

You know it was a stupid thing to ask her. What if she ever met herself over there? Could the universe handle such an imbalance? "But would you at least ride with me to Versailles?"

"I can't," she said again. And then with a knowing wink, "But I'll know where to find you. I'll know." She gave you a warm hug and a kiss on the cheek and then you ran to catch that E-Train to Penn Station.

You don't know how much power this external battery was meant to provide but the machine doesn't appear to be slowing down any. The extent of Zoltan's technology is a complete unknown to you; you only hope that it won't run out of gas in the next few minutes. And that it works as promised.

You don't know what to expect once you start it up. You literally have no clue at all. The Proto-Tech is crackling madly in this spot so you assume the presence of shadows — or slivers, or patches, or ghosts, or whatever you might try calling them — is strong here. Maybe even stronger than what you were witness to in Penelope Park.

You don't adjust any settings on the dial, simply assuming everything is ready to go. Besides, there's a severe lack of complication in regards to this device. There's a big green button labeled "ON" above a smaller red button that is marked "OFF." There's a dial too, similar to an old radio. The dial is held in one specific position with two strips of heavy duct tape. You assume this has something to do with the frequencies Zoltan liked to talk about, but you can't be sure. You push and hold the green button and remain motionless, crouching before the Proto-Tech and waiting to see what happens next. Waiting for your world to open up.

Almost instantly, there is a small, rectangular-shaped glow flickering in the space before you; its edges are fuzzy and hard to really make out but you guess it's about the size of a book. The size of *The Third* by Jean Trepanier. You know immediately this is the same phenomenon as what you saw in the park with Abi, though this one does not fade away. The strange, dark energies within it seem to be spiraling, rising and falling over and under themselves.

The first thing you plan on doing as soon as you cross through is to destroy the other Earth's Proto-Tech. You're optimistic in your hope that the other you will do the same here once he's through. You keep the clothes you're wearing on, but you leave your keys, wallet, and the return ticket to New York on a dry patch of grass a few feet from the machine. And even though you've never been extraordinarily sentimental, you bring your father's coat with you too. You don't want to forget the smell of it, in case smells work differently over there, that is.

At first you don't notice it, but the shadowy patch is beginning to grow in size. It's the shape of a smoke-tinged metal box full of peculiar mementos; a mustard-yellow journal labeled *Graves, Reya* on the spine; a framed poster of the Demon of the Surf; a window overlooking Surf Avenue. You tell yourself you'll know for sure when the time is right to step through.

Before long, it is the size of a doorway; like the empty frame that remained after your apartment door was battered in. But crossing this threshold will not lead to your sad, erroneous home, but rather to your destiny. Your intended world. The one that fate and chance could only temporarily procure from you.

And you step in.

As you merge with the shadow for the first time it begins to change again. It actually looks and feels more like a light now.

The same light they tell you to walk toward when you're dying.

You cross through fully, completely, and there she is.

Finally, there she is.

One hundred centuries ago, when the world's population was around four million, mankind was beginning its transition from hunters and gatherers to farmers. And as Earth's last glacial period — the world's final Ice Age — ended, as wild horses completely disappeared from Great Britain, and as Chinese farmers began harvesting rice and soybeans, a black hole collapsed somewhere far beyond where man ever knew about. The resulting wave of cosmic light hit the planet Earth ten thousand years later; in the same instant two baby boys named Cepik Small were born.

Twenty years after that, the same two boys were born once more.

ooo

The brand-new deadbolt lock clunks smoothly into the door as I unlock it. Stanley must have used the same old rusty hinges however, as the familiar creaking remains. Familiar, but for the first time, really.

It's hot in here. Hotter than I imagined it would be. Pulling the chain, I click the overhead lightbulb on and immediately spot the note on the kitchen counter. I ignore it for now though, having more important demons to lay to rest first.

In the bathroom mirror, I take a look at myself. The same person I expected to see, but I've been fooled before. I close my eyes and remove first my hoodie then my shirt, dropping both into the sink.

Deep breath. Eyes open.

They are no longer there. In my dreams, this threadbare apartment is where I was meant to be, where I've *wanted* to be, but in my dreams, I always had the scars. The horrible reminders from the worst of my recurring nightmares are not there.

I breathe out and reach for the shirt in the sink to wipe my tears away. But the tears keep coming. Let them, I finally say.

The folded letter is not sealed inside an envelope nor are there any markings on it. But I know exactly from whom, when, and where it came. Pulling the Murphy bed down from the wall just as I've done in my dreams countless times, I decide to sit and read the note. But I find another letter stuck to the sheets, this one sealed in a small envelope that is only marked with a "CEPIK" in unsteady handwriting. I recall the dream I had recently in which my apartment was broken into by that stranger in the mask. The letter from my father — my *real* father — was inside that book the man threw at my head; it must have fallen out onto the bed unnoticed. I save it for now and unfold the letter from EPOCH-A instead. It reads:

> Cepik Small,
>
> I know you will not recognize the handwriting in this letter, but I also know for certain you will not mistake who it is from. In your dreams, you injured your right hand when you were ten years old. You remember. You were foolishly riding your bike down the stairwell of a condemned building when you lost control. I remember too. You had to learn how to write and throw a baseball with your left arm instead. Turned out, this was actually your better throwing arm, though your handwriting never looked quite as good. In your dreams, you threw a plastic cup across the room and killed a buzzing insect. You remember. I remember too.
>
> I am confident you will find this letter because I know in your dreams you live with your father in this small apartment on Mermaid Avenue. And in your dreams, it's really not so bad here. Because here, you're exactly where you want to be. You're where you are meant to be.
>
> In your dreams, you almost died. I've heard before of a popular belief that if you dream your own death while you sleep you will never wake up. You remember how close you came. I remember too. I'm sorry for everything horrible you might have experienced in your dreams. I apologize for the things you've had to endure. But there's probably some good in there somewhere too. Or maybe you *only* remember the good stuff? I hope that's the case. Why else would you be here now?
>
> Don't worry about finding Abby. She'll find you wherever you are. Things just seem to go that way with that girl.
>
> Recently in your dreams, you've been seeing a therapist. You found a book on the subway. You smoked pot and quit your job. You dreamed all

of this, unless you've been sleeping as little as I have, that is. None of these things matter. You'll be fine with or without any of them.

But in your dreams, I do not know how sick your father has become, which is probably my fault for not seeing him enough. So, I'm pleading that you visit him. For the first time. For one last time.

He's been waiting twenty years to see you, too.

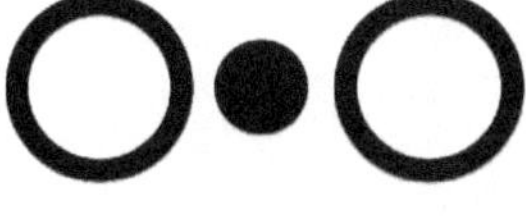

END

From the Author

When I write a book, I put a lot of thought into it. I try to leave enough clues and breadcrumbs and hints of things to come – whether as major plot twists or just a thought which harkens back to an earlier idea – so that the reader would likely have a far different (and hopefully better) experience upon a second read. I re-read books all the time, so it's the kind of detail I appreciate myself.

This Never Happened is my most ambitious work in this regard. Inspired by the Speculative Fiction genre I'd only just discovered, I wanted to craft an atmospheric tale which not only made the reader a bit uncomfortable, but also had them questioning the reality of everything they experienced within. Taking the all-too common feeling of "I don't belong here" and turning it on its head was my starting point for this novel about identity, reality, depression, parallel worlds, and the human condition. Along the way, there lies a wealth of metaphors, coincidences, red herrings, and flat-out unanswerable scenarios. Hopefully not too many, though!

Adding unnerving elements was a fine balance too. Epic Small's face-blindness, or prosopagnosia. The incessant Coney Island heat wave. The constant buzzing of mosquitoes. The awkward therapy sessions with Dr. Gideon Flat. How finding a poorly-translated French novel on the subway strangely begins to mirror occurrences in Epic's own life.

And the key to unlocking the desired emotions from the readers was not only making Epic just as lost as them, but by telling his story in a second-person narrative, a tricky way to incorporate a bit more distance while also allowing for more questioning and doubt.

I'm extremely proud of how this novel turned out, and if you enjoyed it the first time around, why not flip back to the start and read it again? You might be surprised at what you discover along the way.

Or, you might be even more confused. You never know.